# Whatever the Impulse

# Impulse

## By: Tina Amiri

Whatever the Impulse

By: Tina Amiri

Siento Sordida

A division of Caliburn Press, LLC.
P.O. Box 8747
Madison, WI 53714
www.eternalpress.biz

Hardback ISBN: 978-1-944579-63-0
Paperback ISBN: 978-1-944579-20-3
E Book ISBN: 978-1-944579-21-0

Cover art by: Dawné Dominique

*Gerda...I told you I wouldn't forget.*

There is, clearly, a list of people who significantly contributed to me getting to this point where I could finally write an acknowledgement—people who brought me from the caveman version to this. Bish, in less than three days you saved me ten years. Herb, you read your share of versions, preventing more than a few "6-foot-long-arm blunders". Dr. Paul Muller, I hope you're looking down, or up...LOL...to see this. You offered me a university degree in writing and even made me an editor. Those writers who you sent my way have likely heard you in my words; I know I do. And then there's my number one supporter: Karen Folques—best friend and spotter of logistical issues. You've literally read every version, and spent countless hours working as hard as me just to nail one word. Thanks for the laughs! Finally, I want to thank Caliburn Press, previously Damnation Books, for making it all happen. What a perfect home for my cursed book...but that is another story.

# Prologue

"No, Night, it's already blacker than your name outside and even I'm getting tired of this." The polished man lolled back in his armchair, crossed his long legs, and waited.

The student sat in an adjacent wooden chair with a composure that belied his four years. He made another sign, placing his left hand to the bent elbow of his right arm.

"No. That is the sign for 'morning'. Show me the sign for 'early'."

The boy dropped his gaze; his voice barely pierced the somber air. "It's just easier talking."

"Night..." The man leaned forward and lifted his student's chin until their eyes met. "Why can't you trust your father? We would both prefer to have it easy, but you're special...our lives are special. That means we have to do some things that other people do not." He paused to smile before sitting back. "All those bad dreams... Do you want them to get worse?"

The boy shook his head.

"Of course not. And we don't want them to become real, do we?"

"No."

"No," echoed the teacher, after he signed the word. "But believe me, they will if you're not careful. Yes, of course you can talk," he finally acknowledged, "but it's important that no one but me ever hears you do it and this will make it easier. You're learning a language that we alone can share. It's the only way for us to stay safe, and that's all I want, Night...for you to be safe. Do you understand?"

The child blinked his pale eyes and dared to shake his head.

"You will understand—you must!" The boy's teacher and sole guardian rose and snatched the open instruction book from the table, snapping it shut inside his grip. "From now on you will use these signs whenever you have something to say to me. I don't want to hear your voice at all until I am satisfied with your progress—until I can read every sign you make, and you understand every thought that I show you in return. Let that be some motivation to learn because, until then, you speak to no one!"

# Chapter One

1984

"C'mon, you said he's better than anyone on the Oregon coast, but what the hell kind of bartender can he be if he's deaf? Blind I'd believe. I mean, look at his eyes, but deaf...! I can't even tell him my problems."

An *Emerald Shore* regular sat crumpled on his stool in front of the bar. "For God's sake, Ted. He can understand you."

"Good, then maybe I'll get to problems a bit later." The stranger named Ted laughed. "So, what do we call our deaf friend?"

The bartender turned both men's heads with a word.

"Night?" the obnoxious guest repeated, squinting through his chunky glasses at the bartender's naked, nearly colorless eyes, then at the lips that had barely moved.

The man's friend pointed toward the lobby. "See that fellow over there? That's Andrew Shannien. He owns this place, and Night, here, is his son."

"Of course!" Ted boomed, shuffling forward. "You're workin' for Daddy. Or do you just...help out?"

The bartender returned an ambiguous nod.

"Maybe that answer will make sense if I have a drink," the man digressed. "C'mon... Let's all drink to Night. Get me...get me a *Nightmare*, Night...Nightmare." Ted cackled and smacked the countertop.

A mild grin cracked Night's stoic expression before he turned away to gather three bottles and some orange juice. The wood fire surged behind the mahogany counter and heightened the red in his auburn hair. He could feel the man's stare burning on his face as he shook up the mixture and strained it through ice.

Night served the newcomer his *Nightmare* then handed the regular guest his usual beer, which prompted another disclosure.

"I swear, he's like a drink encyclopedia. You can order anything and he never gets it wrong. And if that weren't enough...you should hear him play the piano."

Ted lurched forward and showered the alleged pianist with cocktail spittle. "All right, Nightmare...I have to see it. Why don't you play something for the crowd?"

Night glanced at the baby-grand piano in the corner of the room and turned down the challenge with a quick shudder.

"Oh, go ahead, kid... Show us!" The man spun to face the people dining in the restaurant. "Our deaf friend here says he can play the piano, and wouldn't we all like to hear a tune?"

A few people clapped; there was even a whistle.

"Go on, Nightmare..." Ted expelled the words directly in Night's face. "They all want to hear you play."

Night's stare shifted to the massive lobby doors where his father ran one hand over his silver head and then crossed his arms over a well-tailored suit jacket before tossing back a reluctant nod.

Crouched on the bench, without looking up, Night sensed every set of eyes in the room on him, everyone anticipating what this deaf prodigy would sound like on a piano. The slow tune he chose to play matched his resistance in getting started, but he quickly loosened up. His awareness flitted from one table to the next—until one guest snared it. Different from every other set in the room, her eyes wouldn't let go of his, teasing and challenging him to look just a little bit longer.

His performance suffered as he fought to look down at the keys, but it became next to impossible when the girl dropped her chin and began playing with the rim of her water glass. He could no longer hear his own music as she swept the surface of her drink, lifted her finger to her mouth, and brushed the water across her relaxed bottom

4

lip. Night tipped his face down and clamped his front teeth over his own lower lip before fully surrendering his gaze to her.

She declared her win by rising and striking a victory pose with one hand on a hip and the opposite leg bent and thrust forward. The attention in the room split as she made her way to the piano, but it refocused as she crowded herself next to him on the piano bench.

Night peered at her with caution, but he did not stop playing...not until she placed her hands on the keyboard, at which point he withdrew as though she'd just set the keys on fire. The music vanished into the din of hands clapping.

"I play too," she told him. "You shouldn't have stopped."

The audience now forgotten, he absorbed every detail, following her tiers of yellow hair down past her chest. She appeared to be studying him as well so he took his time. Faint freckles dressed a face without makeup, and while her loose cotton dress kept a few secrets, his heart rate exploded.

He glanced up briefly to see the sharp blue lasers from the restaurant owner's eyes now peevishly directed at the ceiling.

"Finish the song with me," she enticed.

Night, too, recognized their newfound responsibility to the audience. His fingers slid into position and the impromptu *A Time For Us* rendition took form once again.

"How do you do that?" she whispered when he tilted his face to hers. "I mean...if you can't hear."

It took him a moment to churn out an answer.

"I can feel it with my hands."

"Really?" She picked up his right hand and placed the backs of his fingers over her heart. "Can you feel this?"

Without blinking, he nodded.

"I just wanted to say hello," she stated with stark simplicity before releasing his hand and marching back to her table.

Beyond the bustle of applause, Night witnessed how the *Emerald Shore*'s distinguished owner lifted his hands only to show him a curt gesture. Just steps from his father, the girl hustled her friends out of their seats as though she knew it would be anticlimactic to stay around another second. Then, the door closed behind her, leaving him to contend with a less desirable admirer, Ted, for the rest of the evening.

# Chapter Two

Andrew Shannien didn't say a word on the trip home down the US 101. Night glanced his way many times, but the car just sped through the darkness in combustible silence. He sensed that things were about to change as his father turned onto their private, dirt road.

A gust of briny air from the bay tried to follow them through the front door, but Andrew slammed the door in the face of it, and only now, in the stillness of the house, did he decide to let rip.

"What the hell was that, Night? Did we forget something this evening? You're supposed to be deaf!" He ticked his own ear in a sloppy effort to sign the word. "Don't you think people might start to wonder after your little exhibition, complete with dialogue, playing like a damned concert pianist!" Andrew walked away, but then he spun and came back. "Night, you have to be modest or people will demand more and more from you, and then we will both regret it."

"I didn't say a lot..."

"Oh! Can you feel this?" Andrew mimicked in a false nasal voice. "Feel this. Feel this. I can *feel* it with my hands," he persisted deliriously. "Well, feel *this!*" In a flash, Andrew's hand was across Night's face.

Night crossed his arms tightly, leaving it up to the draft in the room to tell him if the ring on Andrew's left hand had drawn blood. *Not this time.* "People make it hard sometimes. It's hard sometimes...pretending."

"I know that, but I've told you how it is. They can't know too much."

Night recoiled from the hand that now tried to offer affection and Andrew's manner turned tetchy again.

"But they will if you're careless. They cannot ask too many questions, and it's our responsibility not to let them. We don't have a choice."

"It would be easier...if I just knew why."

"Trust me, Night. How can you not trust me?"

Night stumbled in and out of a whirlwind embrace, but a grip on his right arm prevented him from leaving just yet.

"A word here and there is fine. Dazzle them with your extraordinary gift to play music, but don't let it go too far. They love you, Night...just the way you are. They admire you—and I need you at the restaurant. It would never be as successful without you. I owe you so much, and after protecting you for nineteen years, I will not let my guard down to this world that is just waiting for one of us to make a mistake."

Night turned away, refusing to look up at his father.

"Why can you not trust me, Night? Do you see how you want to know more? People are all the same and they'll want to know more too. You'll understand everything at the right time."

Night pushed past Andrew. The floorboards yelped under his quick and heavy steps all the way to the top of the staircase and down the hallway. He bashed the side of one fist against the door to his room, last on the left, which opened to the best ocean view in the house—a meager consolation for being denied virtually all human contact, aside from their guests at the *Emerald Shore*.

Like tonight, they often reminded him that even his name was a secret. *That is his mother's tale to tell,* his father would say to anyone who asked about it, but since she died before he ever knew her, he didn't expect to get an answer about his name, his mother's name, his life, or her death—ever.

The annoying man at the restaurant that evening had probably named him best by dubbing him Nightmare, after the blood-red drink. Even before sleep could set in, something would join him on most nights. It would linger above him, or beside him, and he usually had to fall asleep listening to it breathing.

Only in the dream realm could he see it...his aberrant doppelganger. While it flashed around its familiar, pale eyes, it declared its autonomy with pearly white hair and thoughts that came from outside his limited life experiences. It would often beckon him to follow, and then throw a tantrum when he couldn't. It had the ability to impart emotion and impose its distinct brand of excruciating pain, but through all its efforts, it couldn't extort what it wanted from Night. That's when it would distort in some horrific way, then slice through his body on its way to oblivion.

****

In this week of intrigues, the final one came with his father's announcement that the mystery woman, whom he'd been meeting in town for several months, was finally going to visit their home. Other than the occasional repairman and cleaning crew, no one had ever been granted this privilege. In any case, Lila Hughes would be joining them this morning and Andrew flippantly insisted that Night behave as required in the company of other people.

Night studied her from the far end of the corridor and noted that she rivaled his father in height but fell short of his fifty-five years by more than a decade. She had a kind and pretty face and he also noticed that she had almost the same shade of blond hair as the young girl in his daydreams.

She stood smiling in the doorway. "That road is quite a test for someone just coming off a night shift."

"I've often thought that too. Come in, Lila." Andrew took her by the hand and escorted her a few steps into the house.

"Lila, this is Night...my son. Night, may I introduce Lillian Hughes. She's a nurse," he added when Night's focus landed on her gold name pin.

She leaned forward and spoke slowly and precisely. "Hello. It's nice to finally meet this mysterious Night." She spoke with an accent that his father called 'English.' He'd often come across it at the restaurant, but he still had no idea what that meant. He stared back, oblivious to her extended hand until she lowered it. "What an interesting name. How did it come to be?"

"You would have to ask his mother," replied Andrew, without missing a beat. "Let's not stand here. I have coffee waiting for us in the kitchen." He focused on Night before turning the other way. "Why don't you treat us, Night? Play something for Lila."

The woman's right eyebrow perked up, as did Night's.

****

Lila led Andrew into the kitchen. "He obviously reads lips very well."

"When he remembers to pay attention." Andrew seated himself at the breakfast table as if for an interview.

Lila continued standing, craning her neck to admire the shoreline from the window. "This is a lovely place—and you must have spectacular trails right in your backyard?"

"Not quite, but there are more than enough not even fifteen minutes from here."

Lila sat down. "Oh, I'm familiar with those. Running them has helped me lose my troubles for nearly ten years...although my troubles seem to have a much easier time keeping up with me these days."

"Perhaps I can change that."

The music in the next room caused her to abandon her answer and look up sharply. "Is that really Night?"

"Of course."

"But how...?"

"Others like him, without hearing, have learned to play the piano. I taught him myself."

"Yes, you mentioned he was homeschooled. I can see he's a good student."

"He did have an excellent teacher." Andrew's face tensed, in spite of his bright eyes and grin.

Lila giggled shortly. "You're just so far away from everything. Didn't you ever worry about him not being around other kids when he was growing up?"

Andrew's coffee cup clanked on its saucer. "No, Lila. He didn't want to go away to any special school and mainstreaming wasn't even an option until he was ten—at which point they would have stuck him into one of those special classrooms with idiots and morons. No, as you can see, Night's IQ is not a problem, and I was going to make sure he got what he needed, here at home. Listen to him... Should anyone be worried?"

Every part of Andrew's explanation made perfect sense to Lila and she nodded. "I just wonder...what about friends?"

"I'm sure you can appreciate the challenges Night faces. Some things can't be helped. But he does have the restaurant to contend with almost every day. There's a reason why we both enjoy living here. You have no idea what a relief it is to come home some mornings and finally have some peace."

"Yes, Andrew, I do. But some mornings, after a hectic shift, I still get into my car and drive miles out of my way just so I can spend time with somebody else."

Andrew leaned back and chuckled.

The spellbinding music trailed off and Lila excused herself from the table. She stepped into the living room and Night dropped the keyboard cover as their eyes met.

"That was so brilliant." She crossed the room and stopped in front of him. "Perfect."

Andrew sidled up to her as she noticed a heavily framed seascape painting over the staircase banister.

"The artist is among us," he revealed.

"You...? No... Night? He's amazing. I can almost feel the mist in the air."

"I told you," Andrew persisted, "he isn't missing anything."

Lila concurred, but she still couldn't help but wonder how much further Night might have gone with some outside recognition of his gifts.

****

In the light of a west-coast sunset, Night sought out his sole companions. In a cliff-side crevasse between giant pines, he pulled the lid off the dilapidated crate and took inventory of his family of field mice.

While tearing apart some crusty bread from the restaurant, he deliberated over which mouse would have to fight for its meal tonight. As usual, it would be the one that refused to stand up to the others and take what he knew it wanted—the one that reminded him most of himself. He lifted that mouse by the tail and sprinkled some bread into the crate with his right hand while the mouse in his left hand dangled over the others, playing dead as it always did until he placed it back inside. He imagined there would come a time when he no longer required their company and set them all free, but for now he would remain the dominant field mouse. He replaced the lid as he noticed darkness descending fast over him...prompting him, now, to scurry along home.

# Chapter Three

"Night! What the hell are you doing?"

Daniel, the *Emerald Shore*'s friendliest waiter, was the only employee who spoke to him as though he wasn't deaf. After the anticipated poke in the back, Night turned around.

"You're ignoring a customer."

Night turned around to scan the counter.

"I'm talking about that one..." Daniel broadcasted to the whole room, pointing to the lobby.

A teen girl waved back. Everything about this moment matched his fantasy, except that the girl's wild yellow hair was now coursing a fiery red!

With his father away for the evening, a casual air danced around the place and Daniel gave Night a push toward the lobby, offering to cover the bar in his absence. The girl winked at the waiter before she signaled for Night to follow her out of the building.

It smelled like rain as she led him to her car and opened the passenger door of her compact beater-hatchback.

When he yielded to making eye contact, she said, "I just thought it would be easier to talk out here."

It shocked him that she hadn't long written him off as the world's least desirable conversationalist.

"So...you must have a girlfriend?"

He didn't answer her, content at that moment to be lost in the silver on her eyelids and the red on her lips.

"It's okay if you don't want to be here," she said, startling him from his reverie. "I know I'm not exactly in your league."

"What do you mean?" he blurted. He was truly finding it a chore to speak, which added credibility to his performance. "I've been waiting for you to come back."

"Waiting for me? I think I'm about to disappoint you, and I'd rather do it now than later." An amused snort escaped her. "Like, what if I told you I used to dance naked in a club?"

Night's pulled away from her, shocked at nothing more than the word "naked".

"I also have a kid. Big surprise..." she chortled disparagingly. "That was years ago, and I want you to know is that, despite what I just told you, I'm different now. I've gone back to school and another thing...I would never have gone after someone like you before."

Although he sensed her shame, it didn't compare to his own as he accepted, once again, that he understood nothing.

"I've started over," she explained with a double edge to her voice of half pride and half defeat. "I'm not raising my baby. My mother takes care of her and it bothers me every day...but...you don't seem bothered by any of this. Why?"

He crooked his head. "Bothered...by what?"

She giggled with relief. "That's chivalrous, Night—my Knight. So, we're okay?"

He nodded, allowing the mischief in her eyes to invade his.

"Night...you don't say a lot. Maybe I can learn that sign language you do. Maybe you can teach me."

He considered this for a moment. If he talked only with his hands, would it be the same as speaking out loud? Would the threat of eternal doom be realized either way? And he'd already spoken... He decided that he didn't really care. A few words wouldn't hurt...and he wouldn't have to tell her his secret.

"By the way, I'm Daphne."

"Daphne..." he repeated the name as though he needed the verification.

14

"That's right. Can you show me how to sign my name?"

He shook his head. Andrew had never told him what to do for names.

"Well then, show me how to say yours."

This time, he raised his hands and represented his name as the word. He placed his wrists together forming a sort of cross.

"Let me try."

She asked him other words too, but the sporadic intrusion of headlights in the parking lot distracted him more every time.

"I think we should go somewhere else." She'd read his mind. Her hand gripped the key in the ignition while Night's hand went for the door handle, so she followed his lead. She took his hand and pulled him away from the *Emerald Shore*, away from the lanterns and cars and toward the forest. The wind was starting to pour through the branches—a warning about the rain only seconds behind.

Daphne turned to him at the bottom of the hill as rain started streaming down. The delicate white fabric of her dress turned sheer, outlining her body...hips and beveled thighs, slender arms, shoulders and breasts in more detail than Night had ever seen.

Waves slapped against the rocky shoreline, the black ocean trying harder to reach them with every successive miss, as though envious of their enthrallment with one another.

Like a music box dancer coming to life, Daphne drew herself to him. Her hands rose up to move the matted wisps of hair away from his face while she sought permission in his gaze. Satisfied with whatever she saw, she lifted her chin and kissed his lips.

His gaze fell between them as he swayed back to study her and then traced the path of his eyes with his fingertips. He brushed his hands over her cool, wet arms, and he wasn't even sure of his motive when he picked up her hair and dropped it again so that it tumbled across her chest, dividing around a soft mound that supported a well-defined nipple. His fingers caressed one after slipping down the faded neckline of her dress, but he withdrew his hands when she fired a laugh to the skies.

He figured he'd messed up and, with a dropped jaw, tried to back away, but she held on and kissed his mouth before he could close it. Her parted lips traveled upward, collecting the water droplets from the tip and bridge of his nose. She kissed his heated eyelids, his forehead, and grazed his eyelashes with her lower lip as she murmured about the utter perfection of each of his features.

The scent of evergreen and sodden earth harmonized with Daphne's floral perfume. She had more kisses for his face and neck, and an electric current trilled down his back as she teased his ear. His fingers raked down the length of her mysteriously transformed hair before her body sank and her open hands slid down his front. Cool air invaded his skin as her fingers drove two layers of fabric up his chest; her dense cloak of hair replaced some of the warmth as her tongue slid up his breastbone.

With Andrew, he'd never known this kind of attention—attention that held him breathless for each successive move. His father's lifelong proclamations of love had come with the stingiest offers of physical affection—while, in less than a few minutes, this mere stranger had transcended a long list of his latent desires.

Her breath warmed his ribs and her tongue ran like hot steam across his chest. He shuddered from the sensation of her wet hair sweeping his middle, but not like he did when he felt her tongue on his nipple. Her one hand ran gently along his inner thigh before one finger at a time closed around what he'd hoped to keep secret. He pushed her away and tripped backward.

He had long since been warned about how wrong it was to touch it in this state—let alone reveal it to anyone—and he tried to observe at least the latter half of the edict.

Headlights flashed on the hilltop and the muffled sound of an alarm and a car door slamming came down with the rain. Daphne peered sideways to read his frantic expression. Her hand touched his and he grasped it, but only to take her with him, back onto the dirt path. His quick strides punished Daphne for wearing heeled sandals. The lanterns in front of the restaurant pulled him forward—lights that looked ominous and distorted through the rain.

Water splashed up from the rock-studded path as they lost contact. Daphne veered toward her car and Night headed straight for the concrete steps. He turned around to find Daphne unwilling to follow his lead, this time. Her expression revealed hurt and fear, and his eyelids crumpled as she ducked to climb into her car. He had literally bolted from her offer and he no longer had a shred of hope of her ever coming back.

She offered him one last glance through the windshield before her car's headlights severed their connection, yet his gaze lingered long after the car's taillights had vanished. He kicked a clump of dirt before proceeding up the long concrete steps that spilled like puddles out from underneath one another, but in the end, he decided to use the back door.

He removed his sopping sweater in the warmth of the kitchen and loosened his hair. Someone whistled in jest as he crossed the room in a wet short-sleeved undershirt to set his sweater on the radiator, but he barely gave it a thought as he settled into washing dishes. Only then did it become a challenge to ignore the simpering remarks around him.

"I'd say that was a first."

"For what?" asked Daniel in response to the head chef.

"For our bartender getting personal with anybody...let alone getting it on with some chick. I mean, everyone here has tried to break the ice with him at one time or another. Some of us have even attempted signing—which you might want to try yourself if you want to be avoided by him for all time."

"Yeah, he's a little bizarre, but his father can be a little intense. I suppose it's no wonder if Night's a bit of a freak."

"Maybe he just can't read lips all that well."

"Maybe he only reads drinks," Daniel quipped as he loaded orders onto a large platter.

Holding a stack of dinner plates, Night looked at the sink full of hot soapy water and then at the hard tiled floor on which he dropped them. The crash froze everyone in the room, except Night, who pretended to be oblivious to all sound, even as he began firing the broken pieces into a metal garbage bin.

Amidst the cacophony of clashing ceramic, tin, and human squawking, a waiter ended Night's catharsis by intervening with a stand-up dustpan and lobby broom. Quickly thereafter, Night realized his resentment had everything to do with his gross incompetence with Daphne, not with the remarks of the staff, and that's when Andrew appeared in the kitchen. He took one look at Night and smiled.

"That's good, Night. Stay back here and help the others."

Despite the chill he still felt, the reassuring softness in Andrew's light blue eyes made Night begin to sweat.

The last customer and then the last employee left the *Emerald Shore*. The crash and click of the heavy front doors closing reverberated through the deserted room. Night pulled his musty sweater back on and came out of the kitchen.

The fireplace had guttered out and the bar had been organized for the next day. Andrew stood motionless in the middle of the room, like one of the formidable monoliths along the shore. Clutching a turquoise shawl in both hands, he first leaned down to blow out one forgotten candle before he refocused on Night.

"Your friend left something behind."

Night caught the streak of color that came whirling at him, but he threw it aside like he had no attachment to it at all. The essence of Daphne now lingered between them.

"How wonderful that the two of you hit it off so well...or so I hear. Apparently, she's a redhead now... almost like you. That is so darling."

Night took in a breath but abandoned any attempt at a reply.

"No doubt you spoke with her?"

"No."

Andrew shifted his weight. "Well, I sure hope you talked some in all that time!"

Night knew there could be no diffusing answer.

"Did she touch you?"

"No... We went outside and she talked about herself a little bit. She wanted me to talk but I told her I had to go back, and I did, and she left."

"Is that the truth, Night?"

"Yes."

Andrew looked down and let out a breath when suddenly his eyes shot up, flaming. "Bullshit! Do you think I'm an idiot? Why do I bother instructing you when you don't care and you won't listen! I know you did more than go for a walk." He scooped up Daphne's shawl from the floor and hurled it into the foyer. In the same frenzy, he snatched Night's ragged hair and sharply pulled back on it. "Take a good look at the bar because you won't be back here to see it for a while."

****

In the car, Andrew revved the engine to match his rage. "You really don't listen to me anymore, Night, and I know that, but I can make you listen."

Night glared at the windshield.

"You know, if your jaw was broken you wouldn't have too much to say for a while. Oh, do I have your attention now? Because then you would have to have it fixed, which would mean having your teeth locked together with wire for weeks and weeks."

Night tried to imagine it. "Then how would I eat?"

19

Andrew shrugged with a wry grin. "Well, you can't, Night. It's quite possible you would starve to death."

"How could talking to people be more dangerous than that?"

Andrew shed the amused sparkle in his eyes. "It can be a lot more dangerous, Night. Trust me."

# Chapter Four

Then came the day when Lila just showed up at the house, about a week after his banishment from the restaurant.

Night played his expected part by ignoring her knocking, but he couldn't very well avoid her when she let herself into the house.

"Night...did your father go to work without you today? I'd hoped to still catch him this morning."

He stood in the corridor with hikers already on. If Lila had arrived even a minute later, the house would have been deserted. He nodded with a sigh.

"Well you know..." Lila's face brightened, "this does allow us a wonderful opportunity. We can go into town together, and you can help me choose a birthday gift for your father. It'll be fun. And we can learn more about each other along the way."

The ride to this mysterious place that people called "town" felt much longer than his trips to the restaurant, and they traveled in the opposite direction. The fir trees grew scarcer as houses and larger buildings took over the landscape. Eventually, the world turned into an elaborate maze of concrete and brick passageways.

Lila parked her car on a quiet street and she tapped his arm when he didn't make any move to get out. "Night...? What is it?"

His chest felt crushed. *There was no air here "in town".*

In a series of quick motions, Lila turned his face to hers, searched his eyes and then felt one of his wrists. He could feel his own pulse racing beneath her fingers.

"What's the matter with you? He didn't mention you had any other conditions..."

Lila's voice sounded far away, but her little huff, meant for his father, made the world seem familiar again. He had to remind himself that this was what he wanted: to experience more. He nodded like he'd already been involved in a conversation and then slowly cracked open the door. Lila followed and they made their way to the shops in complete silence. With his attention firing around at everything but Lila, it took him a while to notice her frustration at not being able to speak to him.

His awe at the mundane quickly turned into despondency. All the people around him looked so comfortable with their surroundings that, all at once, he knew exactly what a freak was. When pedestrians glanced his way, he figured they could see it too.

Lila squeezed one of his arms and then waved for him to follow her into a shop filled with marble works and decorative items. Her hand reached up and caressed something hanging from the ceiling. "I love wind chimes. They have such a haunting sound, especially at night. ...I'm so sorry. That was incredibly insensitive of me."

"I think he would like it," Night replied, expecting Lila to hear forgiveness in his answer, but when her features twisted, he feared she'd heard nothing beyond his plain speech. She turned away from him to take a wind chime down from a hook on the ceiling. It had a large metal wreath in the form of pine-needle branches surrounding a rectangular plate. "We could have 'Emerald Shore' engraved across here and he can hang it at the restaurant."

It made sense to Night, and he nodded.

Lila turned to him while the woman behind the desk wrapped the gift in tissue paper. "So when is *your* birthday?"

"What do you mean?" he said, his focus breaking up amongst the different objects in the room.

"Your birthday... When were you born?"

He shrugged as though she had asked him something bizarre and irrelevant while an object on a nearby table made him forget she even asked a question. He walked over to the clear ball and lifted the orb straight off its claw-foot base.

He could feel Lila's stare on his back as his eyes widened—just before he flinched and dropped the solid crystal ball that shattered on the granite floor.

When the saleslady cringed, Lila dumped her purse back on the counter and pulled out her checkbook. Lila stared at him for a while after they left the shop, clearly seeking an explanation.

Finally, Night spun at her. "I saw something inside it! It looked like me with—"

"Oh, Night, it was just lined with a mirror and with the glass...it's nothing more than an optical trick."

Night turned around and kept walking. Lila's theory made too much sense to argue with, but if it had been his reflection, and nothing more, why did his image have white hair? Lila wouldn't know about this phenomenon, but the white-haired image of himself, and even the pains in his limbs, were now boldly creeping into his waking hours.

But now he had a bigger problem. Lila had paid for the item that he'd stupidly destroyed and he found himself scrambling for a way to erase the whole incident. Perhaps he could hide some of his tip money and pay her back—but what if she shared the story with his father first, or at any point in the future? In any case, Andrew would learn of this trip.

Lila clutched his arm reassuringly. Some young girls smiled and giggled as they passed by. They were no more than fourteen years old but Night smiled back and it encouraged the girls to keep turning around to stare at him.

"They've taken a fancy to you," Lila remarked. "You are very attractive after all...and also very mysterious." She strode along in silence until she decided they had to go inside another store.

The store turned out to be a café-restaurant. Lila had cleverly found a way to get him to stay face-to-face with her for more than a few seconds. When their food was delivered, she asked him about his smoked fish.

"Is it as good as the *Emerald Shore's*?"

He produced a trace grin as his eyes roved around the quaint, pastel-colored restaurant. "I don't think so," he answered with rare decisiveness.

"You know, you really play the piano beautifully...and you speak very well, too. Tell me...do you have any hearing at all?"

With his fork hanging over the dish, he turned his eyes up at Lila. Nobody had ever probed into the matter of his make-believe deafness the way she did.

He shook his head. "I can feel the sound inside it when I play." He hoped she'd be satisfied with his now-standard answer.

Lila's mouth shifted with suspicion. "Well, you certainly are a fine pianist," she reiterated. "So you can paint, play music. What else? Do you like to read?"

Now self-conscious about his speech, he wanted this experience to end. He had pressed Andrew about how to speak if his speech was to be imperfect, but Andrew would snap back that he should simply refrain from speaking at all, and so he continued to blunder through his act. "Read? You mean words?"

Lila's fork now dangled as well. "Yes, of course, words." After a moment she blurted, "Can you not read?"

Now they shared the same wary expression and his silence apparently answered her question.

"That's why you went with the lunch special that the waitress told us about... Night, for God's sake, why can't you read? Didn't your father teach you?"

He shook his head.

"What exactly did he teach you, then?" She rifled through her purse and pulled out a notepad and pen. She scribbled on the page and then slid it across the table. "That's your name. Let's begin with these letters."

Concentrating as though it were a riddle, Night sized up each character before the point of his pen came down and his hand scrolled across the page. Lila's head twitched when she saw it. His effort was identical to her sample in every way.

"Okay, genius..." She took back the paper and produced his name in cursive writing. "You should at least know how to sign your name." Night examined the artwork before his eyes brightened and the words practically boiled from his lips. "I want to learn this. Show me how to write 'Daphne'?"

Again her eyes flashed at his well-articulated words. "We'll work on this later, all right? I'll visit you when you're alone. Each week you can give me your work schedule or tell me when you want me to come and, when you're ready, we'll surprise your father."

Lila led Night through a shortcut back to her car. An old building along the way distracted him with its elaborate architecture and then he noticed a disheveled character sitting in a doorway. Night stopped when the man mumbled something and answered Night's stare by rattling his tin cup.

When Night didn't react, he rattled his cup again.

"Night, come on." Lila tugged at his coat, but he pulled his arm away.

The man snarled, "That's right, Mommy. Take the little freak out of my sight...maybe teach him that staring is rude?"

"I don't understand what you want," Night answered boldly, clearly, recklessly.

Night glared at Lila when she tugged on his arm again, but this time she gave him an answer. "Money, Night. He wants money."

"I don't have any money!"

A crude laugh, then a cough, escaped the man's throat. "Really? You, with your little shopping bags and fancy clothes...how about that watch? Do you know what that glorified piece of metal could do for me, you tight-assed son of a bitch. Why don't you just go run along home with Mommy now? She doesn't want you talking to my kind. Go on now."

26

Feeling more annoyed than offended, Night opened the clasp of his platinum watch and flung it at the stranger's chest. The cup skipped free and rolled down the sidewalk, spilling all its coins.

The man's features transformed as he clutched the watch in one palm and stared at Night. "You're joking?"

Night had no trouble recognizing the familiar look of bewilderment.

Lila began walking away and Night felt compelled to run after her.

"Sorry man," the stranger called after him. "Really... You know, I wasn't always like this..."

Night turned back one more time as Lila clutched his arm.

"That was very nice of you," she acknowledged. "But what on earth were you thinking? I'm sure your father meant for you to wear that expensive thing, not whoever found it in the pawnshop."

Night knew Lila had it right, whatever she meant.

"Well, if nothing else, I suppose you've made a stranger's year."

In the earliest hour of the morning, Night waited for the front door to open. He sat in an armchair in his sapphire-blue robe, tensely gripping the armrests. Andrew strode in, but stopped abruptly at the border of the living room where one small brass lamp lit the room.

"What happened?"

Night sighed. "I went...I went somewhere today...in town."

There was no response.

"Lila came to the house, and she just walked in, and she asked me to go with her. She wanted me to go. I had to go. ...She made me go."

"I see." Andrew plunked himself down and leaned back in the second armchair before crossing his legs and throwing his eyes upward at Night. "So," he continued, "what did you think?"

"What do you mean?"

"It always shows when you have a reason to stall, Night. Did you talk to anyone?"

"No."

"You spoke with Lila, did you not?"

"Not very much."

"But you did talk to her. Who else did you talk to?"

Night paused. "Just some man..."

Andrew's impatience finally combusted. "Who?"

"There was this man on one street... Lila said he wanted money, but I didn't have any so I gave him my watch because he said it would help him."

Andrew pressed his forehead into his hands. "It's not your fault. What could I expect?" Then he reached for the sky like a half-crazed man. "But you shouldn't have been there...especially since you've come up with this new theory that you can chat with anybody at all— as long as they talk to you first!"

"Nothing bad happened." Then he remembered the glass ball. "Oh...except I broke something...and Lila paid for it. That's what I wanted to tell you."

"Perfect. Thank you for that. So, you gave away your watch to some charlatan on the street, you broke some damn inanimate thing—everything seems so much more important to you than the fact that you keep putting our lives in jeopardy! How do you know that nothing bad will happen? I suppose I'm just stupid—*you're* the one who knows everything now."

"No."

"Why won't you just listen? The world is falling out from under our feet so fast these days. I try to bring back one piece while another is already crumbling away." His blue eyes had turned to dead steel. "I don't need to be dealing with this, worrying about you all the time. If I hadn't taken this on, you could have been the man on the street."

"What do you mean?"

28

"You don't appreciate what I've done for you, Night. You think nothing of what I give to you and do for you every single day and, for once, I want you to think about it! Sit right here and tell me, out loud. Let's see if you can remember even one thing!"

He followed Andrew's outstretched arm straight to the point of his finger and his gaze ended up on the floor. He looked up startled. Why would he sit on the floor? An old clock ticking nearby counted the passing seconds out loud for him and, still, Andrew did not waive his request. Night rose from the armchair and hesitated, but Andrew's eyes didn't even blink. Night came closer, then awkwardly knelt before the self-appointed overlord of the emerald coastline.

"Now...what is the only thing I have always asked of you?"

"Not to talk to anyone."

"No! That you trust me!"

He nodded.

"And tell me... Just try to use your imagination. What should you be grateful for?"

"What do you want me to say?"

"Try love, prestige, everything you know, a future, your life— everything."

*Not everything.*

Andrew stood up from his chair and Night's shoulders lifted so he could follow suit. "No! You need to start remembering things, Night. Stay there and put your head to the floor."

Night glanced in the direction of his bed where his head should have been at this hour; then, gradually, his head sank to the floorboards. The sole of Andrew's shoe clamped down on the collar of the blue robe and Night's cheek abruptly met the wood. He heard a belt slithering out to freedom as Andrew stepped around him and he felt the bathrobe's velvet lift from the back of his thighs. He closed his eyes and tried to remind himself why this was worth it, but all he could conjure in the blackness were images from his nightmares.

# Chapter Five

After two weeks and four visits to the house as Night's English teacher, Lila stepped through the front door in her original capacity, as Andrew's lover...and perhaps as a bit of a sleuth.

Following an extended late shift at the hospital, she didn't feel hurried to announce her presence. She snapped on the table lamp in the living room and let her eyes glide up the banister of the curved staircase, along the minstrels' gallery, and then drop to the door below.

The room turned out to be a small den...a den without any books. She had expected to at least find a Bible in the house, after hearing about Andrew's undiluted Catholic ancestry, but despite the presence of a massive antique cabinet, its compartments turned up nothing but business documents. The last shelf she checked proved her wrong—at least until she realized she'd only found an outdated signing textbook. This implied that Night really did have profound hearing loss, but now she needed an explanation for his flawless speech, or if she dared think it...for the sign language.

She no longer made any attempt at stealth as she climbed to the second floor. Water ran in the bathroom and lamplight spilled into the hallway through Andrew's open bedroom door. In his absence, she sat down on the edge of his bed and, still in snoop-mode, couldn't help but pull on the night table drawer.

Her hand slipped inside to lift out a picture frame loosely wrapped in a woman's silk scarf. It slid off as she turned the oval framed photograph around. Andrew's summer-sky eyes peered back at her in shades of gray, like the rest of the picture. Andrew with a youthful face, stood like a soldier posing for his portrait, while the woman sitting next to him tipped an open smile down at her tiny infant. Andrew's wife had delicate features, penciled eyebrows, and teeth worthy of showing off between her darkly painted lips. Also in contrast with her light skin, she had chin-length, heavily waved dark hair. Andrew's hair appeared light in comparison. He had already admitted to her that it had once been as copper as a penny. Lila could see why their son was so attractive.

"Yes, my family..." Andrew interrupted, sullenly, from the doorway. He came in, stopped beside Lila, and also gazed down at the picture.

"You've never answered me about this. What happened to her?"

"Car accident."

Lila shifted on the bed to peer up at him. "Didn't you say she'd been ill?"

"I say a lot of things. I don't like to talk about it."

She felt she was playing chess. Her next move would have to be less aggressive or her opponent might be tempted to throw the board. "Andrew, I couldn't help notice that you don't have any books in the house." She decided to forget about subtle. "I mean, other than the ones right there, under your night table."

"Lila, why would I leave books all over the house when my son can't read?"

"Incentive? Okay, maybe you want to tell me about that, Andrew. Why is it that Night can't read?"

He finally eased himself down on the bed beside her. "It was a priority for me to teach him how to sign, how to communicate with me. Reading didn't come easy to him, and after a while, it didn't seem important anymore. I know, I should have pushed him, but he never really showed any interest."

"Well, he's showing an interest now." Lila appreciated that she was probably about to stalemate this game. "I have to ask you one more thing, Andrew. Does Night even know when his birthday is or did he, again, never really show an interest in presents and cake?"

"What are you getting at, Lila? We just don't celebrate birthdays, and I'll admit, that's for my benefit."

She sensed that Andrew was just as aware of the need to sacrifice a pawn or two in order to survive.

"His birthday happens to clash with my feelings about that time and since I can't acknowledge his, I won't acknowledge my own." Andrew's eyes turned up as though they were heavy. "It might be selfish of me, but I've honestly tried to make very little of birthdays in this house."

"Thanks for the tip," Lila sniped, dropping the picture on the bed as she stood up. "I don't understand why you've designed this life for yourself, and for Night, that doesn't offer either of you any advantages. He's never been to school—"

"I told you..."

"Andrew, should I really believe that you yielded to a six-year-old because he showed some aversion to the idea of going away for school? He would have made friends. And assuming that you made the right decision, did it make sense to never teach Night how to read? It's strange. You don't have a television, or even one of those devices for the telephone so he could use it...not that he could, being illiterate of course!"

"Lila—"

"He's completely isolated out here."

"And we both like it that way."

"And after the experience I had with Night the other week, I wonder if he's ever been out of his backyard."

"Why are you saying these ridiculous things, Lila? Why would I disadvantage him? How could you question that I love my kid?"

"I'm not saying that." She crossed her arms and dropped a sultry blink over her shoulder. "Maybe I just think it's a...strange love."

The corners of Andrew's mouth lifted and his eyes looked playful. "Well, you seem to quite like my strange love," he purred, setting his hands on her shoulders from behind before pulling her against his chest.

She fought not to smile but lost. "I'm sorry. I don't know what all you've been through and I'm not a parent. I shouldn't have said those things."

"I understand how it may seem, Lila. I never expected to do it all myself, and I know I've made mistakes, as you've so plainly outlined for me, but Night is also a very private and stubborn person. Sometimes I even have difficulty understanding him."

"I don't understand either of you." She sighed and turned around to accept his embrace, but he barely hesitated before he pressed his body to hers, all the way down to the bed sheets.

\*\*\*\*

Night thought little of the frantic breaths that reached him from his father's room as he neared the bathroom door. It pleased him to think someone else might be experiencing a nightmare for a change. Just then, his father called out as though he sensed him in the hallway and had something urgent to confess or report, so Night cracked open his father's door and pushed past the threshold.

Lila gasped and Night shot backward and hit his head as two naked bodies scrambled for decency, conspicuously united, the bed covers hopelessly trapped underneath hands and knees.

His father certainly didn't feel the least bit shamed in his state—in front of Lila. He boosted himself up to free the covers, revealing all before hunkering down between her legs as much as he could.

Night managed to clear the doorway on his second attempt to flee. He locked the door to the bathroom where a thought hit him, even before the whole incident finished playing back in his mind. If his father had lied to him about a man's spontaneous growth being an indignity, how many other dubious lessons could he finally dispense with?

\*\*\*\*

That morning, his father looked a bit sheepish when he came into Night's room, but he only stopped in to report that he and Lila were leaving to drive up the coast, so they wouldn't be back for several hours.

Night could hardly wait for them to leave. When they drove off, he slipped into the den. Unlike Lila, he was familiar with the contents of the wooden cabinet.

He studied the alphabet signs inside the front cover of the book he knew only too well, but for the first time in his life, these symbols meant something to him. He identified the print letters that Lila had taught him and he formed each letter with his fingers. He'd never even realized that his father had skipped this very basic lesson. Half way through finger spelling his name, he thought he heard the car return. He scrambled to get the book back in its place and vacate the room, but the living room window revealed that it wasn't his father's Mercedes that nestled in beside Lila's car... He couldn't get his shoes on fast enough before he calmly opened the front door.

"You're not easy to find!" Daphne called out, emerging from his muted dreams into brilliant reality. "I went to the restaurant a few times, but you're like never there, so I asked that waiter where you lived. He said about twenty minutes south—a beachfront house—but he didn't know the number. I can't believe I finally found you."

He couldn't believe it either.

"I'm sorry I didn't come sooner, but I thought about you a lot."

"I think about you all the time."

She always looked amused when he tried to be serious, but her focus left him to flit around the property before it came to rest on an abandoned pile of logs near her car. "Do you chop the wood?"

He nodded. It had been his job since childhood to keep the home and work fireplaces burning.

"Maybe you can cut some for me later?" She turned to look over her shoulder as though the ocean had just called her by name.

Night showed her the beach, and the window above a vine covered rock-cut that happened to be the view from his room. She winked and, once again, her eyes went in search of a new distraction.

She reminded him of the capricious winds on the bay; each moment carried her boldly in a different direction. Her loose, fiery hair danced in the wind to the beat of her full beige skirt as she flung off her shoes and teetered along the edge of the breaking waves. Likely with numbed feet, she returned and looked up at him. She contorted her hands in an effort to say something.

He squinted at her attempt.

"I've been practicing," she announced. "Don't you understand? ...I guess I'm not very good."

Guilt and resentment caused his shoulders and every feature in his face to fall.

"What's wrong, Night? You don't think it matters to me that you can't hear, do you? It really doesn't matter to me. I know we haven't spent much time together, but I already like everything about you. I love what I see. I love the way you move, the way your hands move, and how you sometimes throw your hair while you're working..." She tossed her head in an effort to imitate him. "You wouldn't believe how that makes me hot. And I love the way you smile, even though you don't do it often—but I have seen you do it. And I don't know if you know this, but when you speak, you have a nice voice. I love being around you, and how you make me feel... It's chemistry. Do you get what I'm saying? Do you understand me?"

Night nodded in a daze. He noticed but didn't care that Daphne seemed to be testing him with increasingly elaborate speech.

"Night, I want you...as much as on that first day when I went to see you at the restaurant and my friends thought you were nothing more than a challenge to me. Well, you're a challenge for sure, but you're way more than that. Please tell me...do you feel anywhere near the same?"

The kiss that followed sent his mind whirling. He closed his eyes and concentrated on every motion of her lips. He sensed exactly how much they parted, and how often, and how her head shifted, and for what purpose, and he mimicked her. Before he knew it, he was leading. His tongue traced lightly across her candy-flavored lip gloss,

36

and then between her gentle teeth. He'd now experienced her through all his five senses and he enjoyed every one of them. Inside the cold air, he was burning up. The salt in the breeze seasoning her skin—his too, apparently—and she began tasting it on his fingers until he felt like he was going to faint. On a blanket of dryer sand, she sank down over him, never letting their lips part. Her skirt billowed clear from under her and she straddled his right hip, letting the hardness he sustained beneath his zipper push up into the burrow beneath her thin underpants. Bracing her ankles beneath his legs, she pressed down on him and stirred, and he found out that he could intensify the effect by joining in. His kisses became hungrier and she eagerly fed them. His restless hands searched for a way to get between their bodies so he could free his pleading parts. Just then, a rogue wave collapsed behind them and Daphne shrieked as she bore the brunt of the icy shower. She scrambled off him and rolled her head onto his firm upper arm.

"Next time, my love," she voiced lightly, through a sigh.

As he stared at the clouds, devastated, Daphne reactivated. She turned toward him and draped one knee over his thighs; then she opened his pants. Far surpassing any of his own past efforts, she used her hands and raised him like dominos to topple dynamically through her prolonged and mind-bending course. He'd never savored every moment quite like this...delivered by hands from a dream, from the sky, from beauty and benevolence itself. What was she promising him...*next time?*

She'd taken him on a trip, without ever leaving the beach, but she took him other places too—physical places—by means of her car. At a roadside lookout, he snatched the binoculars from Daphne when she offered him a turn.

"What's the matter? Haven't you ever seen sea lions before?"

Night took another look. "I've never seen so many in one place."

On a day peppered with firsts, he yielded to one more when they returned to the car and Daphne pressed keys into his hand. In the driver's seat, Night gripped the wheel hard and pretended to watch Daphne's lips for instruction.

As they drove along the seaboard, he glanced at her often, and each time she answered him the same way: "You're doing great."

Daphne reached forward and snapped on her car radio, which made his eyes flash across the dashboard.

The instant the music came on, something sparked from his nightly tribulations like kismet—something he couldn't explain and far less dismiss. It struck him as yet another link between his nightmares and his unspecified destiny. He absorbed as much as he could, all the while trying not to tap his fingers.

Not far from their turn, Daphne lowered the volume and, after one hypnotic minute, Night reached for the dial and turned the music back up. He realized his mistake instantly. Daphne's wide stare brushed up his arm, to his face. Her mouth opened, but she simply sat back in her seat and let the music play.

Night racked his mind for a defense, but he couldn't think of anything to say, even as he parked the compact car in the clearing where his father typically brought his own great beast to rest. The pile of logs that greeted them again saved him temporarily.

"Are you going to cut some wood for me or not?" she asked, hoisting herself onto the hood of her car and crossing her legs over a headlight.

After a loose shrug, he grasped the long handle of the weathered axe and tensed his fingers around it. Daphne placed her fists together at her throat and smiled as she mimed taking off her top. A soundless giggle escaped Night as it dawned on him that this was a playful demand.

"You're laughing! Is that an actual laugh?"

The blush that invaded him made him oblivious to the cool spring air that blew through his short-sleeve undershirt as he lifted the axe. He experimented with showing off as he smashed the blade down, exploding the log in half.

Her head wiggled like she could hardly stand a repeat of the scene and she sprang off the hood, stepped up on the weathered tree stump, and kissed him until he dropped the axe.

"Bye, Night—my knight. I have to go," she announced abruptly. "I'm taking care of my daughter in a bit. My parents are going out."

Night tried hard to comprehend that someone younger than himself could be a parent.

"It's okay," she told him. "I've learned...or we both would have gotten exactly what we wanted today."

She returned his troubled gaze.

"I'll come back..."

"Come when I'm alone."

She started to smile but froze when Night latched onto her arms.

"What's wrong? Your father doesn't like me? I did get that impression."

"He doesn't like people coming here." His grip tightened on her arm.

Her voice now trembled. "I don't understand..."

Night dropped his hands and looked the other way, but Daphne gave him a push and a pull and reset his focus on her face.

"I know you can hear," she blurted. "I mean, why else would you turn up my radio? You can hear at least a little bit, can't you?"

Denying it would only make her more suspicious. He nodded and she skipped forward to kiss him, like in congratulations, but it was also goodbye.

****

In the kitchen, he picked at some desserts that had come home from the restaurant. He only stopped when Andrew and Lila pranced into the house.

His father' acknowledged him dryly. "Hello, Night. Have you had a busy day? I see that you managed to cut one whole piece of wood. I guess that would explain your appetite. Lila wanted to greet you this morning but you locked yourself in your room, at least until we left. Don't worry about what happened... We all make mistakes."

Night didn't pull his dead stare off his father fast enough to avoid another question.

"So, what did you actually do today?"

Night signed his response with a barbed edge. "Not a lot. I chopped a piece of wood."

Andrew flinched, but he didn't say another word.

****

Night stayed awake long after he'd turned off the lights, acutely aware of the proverbial presence hanging around him. It nagged him like a dripping faucet while he stared at the ceiling. The moment he tuned it out and drifted off, it had him—or something did.

With no prior negotiation, its invisible fingers latched onto his throat. His lungs raced for a breath, but they didn't make it and the slaughtering began. He thrashed against the shadow in the void, but the crushing intensified, which had a paralyzing impact. He would never have imagined that he had bones there, but he could feel them breaking, sending the illusion of a sickening sound to his brain.

He perceived a time-lapse and arms closed tight around him, he sensed protectively, but at the same time like a parasite. A voice from beyond his nightmare hurled him back into consciousness where real hands grasped him and sent his whole being into a violent spin.

"It's all right," Andrew repeated, with what struck Night as genuine affection. "It's just another one of your ridiculous nightmares."

Reality returned as fast as his spirit could re-inhabit his body. "Why do they never go away?"

Andrew truly looked troubled. "I don't know. But they're just dreams. Nothing can ever happen to you in real life as long as you trust me."

With open eyes, Night waited until Andrew went away, but the questions lingered. Was it just a coincidence that he would have such a potent dream right after the torrent of transgressions he'd committed today? Did he, in fact, need to respect his father's every word and warning?

# Chapter Six

"I've seen you before," blurted a guest at the restaurant before he even reached the counter. "Didn't I see you on the 101 the other day, at that lookout?"

Night rolled his eyes. He was still very much on trial on his first day back and, to boot, his father had decided to park himself, with Lila, at the counter for the entire evening.

"I'm sure you've seen Night," Andrew intervened in the silence. His eyes revealed a shimmer of forty-proof liquid amusement. "You've been here before, and everyone remembers our bartender."

Night prevented the man from arguing when he spilled the cognac bottle from his double grip, groped along the bar, and bee-lined for the washrooms.

Andrew came in, seconds later. "What's the matter with you?"

"I don't know," Night groaned into the sink. The water kept spiraling, escalating his vertigo.

"Did your thirst for new things possibly have you slipping a few drinks behind the counter this evening?"

Night's sneer flashed in the mirror. "I didn't drink anything...not even water."

"How can you be sick when you've gone nowhere for weeks?"

Night retched into the sink.

"Terrific. Fine. I suppose Lila can take us home now, but try to pull yourself together or she might also come to the wrong conclusion."

But as they settled themselves into Lila's car, only Andrew had trouble composing himself. "I can't understand this, Lila. He's never been drunk before."

"Andrew, it's pretty clear that you're the one who's drunk."

Andrew appeared to sober up instantly. "I have something to confess. You're right. I may have done things...wrong. That's why I need you, Lila. You can tell me when I'm not seeing straight."

Cringing through his mounting symptoms, Night listened in disbelief.

"Oh, Andrew, you've done well for yourself, and Night, but let's not discuss this in front of him like this."

"You're so right," he said, leaning back blissfully. "See, you're going to be good for both of us."

Even Night spotted Lila's opportunity to fish at this moment.

"Tell me a bit about his mother. What was her name?"

"Her name was Brigitte Morgen." Andrew spoke as though his former wife's name had been waiting to leap off his tongue, all evening. "Morgen, like the German word for tomorrow or morning. And she was quite the morning person."

That was the first time Night had heard his mother's name—this woman who had taken so many secrets with her.

"I'm sorry. You must miss her..."

Even intoxicated, Andrew retained his ability to change a topic quickly under duress. "So, do they have you working the graveyard shift all week?"

****

The evening's steady rain had graduated to a monsoon by the time they reached the house. Lila simply dropped her passengers off and continued on to work.

Night didn't bother to wash up or even look at the book that his new teacher had left with him on her last visit. Now feverish as well as nauseous, he stripped off his stylish work clothes on his way through his room and fell into bed. Everything from his blue sheets to his black boxers turned wet in no time. On the plus side, his illness left him immune to the nuisance entity that liked to show up at bedtime. He was almost asleep when Andrew appeared at his bedside.

"Night, forgive me for this evening. I wasn't in control of myself...something I cannot excuse and will never repeat. I didn't know what I was saying and I embarrassed both of us."

Night didn't have the strength or desire to entertain his father's petty woe. "I'm sorry too," he offered listlessly.

The weighty silence intensified as Andrew's eyes narrowed at a chair in the corner of the room. Night witnessed how purposefully his father walked over to it and lifted the sweater from the backrest, and how gingerly he picked off a long red hair that clung to the edge of the knitted fabric. He held it up high and stared at it in horror, as did Night.

His father dropped both and turned. "You let that bitch into my house and I'm apologizing to *you!* How many trysts have you had while I went to work? And the answer you gave me when I asked you about the wood...you were blatantly mocking me!"

Night struggled to sit up, wishing he could just vanish in the way of his nightly caller. "She was only here once..."

"Do you think this is nothing? Do you think there'll be no consequences for trusting that filthy little bitch with your life!"

For the first time ever, he blocked Andrew's punitive hand. Their sightlines clashed as hard as the thunder outside and Night savored the full second of his victory before he dove forward and launched off the foot of the bed. Through his condition, he sprinted to the ground floor, but with no plan, no destination in mind, he made himself easy prey at the front door.

Andrew latched onto an arm, and the door handle.

"It isn't wrong, Daddy...she's a really nice person."

"Oh, I feel so much better now!"

Night tripped onto the veranda.

"You wanted to go somewhere, Night?" Andrew kept him from falling, only to thrust him clear of the wooden steps, onto raw ground.

On skinned forearms, Night lifted himself off the rocky soil and Andrew hauled him upright, just so he could drive him another few feet, onto the broad tree stump that served as their chopping block.

Rain pelted the earth as Andrew plunged one knee and all of his weight over Night's back and pressed his left-hand flat against the deeply scarred wood. He ripped the axe from the edge of the stump while Night battled to curl his fingers under his palm. His frenzied breaths couldn't break through the clamor of the downpour assailing the forest around them.

"I hope this is memorable for you," Andrew pronounced over the chaos, "...every time you think of telling me another lie!" He raised the axe to the unfamiliar sound of Night screaming.

The deed was done in a split second, but in the absence of pain Night realized that the blade hadn't sliced through any part of him; instead, Andrew had buried it deep into the wood within an inch of his knuckles.

"Your insolent little response...not so amusing now, is it?" Andrew released the pressure from Night's spine and stumbled backward. "What the hell were you thinking?"

Andrew's footsteps fled across the veranda and ceased with the slamming of the door. Lightning hammered the bay, followed by bleak darkness as the veranda's lights went out.

Night suffered the molten anger that swirled through him. He swiped a rock from the ground like he'd always known its location and pitched it at the living room window. Not only did he miss, but this action also caused the ground to tilt until he folded back over the tree stump.

With enough rage still circulating to ignite his last reserve of strength, he dislodged the axe and hurled it straight through the colonial-grill picture window.

46

This brought back the light at the door, and undoubtedly, the grief he'd just invited was not far behind. But he wouldn't have to face it tonight. He'd gone off like a firecracker, and short-lived as such, he now felt himself disintegrating...plummeting through blackness.

**** 

Night's stark eyes opened to a fire. With his head on the floor, he sensed his father nearby through the shifting pressure in the hardwood. He instinctively peered at the sunlit window and saw that it was covered with plastic.

"I can always have the stupid window fixed, but it's not so easy when it's a broken life."

Night couldn't stop shaking, even under two blankets. He couldn't remember ever feeling so sick, and the thought did cross his mind that maybe he was dying. His father, on the other hand, hardly seemed concerned.

"Did I mention...your slut friend came by the restaurant yesterday?"

Night's eyelids parted to the sight of Andrew's face turning sharply toward the window—right before he too heard the car enter the clearing.

His father tramped to the front door and Night heard it fly open. The light from outside beamed down the corridor and stayed until long after the rumbling noise had faded. After the thud of the door closing, Night also heard three muffled words...

"No fucking way."

**** 

Andrew feigned delight when Lila paid him another surprise visit, the next morning.

"You don't look well, Andrew."

"And I'm the healthy one here," he replied, instigating the discussion that he intended to wrap up forthwith.

"I certainly hope you've apologized to your son for yesterday?"

"Yes, I did."

Lila grinned. "I kind of like the rarely seen disheveled Andrew, but I guess this was a bad time for me to just drop in."

"It's never a bad time, Lila. Rightfully, you should be living here with me."

"Hm. How's Night feeling? Could I say hello?"

"I don't think he would appreciate company right now."

"Andrew, I'm not company, remember? Rightfully I should be living here with you." She strode past him and he followed her, up the stairs, and into Night's room.

The half-open window drew the sickness from the room and replaced it with fresh salty air. Lila approached Night's bedside and waited for him to open his eyes.

Andrew lingered inside the doorway and crossed his arms.

"Night...?" She touched his face like a mother and her eyes widened. "My God, Andrew. You hardly need a fire downstairs to heat this place up."

"Yes, come now, Lila. He'll be just fine."

Lila ignored him and proficiently slipped another pillow under Night's head. "His lungs sound full. That might help a bit." She felt his pulse at his throat and appeared to be assessing the rate of his breaths. "If he's got pneumonia, he may need more than bed rest, Andrew."

"I know, and I've already been to the doctor," Andrew informed. "It's just a cold."

"A cold?" She gawked his way in disbelief.

"Whatever it is, he'll be just fine in a few days. His doctor gave me this." He pulled a piece of paper from his breast pocket. "If you really want to help, you can go into town and pick this up for me."

****

Two hours later, Lila returned with the antibiotics that Andrew had prescribed using a page from his own doctor's prescription pad. He'd filched it some time ago for situations like this, but he'd never had to use it.

Lila showed him how to dissolve the contents of these capsules in water to get them into his patient. "You want to make sure that he doesn't get too dehydrated," she lectured. "People don't always respect how serious that can be."

"Thank you, Nurse Lila, but he isn't going to die. It's just what we get sometimes for dealing with the public."

Lila smirked. "You're so sympathetic, Andrew. You'd fit right in with the nurses on my floor."

"I trust you work with a brilliant staff?"

Their persistent bantering engaged Night on some level, but his words kept evaporating on his lips. Lila dropped an ear closer to his mouth. "What's he saying? 'It's like' what'?"

"He's dreaming, Lila. Come now."

He hastened her through the doorway, remaining tight at her heels. Before the door closed behind him, Andrew managed to decode Night's uncoordinated, yet defiant effort:

"It's a lie."

After Lila had left the house to catch some sleep before her next shift, Andrew called the restaurant to report that he wouldn't be in for a few days. He stayed with Night in a similar state of dysfunction, resting his head on the blanket at the level of Night's hand. It slowly began to register that he could be reaping the upshot of some unlicensed doctoring. Lila's words taunted him as well. Night would no longer swallow any water, therefore no medication, and after the initial two days of incoherent rambling, he just fell silent.

The tedious accounts of modern people becoming deathly ill from some bug had never impressed Andrew before, but here he was, essentially being confronted with the influenza of the dark ages.

****

Lila reached for the hospital elevator's Hold Door button when Doctor Gardner came strutting around the corner from the adjacent hallway.

"Thanks, Lila," he said, turning to face the front, before he dropped his chin.

She thought he always acted a little coy when he came into contact with her. He was a true South County General relic, having practiced at this hospital since its doors opened in the late 1950's. He'd blushed in her presence the first time she introduced herself as a new nurse, sixteen years ago, at age twenty-five, but beyond his mannerisms, he'd always remained professional.

"How are you tonight?" Lila continued, working her way up to the real question. She peeped at him sideways, opened her mouth, reset her posture, and then repeated this whole sequence.

"Can't complain, but what about you, Lila? It looks like there's something on your mind."

The modest hopefulness in his tone encouraged Lila to go for it. "Doctor...can you recall a case from 1965-66, involving a local woman who died here...last name Shannien?"

He gave her question some genuine thought. "Shannien... That's a name from around that time, but I believe the situation involved a young, unwed mother..."

"No, no," Lila asserted. "The woman I'm referring to was definitely a mature, sophisticated woman."

The doctor chuckled. "I don't think so, but the more I think about it, it was her infant son who was admitted. Shannien...yes. That was the case."

"What are you talking about?" Lila became more obstinate as the blood drained from her head. "That doesn't make any sense. I'm talking about my partner's deceased wife and she wasn't an unwed teenager."

50

It appeared that her charm had limits as Gardner bristled against her contention. He shuffled his whole body in a quarter turn to face her, even as the elevator doors reopened. "Lila, come by my office tomorrow evening. By then I should have what I need from Medical Records and I'll prove to you that my memory is not failing me yet."

****

Almost a week of decline brought Andrew to a long forgotten threshold. He'd nixed the hospital as an option so he had only one hope. He knelt beside Night's bed and resorted to an act that he had refused to perform in almost two decades. At the edge of the bed, he placed his head between his elbows and he prayed. When he felt he'd lectured the Fates enough, he left the room and simply closed the door.

****

Night awoke into a stale blackness of midnight and wondered if he hadn't woken up, if this was another form of nightmare, already in progress. He couldn't convince his body or even his lips to move when panic should have ignited all systems. But this experience, like every bad dream, could not endure the light of sunrise.

****

Andrew kept his relief hidden behind a mantle of guilt. It wasn't until he came to see Night's recovery as a personal win—something to throw back at Lila—that he noticed a clear aberration. Lila hadn't called him or visited him in days.

****

True to form, Andrew made Night feel sorry that he had lived for whatever he did in his virtual coma. Apparently, some sort of doom was upon them both and it was *all his fault*. Sniffing and surveying the waves from the new living room window, still pristine and curtainless, Night watched as though the chaos and destruction would come by sea, and somehow, he didn't really care.

# Chapter Seven

The world looked a lot brighter to Night through the windshield of Daphne's car. While she kept their destination a secret, she didn't hold back about the number of times she'd tried to visit him but had to turn around, as per his instructions. Night tipped his head into his hand against the window, regretting that he'd done this to himself and to Daphne under the counsel of someone who was clearly the enemy.

They arrived at an old cottage where a large group of young people sat around a blazing bonfire, drinking beer. It didn't take long for a bottle to end up in each of their hands and Night tipped his back incessantly. He didn't mean for the sun to disappear before mustering the nerve to tell Daphne the truth about everything, but he couldn't chance her getting angry.

"You look so damn serious and we're here to relax," Daphne chided playfully in the flickering light.

The air had turned cool, and perched on one of his thighs, she wrapped herself around him like a backward scarf. Another couple in their circle started kissing, inspiring Night to show Daphne that he remembered everything from their last visit.

He would tell her the truth very soon, in a moment, or later—or in the morning when they woke up together in her room. He only knew he wasn't going back to his house.

The music picked up—again that peculiar and brilliant sound. A young man with a mustache bounded from the house clutching a cigarette in one hand and a long wooden pole in the other, just ahead of his friend who carried a set of long brackets with many rungs. In two minutes, they had the pole suspended horizontally in mid-air, the soft rock music swapped for something seductively energetic, and the occasion labeled for the one clueless freak among them as someone jumped up and howled, "Limbo contest!"

Daphne lifted her mouth to his ear. "I'll bet you could do that."

Everyone stood up to watch as the first fellow leaned back and bounced his way out from under the pole; the two females that followed turned out to be equally skilled. Night could not only hear the music, he could feel it reinventing the rhythm of his heart and overhauling his whole concept of living.

Daphne shoved him toward the lineup. He glanced back several times out of habitual unease, but he was exactly where he wanted to be. He copied what the others had demonstrated and also emerged cleanly from under the pole. People cheered at the limber newcomer, especially when he cleared it for the third time. It both surprised and encouraged him, but even his newfound confidence didn't help him when the bar was dropped to the second last rung.

By that time, Daphne looked more than eager to have him back. She finished taking a drag on the strange, tiny cigarette between her thumb and forefinger and passed it to her neighbor before he could take a seat. She helped herself to a swig of his beer before she grabbed his fingers and led him into the darkness of a nearby path.

The light of the ancient moon followed them like a magic lantern. Its glow blossomed over the old bridge where they stopped and admired the diamond carpet that rolled out across the black water. Earth's aura lifted between them in scents of mushroom and evergreen.

Night turned from the railing and locked his sight on Daphne. She dropped her heavy knitted cardigan and he hungrily pulled her near. The bridge became a surreal place, with no rules, no right or wrong, nobody to declare his every move and desire a perilous violation.

Daphne stepped back and, in less than three heartbeats, he caught onto her game. She turned her smile away when the zipper on his quilted vest got caught on a thread, but it fell soon enough, leaving him still covered by a tight, thin sweater.

"That's cheating," she teased in a sultry purr. Showing him her back, she unbuttoned her slip-dress and waited to be helped with the rest. Instinct took over and he placed his hands on her small shoulders and traced them down, taking with them the straps of her dress. Then she twirled to face him.

Night had never seen ice-pink underwear like this before, and it did for him everything it was meant to. Daphne stole his turn and pulled up his sweater. When she could no longer reach, he completed the job. His focus returned to her lacy bra, which she reached back to unclasp herself. It tumbled to the wood, but Night didn't notice it land.

Holding his gaze, she backed away and stroked her long flame-red hair while the moonlight presented her skin in milky porcelain-white, the contrast breathtaking.

He remained transfixed and desire rushed his neutral eyes. At once he understood that a flawless veneer, stylish clothes, and flashy accessories couldn't hold a candle to the sublimity of this girl's bare skin, the wind through her already careless hair—mystery, expectation and pure admiration for nothing more than what nature ordained. This was the essence of eroticism though he didn't know it by name.

"Don't worry," she breathed as they came together, which he assumed implied that nobody would know.

Their arms fused around one another and their lips collided with more force at every contact. It helped that on high-heeled sandals, Daphne stood several inches taller. He had learned a lot from their past kisses, and it didn't take him long to master any art. Daphne would just have to wonder how he'd suddenly become the aggressor.

She brought him to the wood planks and pushed him back before he could think of coming forward on her. She kissed him shortly before slinking halfway down his body.

He blushed at the stars as he listened to murmurings of how 'hot' he was while she kissed him all the way from below his navel to his chest where she teased his taut nipples with small shudders of breath, tiny licks and delightfully distressing pinches between her teeth. His fingers coursed through her river of hair while she lifted her head, but his hands went limp when she opened his jeans. He helped her slide them past his knees, from where her hands ran up as she kissed her way up his thighs. There, she began tracing his hips with her nails while she tugged at the damp front of his underpants with her lips. He already welcomed the arrival of the most magnificent feeling of his life and he reclaimed his grip on her scattered mane.

Night appreciated all the tactics she used to drive him to this treacherous brink. He forgot to exhale as Daphne's warm breath continued to circle his *private parts...* This term, which he'd only heard from his father, thanks to his childhood curiosity, breezed through his frenetically blissful mind, and stirred up a grievance. More than any other body part—more than an elbow, knee or a nose—this one deserved to have a specific *name.*

Daphne's fingers slipped inside his underpants to free this special part and his breathing reignited with a gasp. Her mouth sank down and he could hardly stand the few last seconds to touchdown, and then her body collapsed over him to the sound of her shoe sole skidding off the edge of the bridge. A faint splash followed as her shoe met the inkwell below.

Daphne scrambled onto her knees and twisted to peer over the side and Night's intentions split in two. His state had not been abated, but Daphne's attention appeared to have left him, so he stood up and pulled up his jeans.

He left them open, and once he'd climbed down the embankment, he finished the job himself. It didn't take long; then he staggered through the icy thigh-high water until he spotted the pale shoe scarcely hanging onto one of the boulders beneath the surface.

By the time he returned, Daphne looked as cold as the current he'd just waded through, in spite of his gallant deed. He set the shoe down in front of her where she sat crouched against a splintery post, huddled in her wooly cardigan with her arms crossed unyieldingly across her chest, but then she grinned.

"It's all right," she said as she rose and pulled the straps over her heels. "You're soaked and you're freezing. Let's just go."

56

With chattering teeth, Night scooped up his things and followed her to the car. He frequently disappointed his father and so, he concluded, he probably had the same propensity with everybody else. He exhaled as he sat down in the passenger seat. How could he tell her the truth now?

She drove him back to his house in complete silence. In the driveway, she flicked the light on above them. "I had a good time. You probably could have won the contest but you tend to freeze up." She winked and then draped her pink bra over Night's arm.

He didn't know if she'd just handed him a final consolation prize or a pledge of commitment, but either way, it was his cue to get out.

The car's headlights helped him to the front steps. He hated being back, but he felt he could survive on this evening for a while. Even if something trumped it, he would never forget this one experience. He waited until he could no longer see the car's taillights through the trees, then he blissfully swung around and sauntered up the stairs, closing his eyes indulgently, and it was in that moment that the lanterns beside the doorframe came to life.

His father had informed him that he wouldn't be home until the next morning, but the lanterns suggested otherwise. The silent door in front of him now seemed alive and breathing and he feared disturbing it. He hesitated with his hand on the door handle, but he had little choice, now that Daphne had left.

He crept through the foyer, drawn forward by the demure lamplight in the living room that spilled a human shadow toward him. Night peered in the direction of the empty driveway, only to receive full confirmation of his father's presence through a blazing sweep that landed across his face.

"Yes, the car is out there," Andrew barked as he studied Night up and down, wincing at the beacon of pink lingerie hanging over his arm. The malevolent glow in his eyes faded as he turned around and made his way, despondently now, to his armchair.

Night pressed himself against the wall in the living room, now that his legs had lost most of their strength.

Andrew's head slumped over his knees and he rubbed his heated temples. "How could you?"

Night assumed this was all about his rendezvous with Daphne. "She just—"

"Lila's gone," his father's voice rolled like dark, heavy storm clouds.

Night wished his father would just shout through his list of his charges or do whatever it took for him to close the matter, rather than perpetuate this eerie, electric calm. "What do you mean, she's gone?" he finally asked.

"She's gone! She's not the same. She's gone—just like my last shred of trust in you!"

"No..." Night rattled his head. "Everything is a lot better than you think." He rushed forward and kneeled in front of Andrew, who seemed blind to him at only inches away. "Whatever you thought would happen if I talked to people...it's not true. Nothing is going to happen. Nothing ever happens and..." He stopped when Andrew's face shot up.

"You sound like you've been busy, Night. And why don't you keep your liquored breath to yourself. Just go." He waved his hand loosely at the staircase.

Night rose cautiously. "I know you're angry..."

"Angry?" Andrew's words came out like corrosive steam. "Anger is a pitiful waste when it comes to you—but maybe you'll care about consequences."

Water leeched into Night's mouth from the passages of his eyes and nose. He was determined to have his father resolve his anger promptly, even if it wasn't particularly fair. He straightened his shoulders and declared in his new nasal voice, "I'm going to leave."

This finally animated Andrew.

58

"Oh, now you're going to leave?" he roared in demonic amusement, rising from his chair. "Tell me, Night...where are you going to go? Do you, in fact, have somewhere to go?"

"Yes."

"Oh really? Where? Are you going to live with your little slut friend? And as low as she is, you have nothing to offer her! Don't you understand that you do not and cannot exist anywhere else but here? The world would suffocate you...crush you!"

"I can call Lila. She'll help me."

"Call Lila? Call Lila! How are you going to do that, Night?" Andrew took two giant steps toward the telephone and ripped the mounting cable straight out from the wall. "How the fuck can you taunt me like this after everything you've done! I'm sorry if someone confused you, but the fact is that you belong to me—not to any street prostitute female or even to yourself! Do you understand? You belong to me, my dear child, and from now on..." his voice started to break, "you are going to know it!"

Night straightened his back and tried to keep his eyelids from twitching.

"Don't bother with pride. You have no loyalty, no standards, no shame. Call Lila... Isn't that bloody precious?"

Night clenched his hands. He realized he was trapped in the only real nightmare he had ever truly faced: living in his own house.

His father snatched the scant piece of pink fabric off the floor where it had fallen and slammed it into the fireplace. "Does she ever keep anything on?"

Night gave into a subtle grin at this reference to Daphne's shawl that had met the same fate at the restaurant. He turned away from the gushing flame dispassionately. As long as Daphne was still intact, nothing could destroy what they'd already shared and what they would have together in the future.

He took his time in the bathroom, after going upstairs. As he slowly combed through his hair, he took stock of the many features

59

that Daphne referred to as "hot", but a sudden surge of pain through his hand—the kind he knew well from his nightmares—interrupted his musing and made him drop the comb. At the same moment, Andrew's reflection appeared in the mirror.

"Feeling guilty?" his father inferred as he presented his palm. "Here, just take your pills."

Night had continued to take a variety of medication, daily, since his recent illness and his father was right to assume he hadn't taken any of them today.

He felt beyond tired as he sank into his pillows and sheets. They were satiny and abundant, like Daphne's hair against his face and bare chest. He felt content as he drifted off on this reflection...a trip that lasted only seconds.

****

As the light of morning accosted him—or was it the brief appearance of the midday sun—he no longer had that content feeling. Although he had no recollection of what had happened, his flesh remembered every detail and his mouth sprang open against his pillow in a silent, belated cry. He began to cough, which spawned a colossal headache that crippled him more than the scorching pain that now replaced his skin.

He twisted through the searing pain to look over his shoulder. At the slightest effort, he saw blood on his sheets, then on his leg, then everywhere, and this triggered him to flip off the edge of the bed. Too dizzy to walk, he crawled his way to the full-length mirror on the far side of his open doorway where he relapsed into unconsciousness.

When he came around again, he dragged himself within an inch of the mirror and placed his hands flush on the cool glass. He could have stayed that way, but desperate to see the problem, he willed himself to keep climbing, smudging the mirror with a collage of handprints all the way up to the top. His sensitivity to the light caused him to strain as he turned to have a look at his dorsal side. The shallow breaths that he emitted became labored as he blinked around the room, seeking comfort or explanation from anything for the crimson lines that trailed every which way over his back and almost all the way down to behind his knees. They were no longer distinct beneath the global mess caused by excessive swelling and bleeding, but whatever was used to draw these marks had slashed open his skin as though a possessed violin bow had played a concerto all over his body. Night's eyes lifted slowly in his already turned head as he realized the other presence.

Andrew idled in the doorway, as even he appeared troubled by what he beheld in the blatantly sincere light of day. He swallowed and cleared his throat, despite his bold admission.

"I had to, Night...for your sake. Maybe this will help you keep your clothes on...at least for a while."

Night turned his face away as though nobody was there, but he couldn't ignore that he might throw up or faint at any second. His father must have sensed this because, when he did go down, he met with his bed, rather than the floor.

Andrew sat himself at the edge and pulled a thin blue sheet over the mess on Night's body that still quivered from the physical as well as chemical assault.

"I didn't want to hurt you, Night. That's why I made you sleep."

"Well, it does hurt."

"But that will go away." Andrew's words rained down heavy, along with his stare. "The train finally veered too far off its track...and it needed the hand of a giant to set it back on. I hope it will stay there from now on. You know, Night, I've never taken away your freedom, and that's revealing its price... Remember that."

The burning and nausea made every vulgar reality, especially Andrew's foul logic, unbearable at that moment. Night let go of the sheet he'd crumpled inside his clammy grip and buried his face; then his hand and the whole length of his body began to shudder in a different way.

Andrew stood up and left without another word, but first he dropped two pills onto the nightstand.

Night swept them off as though they were spiders. Even without the help of the painkillers, he did fall asleep again, and this time, when he met up with his ubiquitous doppelganger, it greeted him with something other than its usual impatience. For once, it was teeming with excitement.

# Chapter Eight

Serious change was coming. Even as he allowed days to pass in self-imposed seclusion, Night knew it would find him, but he didn't anticipate that it would arrive by the twisted network of vines below his bedroom window. First, two hands appeared on the sunny window ledge, followed by the face he daydreamed about through every waking minute.

"I know he's here," Daphne confessed through winded breaths. "I left my car up the road. Night...I can't stand it anymore."

He strung on the shirt that he kept on standby, at the edge of his bed, before helping Daphne down from the ledge, but then he scooped her head inside both hands. "I know... I have to tell you something, Daphne. I wanted to tell you this all along. I can hear. I can hear you. I've always been able to hear you."

She reflected his desperate nods. "I know. It has something to do with your crazy father, but I don't get it..."

Instead of an answer, he gave her a kiss. Their lips stayed locked as her hands brushed up his covered arms, down his bare chest and then beneath his shirt to his back, at which point he shunted her away.

"What's wrong?" She came to his side, her hand hovering above his shoulder, hesitant to touch.

Night helped her out. He lowered his shirt, just enough to reveal one shoulder, then pulled it back up. Daphne stumbled back, her fingers pressed to her mouth before she dropped her hands to implore him.

"How could you let him do all these things to you, and for so long—and now *this*? You could have left with me before it got this far." Her voice was quickly spiraling above a hush. "Do you even know how freakish this is?"

Similar to his, her eyes were now loading with tears, but Night shocked her with a grin.

"How could you be smiling?"

"He thought this would stop us."

After one big exasperated breath, she collapsed against him and stroked his arms and chest feverishly. "Well, if you think you've finally had enough, leave with me now?"

Night sent his reply through another greedy kiss, oblivious to his door falling wide open, but Daphne jumped back.

From the doorway, Andrew fixated on her alone. "Get the hell away from my son, Aileen."

Night stepped in front of Daphne, but she shuffled sideways, refusing to lose eye contact with her monster as she stated: "My name isn't Aileen. I'm Daphne."

Andrew's glare ignited into a vehement blaze that made Daphne recoil. Night shoved her out of his father's trajectory, but Andrew kept advancing.

Daphne jumped onto the bed. "You're really some kind of psycho!" She now towered over Andrew—a sleek, panther-like silhouette in her ribbed sweater and tight blue jeans, baring her incisors. "He's leaving with me, and if you try to stop him I'll go straight to the police!"

But she screamed when Andrew swiped at her. She leapt off the bed, inciting a chase down the hallway that ended on the landing when Andrew caught her hair.

"You want to go to the police, you little bitch! About what exactly?"

Daphne bashed at the hands that swarmed her when the grip came off her hair, but her whole body melted once she realized the hands belonged to Night. He gathered her against himself, aware of her racing heartbeat and breathing being out of sync with his, and he peered at the staircase. Andrew stepped out of the way.

"Go, Night... I'm not going to stop you. ...You can go. I promise."

Slowly, Night unglued himself from Daphne so they could hurry down the stairs. She still gripped his hand, which is why he felt it when Andrew's shoe sole slammed blunt against her spine. Her shriek ripped through the shadows on the staircase, ending abruptly with a sickening crack between two rail posts that had snagged her head about halfway down.

Night couldn't recall getting there, but he found himself at the bottom, groping her arms, then her head, until his fingers could no longer crawl inside the web of red hair.

Andrew ripped her away and just stared at the detested ragdoll in his grip for a few seconds before he heaved her slight body over his shoulder; then he ran out the front door, leaving it wide open.

Night felt almost too numb to walk. He staggered to the gaping doorframe to see his father throw a shovel into the trunk of his car. He didn't see much after that, but he heard the consecutive thuds as his father closed the trunk and the car door. He didn't hear the engine engage.

On the veranda, Night gripped his arms as he began to shake like no amount of heat could ever end the chill. He could already feel himself reeling back into the insufferable void...his true eternal nightmare.

He returned to the living room, in a virulent haze, and crafted a wall of fire inside the fireplace. In front of it, he sat quivering, even as the front door creaked open, hours later. His trance was shattered only by the strange presence of mud on the typically gleaming hardwood floor, in the trail of his father's footsteps. Night had never seen Andrew covered in dirt. The sweat on his face had made the silt that dusted it run into dark streams and form into blotches. Only the pristine blue of his eyes remained recognizable.

"Now do you see it?" Andrew barked, his voice as gritty as his exterior. "Do you finally understand what I've always told you? Do you want to destroy any more lives? ...Your own? Mine? ...And I still have to deal with her car." He marched on but stopped in his tracks when Night suddenly barked back.

"What did you do with her? Tell me where she is!"

"She's in the ground! I did what one must do with someone who is dead!"

Night continued, just as Andrew turned to leave. "If I would have told her the truth sooner, this wouldn't have happened."

"The stupid girl did it to herself. It's not your fault."

"No, it's yours!"

Andrew's hands smashed down at his sides. "Fine, it's *my* fault! But is it not your fault that Lila's gone?"

"Lila..." Night said, trembling like a bomb getting ready to detonate, "Lila...is not *dead!*"

"I am sorry for you, Night..." Andrew replied, replacing his red-hot anger with a cool condescending air. "Sorry that you are so uncomplicated that it gets you into trouble..." He planted himself on the floor beside Night and even dared to stroke his hair with his filthy hand.

Night didn't move, but his eyes shot stakes of ice into the flames. "Who am I hiding my body from now?" he blurted when the tension hit its pinnacle.

Andrew's fingers tightened for just a second before completing their path. "Soon you'll go back to the restaurant and then everything will be like it was before."

Glaring through the water in his eyes, Night foresaw one thing clearly. Nothing would ever be like it was before.

****

A few days later, Night confirmed that his family of mice had perished through his neglectful absence, so he sank the crate in the bay in salute to former ignorant bliss as it too would never be seen again.

Inside the more elaborate crate that he once called home, Night finally mastered the lifelong command, never to speak, yet Andrew did not seem pleased.

"Think about your fans," his father chided as he parked his car at the restaurant. "They've all missed you, and you'll only be embarrassing yourself if you insist on punishing them like you are me. By the way, I suppose I should thank you for the gift I found in your room the other day. The wind-chimes are quite nice. I hung them up here, as I'm sure was intended. It's only a shame that I can't thank Lila for them too."

Steaming in his seat, Night made no move for the door handle.

"Everything that you should care about is right here, Night. Soon, you'll forget about what happened and then maybe I can start to forget about this whole hellish mess also."

But it could never be that way. Night no longer felt at home at the restaurant. A strange aura lifted off the floor and walls that made him feel disconnected and unwelcome.

His resentment spiked when he learned that Daniel had long been replaced, but the new waiter kept him from dwelling on it when he announced that somebody wanted to see him at the back door. He foolishly hoped that it would be Daphne, but it was Lila who greeted him with no time for pleasantries.

"I didn't want to come here, but I couldn't just forget about you. We have to talk, Night...but not right here."

Her confident strides led Night all the way down the dirt path to the water's edge where he knew Lila was about to confirm that she didn't plan to ever offer him another reading lesson. Holding his elbow and gazing at oblivion beyond the whitecaps, she spoke.

"Is there something you want to tell me, Night...before I talk to your father?" She started pacing in a circle, coming to an abrupt halt behind him. "You can hear me, can't you, Night?"

He clenched his teeth and his breath quavered when he exhaled. He wanted to confess, but he had to take into account her primary, or at least former, allegiance to his father.

She sighed heavily and returned to his side, but she didn't look at him. "I want to know about your hearing loss, and I want to know about your mother—and I don't mean Brigitte Morgen—but your real mother who is more than likely still alive."

Night threw his head to look at her, but now he truly couldn't speak.

"I apologize, Night. I may have been bluffing somewhat. But which one of us pulled the bigger bluff?"

Somehow, Lila knew. Night waited for the sky to fall or the sea to lurch up and swallow the earth, or for everything around him to burst into flames—for whatever this thing was that would in some way eradicate the world as he knew it.

"Night, why the hell are you pretending to be deaf?"

"I don't know! Ask my father and then tell me!" He bounded up the path. He wanted to get away from Lila and all her questions—away from the possibility of making everything even worse. Halfway to the parking lot, he veered toward the woods. He only looked over his shoulder after crossing the tree line and he spotted Lila, no more than ten yards away. She abandoned her pursuit of him when she too heard the footsteps descending on the path.

"Lila? I noticed your car. What are you doing out here?"

"Hello, Andrew," she acknowledged flatly. "Night and I were just having our first really uninhibited conversation together."

Andrew glanced both ways. "Where is he?"

She flipped her hands theatrically. "I'm not sure. When I asked him why he's pretending to be deaf, he just ran off."

"Lila, why would you do that?"

"Just stop it, Andrew. It's not a secret anymore that he's been pretending—although I can't for the life of me understand how his father could be involved in this charade."

Andrew's expression turned oddly placid. "I've been waiting for you to come back. We should talk."

"I agree, Andrew. I've recently discovered why you don't like to discuss the past—why you lie about almost everything that pertains to your family."

Night heard his father laugh. "Your source must be a mystic, Lila?"

"Hardly! My source is a hospital file. I only wanted to know the truth about Brigitte's death, but instead I found out that the only Shannien who received treatment at South County General in 1965 was, not Brigitte, not Night—but a Morgen Shannien who was brought in at two weeks for failure to thrive, by his mother...a fourteen-year-old girl named Aileen Coleman."

Night waved a leaf out of his line of sight to see his father finish smearing his face before he showed Lila a dead stare.

"For God's sake, Andrew—a fourteen-year-old girl! All the ideals you spoke of with me, all your righteous notions—all just a big farce!"

"No!" Andrew erupted. "Your file didn't give you all the facts."

"Is that right? Did some other Shannien family pass through Lincoln County in the year that Night was born? And if Brigitte Morgen was really your wife, then Aileen Coleman could only have been an affair..."

Andrew fired out a grim chuckle. "In someone's demented fantasy, perhaps. No...Brigitte was my wife, and we were very happy."

"So, Aileen Coleman...?"

"Was the mangy slut responsible for the death of my son and who eventually paid me back with Night!" Andrew crossed his arms and glared down at the dirt beneath his expensive wing-tipped shoes. He stayed silent like he needed to digest his disclosure, the same as

Lila. Against the breeze, Andrew again showed the world his faultless blue eyes through fallen wisps of silver.

"Night is your grandson."

"Yes," Andrew grunted. "If it were only as sweet as that sounds. I cherish the part of Night that is my son, but I could never help but loathe the whole half of him that is *her*."

"How could you confess to feeling that way? Why, what happened? Did your son run away with this girl before he—?"

"No! He did not run away with her. My son, Reade—at fifteen-years-old—killed himself with alcohol and a bottle of sleeping pills. Didn't you find that file?"

"No," Lila uttered. "I'm sorry. So, you had a son named Reade... Red hair?"

"Of course. Runs in the family."

"Why didn't you just tell me about him? Why all the lies?"

"Why would I want to share the details of that mess with anyone? I allowed some little plebian bitch to destroy my son's life, and in the end, my life as well. It didn't help that Brigitte had always welcomed her. A few months after Reade was found dead, that creature showed up on my doorstep asking for Brigitte, because she's pregnant, and is starting to show, and she couldn't tell her parents... That was when I finally understood what had happened. Reade obviously couldn't tell his parents either."

"Maybe that wasn't so easy for him to do."

Andrew sharply pulled his fingers from his temples. "Don't insult me, Lila. I was right about everything. I told him to stay away from her, but he wouldn't listen—and look how it all turned out. After killing our only son, she still hoped that Brigitte would dig her out of her mess, but by the time she came to the house, Brigitte wasn't there anymore. Brigitte had left me. She just couldn't deal with my grief...but how could she understand it? Reade wasn't *her* son."

Lila didn't react, as though anesthetized against Andrew's shockers by now.

"You wanted to know the truth," he snapped. "Brigitte couldn't have children. The woman in the photograph you found was my first wife, holding Reade. And I told you the truth. I lost her in a car accident. I lived through that accident—she didn't—then Reade, then Brigitte. Do you understand now why I wanted to protect the only semblance of family I had left?"

"To a point," Lila granted. "What kind of arrangement did you make with this girl who you hated so much?"

Andrew continued, half-delirious. "I wanted my son's child. What else did I have left? But I couldn't stand to look at the mother for the next four months, so I paid for her board at a rooming house in town, and I was generous in hiring someone to help her deliver— early, thank God—and tend to their medical needs as they both had many. And yes, there were twins. She didn't even care about giving them up. She only cared about the payment I offered her in exchange.

"You couldn't imagine my relief when she finally pulled up in a taxi to pick up her imbursement and deliver mine. But she only came with Night. The file you found belonged to Night's brother who obviously survived longer than I was told."

"Well, it was all for the best, I would imagine. Hiding away, two could've been a real headache."

"I thought you were starting to understand. Go home, Lila. I have to go find my kid," Andrew muttered before he stomped off like a child himself, into the realm of perpetual twilight.

Night ducked in the foliage and hoped to stay invisible as he slunk toward the open path, but the sticks breaking under his soles gave his effort away.

"Night!"

He reached Lila on the path, with his young grandfather already in tow. "Help me get away from here, Lila..."

72

She flung her keys into his hand. "Go...I'll meet you at my car. See, Andrew, it's contagious."

"Oh, shut-up, Lila."

In his fine suit, Andrew slogged up the path and wrestled the keys away from Night's fumbling hands; then he pitched the keys clean down the hill.

Lila cursed at witnessing them whizz by, and as she ran back down the hill, Night looked at Andrew in disbelief.

"What are you doing, Night? I wish you could be a little more grateful. You would have been nothing but a stray if I didn't take you in. Maybe your brother, the mystery Morgen, would have been less disappointing in the end. Maybe it was a sign when I bequeathed him Brigitte's surname instead of something opposite to 'Morning'."

"Why don't you tell me what happened to my mother? Either way, I'm going to find her and ask her..."

Andrew released a short, derisive snuffle. "Good luck with that, Night. Tell me if you find your Daphne as well."

Even without the sophistication of others, Night grasped his grandfather's admission and he felt the red in his hair flooding his complexion. All his pent up words began to boil from his lips.

"Why...? Tell me why you did all this, and why I had to learn this..." He flailed his hands around senselessly before he dropped them in fists. "Tell me why I wasn't supposed to talk to anyone or go anywhere or learn anything—and if it was all for my sake, why was it so much better to hurt me all the time than just risk that something else *might do it!* Tell me! Tell me right now—and tell me something good—and don't try to tell me that it's not the right time because I've been waiting my whole life for the answer and I just can't wait any longer!"

"Night, I didn't go through all this effort to replace my son just so all the same things could happen. I had to do something different. I found a legitimate way to explain why you couldn't go to school, and I was still able to offer you a life around people, without you getting too close to them. And I have to say...every time we worked on your sign language I felt like I was doing something to succeed at my goal, and the reality is, it did work, because here you are, an adult."

Andrew's voice sounded so far away over the rustling in the fir trees and the breaking of waves growing louder in Night's head. Even the tiny insects added to his expanding mental din. The world around him started spinning, fading, sinking—the revolt of all his days and nights of painful wondering. He held the top of his head and let out a shriek before he managed some words.

"All for nothing! This is why I'm such a freak and why Daphne's—?"

"Night, shut your mouth, for *both* our sakes! You can't tell anyone about what happened to her. There is no way for me to make you understand the consequences. Now, calm down!"

Tears choked Night's airways as he scuffled past Andrew and charged toward the concrete steps of the restaurant, but Andrew caught one of his arms before he reached the doors. Night tore free and spun around—poised with his fists wrapped tightly around a phantom pitchfork.

"You want me to calm down?" Night dropped his hands and shoved Andrew clear off the top step before he resumed his course.

"Night, don't you go in there like that or I'll never forgive you."

Night balked in the face of the restaurant's grand front doors. "Like it matters." Then he stormed into the restaurant, tear-streaked and breathless, and he ran to his usual post at the far side of the bar.

All the pain, torment, evil and anger from Hell channeled into his feet and through his body. "Look at what you've done to me! You did all these things—just in case something went wrong?"

Andrew pleaded, in sign, for Night to stop while everyone in the place watched their typically passive bartender go off.

"Daniel was right...I'm a freak and it's *your* fault! I don't know anything! All I know is drinks!" Night picked up a stemmed glass and hurled it at the side wall. He couldn't even hear the gasps. "I also

74

know what glasses to use for everything. Red wine!" he called out as he pitched a second glass at an abandoned table where it skidded and crashed on the floor.

Andrew strode forward, no longer silent. "Night, control yourself!"

"White wine!" Night screamed as he whipped a third glass across the room, then a fourth and a fifth... "Champagne...Old-fashioned...Brandy snifter...! Should I flame you a drink?" he inquired hysterically after the sound of breaking glass. He smashed a full bottle of Cognac over the counter and set it ablaze with a match. The flame burst over the entire bar, evoking a few screams and sending a few customers scrambling away from the blaze.

Andrew clutched his arms from behind and held him back from the counter, and for a moment Night didn't struggle.

"It was all for nothing. There was never any reason..."

"Everyone, leave us!" Andrew commanded, abandoning Night to usher his customers into the foyer.

"Why don't you tell them the truth?" Night persisted. "See if *they* understand."

"The show is over! Leave us!" Andrew roared, sweeping the room with a glower that chased a few more people toward the exit before he returned to the bar.

Night snatched another bottle of hard liquor from the wall and held it out in front of him. "Stay away from me! Tell them the truth! Tell them what Lila thinks. Tell them what Daphne thought! Tell them what my real father would have said about you if he were here!"

"Night...!"

"At least he was smarter than me... I never even thought about killing myself!"

Andrew gripped the rye bottle on both ends and used it to drive Night into the busy wall behind him. Night crashed onto the floor tiles, taking with him many glasses and glass shelves, but he didn't linger in the rubble; he sprang up and hurled himself full-force into Andrew. The bottle in Andrew's hand flew free and shattered, creating an even greater flame-barrier between him and his remaining spectators, some being moved to intervene.

"Get yourselves out of here and let me deal with this!" Andrew tried pulling Night forward but he stayed put like cement brick, unlike the walls around them that quaked through the livening fire, and the wrath from Andrew's personal desecration.

Night stood there impassively, surrounded by the inferno as though immune to the heat.

Andrew glanced around. "Look at what you've done to this place—and to us! Look around! Look!"

The fire burst across the floor and onto the tablecloths. A vertical wooden beam between the counter and the ceiling became a crackling orange mass and the solid-wood rafters above them lit up like flaming crossroads. The usually pleasant smell of burning wood started to turn caustic. The grand fireplace blackened behind a sheet of fire and another vertical post snapped and rolled off the furniture like a flaming barrel. Everything that had once been beautiful furniture was now reduced to fuel. Outside, a terrified wind-chime rang out frantically through the mutable air pressure and stirred Night out of his trance.

"Why did you even bother if you *hated* me so much?"

"Night, I loved you."

A moment lapsed. "What does that even mean?"

Lila suddenly appeared through the smoke with her keys in one hand and the other extended. "Here, come with me, Night... *Just come!*"

"No, Night. Don't listen to her. Stay with me or, I promise, you'll regret it."

Night crept toward the door and Lila snatched his arm. In front of the exit, he braced himself and looked back at Andrew, one last time, as he raised his hand and signed just three letters...

76

"B-Y-E."

# Chapter Nine

The site of the *Emerald Shore* still smoldered as police interviewed Andrew at his house. One of the officers hovered over his notes with Andrew, at the kitchen table, while the other completed an inspection of Night's room.

"So you're saying you have no pictures of your son?"

"That's right."

The roving officer arrived in the doorway just in time to supplement his partner's line of questioning. "I notice you don't have a television in any of the rooms, or even a radio. Is it some sort of religious thing or something like that?"

"Something like that." Andrew leaned back and swung his gaze up, becoming less accommodating by the minute.

"Well, we're going to need something to work with. We can arrange for you to meet with a sketch artist at the station, tomorrow morning. For now, give us a description of him so we can alert the media."

"I just don't see that it's necessary. My son isn't running from anything. He won't stay away for long."

"First of all, he has every reason to run, and second, the opposite seems more likely, Mister Shannien. That young girl who's been missing, Daphne Swanson...she was pretty smitten with your son and, according to her friends, she'd made several comments in recent weeks about running off with him."

Andrew shuddered at the sound and syllables of Daphne's full name that echoed back at him: "Aileen Coleman".

"Another thing we don't understand is how you can insist that the fire was an accident when witnesses say that your son willfully started it during an intense altercation with you."

"We understand that you may not want to implicate your son..."

"No, I don't, because it didn't happen like that. Night was completely hysterical over something that I still have no idea about, but I assure you, he would never have intentionally set fire to the restaurant. He's not capable of that kind of premeditation."

"What exactly are you saying?"

"If you must know..." he paused before his most brilliant line yet, "Night is a bit...simple, and what happened was an unfortunate consequence of his agitated state. Now, I just want to find him before something else goes terribly wrong. You wanted a description..."

****

"Is this where you live?" Night asked when Lila pulled her car up in front of a long, flat building, at dusk.

"It's a motel. It's just where we're going to stay until I know that your *grandfather* isn't going to show up at my door and start God knows what. I always thought something wasn't right with him. I suppose I just didn't want to see it. I'm sorry, Night...really sorry."

Night followed her inside without saying anything. It took some work to remember that he could now speak freely. He looked around at the old paint job on the walls and the shoddy furniture in the office while Lila obtained a key from the man behind the desk.

Inside the modest room, he had a minor battle with one of two narrow beds that Lila indicated would be his for tonight. He wanted to crash, but he couldn't help but pound on the bedsprings that kept pushing him in the chest. His sores pinched him, high and low, on his opposite side, but this didn't compare to how he was otherwise destroyed by the day.

Lila sounded cheerful. "Are you going to sleep in your clothes? Remember, that's all you've got to wear for now. I, at least, can grab my work clothes from the car." She stopped talking for almost a minute and, when she continued, something had extinguished the chirp in her voice.

"What happened inside the restaurant, Night—I mean, how did the fire start?"

Night simply shrugged. He didn't want to talk about anything. Despite all the other lies, he couldn't dismiss Andrew's frantic warning, never to divulge what happened to Daphne, and so he thought better of trying to explain things to Lila.

"All right...I'll start making some calls, first thing in the morning. I'll find out where you stand in what's likely turned into an investigation, and if you're in the clear, I'm going to call a social worker to help you. Is it safe to do that, Night? You have to tell me if it isn't."

The question disturbed him because he didn't know what she meant. As long as she didn't plan to call Andrew, he couldn't see a reason to worry.

"You know, Night, you'll always be welcome at my house, but you'll want a place of your own someday. And you might even want to go to school." She finished opening her bed and then drew the curtains.

Meanwhile, Night had silently climbed off the bed. Lila jumped when she turned and found him standing right behind her.

"Are you okay?" Her hand slid on his arm while she searched his face for a subtle clue.

He wanted her to kiss him. Considering all she had done to improve his life from the day they first met, this had to be real love— like Daphne's love. He closed the gap between them, preparing for the kiss that would confirm it, but her cheek brushed past his ear as she simply gave him a hug.

"Despite what I now know," she uttered, "I probably still have no idea."

He felt much the same as he stood there, abandoned.

\*\*\*\*

Andrew was not surprised that Lila didn't answer her phone throughout the evening, but he didn't expect to find her driveway empty when he arrived at her house in the middle of the night. He knew she had no family in the area, or even in the country, so he assumed that she made the smart move of taking Night to the next most logical place.

Back at home, he finally replaced his telephone's mounting cord, got comfortable in his armchair and opened *the Oregon Coast Travel Guide* that he'd picked up with Lila on their last day trip. Inside it, he found a list of every hotel, motel, B&B and hostel in the region, and beyond—each represented as a numbered dot on a map so he could see their proximity to one another. He decided he would start by calling roadhouses along the 101, but not any too close to the *Emerald Shore*. He thought he'd start at the southern end of Lincoln County.

"Yeah..." Andrew began on his first encounter with a motel clerk. "I seem to be a little lost. I'm supposed to meet my wife and son at the motel and I can't remember if she said 'The 101 Inn' or 'The Dream Inn' on the 101... Is there a chance you've seen them...an attractive blond woman—?"

The clerk cut in with a cough, or it could have been a laugh. "I wish. You might want to try that other place you mentioned."

"Thank you for your time." Andrew hit the shallow disconnect button above the mouthpiece. He called a neighboring motel and repeated his story. His eyes wanted to cross by the fifth call, but he kept trying.

"They would have checked in...maybe around dinner time or later?"

"A blond woman came in with a kid...well, he was older...but she treated him like a kid."

Andrew laughed. "Stupid me... Once again, I've probably made them sick with worry, but I don't want to wake them up. Just give me their room number and I'll call them in a few hours."

****

Sunshine filled the streets of a nearby town where Lila took Night, early the next morning.

The scenery no longer shocked Night, so his scattered thoughts now converged on the one diamond that had surfaced from the hell of last evening.

"Does anybody actually know if my brother's alive?"

"He could be alive. I know he had an extremely rough start, but I also know he was discharged from the hospital in guarded health."

"Well, what does that mean? What happened to him? Maybe we should try to find him. I wonder what he's like."

Lila grinned. "If he's alive, I would suspect that he's very much like you. But don't get ahead of yourself. That's something you can do when you have your own life sorted out."

Night gazed at the apartment balconies above the stores along the sidewalk before he wandered into the middle of the street and turned in a full circle with a resurgence of awe. "You said he's probably like me. But he can't be like me. Nobody's like me."

Lila stepped off the curb and pulled him back. "That's only true for now, Night. Just give it some time."

****

They arrived back in their motel room with a few items of clothing, socks, underwear, and one purchase of casual footwear. Lila had bit her tongue when Night went for a pair of designer label hikers that resembled the ones he'd left behind at the house. She could accuse Andrew of many things, but not of being cheap. Lastly, she'd bought Night a duffel bag to carry all his things, wherever he went. It had occurred to her, at the first checkout, that one of them should have taken the money from the bar instead of leaving it all behind to burn.

While Night used the shower in the tiny bathroom, Lila glanced at her watch and turned the radio on beside her bed. She realized she'd tuned in seconds too late to hear the latest on the *Emerald Shore* fire when the newscaster quoted some phenomenal property damage before moving onto a minor story. She'd hoped to find out if a cause had been determined and, at the same time, she dreaded the truth. For a few minutes, she half listened to the gibbering as she considered her next move. That's when the telephone rang.

"Lila..." demanded a voice, even before she could say hello. "I wish you'd show more consideration for me. I've been trying you all morning."

"Andrew?" Her hand on the receiver tensed. "How did you...?"

"You're such a smart woman, Lila. You've proven that, so figure it out. Now, please, put my son on."

When she couldn't find any words, Andrew continued to speak in the same monotone voice.

"I know he's with you, and he can't stay hidden forever."

"No," Lila granted, "nineteen years is plenty."

Night stepped out of the bathroom wearing his new jeans and an undershirt, carrying his duffle bag under one arm.

"Don't get too cocky, Lila. You've already made a few mistakes."

"Is that a threat, Andrew?"

Night dropped his luggage where he stood, between the two beds, with his back to Lila.

"It doesn't have to be a threat."

Lila missed her chance to respond as some red flecks on Night's white undershirt moved her to latch onto the base of it. He quickly twisted and pulled free, but this granted her a hardy glimpse of the bloody marks before the fabric released and fell.

She slowly put the receiver down, and Night looked at the wall.

"Rightfully, you should press charges," she managed, her voice thin.

"What do you mean?"

She began flipping through the telephone book that she'd borrowed from the front desk. "I mean, he's a soulless criminal. I had no idea what I was sleeping with," she added, more to herself.

Lila started making another call, and Night sat down across from her.

"I have to tell you about Andrew Shannien," she told the deputy who answered at the Lincoln County Sheriff's Office, after being transferred by the operator. "...Yes, the restaurant owner. I have to warn you that he's looking for his son."

"We're all looking for his son...us, the OSP...specifically because he's wanted for questioning in regard to the fire that completely destroyed the *Emerald Shore*."

Lila groaned indignantly. "Trust me when I tell you that things are not as they seem and you should know who the—"

"What you should know is extremely plain, Ma'am. Night Shannien is more than just suspected of arson. Is he with you right now?"

She paused, aware that she had to change her course immediately. "No. But you have to understand, that kid cannot be held responsible for what happened at the restaurant. He's the victim in all this. Andrew Shannien has committed acts that go against every human right and now he's even threatening me!"

"Ma'am, we can talk about these charges of yours, but right now it is very important that we get Night Shannien into our custody so we can sort this whole thing out. Now, do you want to tell me where we can find him?"

"Uh..." She couldn't decide whether to hang up or make something up.

"What did you say your name is, Ma'am? We'd like to meet with you as soon as possible."

She rattled her head. "I suppose I can go to the station. I'd be happy to tell you everything I know...in person." The receiver missed the cradle on her first attempt to set it down and a pair of desperate eyes met hers when she looked up. "If even one employee of the restaurant saw you leave with me, the law will be at my door when I get there, and I will do everything I can to slant things in your favor, but Night...you need to disappear."

It startled both of them when the telephone rang again; each successive ring sounded more aggressive. Lila drew in a deep breath and slowly brought the receiver to her ear.

"Yes?"

"Who were you on the phone with, Lila? The police?" Andrew gibed. "I was talking to them too, not so long ago, when I made that generous donation to their department and pleaded with them to do everything they could to find my son."

"Andrew, isn't this game a bit pointless? You can't possibly claim to care what happens to Night—"

"That's all I've ever cared about! But there's something else I care about now—restitution—and Night will damn well pay me every last cent!"

"Night will pay you, even a penny, over my dead body."

Andrew cackled as though she'd presented him with an enticing dare. "Come on, Lila. We both don't want the police to find Night. Just bring him back here, to what he knows."

"Really? Why, Andrew, so you can cut him into little steaks and serve him to the guests of your new restaurant?"

"Tempting," he quipped, "but I'm still more forgiving than that—
"

Lila slammed the phone down.

"Time to go, Night."

"What did he say? Is he coming here?"

She rubbed her face. "I don't think so or he would have already. I'm sure he's aware that would create quite a scene, but I'm more concerned about the police. I'm not going to leave it to chance that you might end up in prison, or worse...back at home. "Make sure you have everything. We're leaving."

Night climbed into the car a few seconds after her. "I thought you said the police were people who could help me?"

"Yes, perhaps if you hadn't lit up the *Emerald Shore*." She huffed. "I'm sure the law would eventually recognize that you weren't completely responsible for what happened, but there are no guarantees. And I don't want to see what will happen to you until it's all sorted out. Right now, the police are all about arresting you for arson." She paused before delivering what she thought would be a shocker. "Night, I have to get you far away from here—and you don't have to tell me that it's too soon."

He didn't even blink; in fact, he looked relieved.

"Help me find my brother. If we're so much the same, like you said, wouldn't he want to help me?"

"Yes, I'm sure, but we don't have a lot of time." She now grasped that Night's mystery brother would never leave his mind until he found him, or his headstone.

"Where else can I go, then? That would be the only place."

Lila tried not to lose sight of the road as a possibility sprang up right in front of her. "Indeed."

****

Lila seemed to be accelerating to nowhere, until she swerved off the road and brought her wheels to a halt on the gravel shoulder, past a phone booth. She turned off the engine and faced him.

"I do have an idea. Finding out the truth about your brother may not be such a difficult thing. I didn't have time to turn the pages, but I saw some key names in your brother's hospital file."

Night batted his eyelids to hurry her point.

"I know that your young mother, Aileen, got in touch with Brigitte Morgen after she brought your brother into the hospital. She named Brigitte as her guardian, and there were a lot of notes. But

Doctor Gardner took the chart out of my hands as soon as he'd made his point about Aileen Coleman."

Despite feeling some relief at this lead, he felt even more resentment. "So, Brigitte, who left my father like I did, might know what happened to him. Why didn't you tell me? Nobody wants me to know anything...even you."

"I wanted to wait until... I don't even know." She flicked her hand dismissively and opened her door. "We don't have time for this. Just trust me."

Night almost vomited at those words, but he did trust Lila. Even so, he followed her to the glass enclosure and held the door open to watch her every move. She didn't object either. She shared her view of the page with him while she looked for the last name "Morgen" in the telephone book.

Lila found only one listing for that particular spelling of the name. She explained that it wasn't likely that Brigitte would have retained her maiden name for the last nineteen years, but it had to be a lead.

"Yes, hello," she said, mimicking the soft greeting of an elderly woman. "I'm looking for Brigitte...she used to be Brigitte Morgen?"

"Brigitte doesn't live here, dear, but this is where she grew up."

"Oh," Lila chirped. "Well, I'm an old friend of Brigitte's, from school, and I was hoping to get in touch with her again. Would you be able to help me?"

Night could faintly hear the woman's response.

"Brigitte got remarried quite some time ago...to a Mister Frederick Dahlsi. She's been living in California for, oh, almost twenty years now. But I could give you her number if you'd like... Just wait 'til I find it..."

Lila flashed Night a broad smile. She took a pen and paper out of her purse and, after an excruciating minute, began scribbling a phone number down, and then a name that Night hadn't heard yet. "Thank you, Mrs. Morgen. Thank you so much. Also, if you don't mind giving me her address, I might start by mailing her a letter."

\*\*\*\*

Lila's request to speak with Brigitte was answered by Brigitte herself.

"My name is Lila Hughes. We've never met, but we're connected, in a way, through someone: Andrew Shannien."

"What is it you want, Ms. Hughes? For twenty years I have not been connected, in any way, to Andrew Shannien."

"It's precisely something about that time, twenty years ago, that I want to ask you about. I'm trying to assist someone who is with me at this moment. I'm sure that you remember a girl named Aileen Coleman. I understand she felt quite a trust—"

"Ms. Hughes, please remind Aileen Coleman that we had an agreement when the adoption was finalized. She forfeited a part of her life when she signed those papers and she was more than happy to do it back then. Please do not call here again."

Lila held the dead receiver on her ear as she turned to Night. For a moment, she couldn't free her jaw from her gaping grin. "I didn't think it would be so easy," she remarked with a giggle. "You will have your wish, Night. It looks like you're finally going to meet your brother."

\*\*\*\*

"No reason I couldn't make it in for my shift tonight...*with* time to spare," Lila announced proudly as she steered the car to another undisclosed location. Yet, her tone was fragile, and all at once it flattened. "They will know that we were both at that motel, so when they question me, I'm going to tell them that you disappeared. I'll tell them that you probably got scared when your grandfather called the motel. It'll reinforce my story, that you had reason to run from him. In any case, you'll be long gone. ...It will all work out, Night. Just remember everything we talked about."

He sat quietly, beside Lila, and tried to organize all her instructions.

Lila pointed to a taxi driving in the opposite lane. "See that...there will be many of those when you get off the bus in Los Angeles. And you can always ask others for help once you're there, but it would be best if you didn't go into any bus terminals along the way." She glanced to her right. "How are you feeling, Night?"

His nod became increasingly explicit. "I can do this. I'll never be like I was before, and I wish my father...grandfather could see that."

Lila grinned. "He already sees that. That's what's making him crazy."

Night let his head fall into his hand against the window as he felt his confidence sliding down the crag of reality. At the same time, Lila pulled into a picnic area, a stone's throw off the highway.

"You'll walk ahead a little bit and I'll wait here to make sure you got yourself on the bus without a problem. The bus from Portland should be passing through here in the next half hour." She handed Night the rest of the money that she'd stopped to withdraw from her bank and he put it in his pocket. She also gave him a paper that contained both her home and work telephone numbers. "In case of an emergency...and *only* from a payphone."

They walked together in silence before Lila aired some final advice. "I put sunglasses in your bag. I would put them on if I were you. You can be anybody you want to be now—but you cannot be Night Shannien. You should think of a new name while you're sitting there for the next twenty-three hours."

He nodded and took a step back.

"Oh gosh..." she breathed. "This is the most irresponsible thing I've ever done, but if they find you, it'll be hell. They won't understand where you came from, that you're..."

"A freak," Night supplied. He nodded for her, then stared at the folded paper containing Lila's telephone numbers as though he wanted to call her already.

He welcomed her embrace, and she even kissed him, but not like Daphne. Walking along the highway, he imagined there would have to be others in the world waiting to show him real love...now that he knew exactly what that was.

# Chapter Ten

Several witnesses, many of them employees of the restaurant, remembered seeing Night leave the scene with Lila. A Lincoln County Sheriff's Office vehicle greeted her in the driveway when she arrived home, after dropping Night off to catch the California-bound bus.

"I didn't want to get into it over the telephone," she explained calmly in the presence of two uniformed men, one being the officer she'd hung up on earlier that day. "The truth is, Night disappeared on me while I was taking a shower in the motel."

"Why didn't you report his disappearance the minute you realized he was gone?"

"Well, at first, I had no reason to think that he didn't plan to come back. I mean, it would be totally within his character to slip out for a walk rather than sit around in a stale motel room. And I did call the station *before* he disappeared, but truly, nobody seemed interested in what I had to say at the time." She crossed her arms.

"We're very interested, ma'am. That's why we're here. Can you tell us where you went for the rest of the day?"

"I tried to find Night, of course. I drove up and down the highway and I even looked for him in town. To tell you the truth, I didn't want to be alone...and I wasn't keen on being harassed by Andrew if I came home before my shift—which I'm going to be late for, by the way, if I don't start getting ready, soon."

"Ms. Hughes, you're quite safe with us, right now, and you might just have to be late. You're the only person who has seen this man's kid since he fled from the restaurant. And if you have any reason to fear Andrew Shannien, then I advise you to make a statement now."

"Oh, I can give you more than a statement," Lila chortled, shedding any residual show-quality. "Let's go inside and I'll tell you boys everything you need to know."

****

By now, most Oregon bus terminals had received appeals to look out for a nineteen-year-old male with light brown hair and hazel eyes who also happened to be deaf. Night shook his head at the poster on the main door as he assumed it was meant to depict him, but he could have stood beside it until morning and not a soul would have looked at him twice. In spite of the break Andrew granted him by skewing the details of his appearance, Night tensed when the driver paused and studied him during headcount. It wouldn't have been the first time someone perceived his rich auburn hair as a dye job, but in the end, the driver must have concluded that a deaf person wouldn't be chatting it up with some random traveler in the neighboring seat.

\*\*\*\*

The Newport deputy shuffled impatiently. "So you're saying that this kid wouldn't know the first thing to do if he was left alone in a strange place, yet you allege he just took off from some highway motel in the middle of nowhere?"

Lila also became tetchy. "He definitely hadn't been out much, so I can only assume that to be true. What I know for sure is that he didn't want to go home. Maybe he managed to get a lift to another town. I don't know. He could be anywhere..." Lila's whole body twisted through her shrug. Lying was exhausting. She wondered how Andrew could do it so consistently and with so little effort. She was grateful that, at least for now, she was up to the challenge.

"Ms. Hughes, at this point our primary objective is to apprehend Mister Shannien's son, or grandson, or whatever he is, for his part in burning down an insured business. Anything beyond that will certainly be investigated when we find him. Now, so far, everyone at least agrees that he's nineteen and if he wasn't happy living at home then, as an adult, he wasn't obligated to stay there."

Lila put on a mild act in touching her forehead. "I would hardly have gotten involved in all this if it were that straightforward."

The second officer gave his partner a nudge and mumbled in his direction. "He did say Night was a bit simple' remember?"

Lila shook her head in wonder of Andrew's strategy for coming up with that line. "Yes, Night is 'a bit simple', but only because Andrew had this bizarre agenda to control his life and keep him that way. I told you about the marks I saw on his body, and everything that has happened in the last two days is proof that Night just couldn't take it anymore and needed to get away—and Andrew isn't pleased that I helped. So what are you going to do to ensure my safety, or will I have to run away too?"

The interrogating officer pursed his lips. "Andrew Shannien is not only upstanding, but a model citizen in this area. He's been nothing but helpful in this investigation and I don't really want to say what I'm inclined to think about your story."

"Enlighten me."

"First of all, you say Night isn't deaf, but how would it serve Mister Shannien for us to discover that upon finding his son? Are you going to tell us, next, that Night doesn't have light-brown hair?"

She wanted nothing more than to tell them that, and prove Andrew a liar, but not at Night's expense. "No, that sounds about right."

"Right... So, Ma'am, when we put all the facts together, Mister Shannien just sounds like a man who is desperate to find his son and has some cause to be angry. After all, he just lost his business, his son, and judging from your own account of things, his fiancé. Perhaps you're just a little angry with him about some private matter and maybe you want to hurt him back a little?"

Lila's mouth dropped in genuine disbelief.

"Call us back if you receive any serious threats or have some tangible proof that you're in danger, but I suspect that Mister Shannien has more than enough on his plate right now and doesn't have any plans to devour you too." He grinned at his colleague shamelessly.

Lila did catch the shadow of uncertainty cross the other man's face as he offered her a few compassionate words.

"We'll pay Andrew Shannien another visit, and we're here if you need us, Ma'am. Remember to keep your door locked."

****

Nothing Night had been introduced to in Oregon compared to what he saw when he woke up in San Francisco. He had to close his eyes to prevent a repeat of what had happened the first time he went into town with Lila. Every manmade structure was gargantuan, there were no forests in sight, only some unrecognizable forms of vegetation, and his introduction to the freeway nearly shut all his systems down.

He quickly trained himself to breathe through the panic, to welcome novelty—and just in time. The bus driver made the announcement that they had arrived in L.A.

Night tripped from the bus that had taken him almost one thousand miles from his former life into a world of stewed sunlight, heat and car exhaust. He threw on his sunglasses, now exceptionally glad to have them. Taxis dominated the street and he climbed into the front seat of the first car that rolled forward.

"Fine address," remarked the driver after Night recited the street name to the young man who he couldn't help but notice had the darkest skin he'd ever seen.

Night tried not to stare.

"You live there?" the driver persisted.

Night nodded then flinched at the fellow's explosive reaction.

"Get outta here! I would have sworn you're only visiting L.A. I can always spot 'em. Hey, you know that guy, Frederick Dahlsi...he's running for District Councilman? Did you know he's from your neighborhood?"

"Yes. He's from my house."

"No shit. You ain't Morgen Dahlsi by chance? I never got a real good look, but your band was doin' some gig at *The Stardeck* one time. You guys got something goin' on—I mean, that place was packed!"

Night gazed through his tinted lenses at the young driver. This was truly how it felt to be without language. A single question registered with him, so Night responded to that one.

"Morgen's my brother."

"No shit! Well here..." The driver handed him a business card. "I'm J.P. Maybe you'll send me some tickets to see his band when he really hits it big...since you and me are practically friends now."

Night stared at the card before mindlessly putting it away in some side compartment of his luggage. He turned to look out the passenger window while the cab driver talked on and on. They rolled into a residential area and the atmosphere inside and outside the car became more serene. Houses grew fewer, but more stately. Climbing ivy sprawled over most of these pale houses, often behind a defense of mature trees or huge fences. The driver slowed down in front of one such home—not the biggest one by far, but definitely an elite home. It too had vines that fanned diagonally toward one-half of the house and all along its flowered base. He could see an alabaster statue of a man close to the end of one of the two brick driveways. It stood on the lawn as though guarding the property.

"This driveway the one you want?"

Night had no idea, but he pulled out two twenties and didn't wait for his change.

"Man, you sure you from around here?"

Night couldn't stop his hands from shaking as he fumbled with the door handle, not saying a word.

"Don't forget about them tickets," J.P. called out through his open window as he sped off.

The taxi had barely turned the corner before another voice, with yet another accent and strange vernacular, accosted him from inside the front gates.

"Morgen, where you been, man? I been trying to call you for days."

"Why are you calling me Morgen?" Night blurted, clutching the strap of his duffel bag against his shoulder with both hands to control his shaking. In contrast to J.P.'s short afro, this tanned-looking fellow's black hair fell shiny and long in a gleaming tail down his back.

"Why am I calling you Morgen...?" There was a long pause. "Well, you got real mad the time I said Asshole." Though grinning, he recoiled. "Are you high, my friend? And what did you do to your hair?"

"What do you mean?"

"*No!* I mean it looks great. I jus' didn' know you were changing your look. You're acting funny, my friend." He walked past Night and opened the pedestrian door to the garage like he lived in the house. Night followed him past a white convertible, to the back of the room and up a narrow staircase that led into the upper level of the house.

At the top, one more door stood between Night and...he could hardly wait to see. The south hallway they entered eerily reminded him of his house in Oregon, but when his brother's friend threw open the last door on the left, they stepped into a realm that no longer resembled anything he had ever known. Night removed his sunglasses and glanced around. He couldn't decide if this was a living room or a bedroom, and then he noticed adjoining rooms on each end.

"What is this...is it all one house? Do you live here?"

The Hispanic fellow just stared at Night for a few seconds. "Morgen is going to freak."

Their matching gazes suddenly turned to the west end of the room where a human form emerged from another doorway and complacently came over to complete a triangle.

"I never knew you had a brother, man."

"Guess that makes two of us."

If Morgen's response was intended to be a pun, he certainly didn't care if anyone knew it. His attention transferred to Night.

"Before you say anything, let me save both of us a lot of time. I'm not interested in the tales of my long lost twin, and I don't foresee that changing in this lifetime, so if you've come from any sort of distance, I recommend you have yourself a blast in Hollywood for a couple days. Go check out the Walk of Fame or Magic Castle or whatever turns you on, but don't mistake me for someone who might join you."

Night could hear his brother's blast of contempt but he couldn't digest a single word. Here stood his blanched replica, his reflection with the identical pale eyes, and the inexplicable ivory hair, the image he had seen in the ornamental crystal ball, the one that pestered him at the end of every day, and never allowed him to experience a simple dream—his lifelong nightmare!

"You're my brother," Night stated, "and I need your help."

"How 'bout I see you later, Steve?"

"No way, man. I wanna hear from your brother—"

"Steve... Get the fuck out!"

Once he did, Morgen's tundra-like stare fell back on Night. "Look, I'm not interested in your story, but you can crash here if you'd like. There's a bathroom through that door at the back and a guest room on the other side of it. It all connects, so there's no reason for you to show your face outside this suite. All I need is for someone to see you and end up in the middle of some big family drama."

"Morgen?"

"I said you can crash here...no questions, no debate."

"Aren't you wondering...if you've seen me before?"

"No. Never seen you."

After Morgen retreated to his bedroom, punctuating his declaration with a slam of the door, Night became acutely aware of the waning light outside the common room window, and how his

98

time here might be just as fleeting. Was this really it? Following nearly two decades of visits from his brother's turbulent energy, countless appeals from the essence of his platinum-haired twin to acknowledge its tangible source—all from across the almost impassable expanse of lies that Andrew had surrounded him with—did it all amount to nothing but a bout of hot air? The heat that climbed Night's face induced images of the restaurant inferno everywhere he looked. Morgen hadn't even asked him his name, but with or without an invitation to share, his brother was going to know it.

But right now, he just needed to pee. As Morgen had offhandedly described, the bathroom separated his common room from an extra bedroom, which he had just offered to a complete stranger. Clearly, his brother's life wasn't governed by an Andrew.

He couldn't believe how this normally utilitarian room outshone the rest of Morgen's suite in swirling grey-green marble, from the floor, up some steps, and down into a sunken tub that resembled an oceanographic whirlpool. Morgen appeared to have it good, in all ways, and it begged the question: why was his brother so miserable?

Adding to the noise of the toilet flushing, Night ran the faucet over the sink. When the temperature was right, he leaned forward to wash his face, but he froze when somebody knocked on the door on the common room side. His mind started to race, wondering what Morgen had come back to say, but the voice that followed belonged to a young female who spoke his brother's name.

"Yes?" he answered, cringing.

He heard a short giggle on the other side of the door. "Are you coming down for supper? They want you to eat with us tonight, and you can't say no. I'm supposed to tell you that."

"...All right."

"Good. And don't take forever." The pleasant-sounding intruder finished with another tiny laugh. Something about his answers elicited this reaction.

Like he'd been doing it all his life, Night ran to warn Morgen, who he nearly collided with when he opened the door.

"What the fuck just happened?"

"A girl asked if you were coming down to eat so I said 'yes.' But it's okay. She didn't see me."

Morgen rolled his eyes and stepped behind a bar counter tucked in the corner between the main entrance to the suite and his bedroom door. Night noted that it was a much smaller bar than the one he'd set fire to the other day, but a bar nonetheless.

"That was my sister, Beth," Morgen disclosed. "I mean, she's not *really* my sister. Mom can't have kids, and we both know we're adopted. That's why I'm not exactly shocked about you." Morgen squatted behind the counter to pull something from a shelf below. "But twins...separated at birth... There's a cliché I wasn't expecting." Morgen's hands reappeared on the surface of the counter in the process of wringing the cap off what was unmistakably a prescription pill bottle.

"Why are you taking those? Are you sick?"

Morgen balked and then threw a couple of pills in his mouth, swallowing them effortlessly before speaking. "Let's just say, thanks to you, I now have to make sure I can get through dinner without being sick."

Night curiously observed as his brother pressed a small mirror against the countertop and sprinkled it with a ration of white powder. Using a small blade, he tapped at the substance diligently until he'd divided it up into little rows. Night flinched when he saw how Morgen ingested it.

"What are you doing?"

"Oh please," Morgen glanced up shortly. "Do you want some?"

"No."

Morgen sniffed and straightened his back. "Then excuse me while I go ahead."

100

Night watched the familiar expanse of eggshells that he'd known in Oregon spring up between them, but somehow he didn't feel the need to approach Morgen with the same level of caution as Andrew. Morgen was nothing more than his twin...not even equal in weight, and evidently not in health.

Morgen threw his equipment, and the pill bottle, into a small box and carelessly tossed it all under the counter. "Gotta go. I won't be long, but stay quiet until I come back."

They both stepped forward and almost collided, which only stretched the tension between them. It didn't faze Night.

"Morgen? Can you get me something to eat?"

"Look, you're not my problem... *Oh shit!*" Morgen shoved him out of the way to get to the phone. "I forgot about Steve! I have to stop him from blabbing about you to the whole world. Pray that he answers and, if he doesn't, pray anyway, because I *will* kill you if I'm too late."

****

It turned out all right, in terms of Steve, but Night missed his first California sunset while inspecting the details of his brother's life. Morgen possessed a multitude of strange objects—the most intriguing being an acoustic guitar, which he carried back to the couch. It didn't take him very long to figure out that the frets had a purpose, and that there was a correct way to hold the thing. He analyzed each twang produced by every string, in combination with every fret, and then, just as he had learned to do on the piano, he plucked out a few scales in major and minor until he got bored and turned to another interesting object: the television.

The recent phenomenon of MTV captivated Night, as much as it had the rest of the world. Morgen must have watched him for some time before he sailed up beside him where he sat, only inches from the screen.

"Didn't they have MTV on your planet?"

"No," Night replied, detecting the insult only after it was too late.

The image on the TV suddenly imploded and the whole screen went black.

"Don't spaz out," Morgen said as he tossed the hand remote aside and then slid a cassette tape into an elaborate stereo system beside the TV. "There's something I want you to hear. Tell me what you think."

Despite his belated introduction to pop music, Night quickly ranked this particular number above many songs he'd heard. "I don't know that one yet, but I like it. I think I even like it better than most of them," he said, enticing a genuine smile out of Morgen for the first time since they'd met.

"It's better, isn't it? You haven't heard it before because it's only on my demo tapes. That's me and my band."

Now it made sense to him, why Morgen had so many instruments and related paraphernalia that he couldn't identify.

"So, why aren't you on...?" He motioned to the magic box on the carpet.

"On TV? Yeah, it's a crime, isn't it? But keep watching. Our big break is coming."

"What do you mean?"

"I mean, we got a bite from the last batch of demo tapes I sent out. *Morning's Desire* is going to be the opener at an amazing venue in just a few days." His tone eroded as he added, "Last chance for me, but it's all I need."

"I don't understand anything you're saying. Are you going to be on TV?"

Morgen gawked at Night for a moment as his music surrounded them. "That's not what I said, but yeah, eventually. What the hell is your name anyway?"

"Night."

"No way. Night, as in midnight?"

"As in morning and night."

102

Morgen sneered and flopped on the couch. "That must have given somebody one big laugh—right before they decided to split us up anyway."

"At least you got to have the real life and a real name. You were named after—"

"Brigitte. I know. She's my adoptive mom."

"I know. I lived with Andrew, and Brigitte used to live with Andrew. I thought he was my father," Night explained, "but I just found out he's my...our grandfather."

Morgen turned a shade paler. "You're saying my mom is technically *Grandma?* Shit... Our real dad must have been twelve."

Rather than correct him, Night simply shrugged. "Morgen, do you think she knew about me?"

"How am I supposed to know? She never talks about the past."

"Well if she did...know about me...she let him ruin my life. I could have been normal if I'd lived here too. Do you know that I never even spoke to anyone, except to Andrew, until a few months ago? I never went anywhere... He always said there was a reason I couldn't be like other people, but there was never a reason. Not a real reason."

Morgen looked dazed, but he managed to eject one word. "What?"

"It's true. I've never been any farther than between the house where I lived and the restaurant where I worked. Andrew even had me pretend that I couldn't hear. I even learned this sign language..." He echoed his last few words in sign. When Morgen stopped being speechless, he uttered, "I don't believe it. Of all the lost twin brothers in this world, how come mine has to be such a...?"

"Freak?"

"Freak," Morgen accepted. He looked bored now, or tired, as he lifted his head off the couch and stood up. He plucked his demo tape out of the stereo and looked at Night. "If you're such a recluse, why'd you dye your hair like that?"

"What do you mean? This is just how it looks."

Morgen's glare sharpened. "You're the freak, so how come I got stuck with all the aberrant genes? Clearly, I have my own problems, and I don't need one of them to be you," Morgen stated, grabbing a set of keys from the sofa table near the exit. "Make sure you're gone by tomorrow."

****

A hard push on his shoulder blade was Night's first indication that he'd fallen asleep. Just for a moment, he thought it was Andrew waking him out of a typical dream. Then, reality set in and he noticed the object of his lifelong nightmares standing right there beside him, in the daylight, in the flesh, with arms crossed.

"You got blood on your shirt. You know, they put seats in buses so you don't have to hang on underneath."

Night turned his back away from Morgen as he sat up.

"Where did you say you were from?"

Night hoped his brother's questions would keep coming. "Lincoln County...Oregon."

"That's too bad. I hope you have enough money to get back because it's check-out time at the Dahlsi hotel."

"I can't go back. Lila said I had to stay out of Oregon...and you're supposed to help."

"Who the hell is Lila? What do you want from me?" Morgen threw up his arms and then let them fall limp. "I don't want you around. It's not like we're going to be best friends or anything. I'm not suddenly going to recognize the virtues of brotherhood or what a gas it can be to have a twin. We're not going to start dressing the same so we can play pranks on people, or spend hours together comparing our experiences."

Night did want most of these things, but he no longer expected anything except to hear how Morgen would wrap up his eviction.

"Look, I have really important things to do today, and I may even have company, so you have to get the hell out before someone sees you. Now, hit the road. *Hasta la vista.* Good-bye."

After being handed his bag of meager belongings, Night quickly found himself alone on the doorstep outside, like a discarded stray—Andrew's threat realized! He felt some relief to be out of Morgen's caustic little world, and he still had some of Lila's money, so he knew he wouldn't starve right away. He also had Lila's number...if Morgen really didn't want him around.

With an inherent good sense of direction, excellent endurance, and a keen eye for landmarks, Night cleared the neighborhood and walked well into a commercial district before he started to slow down.

He found a restaurant and ordered off the menu for the first time in his life, although the bill brought with it a realization: he would be broke in no time unless he found cheaper food, or got some more money. Briefly, he fantasized about asking the manager for a job, but when he failed to decipher the conversation at the next table, he remembered that he was a freak...a childlike one at that.

When he got back to the house, at dusk, Night stared at Morgen's bedroom window for a long time, after finding the pedestrian door locked. He recalled what worked the last time someone shut him out of his home and he picked up a rock, then hurled it straight through one of the glass panels of Morgen's wide-open, shutter-style window.

Morgen's short platinum mop tipped over the window ledge, but in less than a minute, he reappeared in Night's face, clutching him by the shirt.

"You're a bloody psychopath!" Morgen blasted, yanking Night inside and spinning his back against the stone wall.

Night didn't even flinch at the pain. "I need your help," he asserted. "And I can break more windows..."

"Fuck!" Morgen let go with a push. "My family could have heard you. Ever think of that, asshole?"

Night followed his brother up the now-familiar staircase in the back of the garage. A third of the way down the upper hallway, Morgen stopped and gestured at the first door on the left.

"Park your ass in my guestroom, for now, and don't make a bloody sound—even if you think it's just me in the suite. My window will have to be fixed so it could be anyone going in there in the next while. I'll look for you when it's necessary—not the other way around. Got it?"

\*\*\*\*

Night couldn't understand how his brother never developed the slightest interest in him, even after their fairly intimate conversation, now three evenings ago. While Morgen came and went, Night continued to siphon any clues about the world through the television in Morgen's common room. Sometimes, he too slipped out of the house, like every time he got hungry. He discovered where to buy cheap, fast-food, and even groceries to stretch his dollars, but regardless of when and why he left the house, Morgen had learned not to lock him out.

He gained clues about his brother's health from the number of times Morgen's head went into the toilet. It didn't make sense to Night that someone could be sick and then healthy again, often within the same day, and seemingly without end.

On one occasion, Night skulked back into the house and found his brother holed up, like a wounded animal, in one corner of their shared bathroom. Morgen didn't even move as Night stood in the breached doorway and stared down at him.

"What happened?"

Seconds passed before Morgen lifted his face from between his bent knees. Although he wasn't crying, the charcoal under his brother's eyes had migrated south and Night gathered that the emotional phase had long exhausted itself by now.

106

Night finally noticed the empty pill bottle, and its contents strewn all across the marble floor. Morgen sat amidst this evidence, decked out in telltale attire: a sleeveless black shirt, silver and crystal studs on both ears—all plainly visible beneath teased hair—leather bracelets on his wrists, a bandana loosely twisted around his neck and a studded double belt—everything screaming that this was the night of Morgen's epic event.

"Your telephone keeps ringing. Why won't you answer it?"

In his unwavering trance, Morgen turned onto his knees and faced the water in the toilet bowl as though he was completely resigned to this routine by now.

Night lingered as he retreated and then laid his head against the flipside of the doorframe to listen. He wasn't sure why, but something made him envious of this room that already knew more about his brother than he did. This feeling began to extend to the whole house and the people that lived in it, and he resented being so behind when it came to setting things into their rightful order.

****

Andrew grudgingly welcomed a detective, along with the two familiar cops, into his home.

"This case keeps getting more interesting, Mister Shannien. Your ex is coming up with some pretty serious allegations, and we'd like to hear from you now."

"Of course, but I don't understand..."

"Even Ms. Hughes doesn't deny that Night meant to burn down the restaurant, but she says he was driven to a desperate, irrational state by abuse—at your hands. She claims she saw unmistakable marks on his body."

Andrew tipped his forehead into one hand and paced opposite his audience. He stopped and gripped the top of his armchair with his free hand. "I'm sorry... Give me a minute. This is terribly embarrassing for me. That's why I wasn't forthcoming when you asked me about the altercation that led to the fire."

107

"Mister Shannien, it's not in your best interest to withhold anything right now."

"I know, I know." He turned to face them when he sensed that their curiosity had peaked. "This explains so much about Lila's behavior." He chuckled shortly. "It isn't her fault that she's accusing me of this—anybody would think the same thing if they saw him. God, no...it most certainly was not me who did that to Night, it was that little tramp who he's obviously in the company of, right this minute."

"You are referring to that missing girl, Daphne Swanson?"

"Yes! Only now they are both missing—together—and there is still nothing I can do about it, just like I couldn't do anything to stop him from seeing her in the first place. Like I told you, Night is a bit...slower than most teenagers, and him knowing that, and with his hearing loss, he always wanted to prove that he could fit in with anyone. So, yes, I sheltered him, a bit too much, but for good reason because this girl, this freak...she came into his life and introduced him to her vulgar lifestyle and kept him hooked—God only knows how that's possible. I started noticing bruises... Really, I can't talk about this."

"We understand she was once a stripper—but much reformed, according to her friends." The officer chuckled while his partner grinned. "It seems she just moves around in her field."

Andrew expunged their amusement with a scowl. "I can only tell you that we had some horrible fights, the worst being after he came home virtually disfigured. Your marks... You guessed it...courtesy of Miss Swanson. That last morning, I vowed he would never see her again, and Night decided to put me in my place."

"So, when the fire happened, tell us how Ms. Hughes got involved."

"She was simply there, and Night had become so resentful of me... I'm sure he said, and would continue to say, anything to defend this little slut and make me the villain. I'm sure, after using Lila to make his getaway, he found his way back to the bitch. Pardon me..."

He took a seat in his armchair and stared at the floor as one of them scribbled some notes.

"Thank you, Mister Shannien. Although what a nineteen-year-old chooses to do with his own body is not our concern, the restaurant arson is, and you just connected a whole lot of dots for us. I'm sure we'll have a few more questions before this is all over."

"That's fine. Just find my son and do what you have to. Sadly, he does need a lot of help—which is why I dreaded police involvement, at first. But the truth is, I would rather see him in prison than with her."

\*\*\*\*

Night could no longer stand being ignored and he thought he might burn down another building if he didn't get some acknowledgment soon. The ringing of the telephone started to peel the air until he forced Morgen to deal with both him and the call by lifting the receiver and bringing it to his own ear. Morgen snatched it from his hand.

"...I know. ...Probably not. ...Yes, sorry! ....It wasn't my fault. ...You know why!"

Night lost track of how many similar sounding retorts Morgen fired through the line. He could sense his brother struggling just to articulate the words, groggy from the combination of substances he'd gulped, snorted and injected into his body the night before. Night found himself strangely vigilant over the ungrateful creature when the cycle repeated itself after the call.

Facedown on the couch, Morgen didn't even stir when Night tripped over the electric guitar, still in its case, and abandoned near the common room door. He picked it up and carried it over to the rest of his brother's mystery equipment, but this time, he didn't ignore the cloaked object within the mix.

He spread his arms along the width of the thing and carefully lifted the black leather protective cover off. His heart skipped at the sight of a piano keyboard, although it didn't look much like any piano he'd seen before, except in music videos. He had to pull the unit away from the wall to really examine it and that's when he realized it consisted of two parts: the keyboard and a metal stand...and the keyboard tempted him.

Night glanced at his brother who didn't look like he would notice if his ceiling caved in. He looked back down at the keys and struck his first chord, but his action produced no sound. He hit the keys harder, and harder again.

"You're a real genius, aren't you?" came Morgen's voice...the only noise to stab the air above the dull plunk of the keys hitting the frame. "Try turning it on!"

Night twisted around. "I almost had it."

"Right. Even if that were true, you'd probably just end up launching a magnitude seven earthquake across Los Angeles."

Scowling, Night searched the mass of controls all along the top and soon found what he wanted. Power surged through the keyboard, as it did through his arm, and he didn't wait to begin his angry recital. By now, Morgen had wandered off and closed himself inside the bathroom.

But the music brought him back. When Night looked up at Morgen's face, now only inches away, he saw something familiar, and it had nothing to do with the likeness of his features. One time, on his way to the restaurant, Andrew had accused him of having stars in his eyes, and now he knew exactly what that looked like. He broke off in the middle of a haughty crescendo and turned to Morgen, awaiting his reaction.

"What the hell was that? I didn't know you were into music. Why the fuck didn't you say anything about that?"

"I didn't know you had a piano."

Morgen slapped his sides and groaned. "It's not a piano, by the way. It's a synthesizer—a keyboard."

"It looks like a piano...and I've played piano all my life."

"Have you ever considered learning guitar?"

110

It seemed like a good time to confess. "You mean that thing?" Night pointed to the acoustic guitar on the floor. "I think I figured it out, but I can't play it like you."

Morgen's eyes peered right through Night, at something that thawed his stare for a second time. "What would you say if I offered to teach you to play it...just like me?"

His expression must have given away plenty because Morgen grinned.

"Come on. Let me see what you already know."

There was a slight hobble in Morgen's gait as he moved toward the couch, but Night couldn't help notice that an uncustomary spring also came with his brother's newfound purpose.

****

Morgen's tune had completely transitioned, like Night's hair, by the end of the evening. It appeared that Morgen now required his "pain-in-the-ass brother" to stick around.

"It's not going to work, Morgen. We're still going to look different."

"Just shut-up. You can't stay here for much longer without ever being spotted." Morgen sniffed neurotically as he combed the peroxide solution from a bottle through Night's rich auburn hair.

"But can't people just know who I really am for a change?"

"If that happens, I'm done, you're done."

Morgen left him sitting on the marble rim of the sunken bathtub without explaining that the bleaching process would take some time, and when he came back, he still had the nerve to sound irritated.

"Lean back," he ordered, already yanking Night's head into position to rinse his faded strands.

Night couldn't wait to look into the mirror. "What did you do? Look at it, Morgen. It's pink!"

"I'm not a goddamned hairdresser. We'll just do it again, okay?"

Night sat through another application of the stuff that burned his scalp more than the first time. Some of his hair fell out, but the end result startled both of them.

"Nobody'll question it," Morgen pronounced, in spite of Night's healthier complexion and yellower shade of blond hair. "Just don't let me down."

Night stared through the mirror, into his nightscapes, while the most profound sense of *déjà vu* swept over him. Maybe not in one succinct phrase, but Morgen had been thrusting this sentiment at him for as long as he could remember. His nightmares had altogether ceased since his arrival at the house. Instead, each night he slept with a feeling that he had answered Fate. At last, he had answered Morgen.

# Chapter Eleven

Morgen kept fidgeting in his movie theater seat as though he really didn't want to be there. Night couldn't be certain, but it occurred to him that Morgen had only brought him to see the big screen so he could watch his freaky brother's reaction to yet one more ordinary experience.

"Isn't anyone wondering where you are these days?"

"I already told you...only Lila knows where I am, and I'm supposed to be hiding from everybody else."

This was the life Night had pictured when Lila told him he would meet his brother."I guess you really aren't full of shit after all," Morgen granted, witnessing Night's anticipation as they waited for the curtain to rise. "I assume that you never went to school either?"

"Lila mentioned school, but no... Why, did you?"

"Of course, but I didn't exactly qualify for the attendance award. I was always a little busy writing songs."

Those were his last words before the lights dimmed and the curtain lifted as though rising to the theme of his new life.

****

Night gained hints about his progress in conquering both the acoustic and electric guitar by reading his brother's face. It tended to be during a music lesson that Morgen would open up about other things, like who lived inside his enormous house.

"There are four of us: Dad, Mom, Beth, and Sandy. Sandy's our housekeeper, and he's a guy, just so you're not confused...and he's an idiot. He's always trying every sort of get-rich-quick scheme—yet he's still our housekeeper—so you can figure out for yourself how well they've paid off. You don't have to worry about Sandy barging in here, though. He doesn't come into this area because Mom doesn't believe he should have to clean any of the private rooms...so if you ever feel like doing some cleaning, feel free."

Night found it interesting how Morgen's family had a housekeeper that lived in the house. Even before Andrew stopped the cleaners from coming to their house, he'd never even seen them.

"Beth, as you know, is my sister... You keep getting that chord wrong!" Morgen fired, making Night jump before he continued, calmly. "I already told you that we're both adopted and that Mom can't have kids, but nobody is supposed to know that. She tries to pretend that this fucked up family is perfect, just like Dad does."

"Make it sound more like this..." Morgen plucked out the same melody with a different modulation. "Dad's a corporate lawyer, but he's hoping to become District Councilman after the next election, and eventually, Senator. You may have heard of him by now: Frederick Dahlsi? Then again, you probably haven't. Anyway, he's really playing up the nice family thing right now, with the election coming up." It took a moment for Morgen's voice to run clean again. "I'm kind of Mom's favorite because, as you know, we're joined by our history...which, I'm sure, Dad resents. But he's always been nice to me."

The thought of seeing Brigitte made Night's insides lurch. Although she'd left Andrew a long time ago, Night couldn't ignore that they had once been together—married—and he still saw her as the woman who guarded many secrets in death. What would it be like, he wondered, to finally confront the dead?

"Creepy," Morgen proclaimed. "You're so fucking good at this. You've probably got a hundred percent of your brain cells dedicated to this one skill, never having devoted any to anything else."

"Morgen, when am I going to get to meet any of these people?"

Morgen just continued to flip the pages of his handwritten music that sprawled all over the coffee table.

"And what's going to happen to me when you get well? What if I learn all this stuff and you don't need me anymore? Are you going to tell me to leave?" Night focused on his hands and worked on polishing an intricate sequence as he waited for a response. When one didn't come, he asked again. "Is that what you're going to do, Morgen, because I can't go home, ever?"

Morgen slammed down his sheets, then reached over and ripped the power cord from the body of Night's guitar. "I'm not going to get better, you moron!"

"Why wouldn't you? I was really sick once and I got better—and you don't look half as sick as I was."

"Well, I'm sorry I'm not limping around on crutches or dragging around an IV pole to make it more convincing! You want to know the truth? Fine, let's launch this epic pity party. I'm already having more days where I can't stop puking, or even use my hands properly...and they said that when this gets worse, my lungs are going to fill up with all kinds of crap and I won't even be able to talk or breathe, let alone sing. Not such great news when you're a lead singer in a band. So, I hate to break it to you, brainwave, but I'm not that kind of sick!"

Night set his slain guitar on the floor. "But you'll get better someday, won't you? You're not going to...?" His brother's exaggerated nod prompted the next logical question. "Can't anything help you? Aren't there any pills?"

"Yeah, I think they're called 'wishful thinking' and I've been taking them for weeks. And to answer your next question, I'm not going for any more treatments. The fact is, my chance of recovery is about five percent, and if you'd gone to school you would know that five percent is not good—so there is no point. I don't plan to trade what useful time I have left for months of bullshit in hospitals that won't change anything in the end."

Night could feel the world grinding to a stop like it had only once before: right before he set fire to the *Emerald Shore*. "I still don't understand what's wrong with you."

"It's bone cancer, this time...Ewing's Sarcoma. Same shit as before...much bigger bucket. I'm over it—believe me—but it's the timing that really bites. That concert we missed because of me...it would have launched the band. We would've got at least one album

116

recorded before I croaked, and that's all I wanted. The agent who got us that gig told me it was 'in the bag.' There were going to be some big-label reps at that concert and all we had to do was show up and play. Now I'm back to square one and I just don't have enough time to go back there."

It couldn't have been any worse for either of them. Although Morgen already told him he could stay, the world now imposed a strict time limit in which he had to catch up on nineteen years of missed learning, or else suffer the consequences. Memories of the homeless man he'd met on the street in Oregon flashed through Night's mind.

"Listen... I can't just wait around for another big opportunity to fall on my lap, and I can't even promise the others that I'll always be able to make it to our gigs, but you..." Morgen continued, as feared, "*you* can do this. This isn't impossible. My family thinks I'm better than ever, and I haven't told the band, or even Steve, what's really going on. And you keep on whining that you need a place to live... The truth is, you need something more than that. You need a life...and I'm in a position to give that to you."

Night didn't react. Andrew would have been pleased if he'd always been this mute.

"Look, all I want is for you to see me through one recording contract, one album that will put a handful of my songs on the charts, and then you can do whatever you want—and it's not like you won't be well compensated."

"I don't even know what you're saying."

"Night, I'm offering you my life, my family, my friends, my home, my car, my name and everything that would be due to me in the future—in other words, a shitload of cash. You can keep the whole package if you want or take the money and run. Start a new life, if that's more important to you, although you'll already have what most people can only dream of...you'll be famous...a rock star." Morgen's predatory eyes closed. "What can possibly be wrong with this offer?"

A hush swept the room as both minds flailed in chaos.

"It's not all going to happen overnight. I'll teach you everything you need to know and I'll even get you a voice coach—since talking is still kind of a new thing for you. This was meant to be, twin brother. Just think about how you existed for all this time but were hidden from the world. It's destiny...and there is only one for the both of us."

Night knew better than to voice his contention, but it refused to be hushed. "I just thought I was finally done with secrets and pretending."

Morgen stood up and banged his guitar on the table. "Will you stop being such a pussy? You got only two choices. You can get the fuck out of my house and go back to your freaky life with your freaky father, or whatever the fuck he is, or you can stay here and get with the program that actually makes sense—especially if you're running from the law! Leave if you want, but if you do, then neither of us will stand a chance."

Night flushed at the vision of his new puppet master—but at least this one wanted to teach him things and flaunt him in front of the largest audience imaginable. "Do you really think I can learn to be just like you?"

"Christ no, but your only mission is to get my songs out there. It's not my problem if people want to think I had a personality transplant."

Night became transfixed. He saw something compelling in Morgen's ridiculous scheme when he focused beyond the depressing reality of his brother's illness and that his life would once again revolve around a charade. Regardless of the name he used, it would still be his face and his voice that the public would come to know...even across the border, in Oregon.

****

A call came through on Lila's floor, shortly after she began her evening shift. Her skin prickled when she heard Andrew's voice, in spite of his new, gentler approach.

"To what depths of hell do you plan to send me, Lila? I just want to know where Night is...and that he's safe."

118

Lila's voice emerged, choked-up and guttural. "I assure you, he's very safe...finally. I knew you owned a restaurant, Andrew, but you never told me that you were also a butcher."

"It can be dangerous to jump to conclusions, Lila. You got the Sheriff's Office all riled up about those marks on Night's body, for nothing. I had to explain it to them, that no matter how much we try, we can't always teach our children well. Sometimes, they just choose the wrong path, get in with the wrong crowd...partake in the unthinkable."

"What?"

"I never would have pictured that little girl, Daphne, all dressed in black leather."

Just for one second, Lila considered his innuendo and then, brimming with revulsion, shook it off as a lie. "What is wrong with you?" She blocked any attempt for Andrew to respond. "Don't ever call me again, you sick son-of-a-bitch—and don't even think of coming here or to my house!"

"I won't come to your house, Lila, but you will tell me what I need to know."

Then he simply hung up.

****

Despite his condition, Morgen held to the task of teaching his obscenely naïve brother about the world.

It continued to astonish Night, how someone could function while eating almost nothing, but Morgen's cocktail of drugs and tenacity kept him going, at least most days.

One morning, when Morgen failed to meet him in the guest room, Night crept into his room and used his brother's bedside telephone to call for breakfast, mimicking what he'd once observed. Sandy informed him, with a cool graciousness, that he was in the middle of handling other requests and he would have to come down and get what he needed himself.

Night accepted the challenge and went into the kitchen, finding the man who, until now, he'd only known by name and position in the house. Sandy, a tall, young individual, with a narrow face and hair reminiscent of the previous decade, turned to Night and gave him an indulgent smirk. He granted Night a quick flashback to his life at the *Emerald Shore*, especially when Night saw that Sandy had already prepared and set aside his order, complete with garnishes. He grabbed the plate with the omelet for himself and the orange juice for Morgen, thanked Sandy, and fled the kitchen.

He stopped abruptly, on his way through the foyer, and stared down at his feet where a small animal tried to challenge him, unlike any of the skittish creatures of the emerald coastline. The protests belching from its foxlike snout increased by the second and he wondered why Sandy didn't care to see about the problem. Night set the meal down on a console table and turned to the menace that shrieked with astonishment when he snatched it by the scruff of the neck, carried it to the front door, and promptly cast it out of the house. Finally, Night gathered the two breakfasts that looked like one and returned to his brother's bedside.

"Go away," Morgen responded listlessly to Night's tap on the shoulder.

"Morgen...you're sick. You have to eat or you'll die."

Morgen's fist came up, lightning-fast, and sent the glass flying across the room. "Yes, I'm going to die, but I'm not going to die right now, okay? Now screw off and leave me alone if you can manage that for an hour!"

There were days like that. Night occupied himself by studying photographs or looking through books that Morgen thought would help him with his crash education.

When Morgen joined him, hours later, Night saw that his brother was starting to grasp the magnitude of his undertaking.

"I thought you said you could read! What, like a *Dick and Jane* reader, maybe?

But his progress annoyed Morgen just as much—when it threatened to expose his brother's secrets.

"I don't always understand what you're trying to say in these songs," Night admitted. "Except in this one..." He pointed to a title and leaned closer to Morgen, who refused to stop flipping through his sheet music. "Listen to what you wrote..."

Inside the blackness

Like a spark from flint

Another glimpse of the familiar

A tossing head with an auburn tint

Morgen tried to brush him off with a sneer, but Night didn't give up.

Just one soul

Though lives there's two

It's a low-frequency thunder

In the rift between me and you

"You knew about me, didn't you—I mean, not exactly—but in the same way that I saw you all the time? You say you never felt anything, but that's what this song is about, isn't it?"

"Will you knock it off? It's just a generic theme. I'm just talking about how two people had a connection before ever meeting, like soul-mates."

"I know—"

"And I'm hardly talking about you. Anyway, it's just a song."

"They're never just a song, and you called it *My Other Side.*"

"As in 'other half, partner, some chick'—not my idiot brother. Just keep reading and make sure you don't get stuck on any words." Unable to find a particular song, Morgen threw all of his papers aside and headed for his minibar where he grabbed his trusty box of supplies and performed his strange ritual for the second time today.

"What is that stuff?" Night asked, at last.

Morgen turned his eyes up, revealing a hint of amusement. "It helps kill the pain."

"You know, Morgen...I really did see you in my dreams. I thought I was just seeing myself with white hair, but it was obviously you trying to tell me something. And not only that... I've also felt your pain."

Morgen flashed a disturbed glance his way. Perhaps the solidity of his narrative kept Morgen from mocking him.

"Sometimes, I still do. I feel it mostly in my right hand," Night added as he uncurled his fingers, "and then it goes away."

Morgen's face now displayed unadulterated fear. "Wouldn't it be just my luck if you had it too? Just keep it together until after the first album's recorded."

****

It became a priority for Night to also get familiar with the grounds in back of the house. He'd only seen the swimming pool from the common room window, until today.

"Morgen?" a girlish voice tickled the air as Night sniffed around the pool house like a new housecat.

By the time he'd turned around, the teen girl had closed the distance between them. Even in her flats she stood taller than Daphne, with a curvier silhouette. The short cover she wore over her swimsuit invited his evaluation.

"Yes, it's me, Beth," she divulged as though she had read his thoughts. "Or is there something in my hair?" she added, scrunching her bushy, ash-blond ponytail with both hands.

A persistent barking in the distance pulled his attention the opposite way. "Hi...no...I like your hair," he managed, once he focused on Beth again. He liked everything about her.

"'Hi...I like your hair'?" she echoed. "You're not going to give me a hard time about anything? My dress is not too short? My hair is not too poufy?" she swayed with a giggle.

Night retorted with a defensive shrug. He had no desire to be just like his brother.

"Oh, you're no fun lately." Her shoulders fell. "Is there something wrong with you, Morgen? Are you sick again?" Her eyes grew big. "Did they find something else?"

"I'm not sick," he snapped.

Beth scowled. "Then it's drugs. Don't lie to me, Morgen. You've been acting pretty weird, lately, and it wouldn't be a new thing."

If Beth thought the real Morgen seemed a bit off, how could *he* ever pass her inspection? "I'm fine. There's nothing wrong me, and I'm not taking any stuff."

Her pout remained. "I'll be watching you, Morgen Dahlsi, so you better not try to hide anything from me. I always know."

****

Night both dreamed about and dreaded meeting Brigitte Morgen Dahlsi. He didn't know if he could face her without confronting her about the past, so he stalked her instead, watching her flit in and out of the foyer until his curiosity drove him to ask her what she was doing.

Even at close range, Brigitte looked young for her age, her face meticulously made-up, her dramatic dark waves strategically arranged around her face, and her body trim and well dressed. She clearly devoted herself to the cause.

"Oh, Morgen, we can't find Lexi..."

*Lexi?* he wondered as Brigitte slipped into the living room.

"What if she got outside? Oh..." she wailed from the other side of a wall.

Night ran straight to Morgen, who remained as he'd left him, sitting at the edge of his bed, plucking away at his guitar strings.

123

"Who's Lexi?"

"Oh yeah, I forgot to mention the dog...Mom's Pomeranian. She's got one." Morgen looked down and continued to pluck.

"Dog? You mean Lexi's an animal? Because one got into the house the other day and I threw it outside. It looked kind of rabid."

Morgen doubled over his guitar and began laughing, then coughing. "You threw out Mom's fucking dog, you cretin..."

Night dashed from the suite, down the stairs, and toward the front door that had seen the animal out, but he stopped when he found himself between Sandy and Brigitte.

"It's all right, Morgen. Thank goodness," she cooed, already holding the small, sable-colored creature in her arms. She gave it an adoring squeeze. "Sandy found her in the back. I guess somebody wasn't watching, probably when they opened the patio door."

The animal's shrill rumbling now ignited into fireworks.

"What's the matter?" Brigitte fussed, instinctively turning the dog away from Night. "Make sure you tell your friends to watch out for Lexi when they come over," she said before carrying the noisemaker into the kitchen.

Sandy, however, didn't budge, his glare fixed on Night. "The dog's been safe in the outbuilding ever since you heaved it into the front yard the other day. I saw you do it. I just wanted to see how long it would take you to go back for it, but you never did. Maybe you really shouldn't be such an asshole to me all the time. See how I didn't even rat you out?"

Night winced at the mess he'd assumed along with Morgen's identity. Lost for words, he raced up the stairs to recount the scene to Morgen, but he quickly regretted mentioning it when his brother promised that "for once, the prick would be sorry for fucking with him."

****

124

Lessons about living in the real world sometimes called for a field trip. Night commented how he liked Morgen's convertible car and Morgen brought up, once again, that everything of his would belong to him soon enough...as long as he didn't "fuck it all up."

But Night felt little appreciation for this future reward; gauging his relationship with his brother consumed him much more. It didn't promise to evolve into anything like he'd had with Daphne, or even Lila, but despite the fact that Morgen was testy and mean, it also wasn't the same as what he'd known with Andrew.

"I wish it could have been different," he aired as Morgen drove. "I wish you weren't sick and that I didn't have to pretend anymore."

"Maybe you should just be glad," Morgen suggested, his platinum hair blowing straight back as their speed reached sixty miles an hour. "Most people aren't just handed a new life when their old one's a bust."

Night crossed his arms and Morgen turned up the radio.

"Listen... You've heard this song before. Tell me what this part of the song is called."

"The intro."

"Okay. Keep going."

"This is easy, Morgen. The first verse is coming up and then the chorus. This song has three verses."

Morgen peered at Night through his peripheral vision. "You actually remember that?"

"Like I said, this stuff is easy."

"Well, you forgot about the pre-chorus...and there it is."

The streets widened and the buildings along them started to spread out and up, and Night could no longer contain what Morgen would call a stupid comment. "Everything is so different, here. Are all of these houses?"

"No, they're office buildings...where people work."

"I never realized there were so many different kinds of work. All I ever knew about was working at a restaurant." He lifted his hand as if to put his own words on hold. "Here's the bridge."

"What bridge?"

"The bridge in the song."

Morgen did a small skip in his seat. "No way... I only mentioned that term once. It's just like with the guitar; you're a bloody natural or an *idiot savant*," he cackled. But as they drove, Morgen's mood began to slide. "You know, I would gladly die tomorrow if I knew that even one of my songs would live on—or that my name would be recognized like John Lennon or Freddie Mercury or Bowie...Any amount of fame would be nice—and I have what it takes. I just don't have the time. You would understand if you could feel even a quarter of what I do, but you might feel it yet, because you do have it...you have the gift. You probably have it a little bit more than I do."

Night's mouth dropped open at the startling compliment, but he abandoned his response. Morgen wasn't hearing the world outside his head, and Night felt it could be treacherous to force him to listen.

When Morgen reached his first destination, he showed Night a small cove that he called *his beach*, a place separate from the rest of the sandy shoreline that snaked on forever. There were no cliffs in sight, just sunbaked sand and a few blissful pedestrians.

"I feel like I was dead for all these years," Night said, more to himself. "I can't believe all this existed and I didn't know."

"Maybe I'll come back and let you know how 'dead' really feels."

Morgen clearly didn't know his potential for doing just that. He still didn't believe that he'd already invaded a few waking moments, and countless dreamscapes, while still alive.

Morgen grinned at his brother's scowl. "Come on. Let's get the next stop over with."

Walking back to the car, Night noticed his brother pressing his palms into his hips. He began to realize that, if he tried, he could feel Morgen's exact malady of the moment and that he could expel the sensation as readily. This control over what he experienced suggested to Night that he didn't have the condition, as Morgen feared.

They left the last neighborhood behind and soared into wild vegetation. Dense chaparral gave way to evergreen and walnut trees as the car reached high into the San Gabriel Mountains. The scenery changed quickly, on account of Morgen's speeding, but somewhere at an altitude of about two-thousand feet, Morgen finally brought the car to rest.

Morgen led him a fair distance from the road and beckoned him over to a particular spot.

"Sorry...but it's a critical piece of the plan, and you need to be prepared to see it through at any time. When you take over for good, it will have to be like I never existed. You understand?"

Morgen's fingers dug through the earth until they found the edge of something beneath the dirt. He proceeded to shift a camouflaged board to one side, which revealed a roughly four-foot hole in the ground.

Night's mood had taken a rare flight after the compliment he received earlier, but it crashed hard at the sight Morgen's final destination.

"I'm thinking it's going to be like a nightclub up here after dark— I mean, with all the murder victims that've been dumped in these parts," Morgen quipped in the face of Night's horror." He stood up. "So, when I die..."

Night turned his face.

"Look at me! When I die, you will have to put my body in there. It's not very deep, but I'll fit. Then you'll pour gasoline on top. I'll leave some in the trunk for you. Then, you will throw a lit match into the hole—and remember to stand back unless you plan to go with me."

The image of that scene already burned behind Night's glassy stare, retrieved from his mental file of unexplained nightmares. This brought up some more of these files—the documentation of Morgen's experiences and impressions over the years—maybe even blueprints of the future.

"I think this is all your fault," Night accused softly. "It's like you don't even care if you live."

With a growl, Morgen shoved Night hard enough to knock him to the ground. He kicked the ground and sent a shower of sand over Night, who scrambled to get away from the edge of the pit that had just collapsed beneath his hand. "Listen to me...!" he continued once Night was upright. "When I'm toast, you'll have to fill the hole again and make it look natural."

When Night released a stressed sigh, Morgen mistook it for objection and gave him another push.

"Someone will have to do something with my body—"

"I know!" Night snapped. He barely turned his head enough to look at Morgen. Here was one thing Andrew hadn't lied about: being dead and being buried. "Just don't make me do it anytime soon." In the light of the setting sun, he found himself accepting Morgen's car keys after making another comment: "I don't even really know how to drive."

# Chapter Twelve

Night's incidental introduction to Frederick Dahlsi did nothing to lessen his prejudice about fathers, but it did put to rest another misconception.

He never understood why Frederick allowed Morgen to have a minibar in his suite, stocked with alcohol for his unlimited consumption. The bar also contained snack foods and soft drinks, but it was behind these benign things that Morgen stashed the rum, vodka, tequila, and the white powder box that still mystified Night.

It happened during a tequila-enhanced guitar lesson that someone in the hallway tried to turn the door handle. Morgen had locked the door, but his father's voice demanded retroactive entry. Night flung the guitar to the side and scurried into the bathroom, leaving Morgen to scramble to conceal their drinks before opening the door.

Frederick strode into the room, turned to Morgen and burst into a lecture about never seeing him anymore, and something about not quite trusting his activities. From the crack in the bathroom door, Night peeked at the man who Brigitte had married almost as soon as she'd left Andrew. Frederick's face was scarcely in view, but his Nordic traits, especially his still mostly flaxen hair, made him look like he could very well have been Morgen's biological father. He leaned closer to Morgen, suddenly, placing the rest of his sentence on hold.

"I smell booze," he said, which made Morgen back away.

"I just had a drink with my friends, Dad. That's all."

"Uh-huh? I didn't notice anybody coming or going tonight." He left Morgen and walked behind the bar where he quickly located Morgen's stash. He pulled out Night's half-glass of tequila and Morgen's empty glass, and each bottle of liquor that he'd tried to conceal behind soda bottles, bags of potato chips, and all the groceries Night had bought in the past and not yet consumed. "This is great," Frederick proclaimed, dropping all the illicit items on the countertop before opening the cabinet doors. His eyes widened before he pulled out the prescription pills and then the box that contained Morgen's white powder. Night couldn't see how intensely Frederick's pinkish complexion had washed over in red.

Morgen stood on the other side, pinching his hanging forehead before staring obstinately at the invader.

"Just leave me alone, Dad."

"I don't think so, Morgen! Why would you do this after everything you've been through? Your health has never been great—you almost died—and now you're just begging for something else to set you back!" He came around the counter and appraised Morgen's weight, visually at first, and then by gripping his arms. "Tell me about those pills. You tried to hide it from us last time. Are you sick again?"

"I'm not sick. They're old, okay?"

Finally, it made sense to Night why Morgen always scraped the labels off his prescription drugs. He carried them around everywhere he went and he'd wisely anticipated some version of this happening.

"And all this other stuff?"

Morgen shrugged, closing his arms. "I'm in a band. It's no big deal."

"This is unbelievable! How many times since you were born has life given you another chance—and not only when it came to your health?"

Morgen's stance, instantly, grew more defensive.

"We've given you everything, but nothing matters to you. I wish you could only remember how your mother took you from doctor to doctor and tried every trick she could think of to beat the odds and keep you alive."

"How frustrating that must have been for you."

Night winced in the split-second calm, and then came the sound he expected...the sound of Frederick's hand colliding with Morgen's face.

"For what it's worth," Frederick continued as Morgen clutched one hand to his cheek, "I'm going to arrange for you to see our doctor. At least, then I'll know what's really going on with you." He gathered the liquor bottles and turned toward the bathroom.

Morgen dropped his arms in full panic and Night backed away from the door. Night's heart almost stopped. He knew he couldn't squeeze through the sticky guestroom door quickly or quietly enough, so he leapt into the sunken bath. Morgen's father charged into the room and, in his tirade, didn't seem to hear the rings that suspended the shower curtain slithering on the rod.

One by one, Frederick poured the bottles of liquor into the sink and then he returned a second time to empty Morgen's white powder into the toilet, but he ignored the pills. He left the suite after making a final decree. "You will eat dinner with the rest of the family from now on and, until further notice, you can also cancel your meetings with those helpful band buddies of yours."

Night wasn't sure about the activity outside the bathroom so he stayed in the tub until Morgen found him.

"And that..." Morgen announced, flinging the shower curtain aside, "was Dad." He barely glanced at Night before storming out again. Night came after him and Morgen spun around in his face. "But *that* never happens. He actually hit me."

"Not until you begged him to. You kind of deserved it."

"Thanks, asshole. And thanks for running out like that instead of doing something useful to help me clean up. And you can start taking over for me anytime now—like at supper tonight."

Night rattled his head. "I'm not ready."

"Oh, you're ready, smartass, and you can go visit Doc with him too. I can't believe this..." He raked his hair. "You said you felt some pain in your hands before?"

"I feel it right now, right here." Night put his palm to his hip.

"Shut up. Just shut up, okay? You're probably just watching how I'm walking and you can tell that it hurts."

"No," Night insisted. "You tell me like you used to tell me through my dreams. I don't know why you won't believe me when you're the one who came to me all the time."

"Will you stop it? Why the hell would I come to you? I can barely stand you, and if you didn't serve a purpose here I would throw your ass to the curb in a second!"

"I'm just telling you..."

Morgen brushed past him to reach his pills. "Just go into my room, open the drawer next to my bed, and bring me one of the packages that are in there. It's all I got left. I'll just have to get more when I see Sean, later."

"Maybe you should listen to your father and not take any of that stuff."

"Night...maybe you should just take that stuff and stop listening to 'father.'"

****

The dinner atmosphere might have been a bit tense if it hadn't been for Beth's continuous chirping. Night insisted he wasn't ready, so Morgen masked his weight loss under layers of clothing and joined his family for supper. But he couldn't quite hide his lack of appetite. He did his best with the food, and when he couldn't swallow another bite, he announced: "I don't want any more. I really don't like this," just as Sandy poked into the dining room. It was unintentional, but perfect. "Can I go now?" Morgen asked, challenging the stare from his father across the table.

Brigitte, who also never ate very much, came to his rescue. "Of course, honey. But you hardly touched anything. Sandy might take you something else later, if you ask him to." She glanced at the housekeeper who suddenly ducked as though he was too tall for the fifteen-foot ceiling.

"Will you, Sandy?" said Morgen, wide-eyed. "Just a sandwich would be fine." He beamed in the presence of Sandy's tart smirk before it disappeared with him into the kitchen.

Morgen rose from the table and Brigitte followed suit, blocking his next step, and confirming for him that she'd been told about the incident.

"We're just worried about you." With both hands, she stroked back his iridescent hair before pulling him against herself. "Tomorrow, your father will take you to see Doctor Barrett. I've made the appointment. You know that this is a time when you have to be especially responsible considering the scares you've had in the past— and with your father working so hard on his campaign. You know he has to stay focused on it if he hopes to win and also go further someday."

Morgen bit his words. He'd have to remember to puke in red white and blue from now on. "I know that. But I have to meet with the band this week. That's still okay, isn't it? Dad doesn't want me to lose what I've been working for...?"

Beth shot up from her chair. "I knew you weren't serious about giving it up."

Brigitte held him to her shoulder for another moment while she spoke the words he predicted. "No, no. That's not what anyone wants. Why would you think that?"

With a mild grin, Morgen lifted his pale eyes to his father's. As he pulled away from Brigitte and moved toward the corridor, Beth looked ready to chase after him, but she refrained and simply admired him as she settled back into her chair.

Morgen found Night in the guest room, playing with the acoustic guitar when he returned from dinner. "I quit. It's your turn. I can't do this anymore—and they have to get used to seeing you." He held his mouth as he raced into the bathroom where he threw up for the next minute or so. With Night lingering outside the bathroom, he continued to speak like nothing was hindering him. "I'm taking off for tonight, and you can stay here and be the jailbird. Sandy will

134

probably bring some food up, later, which you're welcome to. Just check to make sure there're no pins in it or anything."

Morgen phoned Steve and arranged to meet him on the outskirts of the neighborhood park. He instructed Night not to sleep in the guest bedroom tonight, in case someone insisted on barging in again, and with that resolved, he threw the strap of his guitar case over his shoulder and slipped out of the house, into the coal-black air.

****

The lights of Steve's gray Datsun highlighted Morgen's fair head where he slouched on a bench, in front of the park.

"How long you gonna be?" Morgen's soft-spoken friend inquired.

"Don't worry about it, Steve. I'll get one of the guys to drop me off later."

Sometimes "one of the guys" also meant Doris, the band's keyboardist, who was going to demand a hefty explanation for his glaring absence in recent weeks. Steve jarred him out of this thought.

"So, tell me, my friend...why can no one know about your brother?"

Morgen decided to draw on the truth. "He doesn't want anybody to find him. They're looking for him because of something that happened in Oregon that wasn't really his fault."

"You mean the cops are looking for him?"

"Very good, Steve. You sound just like him now. Look, you have to pretend you never heard of him...like I'm doing. All right?"

"Your brother left your house?"

"What do you think?"

Steve's tanned fingers left the steering wheel to tug at the small gold hoop earring on one earlobe. "I don' understand you, my friend. He's your brother. He looks like you. How come you don' care what happens to him?"

"What am I supposed to do when he's the one who wanted to leave? I don't really know him... And I care about my band," Morgen affirmed. "Thanks for the lift."

The car slowed down in front of a warehouse that had been turned into a semi-equipped rehearsal space. Two familiar cars were already there and the owner of one of them greeted him at the entrance of their unit.

Sean's hand latched onto Morgen's sleeve and yanked him inside. "Don't ever pull anything like that again because I won't be showing up the next time you fucking try it."

Morgen swerved out of his reach. "It's hard to make anything else a priority while you're puking your brains out and you think you're dying."

Across the room, in a chair, Aden continued to pluck out a groove on his bass guitar, taking little notice of either of them until his latent annoyance finished setting. "Looks like you've still got a few more breaths left inside you, and I wouldn't have quit...not until I couldn't see for gasping." He stood up and let the guitar dangle from his left hand.

"Trust me, Aden...I do feel that way."

"Good to hear. Then welcome back... Now, are you going to give us your word that you're in it for good?"

"Why do you think I'm here?" Morgen's tone erupted through a fusion of irritation and enthusiasm. He stooped over and began opening his guitar case. "I need an amp."

"There's a PA system in those lockers over there, remember? Man, get your shit together or are you stoned?"

"No, and my shit's been together for years. Don't give me that shit. Look...I know I fucked up our big break, but I'm also the one who got us that offer in the first place."

Everyone looked at the doorway as Doris strolled in. She only smirked at Morgen like she knew the others had already punished him enough, without any contribution from her.

"Sounds like you're back. So...are you only back for the band or are you back for me too?"

Aden slammed the strings on his bass. "Please, save it for after practice. Can we just plan our next move, now that our savior has returned?"

"Amen," Sean mumbled, adjusting his seat behind the complimentary low-end drum set.

Doris had her own massive keyboard, which she slugged halfway across the room before Morgen intervened and helped her place it on a stand. He tried to hide his thoughts. He had to start distancing himself from Doris, or else allow Night to take over where he left off with her as well. He wasn't prepared when she leaned over the keyboard and kissed him.

"Are you really okay?" she asked. "Why were you so sick that night if they didn't find anything wrong with you?"

"I don't know. They said it's like aftershock from all the transfusions and meds."

"After all this time?"

"I guess," he said, deserting the topic as fast as he could. The room was already pulsing with test sounds and he needed to start backing them. He connected all the cables and monitors in a hurry and then laid his hand on the mixing board. "Okay, go ahead, Sean."

Their ears filled with Sean's rhythm and Morgen signaled to Aden to start, once he was satisfied with the level of kick and snare drum from Sean.

"Let's find out if we still got it!" Aden called through the mic. "Why don't we try *Better Tonight?*"

This allowed for a long introduction, first by Aden and Sean, then by Morgen's guitar and Doris's keyboard, before Morgen's voice finally poured into the microphone. He stopped to boost the volume of the vocals and then resumed his dual responsibility like they'd never missed a rehearsal. They practiced for a good part of the night and as they wrapped up, Aden pressed Morgen for his word that he would reintroduce the band to his former contact.

"For sure, I will," he replied. "I'll explain what happened and, just maybe, he'll give us another chance. ...Look, I'm sorry!" he flared in the unforgiving silence.

Doris had readily agreed to provide him with a lift home. She took her time disassembling her equipment and debating a melodic change with Aden while Morgen cornered Sean at the lockers.

"I need more coke," Morgen told him and Sean's shoulders fell.

"What're you doing with it, man? I give it to you at cost, so you better not be flipping it for double on the street."

"It's not that. My dad flushed it, okay?" When Sean nodded, Morgen continued. "I need something else too. I need a favor." His sudden coughing spell splashed concern over Sean's face. "Listen, we have this housekeeper—"

"Don't ask me to call a hit on some little old lady..."

"He's a cocky little prick who just needs to be taken down a few pegs. Can you do that? I'd like you to do that."

Sean grinned as he locked the metal doors. "I'll have to get back to you about a price."

"It really doesn't matter, Sean. Just tell me if you can make it happen."

Doris cleared her throat in the doorway. "Aden's going to help me load, and I'll wait for you in the car."

"I'll be right down."

Sean finally turned to face Morgen. "All right...describe the guy to me."

****

Morgen slipped back into the house at three in the morning. He announced his return by ripping away Night's covers. "All right, freak. Time to get out of my bed."

138

Night straightened his undershirt over Morgen's borrowed sweatpants before crawling off the bed. "Morgen, Beth came in here earlier," he reported through his grogginess. "I think I did okay answering her questions, but she kept looking at me like she knew."

"She can't possibly know," Morgen insisted. "And between school and her friends, she's hardly around. Anyway Night, when you see Doctor Barrett, don't mention anything about those pains you say you feel sometimes."

"I told you, they're your pains."

"Whatever. Just don't mention it because if you got what I've got, there won't be a damn thing in the world you can do about it. You're still healthy enough to finish what I've started, and nothing else matters."

"Morgen, I still don't understand what's going to happen tomorrow."

Morgen's eyelids dropped. "You're not going to tell me you've never seen a doctor before? Oh, for fuck sake..." Morgen stared at the carpet for a few heartbeats before his eyes popped up again, full of light. "He'll probably start by asking you some questions. Then he might check your breathing, your blood pressure, and then he'll probably order some tests...maybe just some bloodwork, but if he suspects there's something wrong with you, he'll need a tissue sample, in which case he'll have to hack a piece of flesh off some part of your body where you won't notice it missing—like in your case, your dick." Morgen clutched himself through his jeans and cackled in turning.

"You're just like Andrew," Night huffed. "I don't believe you."

Morgen dropped his humor as he swaggered toward the door. "Good. Then maybe there's still some hope."

****

Hope barely registered on the police meter, in Oregon, when it came to finding the *Emerald Shore* arsonist. As far as the law was concerned, Night Shannien and Daphne Swanson had slipped into the underground world in some other state, or even Canada.

The thought crossed Andrew's mind, to hire a private investigator—who he would equip with an accurate description of Night—but he couldn't guarantee that this pro wouldn't uncover too much. So, with what became mind-numbing time on his hands, Andrew visited every shelter and group home in his vicinity—and then beyond. He stood in alleyways and pestered people who barely had the mental capacity, or desire, to process his questions. Some of the vagrants and junkies mistook him for a cop or detective, and out of the ones who didn't slight him, a few rummaged drunkenly through their imaginations to produce a memory of Night. In any case, he gained no leads.

Andrew had seen the truth at the end of every road and on every road sign throughout his travels. Lila held all the clues, and the time for nonsense was over. While watching her house, he never saw Night, but he did witness Lila coming and going dressed in two distinct ways: either in a long coat for going shopping or to work, or in sweats for jogging. He even became aware of her loose schedule for hitting the trails, and he made note of this. He couldn't bear another month to go by without getting any closer to a lead, to avenging his pride and his livelihood, or as he'd put it for Lila, to getting his restitution...now from her as well.

# Chapter Thirteen

Sandy cruised out of the grocery store with bags strung up to his elbows. His tall frame wobbled on the paved slope, in the back parking lot, so he hardly needed help from two meaty hands to end up careening into one of the big metal garbage bins behind the store.

In the rubble of strewn groceries, Sandy tried to turn his head, but his assailant gripped his hair so tight, he could only shift his eyes. His chin jutted within an inch of the metal bin and he suspected he might end up tasting it if he attempted to struggle.

"Shortcuts can be hazardous. What's the rush, buddy?"

Sandy paddled with his arms to back up on his knees but he stopped when he felt a knife rip up through the denim seam at his rear.

"Yummy. Check out the merchandise. Fish-eggs...Steak... I guess I'm going to eat good for a few days." The thug fired a derisive snort, and at the detection of movement at the end of his knife, jabbed the blade further in between Sandy's buttocks. "I don't wanna be feelin' bad about anything, so I hope you'll just tell me you want me to take what I need."

"Take what you need," Sandy croaked, feeling the vomit rising in his throat.

"Good boy. And you don't wanna be puttin' yourself in any more danger by carrying around a lot of cash, now do you?"

Sandy grimaced at the reality that he was being robbed, and at the attacker's degrading method that had already sliced one of his cheeks.

Sudden voices in the distance must have spooked the perpetrator because he finished with his victim abruptly. He pulled back his knife, then smashed Sandy's face against the metal bin before feeling through his pockets and confiscating all the remaining cash from his wallet. After seizing the grocery bag loaded with meat, the man sauntered away to a waiting truck.

****

Doctor Barrett's cordial manner quickly dissolved Night's apprehension about the visit. He also spent more time on small talk with Frederick than on the examination of his patient.

"He's concerned about you," the doctor told Night, trying to excuse Frederick's odd and willful intrusion in the room. "It's been a little while," he commented as he held the chest piece of his stethoscope against Night's back beneath his opened shirt. "Breathe out," he said, and Night nearly did the opposite as his shirt began to lift. Morgen didn't tell him about this, but with his back to the wall and his shirt still on, it all ended without incident with the doctor pulling the apparatus from his ears. "You certainly look better than the last time I saw you. That was quite a miracle...your previous remission. How are you feeling these days?"

"I'm fine," Night answered so quickly that it made the doctor grin and Frederick cross his arms.

"Okay...so, let's just make sure with some routine blood work."

Just like Morgen's account of an exam, the doctor had checked his lungs and blood pressure. He also asked about pain, and Night knew to say no to any questions related to pain symptoms.

"Have you been losing weight?" the doctor inquired, undoubtedly based on Frederick's private, preliminary report.

"I guess so. I haven't been thinking a lot about eating...with all the rehearsing these days." It helped him, and Morgen, that his gradual weight loss, since arriving in California, had blended their alternating appearances.

Doctor Barrett turned to Morgen's father. "My guess is that your son is healthy, but here's a lab rec, just to be sure."

"I'd like you to call me with the results," Frederick insisted.

Even Night caught the doctor's hesitation, but Frederick's long-standing relationship with Doctor Barrett, and whatever it was in his tone, forced a nod from the doctor. "If Morgen's okay with that," he included.

Amidst the prickly hush, inside the car, Night flinched when Frederick's hand sailed toward him when its aim was to simply brush over his hair.

"Well, that's a little unfair," Frederick remarked, clutching onto the steering wheel instead. "But I'll tell you the truth, Morgen, I'm not finished with being angry about the other day. You can be grateful that I didn't mention your new pastime to Doctor Barrett or you might have found yourself with commitments to some rehab program that truly would have messed with your big plans. Just be advised, I have all the resources I need to make that happen anytime I choose."

Night looked his way and tried to comprehend.

"But it's also important to keep this thing quiet, at least until the election is over. It's not exactly what I need, right now, for the whole world to find out that my son is an alcoholic and a drug-addict."

Flickers of understanding began to distort Night's features.

"If you really care about your goals as much as I care about mine, then I hope you'll get familiar with what it takes to achieve them. And even if you blast into stardom, you're still someone's kid, and you will respect us. Do you understand that?"

"Yes, of course, Daddy," Night answered as he pushed Morgen's sunglasses onto his nose to hide his flooding eyes. He ached to trust Frederick's intentions and dismiss Morgen's theory that his adoptive father could barely tolerate him. Absorbed in his thoughts, Night didn't notice the double strobe of Frederick's eyes at his response, or the contemplative silence that followed.

****

Beth found Night in the living room, one evening in December, examining the Christmas tree, and the wrapped boxes beneath it.

144

"Don't tell me you don't care what you've got under there," she blurted.

"What do you mean?"

Beth tossed him a reticent grin and knelt in front of the tree beside him.

He tried to look indifferent to her presence when, to his utter amazement, she leaned over and placed a kiss on his cheek. A few seconds went by, and then she exploded.

"I knew it! I wondered why we had so many presents this year, but I guess it's because they're not all for me and Morgen. Mom and Dad bought some for you too!"

She seemed so confident, he didn't dare try to defend himself. "No one can know," Night whispered. He'd already felt that Morgen was moving too fast to induct him into his new life—and this proved it. Night's eyes scanned the room as though they could penetrate the walls.

Beth snickered. "If you don't want anyone to know, then you'd better start keeping your mouth shut. You're totally unlike him, you know. It was pretty obvious when I talked to you in Morgen's room the other night. But I also noticed your tooth." She pointed to her top right lateral incisor. "Morgen once tried to pull a bottle cap off with his teeth and he chipped his tooth." She shrugged. "Maybe no one else remembers that, but I remember. I remember most things."

Night looked at the floor, blinded by his nervous head rush.

"So, are you going to tell me what's going on? I'm not that surprised, you know. We're both adopted, Morgen and I, so anything's possible. I just can't believe that jerk tried to keep this from me. Let's go see him..." she said, bouncing off the floor and racing for the south staircase.

Night's heart felt like an olive being sucked through a straw as he ran after her. "Don't, Beth," he pleaded as she neared Morgen's suite, but she simply charged in.

"Morgen?" she called, standing in his doorway like a lioness on a crest of land. "Get in here! Me, you, and this person who looks like you, need to have a little conference!"

Morgen emerged from his bedroom looking like something was prodding him from behind. His glare shot over Beth's shoulder and splattered on Night.

"You don't even look the same," Beth articulated, "now that you're together."

Night had thought so all along. It couldn't be missed— the difference in their hair color and cut, the tone of their skin, the prominence of Morgen's cheekbones compared to his own and, probably most of all, how even their demeanors conflicted in such close proximity.

Morgen finally piped up in a huff. "Beth, this wasn't supposed to happen, but since it did, let me introduce you to my idiot brother, Night." He stamped past Beth and shoved Night in the chest. "Get out so I can talk to my sister!"

****

"Well...?" Beth demanded.

"Well, I guess now you know." Morgen plopped down on his couch and waited for her to join him. "Night showed up here completely out of the blue. I wanted him to leave, but just before I kicked his ass out, I realized he was a musical genius. He's going to try to help me, Beth—but you need to help me too, by not saying anything to Mom and Dad."

"What's going on Morgen? What's he helping you with? You look so serious." She shrugged with a tiny simper. "My friends are going to die when they find out there're two of you."

"Beth, listen...no one is allowed to find out about Night." With his elbows pressing hard on his lap, he dropped his face into his hands. "You know I've always been sick?"

"Yeah, but you're not now..."

146

Morgen nodded, even with his head in his hands, before he lifted his face. "Yeah Beth, I am. You also know how hard I've worked with the band to make it." He breathed a laugh at the drama of his own words. "Well, we're close, we're really close, and we can still have what I want—what all of us in the band deserve—but it's not going to happen anymore without Night."

She looked contemplative for a moment. "Why? Will you be in treatment again for a really long time? And what about Night? Won't anyone miss him?"

Morgen spoke gently, hypnotically. "You can ask him about that if you want, but there isn't going to be any treatment for me, this time. That's why no one can know. If you tell Mom and Dad, they'll just freak out. They won't understand that my life's ambition is more important than their need to pretend that there's hope. If you tell them, everything I've worked for will be for nothing. Is that what you want? And we don't even know if they'll accept Night. They may just tell him to leave—and he needs my help too. Do you understand, Beth? He needs my name and I need his life."

"Morgen...?" she whimpered. "What are you saying? Are you going to die?" She bowed over her knees as a thin, strained cry escaped her. Morgen fought to appear unaffected. He looked the other way and eventually left her sobbing while he stood by the window.

"Morgen, are you absolutely sure?" She took one look at him and nodded at the floor. "How can you ask me to ignore that you're letting yourself die without a fight?"

"Why does everybody say that to me when I've explained it already? Are you going to take everything away from me, and from three, no, four other people? There is no goddamn help and the only thing I can change now is my legacy, and Night's fate, and it all comes down to how I use the time I have left."

Night creaked open the bathroom door like he'd been listening from behind it all along. Beth turned her watery eyes to him.

"Why are you helping him do this?"

"It's not all about Morgen," he said. "I'm just helping myself."

****

Sandy entered the house, long after dark, with a few torn grocery bags and his navy-blue windbreaker tied around his waist. He hadn't expected to black out in the car when he thought he'd close his eyes for a minute, after the incident. He grew defensive when he caught Brigitte staring at him, or rather at his bloody nose, crimson cheek, and black eye.

"Sandy, what happened to you?"

"I got my ass kicked behind the grocery store," he stated as though it was partially her fault. "I'm sorry about the missing groceries."

"Oh, Sandy, don't worry about that. Are you all right? Your poor head...you might have a concussion."

"No, it's fine. I'm fine."

"Did you go to the hospital?"

"It isn't that bad," he insisted, attempting to bypass Brigitte, only to stumble into Frederick at the edge of the lobby. Even Beth arrived, with Morgen, likely after hearing the commotion in the lobby. Beth held her hands over most of her face and her brother looked confused, or shaken. Even in his present state, something made Sandy look at Morgen twice.

Frederick began with a stutter. "I hope you'll just rest for as long as you have to, Sandy. Did you see who did this to you?"

"No, I didn't see him. But it's fine, really. It's fine!" He strode through the crowd that seemed amplified in his dizziness and fled up the stairs.

On the landing, he heard the sweep of footsteps at the end of the hallway, and even more clearly, he heard a door handle being released. Any other time, he would have investigated the noise, but tonight, he only wanted to hide in his suite where he could sulk in peace, and tend to his torn flesh.

148

****

Morgen didn't complain about the pain in his arms and legs, but it showed in the dimness of his eyes and through his erratic breaths. The only hurt he ever blatantly expressed followed a short telephone conversation with the music agent who he had hoped to reconnect with. Night rushed into the common room after the sound of an airborne telephone crashing.

On the carpet, sitting against the couch, Morgen sat wheezing and bawling over his knees. "I don't have time for this...I don't have enough time to start from scratch! I tried to explain it to him, but he doesn't want to have anything to do with us now."

Night looked irritated. He saw himself on the floor, not his brother, and he despised the image.

"He said it wasn't worth it to him either if I could take this long to explain myself—and he's right." He looked up. "I couldn't make a move until you were ready—I couldn't risk letting the band down again! But I couldn't tell him that! It doesn't matter what I do now, I'm going to be completely finished before we get another bite." Through a series of gasps, he regained his composure, stood up, and pronounced: "Well, I don't have a choice. I need a contract—even if you have to be the one to get it for me."

"Morgen? What if it doesn't work out?"

Morgen glanced at him sharply. "If you think it's not going to work out, go home."

"You know I can't do that. And you wouldn't want me to go really, would you?"

"Don't test me, Night. You know the deal."

"Yes, and I want it to work," Night said, stopping his brother before he could retreat to his bedroom. "I need it to work—just like you—but this is all really hard. Sometimes, in a way, I wish things were simple again like they used to be. I think sometimes that I would've been happy, and could be again, if I was back in Oregon, and just working at the restaurant, but not all by myself...if you were there too."

Morgen balked. "Oh yeah, that would be great. You're testing me, Night. You're creeping me out!" He barged into his bedroom and tried to slam the door behind him, but Night caught it.

"There's something wrong with you, Morgen."

"No shit!"

"Not in that way. You even scare Beth, and I don't know if I ever want to be exactly like you."

"Listen," Morgen hissed, leaning forward, "you're the freaky one! That's what the problem is. And you'd better start to lose that sick side of yours if you plan to get anywhere in this world. Did you see Sandy's face? Huh? I have to try to amuse myself in any way that I can, these days, and if you piss me off enough, do you think I wouldn't arrange to have something creative done with you too?"

Night's brow pulled together at this revelation and he scrambled out of his close quarters, feeling much the same as when he'd fled the burning restaurant that incomprehensible day, almost six months ago.

****

On a cooler latitude, Lila kept pace with the sunrise on her favorite scenic trail. She barely slowed down as she skirted along the crest of rock that offered a hint of danger to her run. With the sky brightening before her, she glanced at her watch and confirmed that she'd never reach the halfway point before the top of the hour, so she came to a clumsy stop before turning around.

"It's a perfect day to be up here. I didn't think you would miss it."

Lila's eyes flashed to the right, wondering how someone could have appeared on the path without the normal prelude of footsteps.

"Your problems, Lila... Are they still catching up with you, these days?"

Andrew stepped down from the treed slope along the hiking trail as a double alarm triggered inside her. He wasn't dressed for hiking like the one time she'd convinced him to at least somewhat experience her pastime. In fact, he looked "all business" in a pressed shirt, dress pants, and an expensive woolen trench coat.

Her hands slid into her pockets on both sides, since she couldn't remember which pocket contained her jackknife. "I told you not to come near me, Andrew."

"You told me not to call or visit you at home or at work. I did none of those things. Enough with the games, Lila." His face flushed. "I'm just here to find out what happened to my son."

"Oh Andrew, he's not even your son. You're delusional and you're obsessed, and you're really scaring me, so why would you think I'd ever help you find Night?"

"Lila," he said, stooping to look pleadingly up into her unadorned face. "Why are you keeping me from the only family I have left in this whole world—the only one I managed to save?"

She pulled out her puny weapon and opened it as he watched.

"Ridiculous, Lila. I'm not here to hurt you."

"I don't know that. You know that I spoke to the police..."

Andrew gripped both of her forearms and the jackknife skipped from her right hand. "It's all fine. I spoke to them too and straightened everything out. Misunderstandings happen, Lila. I'm not mad. Now, I only want to know what happened to Night—I only want to know where you sent him. This is not an unreasonable request."

He let go of her arms, swooped down, and pocketed the jackknife himself; then he faced her again, with his hands inside his coat, like he'd never moved. "Come on, I'll walk down with you while you tell me what happened."

She did feel less threatened with both of them strolling along, like in the past. "I don't believe there's been any misunderstanding, Andrew, so what are you going to do if I don't tell you anything... Kill me?"

"I've already been hassled enough by every form of police—thanks to you—without another dead body..." He halted and sighed. "I meant...without a dead body being thrown into their investigation."

Lila faced Andrew, calculating her chances of making it back alive... "No, you had it right before. That missing girl...just another 'plebian bitch' about to ruin Night's life, like what happened to Reade. And it's easy to accuse someone of all kinds of infamy when they aren't coming back..."

Andrew's blue eyes unsheathed like a sword to become metallic and deadly. She backed away but a schoolyard bully shunt sent her reeling over the crag. A full somersault later, she caught some shoots that protruded from the rocky slope as she also gained some footing on a minuscule ledge. She peered up to see that her cap had been saved by some impish twigs above her, as the one inside her grip gave way. But it didn't matter... She was still holding onto Night's secret.

# Chapter Fourteen

Rather than celebrating on Christmas Eve in their European tradition, the Dahlsis toasted the holiday with wine and opened presents after an elaborate lunch...only because Brigitte had obligated the whole family to a charity function that evening. Morgen, who could rarely keep food down anymore, sent Night to experience Christmas for himself.

Before this, Night had only known Christmas as that time of year when Andrew chopped down a spruce or pine tree, for the restaurant, and asked him to decorate it. Morgen's explanation of Christmas helped, but when it morphed into one about religion, Night shut the conversation down fast. The very suggestion of rules sent him back to the Hell he'd known in Oregon, under the charge of a man who probably thought he was God.

He had begun to appreciate the "merry" aspects of Christmas, so he felt a sense of tragedy for the spindly housekeeper who insisted on working through the holiday rather than admit that he had nowhere else to go on his days off. It bothered him even more to know that a member of the Dahlsi household had literally bought Sandy the angry swarm of colors that spanned over one-half of his face.

Beth had maintained a solemn air, ever since Morgen shared his plight, and Night, through his usual passiveness, seemed unenthusiastic enough to genuinely pass as Morgen. He stared at one of his gifts for a few second, before realizing it was a music book for guitar.

"Oh, Beethoven..." he blurted. "Did he write something new lately?"

Beth slapped his arm and giggled nervously. Sandy shook his head and rolled his eyes—as did Frederick, who had always tried to steer Morgen toward the classical. Night watched all this and realized he'd messed up, saved only by Beth's effort to turn the blunder around.

"You said you wanted to try some classical, and I didn't even tell Dad about that..."

Luckily, Morgen saved him from wreaking any more Christmas chaos by ordering him to stay behind from the charity event so he could rehearse with him. It was precious time whenever they could perform in tandem, without restraint, and work on matching their voices. Private vocal lessons gave Night the edge he needed to breathe life into Morgen's compositions, but voice lessons alone couldn't instill Morgen's personal style.

After just one hour, Beth surprised both of them when she returned from the function, alone, having faked a sore stomach. She admitted she'd come to challenge their scheme, one last time.

"What if they can cure you?" she implored.

Morgen slammed the stop button on the tape deck that he used to demonstrate his sound for Night. He walked away, grabbed his newly purchased bottle of tequila from the bar, and planted himself on the carpet again. Without asking anyone what they wanted, he poured a glass for Beth and refilled Night's.

"I really expected that after the big shock wore off, you would start to support me a little bit...but I guess not. Well," Morgen continued, in a voice of dry ice, "it's Christmas Eve. I think we should make a toast. How about 'to my last Christmas' or to fate for being so fucking clever, and for awarding the realization of all my hard work to either nobody or to someone who doesn't even give a shit."

While Morgen took a long drink from his glass, Night widened his eyes at Beth who returned his helpless expression before standing up.

"You really are sick, Morgen, and I mean sick with hate. Maybe you'd get better if you actually tried."

Morgen rammed his drink down so it lapped onto the carpet. "For Christ's sake! You sound like you've been taking lessons from this asshole, here. Will both of you just fuck the hell off? I feel like shit anyway, and it's not safe for us to be together like this with Sandy lurking around all the time."

Night rose with Beth, glad to follow her out of Morgen's suite. She paused in the hallway and lightly clasped his fingers in hers.

"I've never seen him this mean," she whimpered. "...Night? Will you tell me if he gets really bad? Will you make sure I know what's happening, even if he doesn't want me to know?"

He nodded.

"I'm so glad you're here. Maybe you'll teach him a few things. Maybe he'll start to become more like you."

Night stifled a cough. "I doubt I'll ever be able to teach him anything." He longed to take her into his intimate realm, where Morgen refused to venture. He hoped she might invite him.

"Will you sit downstairs with me? I like to look at the tree."

It might have been the request he'd waited for. He kneeled beside her and listened when she started to talk, but she sounded removed, almost feverish.

"In a few days, we'll have to take it down already... Not that I care. Not that it matters. Not that anything matters." She started to sniff in an effort to keep her face dry. "Tell me what you meant... Why do you think you don't know a lot?"

Through his own glazed vision, the staggering number of white lights on the Christmas tree became hypnotic.

"Remember...I told you that I lived with Andrew, my grandfather? Well, I didn't tell you everything about that. I didn't tell you how he made me a freak, like Morgen says."

"C'mon. He called you a genius, and I have no doubt that you're smarter than he is."

Night smiled at the sound of those words, but he didn't know quite how to respond.

"Night, how can Morgen expect you to be him forever, or for any length of time? Don't you ever want to go home?"

"Sometimes I do," he said, ashamed. "See... I really *am* stupid."

"What can be stupid about wanting to go home?"

Night debated for a few seconds. Finally, he twisted at the waist and pulled his shirt out of the back of his pants. He rarely thought about it anymore, but suddenly he had to know what Beth would think if she would still find it so shocking that he would rather consent Morgen's crazy ploy than go home. He slowly raised the material and waited for a reaction.

He heard nothing, not even her breath, but Beth's fingers suddenly curled around his while her other hand continued to drive the material up over his back; then his shirt dropped like a curtain, and it took him a moment to feel that Beth was crying.

"How could anyone do that?" she choked out. "This is awful. Everything is awful."

That might have been true if Beth had retreated in horror, but even Daphne hadn't done that. If anything, Andrew had only succeeded in cursing him with a conversation piece that required much tedious explanation every time he chose to reveal it.

"You're nothing like Morgen," Beth uttered, positioning herself opposite him. "I said it before... You don't even look the same."

Night felt his eyes brighten like the lighted snowflake at the top of the Christmas tree as she leaned in to kiss his mouth. He reached behind her and pulled her down over him, welcoming a few of her light brown curls to spill into his face. Her neckline gaped and he could see her cleavage past her diamond teardrop pendant. His eyes pleaded with her, and at long last, they drew her into his common reverie.

The diamond around her neck sparkled in his view each time he opened his eyes. The tree behind Beth grew even more brilliant with reflecting, refracting, and actual lights. They glimmered like thousands of Beth's diamond pendants, but exaggerated, all surrealistically decorating the tree's boughs. It felt like waking from a dream...thousands of shapes and colors lifting him from the dreariness of where he'd come from.

She wore some kind of spicy scent. Her nails were light-pink, her short-sleeved sweater a white angora, and her skirt a pink and green plaid. He loved the feel of her: the texture of her hair, her skin, and even her clothes. Although it became tempting to close his eyes, he just wanted to keep them open so he could drink her all in.

As she kissed him, the technique started to return to him. His knees tightened around her while her feet slid up and down inside his legs. Moist heat clashed between them and although Beth's knee and thigh against his crotch felt extremely pleasurable, the feeling that erupted there demanded more contact, more stimulation. Just then, her hand answered his plea.

"It's not fair," she breathed. "All my friends want Morgen so bad because he's older and hot, and has his own band, and I have to pretend he's just my stupid brother—and now I can't even tell them about you. They'd be so jealous..."

\*\*\*\*

Sandy ambled down the south hallway to get to the staircase, which had him passing the two doors of Morgen's suite. He wrinkled his nose in Morgen's general direction when he heard heavy coughing in the vicinity of the bathroom, followed by the sound of the toilet flushing. He sneered at the wall and continued down the darkened staircase.

\*\*\*\*

"You're nothing like my brother," Beth whispered as she undid the button on Night's black jeans and slid the zipper to its base.

Being himself appeared to be paying off for a change, but he didn't dwell on this as she began touching him. Amidst all the hellish turmoil that surrounded him, constantly, a protective spotlight beamed down on him now, perhaps from the moon. It had to be the moon, he decided, as she clenched the flimsy waistband of his underpants between her teeth and one hand and ripped the elastic

158

apart. It seemed a familiar light bridging the present to the past, to that glorious moment on the moonlit bridge in Oregon—only this time, nobody's shoe would drop into icy water to ruin everything. Only his mind was tumbling, whirling in timelessness.

"I hope you don't mind," she murmured, "but I won't go all the way until I'm married."

The blood in his parts almost ceased to pulse now. He thought them in peril like a furnace kicking into higher and higher temperatures. Then her mouth granted him the tiniest bit of relief. A shy opal leak had sprung and he hoped that she wouldn't be shocked. She didn't seem to be. In fact, she just took him more into her mouth and drew the fiercest current yet through his entire body.

The muscles in his limbs quivered, his skin dampened and tingled, his mind flashed through every desire and actual euphoric encounter he'd ever had with Daphne, or alone, and his heart's generous effort fueled all of these responses.

For the first time ever, he pardoned his brother, and Andrew, for their stinginess as he considered that maybe only women imparted such gestures. He thought he preferred it that way, anyhow, as just the sight of them inspired this kind of longing. He wanted to draw them near and feel their distinct sinuous curves. He wanted to see them undressed so he could touch their plumper skin and explore something new and mysterious. But at this moment, he hungered for nothing other than more of Beth's immediate offer.

****

The tiny sounds he produced stirred the curiosity of a soul in the corridor making his way to the kitchen. Sandy leaned forward, peeked around the doorframe and flinched. He gaped at the lovers for another moment, just to be sure, but even half shielded by Beth, there was no mistaking the hair and the whole general physique of the young male beneath her. Feeling a sickly numbness come over him, he stepped back and lightly plodded up the staircase. He wore quiet enough runners, but in his room, he threw them off. He located his ten-dollar camera and disabled the flash before he returned to the action, downstairs.

159

Night seemed in the process of dying at the exact moment when Sandy eased the lens of the camera, along with his left eye, clear of the door frame. A subconscious cry shot from Night's mouth as his spine formed the telltale arch of arrival. Beth withdrew only at the faint click that split through the large room and caused her to look around. Sandy withdrew as well, but unlike Beth, he shuffled on his socked feet back to the staircase to make his escape before Night could even think of closing his pants.

The housekeeper now sauntered over to Morgen's door and knocked on it before letting himself in. "Are you all right, Morgen?" he almost drawled with indulgence. "I thought I heard you being sick."

"I'm peachy!" Morgen fired back from the bathroom.

"Just checking." He closed the door and waited in the dark of the hallway until Night finally swayed by him, a few minutes later. "So, which present did you like best this year...Morgen?" he asked, but he received no answer from the imposter, only a blank look.

Sandy scuttled to his own suite and jumped onto his bed. On bent knees, he flexed one bicep, then the other. His newest scheme was unlike anything he'd attempted before. This time, he had an ace.

# Chapter Fifteen

While Frederick Dahlsi stood for his campaign flyer photo, surrounded by his attractive family, the Dahlsis' housekeeper also hustled for favors in an office downtown.

"What if I told you I had a story so scandalous that I could be paid just as much to keep it quiet as I could for selling it to you?"

"Who's the celebrity?" chirped the editor of Storm, Oran Twaites.

"Not a celebrity, but close. In the interest of current politics..." Sandy tossed a photograph onto the desk. "I give you our hottest candidate's son, Morgen Dahlsi, and....*his sister*."

The man tried to stifle his reaction, turning a laugh into a hiccup. "Wow."

"The thing is," Sandy persisted, "this family's a goldmine. I can have another story to you in just a short while that will blow all the newsstands in L.A. over for weeks."

"Go on."

"Not yet. This is my offer to you," said Sandy, his voice cool as he crossed his legs. "I will get you the story...detailed reports, photographs, even taped conversations, and I will grant all of it to you, exclusively. You won't have to fight for it or try to outdo your competition. All I want in return is to not be a housekeeper anymore, after this. I want to be assured."

Oran Twaites crossed his legs similarly. His neck muscles twitched like he wasn't sure whether to nod or put the housekeeper in his place.

"I could go down the street to the next guy..." Sandy intimated. "You have absolutely nothing to lose. When the time comes, if you aren't satisfied with my presentation, our deal can simply be off. But if my hunch is right, you'll be begging me—"

"All right," said the editor with a leery grin. "So, exactly how impressed do you suspect I'll be?"

"At least a hundred-thousand-dollars impressed. And I'm being modest."

"That a boy," said the skeptic, reaching for a notepad. "First things first...this photograph in front of me... Then, if you can deliver what you're suggesting, then rest assured...you won't have to be a housekeeper anymore."

****

Beth hopped down the staircase to the sound of her mother humming in the living room. She found Brigitte studying her agenda book.

"Mum?" she began. "How exactly did Morgen come to live here?"

Brigitte's focus shot up from the page. "Why is that important?"

"I just want to know...like did he have any brothers or sisters, and if he did, would you have brought them here too?"

"Morgen didn't have siblings," she answered indignantly, "or I certainly would have. Morgen's mother basically deserted him in the hospital. His father was dead, and she was just too young to take care of him."

"What about the man you married before Daddy? Didn't you say that his son died?"

Brigitte tossed her gold pen on the table. "Why does this matter to you, Beth? Morgen is his grandson, but that man could never have taken care of a sick baby. He needed to get help for himself after losing his own son, but he refused to see how his loss affected him and everyone else. I like to keep those wasted years out of my mind. If I'd had any sense to begin with, I would have just married your father the first time he asked me, years before. Your grandparents knew he was the one, right from the start, but I thought I knew better. The important thing is, everything worked out fine." She reached for her pen and turned a page in her book. "Here is something we really need to be thinking about, right now. What else should I ask the caterers to bring to our New Year's party?"

****

The last few days of 1984 tested Sandy's patience. An AV magazine had alerted him to the security trade show coming to the area, right after New Year's. While browsing its pages for ideas, he'd stumbled upon the perfect device that would be making an introductory appearance at the show. Now, he really appreciated the VCR that the Dahlsis had given him for Christmas.

He had to have all angles covered—literally. The private staircase that led into Morgen's garage would be his low-tech starting point. If he stood in this narrow passageway and drilled a hole through the west wall, he would have a small window to Morgen's guestroom.

The high-tech and best set-up would be to create an aperture into Morgen's area by drilling through his own living room wall, directly into Morgen's bedroom on the other side. He would have to contend with the solid wood, open-faced bookshelf that spanned the entire length of his south wall, but at least the shelves would provide a home for his spy equipment.

A sizable problem was not knowing precisely where to drill, and when. He'd become adept at tracking the movements of his subjects inside the house, and he would have to rely on his skill to determine when to enter Morgen's suite, survey the other side of the wall, and do the whole thing right.

****

Morgen took his understudy to his rehearsal space where he could, in privacy, witness a performance that might reassure him about Night's purpose here. But the more Night proved himself, the more irritable he became.

Night's voice in the PA soared above the support that Morgen's tried to offer. Even when words and melodies were soft, Night's lips seemed to beckon the microphone to come closer. It widened Morgen's eyes: what had once served his lips alone now gravitated toward a new and more powerful master.

164

"All right..." Morgen grunted at the song's finish. "Let's do *The Core of All Hearts*. You're still not so great at that one."

"I like the louder ones," Night confessed. Morgen had already noticed his brother preferred the harder tunes that allowed him to flaunt all the breath he'd been forced to keep inside for the past two decades.

After the two-hour assault on their eardrums, it was a wonder either of them heard the knock on the door at the close of their session. Night crammed himself into one of the equipment lockers when Morgen suggested it could be the warehouse manager, but it was Beth who sprang into the room.

"Hi, Morgen, where's Night? I have some totally rad news!"

Night climbed out of his hiding place and Beth giggled at their cautiousness.

"Listen... I told Dad about what happened with that agent..."

"Night, you asshole, did you have to tell—?"

"Just shut-up and listen, Morgen! I told Dad what happened and now...get this...he's going to let your band play at the New Year's campaign party where there's going to be a lot of people..."

Morgen waved her off and started walking the other way.

"People like this entertainment lawyer he knows."

Morgen spun back around. "Are you kidding?" he shrieked, even rousing Night with his rare display of excitement. "Dad's actually going to bring this guy in as a favor to me?"

"I guess. I know he's inviting this particular friend of his just so he can check you guys out. Dad also thinks this will really appeal to the Young Republicans who are coming to help out. He wants you to keep to your lighter stuff, though."

Morgen stood there, his palms slowly finding their way to his face. "Holy fuck..."

"That right," Beth affirmed. "Dad usually gets what he wants, and if his intention is to showcase the band, he has to think something's going to happen."

"I gotta call the others. ...Yes!" he screamed, smacking Night in the chest, but it was he who began coughing. "You didn't tell Dad that I missed that show because I was sick, did you?"

Beth's humor crumbled instantly. "No. I told him one of your buddies got the date wrong."

"So who's going to do it?" Night asked, point blank.

"I will, of course. It'll be my last show—but it will be our breakout show. Everything has to be perfect."

"Just don't mess this up," Beth advised before she twirled around. "My friend's waiting for me outside. I better go before she decides to come after me."

Night got in Morgen's face after Beth closed the door. "I don't know if you should do it. I'm ready, Morgen. I can do this for you."

"*I'm* doing it. Your turn is coming, but I'm not letting my substitute find out if he can land a contract on a dry run performance with the rest of the band."

"How can you still say that?" Night demanded, fists tensing like he wanted to seize his own temper. "I'm better than you are. And if I left right now, you would die alone without ever getting your wish."

"If you left now... If you left *now*, you'd be going to jail—so just shut up and be glad that I have a use for you, and that my dying is going to keep you, not only rich, but free."

****

New Year's Eve turned the front of the Dahlsi house into a parking lot. Night watched the scene from Morgen's bedroom window, stewing over the fact that it should have been him performing for the fancy and important guests tonight...until Morgen moped into the room.

"Night?" he beseeched in a voice that manifested barely above a whisper. "I blew out my voice. You have to perform tonight...instead of me."

Night felt sure that Morgen didn't just blow out his voice, but he nodded.

He experienced emotions that sent him back to the restaurant as he pulled on the fine clothes that Morgen suggested he wear. Over black trousers, the gray silk sleeves of his jacket rippled down his arms and gleamed down his back and his false platinum hair, which had been perfected in color by now, shone through the hairspray like a frozen falls around his ears and along his neck. In the dim light, he faced Morgen before leaving the suite. Morgen looked faded and tired. It seemed the more Night became his brother, the more his brother dissolved into air.

"This is it," Morgen said in a voice that had transformed from airy to coarse. "You better be ready. You better be stellar tonight."

"You know I'm ready," Night said, but it challenged his confidence when he heard the music and the din of the crowd in a part of the house he'd only seen once.

The ballroom had been cleverly decorated for two occasions. Above campaign posters and banners, white lights dazzled the perimeter of the room, as well as the tail of a shooting star that cascaded from the central chandelier. A shallow platform stood vacant at the head of the room and Night tried to picture it later, presenting him and three of Morgen's friends who he'd never even had a chance to rehearse with. Beth found him and linked herself onto his arm. She had to look twice to confirm his identity.

"Dad's on his way in. Do you see that guy over there?" Her eyes directed his. "That's Dad's lawyer friend, and those guys next to him...they're A&R people from *Detonic Records*."

The way Night's stomach reacted was just about *Detonic*—as Morgen's wrath would be if he didn't stake his legacy before the end of the night.

People started to shuffle and a rift spilled through the center of the room to let the party's host, and popular election candidate, make his way to the stage.

"I wish I understood more about what he's doing," Night whispered to Beth.

"Don't you know anything about politics?"

"I know about restaurants, and maybe the music industry...a little bit."

"Just listen," she said as her father's voice reverberated through the room, engaging the crowd with a casual and humorous welcome before acknowledging his campaign.

Press agents dotted the room and only now started to make their presence known.

"Mister Dahlsi, how familiar are you with the issues specific to this area?"

Frederick steered his answer toward the microphone. "I've been serving the people of this district, as an attorney, for almost thirty years. How could I not be completely familiar with every one of those issues?"

The same woman kept on. "But who have you been serving as an attorney, aside from your wealthy clients? I mean, how concerned are you about initiatives that affect those on the opposite end of the spectrum—like the community development projects beyond your affluent neighborhood."

Charles Lehman, Frederick's campaign manager and lawyer, suddenly piped up. "This isn't a formal press conference. We're here to celebrate our finest candidate, along with the New Year."

"No, no," Frederick insisted. "I'll answer that before we pull out the program. There is price to pay when people don't have a sense of self-worth—the same goes for communities. So, I support these projects, one-hundred percent. My views on this, and on a variety of other topics, are listed in the literature you'll find around the room."

The next speaker had an entourage of cameramen from the local TV station. "Polls indicate enormous public support already. Are you confident you're going to win, Mister Dahlsi?"

"I will only feel that I've won only after I've made a positive difference for the people in this district, including my wonderful, talented family...something I hope to bear witness to tonight. For those who aren't aware, we have a few guests in the room from a record label, and my son, Morgen, with his band, will be entertaining you shortly." Frederick offered Night a quick wave across the room. "I'm sure he will far outshine me in every way, but to answer your question, yes...I plan to win."

Applause followed every successive response. It served as the final ovation for Frederick, and the band's welcome, as he ushered them onto the stage.

Morgen's friends, Aden, Sean, and Doris, found their respective stations on the platform where their equipment, already assembled and sound-checked, had waited since the afternoon.

Beth followed Night, even onto the stage, prepared to buffer any awkward communication between Morgen's longtime friends and their new Morgen. Night had been briefed on the music schedule, but there had been no time for voice prep. He cleared his throat compulsively while the others fidgeted with the precise positioning of their monitors. When he glanced over the room, his sight collided with many inquisitive faces. He felt like he had just taken his seat at the *Emerald Shore* piano, and suddenly he wished he could stop relating everything to the restaurant—or any other aspect of his wretched past.

"I'm starting to miss you, Morgen," Doris's voice lilted as Beth left the stage. "I still exist outside of the band... Is something wrong?"

"No, I can do it. I'm ready."

"Then, why am I hearing doubt?" Sean snapped. "At least you showed up this time." He struck the cymbals, forcing Aden to take his eyes off the imposter and contribute some bass.

They'd agreed to open with an upbeat tune, but nothing "too hard" as per Frederick's instructions. Night's fingers on Morgen's electric guitar jumped into action as Doris's fingers struck the keyboard, and following their short, catchy intro, his voice took off strong.

Within seconds, guests turned to the stage. The A&R people, who Beth had identified earlier, abandoned their conversations and emerged from the crowd to get closer to the band. The music attorney, already in the forefront, whispered excitedly to one of his A&R associates in his vicinity. Even Frederick, who appeared unreachable only a moment ago, now gaped over his shoulder while a supporter continued to speak at him.

"They're ours," said Sean at the end of the first song. "You were kind of awesome, buddy...different...but awesome. I'm actually starting to forget what you did to us."

Unexpected applause bridged their previous beat to the slower and steadier one that opened their next song. Night put down his electric guitar, picked up the acoustic one, and released the opening lyrics in perfect time with his breath. Nobody spoke during this softer number. The other band members noticed the change in their leader's style tonight, but they also appeared more than willing to accommodate his new technique.

Night noticed Brigitte gazing at him quizzically as she clutched a bundle of Frederick's campaign brochures against her gemstone necklace. She eventually blew him a kiss, as though she'd been prompted to do so, and Beth gave him a wink.

Erin Chandler, the music attorney, leaned toward his associate again. "They look great up there. They sound great—and look at *him*. He's already got everything we usually break our backs to infuse into some new guy with only half his potential. Do you see the way he's connecting with the audience?"

"Yeah..."

Through his singing, Night still managed to smile at the other band members, at the audience, and even at himself whenever his eyes squeezed shut over the microphone, but in the next interlude, Aden ousted his bliss with a suggestion.

"I think we should do a cover, now."

Night replied with a stutter. "What do you mean?"

"What's your problem? You know how it is. People also want to hear songs they know. You pick the song."

Sean stood up behind his drums as Night placed his acoustic guitar beside the electric. "What the hell are you doing, Morgen?"

Night ignored Sean, then Aden. He only had a handful of songs memorized to the standard of Morgen's originals. Panic, mixed with euphoria, left him somewhat delirious and unable to recall a single song title. He clumsily bumped Doris away from her keyboard and replaced her hands with his. A light on her synthesizer flashed under the word "piano" and it reassured him in his decision. He addressed the room through the PA that turned his fretful, hushed voice into breathy little sparks.

"Here's something people should know..."

People chuckled as they recognized the complicated classical piece as Mozart's *Rondo Alla Turca*, but the laughter petered off as he continued to play beyond any effort that could be construed as a joke. Frederick watched him for the duration of the piece, clearly paralyzed by pleasure and pride. Beth held her hand in front of her mouth, at first in shock, and then to hide her amusement. Brigitte beamed with a triumphant smile, and Morgen's confounded friends stood back on the stage staring like they were witnessing a manifestation from their fantasies—a music god. Even the most conservative of tonight's guests applauded him genuinely, and Erin Chandler, who had been tossing out favorable remarks ever since they started, still hadn't run out of praise.

"He's brilliant. Look at the crowd. Pop, progressive rock, classical... Is there anything this kid can't do?"

Night noticed how Doris flicked her head toward Aden to see his reaction, which prompted a secretive conversation between them.

Meanwhile, Night tried hard to listen to the action on his other side, off stage.

"Bring him, and the others, in on Wednesday," Erin persisted. "If you know what's good for you, you'll get him signed fast."

The record label rep peered at Erin. "I have a feeling this is going to be a big year for this family. Are you sure that Dahlsi expressly stated that his kid's still unsigned?"

"Do you think he invited us here for a tease?"

The rep shook his head. "He's going to be a phenomenon. So, does his band have a name?"

Night clutched the microphone stand in his fist and pulled it near. "Thank you," he said smiling again at the group of friends he'd adopted from Morgen. "If you don't know us already...we're *Morning's Desire*."

Before Morgen's friends left the house, he botched a high-five with Sean, only vaguely familiar with the custom. But Sean's manner confused him more as he watched the drummer stumble and nearly miss the door on his way out.

Doris lingered in the foyer until the others had left before she kissed Night zealously.

"You were amazing tonight," she said, stepping back to drink him in. "And I've never meant it quite like this. Our duet...I don't know why you've never done it like that before, but it was so right. And I never knew you could play classical—or keyboard, for that matter. I can't believe it." She clasped her hands with a resurgence of wonder. "Did you notice Sean at the end, though?"

"What do you mean?"

"Well, he's high, Morgen. I know he deals, but in the last while, I think he's been dealing mostly to himself." She shrugged. "I guess he has an excuse to celebrate tonight. As for you, Morgen...next time you call me to rehearse, you better want to rehearse with me, and only me."

****

But the reality was harsh when Night returned to his brother's suite. Morgen had landed himself in the middle of the floor with one gaunt cheek against the rich carpet fibers that his fingers clutched onto as though for dear life. Night dropped to his knees and shook him.

"Are you okay, Morgen? Are you alive?"

"Don't touch me," Morgen groaned, alive if nothing else. It took a painfully long time for him to wriggle into a dilapidated sitting position, but nothing about him, or his greeting fazed Night.

"Morgen, it was wonderful! Everything went fine. The music people really liked us. Your father also really liked us, and I know for sure now that I can do it and that everything will turn out great."

"That's just great. Wonderful. *Great.*"

"Well...aren't you pleased?"

"Pleased? Oh sure I'm pleased," Morgen mimicked, gaining more poise with every syllable. "I'm pleased that my clueless, moronic brother is taking the glory for what I've worked my whole life to get. I'm pleased that I'm being erased, day by day. I'm pleased that I'm in so much goddamned pain that I have to fly higher than the freaking sound barrier to achieve a state that's anywhere near tolerable!"

"I'm sorry!" Night fired back. "You wanted me to do this. You were excited for me when I left, and now I tell you that I did well and you're angry..."

"You don't understand anything." Morgen struggled to stand up before he stumbled toward his bedroom, while Night followed.

"I understand a lot more now than I used to. And I know what your pain feels like. I've felt it...over and over again."

Morgen turned and gripped one of Night's wrists as if for blood. "And what if it *never* let go?"

Night's eyes burrowed deeper inside his head. "Morgen, this is stupid. Why don't you let the doctors try to help you?"

Morgen's shove luckily didn't have the power of his words. "How could you go there again—especially after tonight?" his voice strained and cracked. "You're the one living it now. Can't you understand my dream? Can't you honor it?"

Night's eyes filled with tears. He could understand it, but it wasn't only about that.

Morgen staggered off again. "Doctors... There is no cure for me, stupid. How many times do I have to tell you?"

With that, his knees failed beneath the weight of his medication and Night scowled at the bony heap in the middle of the floor. He turned to the guestroom, but on second thought, he laid down beside Morgen to stare at his face like a mirror. Morgen remained unaware, never opening his eyes. Night had felt him this close a thousand times...felt his breath, felt his thoughts...but now, with Morgen physically present, day in and day out, he understood him much less.

# Chapter Sixteen

Lila's funeral spawned as much sympathy for Andrew as it did for Lila's friends, family, and colleagues. People couldn't express enough condolences for the man who had lost his son, his business, and the woman who he called his fiancée, all in the latter half of a year.

"I'll always cherish the time we had," Andrew said again, this time to Margaret, Lila's older sister and beneficiary who shared that she'd flown in from "across the pond." "If it isn't too much of an imposition, perhaps I could come by the house, later. I still have some personal items there that I should take out of your way."

She accepted Andrew's hand and squeezed it inside both of hers as she regained her composure to speak. "I'll be going there after...after the burial." Although more pronounced than Lila's, Margaret's accent generated some nostalgia that caused Andrew to genuinely miss Lila, for a minute.

Sitting amongst a whole crew of her friends and coworkers, Andrew continued to be impressed at how Lila had obviously kept her grievances about him to herself. He didn't observe one shifty eye throughout the ceremony, or at any point before or after.

****

"I'd like to hear that power ballad, *Wingless Angel*, that blew my scouts away at your party."

This demand came from the band's prospective manager, Gin Corbin, following their formal introduction at the music studio. Morgen moved his microphone back beside Doris and wondered how Night had managed to pull off a duet with someone he'd never met. He only knew that, today, he would showcase it properly and finally see his dream fulfilled, or he would see it crash and burn for the very last time. Sean, striking the cymbals, broke his muse and shunted him, full-force, into his atypical masterpiece.

"Wait a second," one of Gin's scouts interrupted. "Sorry, Morgen...but do it like the other night."

They started from the beginning, but this time Erin Chandler, the music attorney, halted the performance. "Do you need like a large crowd to really open up? I mean, the other night you were magic. The other night you were singing to the audience, you were singing to your band members, you were all over the room without ever taking a step, but now you're just singing to the microphone. It's all sounding a bit...labored."

His friends eyed him with the same query.

Morgen suddenly loathed the sound of his brother's name that, disguised as a word, mocked him from all sides. "What do you guys want? I don't see how I could have been that much better. Maybe the stage helps—I don't know—but I couldn't have been that much better *the other night.*"

"Well, anyway..." said Gin. "There's no question about whether I'm going to represent you and your band. I loved your demos, and I'm positive that every aspect of you is going to sell big. I would like to hear the rest, but later, go get some sleep. That's likely your problem. And we can understand why," he added, smiling. "Congratulations, *Morning's Desire.* You're going to be big."

The attorney signaled for Morgen's attention. "I'd like to meet with you later, so you can take a look at a preliminary contract."

"We want to move quickly," Gin continued on the tail of the attorney's thoughts. "If we wait too long, we'll end up on the heels of two other major tours and I want to start the hype about *Morning's Desire* well before that time. We can probably pull off an album before March, but we'll get the obvious hit songs recorded and released as videos ASAP. I want a photo shoot done, right away, so we can hit up the teen magazines at the same time as their début release. We'll just publicize the hell out of these guys, and when they're all up and buzzing, we'll announce our own national tour."

Morgen's head tipped back in a rare display of exultation and his friends linked themselves around him, blissfully unaware that they were saying farewell to the mighty but dwindling force that had, at long last, delivered them into fame.

****

While Margaret sorted through some papers in Lila's office, Andrew poked around the bedroom, until he spotted her purse beside a dresser. He flipped past the credit cards in her wallet, searching for anything that might offer him a clue about her short time with Night.

He took a moment to examine an old receipt for men's apparel that blatantly mocked him with a purchase date of one day after the fire, but then a more interesting piece of paper tripped between his fingers. The name on it made his heart plunge and his hand tense as he brought the paper closer to his face. The phone number of Brigitte and Frederick Dahlsi glared off the page, and he didn't believe in any astronomical coincidence that had Lila corresponding with another Brigitte in recent times. The paper had been ripped in half under the phone number and the peaks of uneven letters still showed above the tear line: "Address". As he strolled into the hallway, he shoved the paper into his shirt pocket, beneath his tailored black coat.

"I must not be thinking clearly," he stated as he reached the office doorway. "There wasn't a lot here after all, so I'll be on my way unless you need me for anything." But Margaret only wanted to be alone.

His mind grew stormy as he drove home from Lila's house for the last time. How did Lila come up with the idea to contact his former wife? What else was in Night's sickly twin's hospital file that had sent her ranting at him about Aileen Coleman? An explanation came to him, instantly. His ex-wife's name, Brigitte, had now surfaced one too many times, and his jaw dropped.

****

1985 demanded much more glam from the already physically stunning group, and Gin Corbin, now officially *Morning's Desire's* manager, introduced the band to a highly recommended image consultant and stylist.

"This is Brandt," he announced in a roundtable setting, two days after their first meeting at *Detonic Records*. "He's going to be the one who sells your image."

Brandt spoke with all of them for part of the morning and later announced that he wanted to meet with each of them individually, starting with their lead singer-guitarist.

In the video department, Brandt's favorite arena, Night was instantly drawn to the effervescent personality of this green-eyed, scarlet-haired, thirty-two-year-old with the style to match.

"This is a dye-job," Brandt stated, grappling like a pirate at the promise of gold through Night's bleached hair. "And not a very good one. I can try something to put the shine back into it, but from now on, consult with me before you do anything else to yourself—in fact, hands off. Are those your real eyes?"

Night pulled away from Brandt. "What do you mean?"

"Well, I just think they're great. I wouldn't dream of changing them. I just wondered if you were wearing some kind of freaky tinted lenses as part of your look."

"No," Night answered apologetically. He didn't need any help to be freaky. "This is just how I look."

"That's fascinating. I love your pale eyes, but I don't like your pale skin. Get some sun. We have enough of it here, but not to worry. I can fix that for now with a lot of make-up. It'll just make your eyes stand out that much more. They're very powerful, very wild. Look... I was studying the pictures in your press kit, yesterday, and I came up with a great emblem for your band." Brandt reached for the counter and then showed him the face of a big roaring beast that Night couldn't identify. "A white tiger," Brandt obliged. "Now, if we transpose your image—of course, picture yourself with a choppy, gravity-defying do..." He slid a set of photos of Morgen beside the white cat. "It's spectacular. What do you think?"

Night stared at the array of images in front of him and nodded guardedly.

"I thought you'd agree. This animal looks like he's absolutely screaming with desire—like people will be screaming for you." He enacted a silent impression of a roar, stooping beside Night to be at the same level. "Just wait until I'm finished with you, Morgen Dahlsi. You're going to be hot."

Brandt's hands were in perpetual motion as though already sculpting Night into the perfection he envisioned in his head. He talked about people and groups that Night had never heard of, even though Morgen had tried to educate him about the major personalities in music. He also talked about Morgen's friends, which provided Night with invaluable details.

"I've also been giving a lot of thought to your costumes," Brandt continued. He suddenly began grasping at Night's shoulders and arms. "You seem to be in good shape, but you'll really benefit from a personal trainer. After all, you don't want to be *almost* perfect when millions of people are viewing your half-naked body."

Night felt the blood drain from his face.

"I'll tell you about the video I've got planned. It all came to me when I was listening to your demos last night. Even our video producer agrees that, at least for your big song, *My Other Side*, we should go with a jungle theme...symbolic of the animalistic side of humanity. I'm thinking some chewed up shirt...the material just barely hanging off one shoulder with your hair all wild..."

"No..."

Brandt laughed. "A star for one hour and you're already refusing advice. Now, are you the expert or am I?"

"I have to go." Night stood up and grabbed the copy of the contract he'd been told to peruse.

"Morgen, we're not done yet."

Brandt's voice only impelled Night to walk out faster.

"*Mister* Dahlsi... I realize you got a big break here, but it'll take a lot more than you to put this star in the sky."

But the sky seemed more than a bit out of reach at the moment. All the way home, he couldn't help but imagine the shallow pit in the San Gabriel Mountains as his more likely destination after his brother learned of his objectionable body art and finished calculating his net worth.

****

Andrew peered out of his living room window and sneered when he saw the vehicle outside that brandished the decal of the Newport Sheriff's Office.

"I understand that you have to ask me these things, but after I told Lila the truth about Night and...his activities, things became civil again. You can certainly verify that with her friends and coworkers. They were all wonderful to me at her funeral. ...I still can't believe that this happened." Andrew shook his head.

"We already checked with them, Mister Shannien, and the evidence suggests that it was an accident. What finally led our Search and Rescue team to her body was her baseball cap. It appears Ms. Hughes may have used some poor judgment when she tried to climb down on a steep slope to get it after the wind blew it off, I guess. We're very sorry for your loss, but it is...*quite astounding* how misfortune keeps showing up for you and the people in your life. We just have to ask you a few more questions, for the record."

"By all means..."

"Ms. Hughes worked an afternoon shift on Sunday, the 16th, and then didn't make it into work on the Tuesday when she was scheduled to work graveyard. So, even though her body wasn't discovered for several days, chances are she went for that fateful run on the Monday. Do you remember what you were doing on Monday, the seventeenth of December?"

"I believe I can tell you....only because I had another appointment with my claims adjuster on a Monday, right before Christmas...you know, because of the restaurant. Let me take a look in my book."

He left the two deputies in the living room while he retrieved a pocket scheduler from the kitchen. He already knew he would be able to confirm his statement. He'd worked like hell to get Daphne's car back into its secret location in the bushes on his vast property, before getting cleaned up for his meeting with the adjuster, set for 11 am. Although he hadn't consciously planned on killing Lila, a part of him must have known it could happen. For that reason, his Mercedes never left the property.

He placed the book, open, on the end table, beside the men. "See, here..."

"Thank you. We will be following up with your insurance company, but this all looks fine. An interesting point... Ms. Hughes' wristwatch didn't survive the fall either. The face was cracked and its hands were stuck on five after eleven..." The deputy finished scribbling a note. "Again, this is for our report, do you remember what you did for the rest of the day?"

The truth was, he spent the first couple of hours making sure the path to Daphne's car, off his main driveway, couldn't be detected at a glance. He had to pull the fallen tree back across the opening and then make sure the car hadn't left tread marks at that turn, or near the highway. Luckily, the old Golf didn't have much tread.

"I probably did some grocery shopping. Should I try to dig up a receipt?" He'd kept one for this very purpose, and when one officer halfheartedly nodded, he fetched his note spike from the kitchen table and made of show of sorting through his stack of punctured receipts. "Here's one from the seventeenth...and one from the eighteenth."

"That's fine, Mister Shannien. I think we've covered our bases." The officer turned toward the entrance and hesitated. "We're also very sorry about your son, Reade," he announced in an abrupt but genuine manner. "Your name incidentally turned up information about his suicide."

"Yes, I suppose it would. Now, I'm sure you can fully grasp why I tried to shelter Night."

182

****

The water was only a swimming pool, but Night watched it from the common room window the same way he used to watch the endless waves on the North Pacific cape. He anticipated Morgen's return any minute, yet he jumped when the door finally swung open.

Beth pranced into the room, modeling a short blue dress with a towel draped across her chest like a sash. She joined him at the window and leaned one elbow on the sill. "Show me your tooth."

He showed her and then let his expression fall flat again.

"I was just testing myself. I'm going for a swim. Want to join me?"

He shook his head.

"Why not? There's no one around to see you," she enticed with a nudge and a grin, but it had no effect. "Boy, are you ever a livewire today."

"I have a real problem, Beth. I went to the studio and, the truth is, I can't do the things they want me to do. I can't even wear the things they want me to wear. What's going to happen when Morgen realizes that I can't do it? He won't want to have anything to do with me then, but...I'll always have you, right, Beth?" He moved in for a validating kiss, but she just wriggled away.

"Night..." she began awkwardly, "you told me about your past, and maybe you don't understand certain things, like that people from the same family don't do what we were doing with each other that one time."

He considered this for a moment. "But we're not really from the same family."

"True, but everybody else thinks that we are, and since nobody even knows you exist, we have to keep what happened between us a secret. What would happen if someone found out, like Mom or Dad? Even if they didn't kill me, or both of us, we would have to tell them about you, and why you've been hiding. Then, they would find out about Morgen being sick. It would ruin everything you've both worked for."

He stepped back, confused and frustrated. Daphne had been a secret and now Beth too? But he had bigger problems. "We'll just be careful," he decided, nodding to himself. "Now, where is Morgen?" His glare seared across the room. "I need to talk to him."

"It'll work out, Night. All I know is, you'll never go back to Oregon." She left quietly as his thoughts alternated between Morgen and Beth. He paced around the room before he returned to the window and witnessed Beth standing before the shimmering expanse of enhanced blue. Her shoulders tipped back as she twirled her hair into a tawny wreath that she secured with a gold barrette, and his stare intensified when she dropped her dress to reveal a neon-pink, ruffled bikini, before she dove into the water.

He felt something that he wanted to classify as "love"—but the word taunted him. One person in his life had claimed to love him but rarely showed it, another had proved she loved him through her selfless actions, but never declared it, another showed him love, but now condemned it—and the one person whom he felt should love him in every sense of the word, didn't seem to like him at all.

His attention returned to Beth as she climbed to the top rung of the ladder. He swayed out of view when he saw her chin start to lift, but he didn't hesitate to look back. By then, she'd planted her feet on the edge of the pool, her back to the window as she pulled off her bikini top and tossed on the nearby deck chair. It occurred to him, then, that Beth could, in fact, love him twofold since she valued him as family, as well as someone who wasn't related.

With the sun caressing her front, she toweled her body from behind her knees, all the way up to her shoulders. She spread her towel like a set of wings that she folded across her chest and used to wipe away all droplets from under and over her full young breasts.

"Hey," Morgen greeted, rather cheerfully, closing the door behind him. "How did it go today?" But as he came closer and took in the view beyond the window, his eyes turned dark gray. "She's your sister you twisted freak! She's *my* sister!"

Night drew a breath.

"Don't say anything!"

Morgen stormed over to his private bar where he scrambled for a vial of his white powder and then clumsily sniffed some into his head. Night waited for a safe moment to try again, but Morgen still looked explosive as he opened a liquor bottle and filled a short water glass.

"Morgen..."

"I can't take this. You're finishing me off and I have no idea if this is really worth it." He took a swig from his glass and slammed it back down.

Night thought he saw an opportunity when his brother let out a sigh. "Morgen—"

"Hopeless! That's what you are. Did you sign the fucking contract yet...because if you didn't, don't bother!"

"Morgen, I didn't know anyone would ever have to see me without my clothes on."

Morgen's head shot up. "What are you talking about? I'm pretty sure *Detonic Records* isn't fronting for the porn industry. I mean, you might have to take off your shirt at some point..."

"That's what—"

"And since when do you have a problem with nudity? You looked quite comfortable with it a moment ago when you were about to jack off—"

"Morgen, just shut-up and look!" Some buttons went flying as Night forced the shirt off his back.

The liquor bottle in Morgen's hand followed suit and crashed on the clay tiles surrounding his bar.

With a triumphant air, Night swept his top off the floor and pulled it on as he headed for the couch.

His brother followed him with frantic eyes. "What the hell happened? Who did this? A-Andrew?"

Night had begun nodding after the word "Who".

Morgen stamped his foot and turned away. "This is a fucking disaster. Why'd you wait so long to tell me about this?"

"You never wanted to know. And I really didn't think it was going to matter."

"You didn't think it would matter? Come on! How could you be such a moron?"

"Because I just am! It's not like you didn't know it!"

"Morgen sat himself beside Night and crossed his arms tightly. "I'm going to kill him," he pledged. "Believe me, Night...you won't see me dead before I make that asshole sorry for causing this mess." He stood up and stamped again.

Night couldn't decide if Morgen was serious or a wee bit delirious.

"Your makeup person can hide it," Morgen proposed. "It'll just be a little more embarrassing for me, but don't worry, it can be done, and it'll be fine."

The room fell silent as their minds took off on different trains of thought.

"Night... Keep your eyes off Beth from now on. I've only ever known her as a sister and now she's *your* sister."

"I know." He didn't need to hear it all again. "She just makes me think of Daphne...and I miss her." He gauged Morgen's expression to see if he should go on and, for once, he saw all green lights. "I think he buried her somewhere so no one would ever know, the same way you want to be buried so no one will ever know."

Morgen rattled his head, briefly. "So, now Gramps is also a killer? What else should I know about our dear granddaddy?"

After bringing out a new liquor bottle from his bedroom, Morgen never interrupted as he listened to some of Night's random experiences. He refilled Night's glass for the fourth time while his gaze hung heavy, like the last drop of tequila, at the tip of the inverted bottle.

"Enough," Night declared, sweeping up the drink that he planned to pour down the drain before taking his shower. He expected Morgen to pass out as soon as he left, but a minute later his brother appeared in the bathroom doorway.

"You've got marks right down to your knees."

"Yes. I know."

"My body used to be just like yours," Morgen persisted, now offering his appraisal of Night's general physique, but something along that thought suddenly sparked an avalanche of panic. "Oh, shit!"

"What?"

"Just turn around for a second—and don't put your hands there!"

Night had only completed a quarter turn before Morgen exhaled in relief.

"Good for you," he said as though he'd never been concerned. "At least you won't have to spend your first paycheck on surgery."

"I don't understand."

"Two-for-one day at the hospital, maybe. I don't know, but it got done..."

His brother gesticulated a clear slice or a chop, but that didn't make any sense. Morgen was so wasted that Night didn't bother to press him for a coherent explanation. But Morgen did offer something intelligible before he shambled away.

"I don't believe I visited you in your sleep, but I promise you, Night... Andrew Shannien is soon going to find out what happens when I show up in one of *his* nightmares."

# Chapter Seventeen

The piece of paper crinkled in Andrew's grip as he stared at his ex-wife's new surname and telephone number. A fire from his core surged into his brain and blazed through his eyes at the thought of Aileen Coleman delivering herself of all liability after devastating everyone else's life. The idea that Brigitte might have made it all possible stirred his fire to its last glowing ember.

In a short time, he would find out how far Brigitte's charity could go. If it had once extended to Morgen, would she dish it out again for Night? Andrew straightened Lila's note and dialed. A dispassionate-sounding male eventually answered the call.

"Hello. Dahlsi residence and campaign headquarters."

"Campaign headquarters?" Andrew paused. "That's great because I have some information I'd like to send to campaign headquarters. If you could, please give me your mailing address."

****

Morgen stopped working the styling product into his hair when Night barged into the bathroom, one evening, without knocking.

"You've been in here forever. I thought you passed out again."

"Hardly," Morgen replied. "I'm going to my beach tonight...to say goodbye to Doris. Leave me alone, Night."

"Are you going to tell her?"

"Of course not," he scoffed. "I shouldn't need to say this, but stay out of her pants when I'm gone. I know you think you've outperformed me in the studio, but don't think you can do the same with Doris. Got that?" He glanced at Night and rolled his eyes. "Oh, never mind. You probably don't even know what I'm talking about."

"I know what you're talking about."

"Oh yeah?" He peered at Night in the mirror. "From what you told me, it doesn't sound like you ever got to know about it."

Night returned an indignant blink and crossed his arms.

"Anyway... I actually feel good today, and I'm not going to waste it."

"Can I go with you, later? I'll stay back, but I want to watch what you do with Doris."

Morgen turned around to find that Night didn't look any less serious than his reflection. "Holy shit... If you really need to know more about sex, then buy yourself a goddamn book."

"You're just like Andrew. You expect me to do everything the way you imagine, but you won't show me."

"A book..." Morgen flared, "will tell you everything!"

Night pleaded with him now. "Why don't you just show me? I'm your brother. We even look the same, so you should love me more than anybody else—more than Beth or your friends, or any of these fans you keep talking about—and definitely more than Doris."

"You don't even know what you're saying," Morgen articulated, tripping as he stepped back. "People don't fuck their own family members—or they're not supposed to. Please don't tell me that Gramps fucked around with you..."

Night was already shaking his head. "But he didn't really love me."

Morgen closed his eyes for a moment. "What I mean is, Grandpa isn't supposed to love you in *that* way. Neither am I. You're a goddamn freak, Night, and I hope you realize that if I hadn't let you stay here, they probably would have locked you up by now, wherever they put crazy people who burn down buildings."

Night held his tongue, but rays of contempt beamed between the wisps of hair in front of his eyes.

Morgen softened his demeanor as he returned to his preening. "Well, he certainly fucked you up, if nothing else, and I'm telling you...one of my lasts is going to feel exceptionally good, and I'm not talking about Doris."

"You're not doing anything to Andrew," Night asserted. "He has to see me on television, and I want him to know that it's me. And if anyone does anything, I'll be the one who does it."

****

After sunset, Morgen skipped out of the house and into Doris's car. From his brother's window, Night watched them leave before he grabbed Morgen's car keys and slinked into the garage.

The car's gleaming white finish cut through the stratum of sapphire that had formed over the coast. He knew where Morgen's beach was since Morgen had labeled it as such on one of their tours. He spotted Doris's car parked on the side of the road, but he drove past it and only pulled over when could no longer see it in the rearview mirror.

The land sloped softly toward the bay and Night found a boulder, close to the top, that eclipsed him while providing the perfect vantage point. The moonlit water illuminated the entire show: Doris giggling as Morgen chased after her and then whirled her into a mutual embrace. Their mouths came together and they remained this way for so long that Night found himself holding his breath to the memory of an identical scene with him and Daphne.

Soft rock music from her car radio swelled over the tiny cove while they settled down on a quilt with two plastic glasses and a bottle of wine. The moonlight cast both human figures a ghostly gray, especially pale Morgen with his platinum hair that gave him a monochromatic look in any light.

It had been a warm day, but the hour brought in a cool breeze that made Night shudder. The two bodies on the beach didn't seem affected by the temperature. Morgen accepted Doris's hand as she stood up to dance to the music and they cuddled like they both knew it would be their last time. It astounded Night that this was the same Morgen...and it angered him.

Morgen didn't appear sick as he swayed elegantly, showing Doris charming smiles and, of course, a chipped tooth that only made him look more sympathetic. His stylish clothes filled him out as he moved unhampered by his usual pain.

With parted lips Night watched how Doris began to help his brother out of these clothes. Morgen's fingers found each of the tiny gold buttons on the front of Doris's dress, gradually parting the silky fabric that billowed in the breeze and tumbled off her shoulders unassisted.

The dress pooled around her feet and she kicked it to the side, along with her shoes. Her black bikini briefs came in a satiny, lacy version of Morgen's, but her matching bra stole the show, charming even distant eyes with its gold embellishments and enchanting gleam.

Night had to switch his focus when she molded over her partner, coating him with honey hair. She seemed in love with his face, kissing his mouth, nose, eyelids, and brow. Night recalled how Daphne had loved his face too. Hauled back in time, he could feel her hot breath on his skin now.

By the time Night focused again, Doris had left Morgen's neck to travel further down his body, using her mouth as well as her fingertips. When she reached his waist, her face lifted and Morgen helped her to pull off his underpants. He unclasped her bra, and she tossed it behind him before her mouth returned to his primed parts.

Beneath his dark clothes, Night's skin became sultry. He pressed his elbows into his groin as the sensation of Beth and the image of Daphne collided. Now hard and ready himself, he sent his hand below, only to end up mindlessly crushing his fingers between his thighs as he watched Doris go down on his brother. He couldn't see beyond her strawberry mane, but he remembered every measure of time from when the action veiled by a girl's long hair had been his pleasure.

But here was something new... Morgen swapped positions with her and threw away her last stitch of clothing. Though she didn't have the parts that he and his twin had, it didn't seem to limit her share of ecstasy. Morgen climbed up between her knees while the moonlight reflected off every curve it could reach. With one hand beneath her to prop her up, Morgen traveled her mysterious caverns with his tongue and even enlisted his free hand until she began to produce cries like Night's mind had already started to conjure. Over the music, and over the whoosh of the sea, the girl's rich breaths and envied whimpers became more pronounced and frequent. Morgen crawled forward and pressed his narrow pelvis between her legs. She guided him, and even without a book, Night understood what she'd just helped him do.

Their breaths stayed out of sync, as though they wanted to pass the moment back and forth to one another. It completely surprised Night when Doris flipped her body around, still beneath Morgen, and they continued in much the same way. Their movement became more aggressive until he heard their successive cries.

The familiar emotions of emptiness, anger and greed converged inside Night's pounding chest as he watched them run into the waves, making it a game to freshen up. Morgen finally looked spent when he returned to the blanket, hardly drying off before flopping on his back. He revived when Doris kneeled next to him. Then, dressed in their beach towels, they picked up their wine glasses, intertwined their arms, and took a sip—toasted, Night assumed, the band's big break that they owed completely to him.

****

Using his skeleton key, Sandy entered Morgen's empty suite through the guestroom to retrieve his long-play, voice-activated tape recorder from where he'd velcroed it, behind the toilet tank.

In his own suite, he rewound all eight hours of it and listened to the exchanges between Morgen and his twin. He shook his head at Morgen's limitless cussing capacity and at the defenseless replies of the brother who Sandy had been ready to indict as an asshole simply for having Morgen's face.

Morgen's chiding voice came first. "Christ, you're not still going out like that, are you? I wish you'd do something with your hair. You look like you're still in the seventies—like Sandy—when you leave it like that."

192

Sandy adjusted the position of his legs beneath his desk and glared at the speaker. "Then are you ever gonna hate your new seventies look on the front page of *Storm,* when you see it, prick." He'd missed a few words beneath his muttering, but after a series of false starts, where the recorder had waffled between whether or not it detected enough noise, Morgen's voice continued. It sounded clearer now, as though he'd made the commitment to fully enter the bathroom.

"Turn your head upside-down, like this. Now stick your hand in the gel and run it through your hair with your fingers... Now scrunch it like this and pull. ...No! Yeah. Like that."

"Uh... Are you sure?" came a cautious reply, obviously from Night when he saw the results in the mirror.

"Do whatever you want. I'm getting' a fucking head-rush." A harsh sigh faded from the bathroom.

Sandy snickered in his palm. This was too easy, and so unbelievably perfect. His recent stab at doing business had turned out to be lucrative and his future projections already blew his mind.

Silence followed and then: "You gotta go, Night. Remember everything I told you..."

"Night...?" Sandy repeated. "Morgen and Night?" He slapped his knees and laughed out loud. He'd long ago learned from Brigitte the many connotations of Morgen's name.

Following some indecipherable rustling, some drawers banging and the toilet flushing, many times, the dialogue from a later episode came through perfectly clear.

But he hadn't counted on their conversations taking such a morbid turn. He considered the potential in finding out more about the mysterious Andrew and the twin from Oregon—and certainly about Morgen's secret illness—but it wasn't crucial to his current scheme. For his efforts to deliver large amounts of cash, he needed pictures of the twins, some jaw-dropping proof that could be captured succinctly on the cover of *Storm.* He would have to put his own curiosity aside and focus on what the public would find even

193

more shocking than today's headline about their enigmatic young idol.

****

"You told me you had a gun, right?" Morgen asked Steve on the telephone, after outlining their mission.

"Yeah. No. I mean it belongs to my brother."

"Bring it. I'll meet you at the park."

Morgen rummaged through his guestroom closet until he found the prize he was after; the duffel bag his brother had brought with him from Oregon. It still contained the dark slacks with pale pinstripes and the mock-turtleneck sweater Night wore the day he burned down the *Emerald Shore*. Morgen threw his personal medications in with the clothes, then discreetly left the house, on foot, through his garage.

Where the grand properties ended and the park began, Morgen collapsed on a bench beneath a towering valley oak tree. The sweet, innocent scent of wild roses still couldn't persuade him to rethink his scheme. He stood up when Steve's old Datsun ripped around the corner.

"Morgen...you not really gonna kill no one, right?"

Morgen sighed as he plunked himself down in the faded passenger seat. "Steve, you were worried that I didn't care about my brother. Well, now you get to help me dish out some justice to the asshole who ruined his life. You should be with me on this—one-hundred percent."

"I don' know. It's a long trip and my car is old. And why you wanna take me to do this? You even know where we gonna go?"

"Don't worry about it, Steve. We're going to have a blast, and all expenses are on me."

Eight hours into the trip, Morgen already writhed in his seat, and an hour after that, he begged Steve to pull over at a motel, hoping he would feel better by morning.

194

While Steve grabbed a meal in the diner, next door, Morgen curled up on a bed, coughing and shivering, in the seclusion of his own musty room. A fever had moved in, along with his usual aches and nausea.

He ignored the knock on his bolted door, not even an hour later, as he sat injecting himself with morphine he'd recently acquired from a brand new source. Then, he opened his pill bottle and cursed. He needed to have his prescription refilled—and soon—but then he questioned if this medication even made a difference anymore.

****

Night steamed when he realized that Morgen had, once again, furtively slipped from the property. His brother had mentioned he might visit someone for a couple of days, *sometime*, but Night didn't expect him to really vanish without any warning.

Also, Morgen's selfish exploit with Doris, two evenings ago, had left her ever more devoted to him—only it wasn't Morgen who had to receive her when Sandy announced she was on her way up the stairs.

He thought he performed well in kissing her at the door, and she seemed game when he proposed lunch on the boardwalk, but their conversation grew more awkward with every nacho they consumed. He couldn't contribute much, every time she talked about something he hadn't experienced, either with her or otherwise. Luckily for him, Doris knew he had to get to the studio by three o'clock, so she simply tried to make the most of their waterfront stroll on their way back to the car.

"If it wasn't for the other night, Morgen Dahlsi, I'd be sure that you didn't care for me anymore." Her fingers tightened on his well-earned calloused fingertips as her eyes pulled the other way. "Oh my God," she pronounced hoarsely, separating from his hand so she could reach the newsstand. She dug into her purse and hastily fed some coins into the metal slot. When she had the tabloid newspaper in hand, she spun the front page into Night's face. "Look!"

Night reeled back as the bold letters of Morgen's family name, and a recognizable image, snagged his eyes and nearly yanked them out of his head.

"It looks so real," Doris chortled, squeezing in beside Night to share his view of the paper. "No wonder you're losing interest in me when you've got a hot sister who'll do *that* for you!"

He gaped at the murky shot of Beth arched over him during their most intimate encounter. Details were unclear, as no flash had been used to take the picture, but forms and colors were all intact, including some details of the Dahlsi's living room. The only other warm bodies that had stayed home that evening were Morgen and Sandy. *Sandy!*

"I...I don't know where this came from," Night stammered, his voice thin, but Doris only laughed and slammed his hip with the newspaper.

"It's just a stupid tabloid, Morgen. Who knows where they get this shit. I just feel bad for your father. I wonder what kind of bastard would stoop this low, for any reason. Here...you'll probably want to save this one." She pushed the paper at him and cracked up with laughter.

"We should get going," Night grumbled. "I don't want to be late."

****

Steve glanced at Morgen as they drove up the coastal highway. "You look bad, my friend. You sick again like two years ago?"

"I just have a cold," Morgen grunted. "What's your problem?"

Steve's eyelids lowered. "I can sometimes tell when you lie."

"Well, maybe you're slipping. Just drive, Steve. I'd like to get there today."

Steve marveled at the ruggedness of Lincoln County. "Your brother is from here? How do you know he didn' go back?"

"I told you, I don't know. I wouldn't be surprised if he did. He's insane, remember?"

196

"I hope you're not insane too, my friend."

Morgen refused to further the conversation, and he didn't speak again until they blew out of Brookings. "We need to stop at a hair salon."

"Man...wha' do you need to do that now?"

Turning to Steve, Morgen's chin dropped like his voice. "Think about it, Steve."

"Oh."

Morgen came out of the small shop in Florence with his platinum hair transformed into a rich auburn. Even his eyebrows and lashes had been tinted authentically. Any differences between Andrew's *Night of the emerald shore*line and the authentic California boy were now minor, disputable, or, at least, explainable.

"You're crazy," Steve declared when he saw him.

Under the increasing cloud cover, Morgen returned a snide look through his shades before he snapped the radio on and grinned.

\*\*\*\*

"How do you like working with a trainer?" Brandt inquired in his studio, inspecting Night up and down as though he could mark his progress through his clothing.

"It's kind of fun," Night peeped beneath the blazing light of Brandt's split-atom energy.

Brandt laughed. "Glutton for punishment, huh? Good." He clutched Night's shoulders and rattled him briefly. "You'll have to maintain this while you're on tour. It may still seem far away, but the tour is coming. Now, it's about time we make some decisions regarding your make-up. I have a photo shoot scheduled for next week and I've worked it around your video shoot."

Night chose to dive in, rather than wait to be thrown into the well of humiliation. "Speaking of make-up...what do you think you can do about this?" He stood up with his back turned to Brandt and pulled off his designer top.

Brandt shot backward and grabbed his teased scarlet hair. "For God's sake, Morgen! What...what the hell? When did this happen? What is this? Don't answer." He held his one hand out while the other one stayed on his head. "If this is some weird sex thing with you? Remember that you have a responsibility to this industry, the public—*yourself*, for God's sake! How the hell could you let this happen?"

Morgen's suggestion had, in fact, been to implicate one regretful night of drugs and sex, which finally led Night to follow through on an earlier recommendation: to buy a book. While he did find the excuse to be valid, it still didn't make any sense to him. "There's more."

"More?" Brandt sighed. "Well...*show me.*"

Night's face tested every shade of natural blush as he dropped his loose-legged khakis and stood before Brandt in just his underpants.

"I assume that your ass matches your legs and back? ...You know, I've dealt with a lot of different things," Brandt proclaimed. "Hairy bodies, tattoos, freckles, birthmarks, but this...this is new."

"I don't want anyone else to know," Night implored after he'd put his clothes back on and sat down. "What am I going to do?"

Brandt mused with his fingers on his lips and then pulled them away abruptly. "You're going to leave it to me. It's not that bad, really. I have to do full makeup on you anyway—at least for any shows and videos. You're so darn pale. And you tan like a redhead."

Night barely looked up. "So you think you can do something?"

Brandt kept his eyes narrowed at him for another moment before he answered. "It'll add at least another hour to your makeup. And you better plan ahead if you're going to be taking off your clothes for any of your fans. This isn't the kind of publicity you want. Shit. If you really want to hide this from people, you might also want to demand that I become your exclusive stylist."

Night nodded at the floor.

"What were you thinking?" Brandt demanded in earnest, this time.

He drew from Morgen's prescribed response. "I guess I just let things go too far, once...a long time ago."

"Huh-huh? A long time ago? You must have been a wild one at twelve." Brandt's crossed arms fell. "Well, I hope you found yourself some different pastimes and friends. I'm definitely not coming to any of your parties."

After Brandt had tested an army of paint tones on Night's skin, he finally settled on one shade of tan. He did the same to darken his complexion, and then pledged to transform his hair color to a gleaming, indisputable platinum, in their next session.

"Thanks to me, you're going to look amazing. You're going to have the power of your signature tiger. Girls are going to build shrines to your image. To the world...you're going to be irresistible."

****

Even Sandy spent the day advancing his business endeavors. Both Morgens were off the property, granting him the break he needed to finally install the Sony Watchcam that he'd picked up at the tradeshow in San Francisco. With his complimentary camera bag slung over his shoulder, which contained the camera unit, cable, and a drill set, he picked the lock to the empty suite and then slipped into Morgen's bedroom.

He surveyed every inch of Morgen's north wall, skipping over the John Lennon poster until he settled on the precise spot along the bookshelf at the foot-end of Morgen's unmade bed. Loaded with volumes of music industry bibles, novels from childhood, a few strangely-random library books, pieces of sheet music, and every odd dust-laden artifact, Sandy rationalized that Morgen was unlikely to notice the small rectangular box among the mess.

The drill bit screamed with excitement as Sandy pumped it through the wooden backboard of the shelving unit, through the insulated wall, and right through to the back of the massive wall unit inside his own suite. He fed the cable through the hole and positioned the camera as far back as possible, between some dusty books that appeared destined to remain that way. The most stressful part of the installation was cleaning away the debris without leaving noticeable tracks in the dust.

In his own suite, he adjusted the contents of one of his shelves to accommodate the four-inch monitor and his new VCR—both of which connected to the covert camera in Morgen's bedroom. Sandy took the four-pin connector and inserted it into the monitor. Then he turned thoughtfully toward his television set on the adjacent wall. He could probably even connect the camera unit to his TV where the entertainment was sure to look that much better. He'd never been such a fan of modern technology.

****

Night had every intention to shred the front page of the newspaper that he'd left in his room, but he really didn't have a plan for the other couple hundred thousand copies still in circulation.

"Morgen!" commanded a foreboding voice as he tried to sneak upstairs.

He turned around to find Frederick at the base of the stairs, already in possession of his own copy, which he held up for Night.

"Isn't this interesting?" he said, but without the humor that Doris had injected into her reaction. "It's not every morning that I get a wake-up call from my campaign manager with this kind of riveting news."

"It's just a stupid tabloid," Night said, borrowing Doris's words.

"That is true," Frederick replied. "However..." he smashed his knuckles on the photograph, "that is my Christmas tree in the background, my floor in the living room, my furniture, my doorway, my painting, my daughter's sweater, and my son's hair!" His face flushed deeply as he suppressed his words. "And I really don't know how someone could have rigged this up."

"I don't know either," Night's voice flared and then cracked, "but it's not real."

200

"I hope like hell that it's not real! Morgen, you've impressed me lately—so much—but I could never excuse this, and right now, I don't have enough faith to discount it simply on your word. If this is real," Frederick decreed, "then you don't belong in this family. If this is real, I'll take it you've chosen to embrace your roots and would, from this point forward, prefer to go by..." he snapped his fingers, coaxing the name from his lips, "Shannien." He pitched the paper onto a bench in the foyer. "Tell me I'm wrong, Morgen."

"You *are* wrong! Why can't anyone see that nothing is *ever* how it looks!"

The frustration of being invisible, behind an eternal wall of secrets, ignited a fire behind Night's eyes that, once again, threatened to incinerate a whole building. He fled the scene and insulated himself inside Morgen's suite before another impetuous thought could shoot from his tongue. Despite his achievements, and the miles between where he'd come from and this, his discarded past still managed to antagonize him. Absently, he drifted to Morgen's bedroom window and waited for his brother's return, which he dreaded as much as he longed for it right now.

# Chapter Eighteen

The 101 North left Waldport behind as the car drifted up the coastline. Morgen, sitting upright and alert since their last stop, reached forward and shut off the radio. "That's the mailbox! This has to be the place. Go back!"

But it wasn't the place and Morgen began to worry about the information he'd artfully wheedled out of his brother about his isolated home.

*"I can see how Gramps got away with what he did. I mean, it's not hard to make yourself invisible on the Oregon coast. It's a wonder your girl, Daphne, ever found you at all—and what about delivery people, and this Lila who helped you? Did your private road have a name or was it just a really long driveway? There had to be a landmark, a mailbox, a number...?"*

The next time Morgen ordered Steve to slow down, he was sure. Somehow, it even felt familiar to him. Steve parked the car on the side of the dirt road, just short of the clearing that surrounded the house.

Andrew's Mercedes was on the property and many more of Night's descriptions came to life through one sweeping glance: the beach, the veranda, the tree-stump... He instructed Steve to join him in about ten minutes, then he made his way to the front door, all the while drawing on his anger to stave off the strange sensation of becoming his brother.

Morgen's nearly translucent hand pressed on the door handle and a shockwave coursed through him when the door easily fell open. Shivering, he glanced around the bottom floor. The sparingly furnished interior and hardwood floor lent to his chill. The emptiness played with his mind, spawning ideas of Night being the true psychopath, or con artist, having made everything up for kicks or some mercenary gain.

It had to be the place... First it had tried to turn him into Night, and when that failed, it turned him entirely against him for one excruciating minute. Back on task, Morgen concluded that if Daphne had scaled the rocks below Night's bedroom window, then his room had to be upstairs, facing the bay. As though stepping into an unknown and parallel world, Morgen opened that door with due caution.

The scent of ocean escaped past him like trapped spirits. The bed had been left crisply made up in blue satiny sheets and covers. The dressers and other odd furniture looked stately beneath a thin layer of dust, and Morgen found himself disturbed only by the insincere luxury here. He walked through the room and peered out the window, just as his twin had done countless times.

Through a casual glance, he thought he caught some movement on the sand, below. He looked again and found himself staring into Daphne's spectral face, but she took one look and faded away in disappointment. Morgen shook his head, not sure whether to attribute this vision to clairvoyance or the needle.

"Night!"

Eclipsed by the window behind him, Morgen returned Andrew's multifaceted gaze.

"You're not Night..."

*"No,"* Morgen thought. It wasn't fair. He hadn't even had his moment. "What do you mean, Daddy."

The confusion on Andrew's face lasted only a few seconds, and then it became clear he'd made up his mind.

"I thought I was deranged when I started to hear noises in the house, but then I saw your door half open. What's happened to you? You're different. You've lost weight. You look terrible." Andrew rushed forward, gripped Morgen's arms, and then embraced him with all of his desperation, frustration, and anger. At no response, he backed away. "What's the matter with you? I want to hear you speak—or are you really a ghost? Speak!"

"Now you want me to speak?"

Andrew's spine went up like a cat's. "Yes, tell me... Didn't you like it out there, Night? Didn't you find everything you thought you'd missed? Was it not fulfilling?" he hammered. "Did you come here with some illusion about making amends, or did you just stop by to taunt me...now that you're so worldly?"

Morgen lifted one eyebrow in a vague acknowledgment.

"If so, then you have no idea. I will never forget what you did to me, Night. I will never forget the way you left me and how you destroyed my restaurant, my life—so many lives!"

Even with Andrew shouting, Morgen became distracted by the calm and tragic howl of the wind outside. His companion still hadn't arrived and already Steve seemed a thousand miles away, or like a memory. Morgen blinked to clear his head.

"Did you rebuild the restaurant?"

Andrew chuckled dryly. "After the scene you made? Maybe once people start to forget and I can stop hearing about how my once-respectable son just up and ran off with his little slut friend. The only good that's come out of the blasted rumor is that nobody believes that anyone is missing."

"Or dead... Yeah, that's pretty lucky for a two-time killer."

Andrew seemed immobilized by the attitude he perceived as coming from Night, so it caught Morgen by surprise when a tremendous weight landed on his face that rocked his balance. His rage swelled at the thought of Night being stuck here for all the years that he'd lived, not aware of the life he'd been deprived of.

"So what happens now?" Morgen asked, incessantly sniffing back the blood that instantly filled his nose. "Are we going to start again? Build a new restaurant and lie to people? Should I pretend I'm deaf again, and never speak to anyone, and stay all by myself all the time, until one of us finally dies?"

"That would have been ideal," Andrew granted, "but nothing will ever be that easy again—least of all, for you."

204

*Where was Steve?* Morgen slipped past Andrew, but the distance between them collapsed at the top of the staircase as Andrew pulled him back into a chokehold.

"This perpetual race to the bottom..." Andrew crooned.

Morgen couldn't breathe. It hadn't been an easy task for days, but the dam across his airway actually made him black out a few times on the steps.

"You don't have any idea what you put me through—all the searching, the restaurant, the police, Lila...! I'd like to kick you straight to the bottom, but I'm afraid you'll shatter."

On the ground level, Andrew hustled him toward the front door. He sniffed at the faint scent of hair dye that lifted under his nose. "No...I don't want you dead," he continued, ignoring the clue. "I've spent far too much time preparing for your return. Oh, yes..." he assured in Morgen's involuntary silence. "I'll show you."

Morgen tried to root himself, expecting Steve to barge in and turn the tables around, any second now. He regretted the belatedness of this trip. He could have taken greater command of the place—when he wasn't dying quite as much.

Andrew adjusted his hold and, suddenly, he couldn't even turn his head with the fierce grip against his scalp. He threw back an elbow, only to lose both his arms to just one of Andrew's, but at least the pressure was off his throat. A last stab attempt to free himself failed when he stamped his heel back, but missed Andrew's foot.

His mind continued to fade in and out. His hands and wrists, and the entire lengths of his arms pulsed with poison blood, and he had difficulty initiating each new breath as Andrew railroaded him into the corridor. Just for a moment, he surrendered to whatever lay ahead as his eyes turned listlessly to see the front door where his recruit should have revealed himself by now.

"Look, Night..." Andrew nodded at another door, directly opposite the main entrance. "It had always been hiding there, behind the paneling."

"For fuck sake... Steve!"

"Did you bring somebody along...*another* problem for me to take care of?"

Andrew reinstated his previous chokehold while his other hand flipped back a latch on the old, narrow door.

Morgen squirmed, but his throat kept paying the price.

"I once kept all of your mother's things down in there," Andrew disclosed as he pried open the door. "But I finally took them all out—so you can try living in a black hole like the one *I've* been living in for so many months!"

As he resisted being pushed forward, Morgen saw the steep line of stairs that angled sharply into the cellar. He also saw how the wood on the inside of the door appeared to have fossilized, in mere decades, through the cool, damp climate that surfaced from the deep. Finally, he dropped all his weight and broke through the chokehold.

"Christ!" Morgen yelled into the blackness as Andrew punted him forward, but he caught the doorframe with his fingers.

"Night..!"

"Wrong!" Morgen pushed himself off. "Don't you see it yet, Daddy...?" He had to regain his breath before finishing. "I'm the one you didn't want."

Andrew's blue eyes darted all over Morgen. He instinctively glanced at his hands and noticed the color that had bled onto them through his clammy grip on Morgen's hair. "I knew it immediately... I knew my Night couldn't have changed so much, so quickly." He shook his head in a quick shudder.

"Your Night...? *Your* Night would shock you ten times over if he were here!"

Andrew's head swayed. "I don't believe it. The sick little Morning... So, you managed to be saved."

"Yeah...you could've chosen me. Who knows how I would've turned out—I might have been easier to handle. Night, from what I've seen, is way too crazy to care what happens to him, so you were damned from the start."

There were tears in Andrew's eyes, even as his anger finally detonated. He plucked Morgen forward and thrust him against the adjacent wall. "So, tell me...! Where is Night? Did he come with you, or did you leave him at home, with Brigitte, in California? Oh, yes...I know where you're from."

Morgen's chronically weak lungs threatened to cave in. His mind battled against a head-rush as his eyes struggled to uncross.

"You're still the same sick runt you were when you were born. Let's return to the question..." He clutched Morgen by the front of his sweater—a sweater he'd once purchased for Night—and smashed his body against the wall a half dozen times before letting him crumble. "I wouldn't hesitate to kill you, you useless curse, so buy yourself some time and talk!"

Blood trickled from the already fragile lining of his nose and he braced for the inevitable blow that would immortalize the silence, but then the door opened.

"Sorry, my friend," Steve began, after assessing the scene. "I never loaded no gun before."

Andrew balked, looking somewhat amused. "Saturday Night Special? Now you think you're going to kill me?"

Morgen scrambled his way up the wall and stumbled over next to Steve.

"Just get out," Andrew shuddered. "I didn't want you here from the very beginning and you are still uninvited! And take this low-bred defective off my doorstep as well." He lunged for the gun in Steve's hand, but Morgen stepped between them.

"Not yet. I want to play a little game, Daddy. You can pretend to be Night." He coughed blood into his hand, wiped it down his side, and through labored breaths, simply continued. "I'm going to pretend I'm you, okay? It'll be fun."

"Get out!" Andrew shrilled. When neither of them budged, he strutted toward a door inside the living room, presumably to find his own source of backup.

Morgen swiped the gun from Steve's hand, pointed it at Andrew's knee, and fired it. By the time Morgen completed a blink Andrew was writhing on the floor. The bullet had missed his knee, but it had drilled through his calf before going on to take out the leg of a nearby chair.

Steve clutched his head for a second. "Man...what are you doing? What if they can trace the gun?"

"Don't worry," Morgen said, his eyes locked on Andrew. "He won't make any problems for us. He's got things to hide, too...much bigger things. Don't you, asshole?"

Andrew groaned and smacked the floor.

"How're you doing there?" Morgen gibed. "I'll hurry this along, for both our sakes, but first I want to know something. Why did you do it? Why did you ruin my brother's life?"

"I didn't *ruin* it," Andrew scoffed through tortured breaths. "I gave him everything."

Morgen sighed. "Yeah, and I go to confession every Sunday. Try again!"

"He didn't understand..."

"Really...? Because I don't understand either. Do you understand, Steve?"

Although half stunned, Steve rattled his head.

"You treated him like shit—my brother—and while I wish it wasn't so, still your own blood!" Morgen gripped the gun in two hands and raised it to Andrew's face.

"No..." Steve beseeched, cringing one second and pulling Morgen's arm back in the next.

Morgen let his arms fall. "Tell me about my brother's friend, Daphne. Do you think Night understands why she had to die?"

208

"She isn't dead."

Morgen kicked Andrew in the chest and knocked him flat; then he kicked him again.

Andrew's breaths became frenzied. "Everything was her own doing... She ruined our lives!"

"So you took hers?" Morgen shoved him with the sole of his borrowed hiking boot, but Andrew barely moved. "How many people have you killed? My real mother, Daphne... Anyone else, lately?"

"I wish I'd killed you, brat. Leave, before—"

"No. I may not be able to keep this up for nineteen years like you deserve, but I'm not going away that easy. To think it could have been me who you put through all this bullshit."

Andrew still gasped for air. "You were never even a thought."

"Well..." Morgen scratched his ear with the gun, "that's not really fair either. I came with a convenient expiry date—and I could've learned the piano. I'm musical...just like Night. In fact, I just landed a music contract. I'm a rock star. Did you know that?"

"Oh, perfect..." Andrew tapped into some reserve of strength and lifted his shoulders. "The authorities will hear about this, *Rock Star*, and I'm sure you'll be a popular little fuck where you're going."

Morgen smirked. He remembered one of Night's stories and abandoned Andrew for a moment. "How are you going to call them?" he asked as he gave the telephone cable a fatal yank.

Andrew gawked, for once, speechless.

"They say twins can feel each other's pain, so excuse me if I'm taking things a little too personal!"

Andrew grimaced, clutching his profusely bleeding leg. "You're nobody's twin... I don't know what you are."

"I'll tell you what I am..." Morgen whispered, leaning close into Andrew's face. "I'm your nightmare." He trudged back over to Steve. "Now...what sort of gesture was that when you put all those lovely marks on my brother who you believe to be such a better pick?"

Andrew collapsed on his own arms, clearly aware of what was coming. His opposite hand left bloody fingerprints on the hardwood floor with every attempt to maneuver away from Morgen.

"No answer on that one, huh? Let's try again. What did you use to do it?"

"I've had enough of this!" Andrew blasted. "Just finish what you came here to do and then get the hell out!"

Unexpectedly, Steve leaned forward. "Jus' answer my friend so we can do that."

"To hell with you both."

Morgen answered this with a pistol-cuff and a swift kick to Andrew's already devastated leg.

Andrew hid his face and refused to answer, but he also briefly passed out.

"Not yet, asshole. Wake up!"

Morgen slapped the gun into Steve's hand and scanned the tidy walls of the living room. He didn't expect the search to take long with the house being so far from cluttered. Like in some benign game of hide-and-seek, he spotted something that struck him as feet peeking out from beneath a thick robe of a curtain. He strode over to the picture window and pulled out the thin metal rod that had supported sheers, prior to one of Night's hallmark window-breaking rock-tosses that Morgen had both experienced and heard about.

Morgen examined the rod and then turned to Andrew, who suddenly had trouble returning a solid gaze.

"I had to," Andrew stated frantically as Morgen approached. "I did it because I had to do something to try and protect us both from what was happening."

"Aw, that's so nice. I feel all warm," Morgen quipped, breathing through an open mouth. "Then, allow me to return that kindness on Night's behalf."

Andrew attempted to back away, but Morgen's pace quickened, forcing Steve to jump out of his way.

"I didn't do it like this," Andrew protested. "I gave him pills! I made him sleep!"

"No time," Morgen grunted. He reached back with the metal rod and wacked it across Andrew's hands as they came up to protect his face. When Andrew cringed, Morgen slammed it over his shoulders, which caused him to double over with an enormous gasp. The rod came down, again and again, until Andrew could no longer resist screaming, yet Morgen refused to stop until he'd depleted his strength—but not his rage.

"There, asshole. Did that feel like love?"

Staring vacantly, Morgen eventually noticed that blood had seeped through Andrew's shirt, delicately...like the whimpering that filtered through the air. Close behind him, his quiet accomplice had winced himself into a tight, upright hunch.

Morgen pitched the rod at the fetal form at his feet and lumbered into the corridor. "This was supposed to be my new room," he presented to Steve, gesturing to the cellar door. "But I think he should have it." He staggered back into the living room, squatted beside Andrew, and planted a kiss on his head. "Nice meeting you, Granddaddy. And to answer your question, Night couldn't live in this world after what you did to him. He just couldn't fit in...so he killed himself."

From the corridor, Morgen nodded at Steve, and then at the black opening, before he shaped a pistol with his fingers and fired a pretend bullet. He didn't witness the final drama as he threw up over the veranda, or after he balled himself up in the passenger seat of Steve's car. He only heard the gunshot.

# Chapter Nineteen

Night kept a vigil at Morgen's bedroom window—at least, this is what Sandy observed through a pixilated image on his television. When this got too boring, Sandy went out to rent a movie, but he couldn't wait to see what his surveillance system would capture when nobody was supposed to be looking.

****

"You latched that door, right?" Morgen slurred, scrunching himself tightly against the passenger door.

"Wha' does it matter? He fell all the way down and...you heard the gun."

Steve's reply sounded ominously evasive. Morgen straightened himself in his seat and took a pill bottle out of the duffel bag by his feet.

"I don' think you got jus' a cold. But you know...I could take you to someone who can help you."

"I'm fine, Steve, except I do have a cold, and I almost had my lights put out by a lunatic. Now drive so we can get the hell back to civilization."

****

Like a bloody, tormented creature surfacing from the depths of hell, Andrew emerged from the cellar, one appendage at a time. By now, Morgen would be well on his way back to California, but he figured he still had at least fourteen hours left to find out about Night's real status and confirm how big a liar his twin actually was. On his hands and one knee, Andrew crawled into the kitchen. There, he pulled a towel from the stove handle and tore it into pieces that he used to seal the leaking hole in his leg.

Using every strip of material barely contained the hemorrhaging, and he dreaded the thought of having to make up a story if he had to turn to the hospital. Aside from his shot up leg and battered body, yet one more aggravation came from having dislocated his shoulder at the bottom of the steep basement stairs. He'd already managed to reset it, but now it begged for ice.

"You just wait, you vicious little shit," he muttered. "Your turn is still coming."

He was a sore hideous mess, but he was alive, and determined to recover. The fulfillment of his plans would be now be delayed for weeks or months—thanks to Aileen Coleman's demon-child—and that truth alone supplied him with the anger to move rather swiftly. He grabbed a broom from the pantry, turned it upside-down, and then used it like a crutch to make his way to the telephone in the living room. He found that the mounting cord was still intact, the jack a bit mangled, but not broken.

For over an hour he played with the prong using a tiny pin and some pliers and he tried and retried the jack in the outlet until a dial tone surged through the line. He laughed with the receiver against his ear and then frowned when he realized that he had to make the journey into his den where he kept the paper he'd found in Lila's purse. Breathing his way through the pain, he limped there, and back, and then dialed the Dahlsi's telephone number.

"Hello," he said, not expecting his voice to come out so butchered. "Would Morgen happen to be available?"

\*\*\*\*

Sandy clutched the receiver between his shoulder and his ear as he rewound the tape in his VCR to see what interesting shots he might have gained during the evening. "Um...he went out earlier, but he might have come back. I don't really know. Do you want his direct number so you can keep trying him?"

\*\*\*\*

"Absolutely. I would love to keep trying him."

Andrew disconnected with a quick tap, grinning as he redialed, but his jaw loosened when he heard the frantic hello at the other end of the line.

"Hello to you, Morgen. You sound well..."

"Okay... Who's this?"

Andrew hung up and looked at the ceiling. "Oh, Night. Don't you even recognize your own father anymore?" He tried to suppress his giddy relief, and amusement, as his body hurt too much to laugh. It didn't stop him from talking to himself, though. "Or should I say, it's astounding how fast you can drive, sweet Morgen? Lincoln County to L.A. in less than two hours..." This time, he did chuckle. "Simply astounding."

****

Night's slight tan drained from his face at the sight of his brother, early the next morning, when he reentered Morgen's suite.

"What did you do?" his voice trembled like distant thunder. "Why are my old clothes on the floor—and why is your hair that color?"

Morgen sat up slowly, dragging his hands down his face. He looked mangier than ever with the addition of bruises along his cheekbones, and yet he smiled. "Just thought I needed a change. You don't like it? I'll dye it back, don't worry."

"You went there, didn't you?" Night voice began to quiver. "After I told you—"

"I made him pay, Night. And I have to say I'm sorry for giving you such a hard time. You really didn't stand a chance of being normal, living there with *Psycho*." He fell back again. "God, I feel like crap. I thought dying would be easier than this."

Night felt himself flush. "What did you do, Morgen? I told you to forget about him until I was ready!"

214

"I can't wait that long and, thanks to me, we can both forget about him, finally. He's already been after you, Night. I did it for you—"

"I don't care! And I think you just did it for yourself!"

Morgen dropped his legs over the edge of the bed. A glare sliced through his stolen auburn bangs that dipped lower than his prominent cheekbones. "Why do you even give a shit after everything he did to you?"

Night smashed his fists against his sides. "I wanted to get back at him in my own way! And now he's really going to try to get back at one of us...unless you killed him! Did you kill him, Morgen?" A few seconds lapsed. "No..."

Morgen rocketed upright. "Christ, you're an idiot. I should've just brought you back there so you two could've lived and died together like the pair of freaks that you are!"

"Oh, shut up...just shut up because maybe this isn't any better— maybe *you* aren't any better! You're just like him...telling me what to do, and then I do it, and then you're still not nice to me! I hate trying to understand everything, and I hate trying to understand you, and sometimes I even hate you!"

"Careful. You need me and my life."

"No...I don't."

Morgen's features contorted. "Excuse me? You can't do shit by yourself. You've never made one move without my help. You came here a freak, and now that you know a little more, you're just a freak with fewer excuses."

Night squashed Morgen's cough when he tackled him to the ground. "Call me a freak if you want—but I'm still better than you!"

Morgen started to both laugh and cough with Night's hands pressing on his chest. "Please, enlighten me... In what way?"

"I'm everyone's favorite...your parents, your manager, Beth... What, you don't believe me?" Night popped up and left the room. He burst back in carrying the infamous newspaper, which he threw at Morgen. "Remember what Doris did for you on the beach the other night? By the way, I was there—and I got there *all by myself*. Well, I know that Beth never did that for you."

Morgen pulled the paper away from his chest and scowled at the front page. His breaths became even more labored. "You're proud of this...?

"Shut-up, Morgen. You know, maybe I don't belong here. Maybe I don't understand a lot of things, but I've done everything you've ever asked me to do. Couldn't you have just been nice to me?"

With his complexion washing over in red, Morgen inched away from Night. "You've lost all possibility of me *ever* being nice to you. Get the fuck away from me—get the fuck out!"

"Good luck, Morgen. You know...you deserve to be sick, and I hope that your pain is as bad as I remember it."

"And I hope you'll enjoy getting fucked for a living because you're no goddamn good for anything else!"

Night came forth and slapped Morgen so hard that it reactivated Andrew's handprint from the previous day. "...And what exactly are *you* good for?"

In the common room, Night slowed down only to recover a small piece of paper from his duffle bag that Morgen had dropped in the middle of the floor. He grabbed his brother's wallet, and car keys, before he marched down the hallway and into the private stairwell that delivered him to Morgen's parked car. Every motion felt mechanical as he reversed out of the driveway and sped from the neighborhood that should always have been home. Driving, he felt no emotion, direction, or worth, whatsoever. For the first time in months, he felt like himself.

****

"Beth didn't see you before she left for school this morning," Brigitte relayed when Frederick stepped into the bedroom. "She's going to stay over at her friend's house tonight. She sends her love."

He grunted. "I think she sends her love too readily."

Brigitte paused at her vanity, letting go of the pin on the lapel of her blouse. "You're not serious... You're actually lending credibility to that ridiculous hoax in that newspaper?"

"I want the list of guests who came to our party."

"How is that going to help? Nobody's going to confess to having any part in this thing, so leave it alone. You have more important things to think about these days. And for goodness sake...how can you doubt your children?"

He was silent as he searched inside his closet for a suit jacket.

Brigitte stopped watching him and smiled at the mirror. "Wasn't Morgen really something that night?"

"He was something...but he wasn't himself. He's like two people all the time. I'm not sure whether he was high, or if he sent his twin to put on that show for him."

Brigitte snapped her fingers and giggled. "That could explain the photograph."

Frederick faced her. "How can you laugh about this? There is nothing amusing about the possibility that this isn't any hoax...that our two adopted kids decided to play Adam and Eve. Maybe we should have opened up to the media, a long time ago, about adopting our kids, but what were the chances that it would come out like this?"

After an uncomfortable pause, Brigitte replied. "I don't believe it's real. And, do you know what else? I don't remember a time when you accepted my decision to bring Morgen into this house. Do you feel the same way now about Beth?"

Frederick balked. "Where's this coming from?"

"You don't even realize how often you imply exactly that—about Morgen anyway. As far as you're concerned, everything about him has been wrong since the very first day."

He walked over to Brigitte and placed a quick kiss on her forehead. "You're right. There's been a lot wrong, but I've never regretted anything about our family."

"You're a very good politician," Brigitte stated wryly. "Just give our son more credit. You saw the real Morgen perform that night, and I'm sure the side of him that we both worry about, at times, will fade away with his success."

****

In the middle of city chaos, Night found a telephone booth and reached into his pocket for the small slip of paper that revealed Lila's home and work telephone numbers. He threw in too much money, but he didn't care. Lila's home number didn't work, so he called the hospital.

"Lila...?" repeated the woman who answered the call. "If you mean Lila Hughes..."

"Yes, I need to speak with her right away."

"I'm sorry, Sir. You must not have heard. I don't know how else to tell you... Lila had a terrible accident on the trails..."

He felt his mind-numbing, and the sensation quickly spread through the rest of his body. "An accident...?"

"Yes, they say she tried to recover her hat on a steep ledge, and she slipped..."

Night hung up the phone and stared through the dirty glass. His real mother, Daphne, Lila... Morgen was right; Andrew needed to be stopped, irrespective of his own petty desire for revenge. He scanned the concrete horizon, crushed by the truth of how much he'd depended on Lila to be his contingency plan if it didn't work out with Morgen.

Tears washed away his view of the city as his thoughts fired down countless dead ends. Just briefly, he hoped he would find Morgen dead when he reentered the house—since returning there appeared to be the only viable option. He would take Morgen's body to the place that had already been prepared for the occasion, and he would bury it, along with all the stress and aggravation that came with knowing him.

But he didn't mean it one bit. Morgen was part of him, a binding curse if nothing more, and somehow he knew his brother would also have come to the same conclusion by this time today.

****

Sweating and wheezing, Morgen scrunched himself against a nightstand in the corner of the guestroom and groped for the telephone behind his head. He figured the strain of this catastrophe would kill him long before the effects of his raging cancer.

He didn't want to call Steve for help and be forced to tell him about his illness. Night would come back, but he had to find a way to explain his own absence from the household, until that time. As ridiculous as it would be to die of starvation within the walls of substantial wealth, he had to acknowledge that possibility. If someone knocked on his door, he couldn't let them see him in his current state—and what if someone decided to come in anyway? It incensed him that he needed Night more than Night needed him, at this point. Even worse, he needed Night even more than he hated him right now.

"Are you crying?" Night asked through a simper, standing in the doorway.

"Asshole!" Morgen pitched the handset at Night who watched it hit the wall beside him.

"You're the asshole, Morgen, and I'm only here because it's the easiest thing for me to do. Why should I lose everything I've worked for when you're not even going to be here for much longer?"

Morgen answered him with a simple hand gesture.

Night showed him a more complex one before swaggering past the bed to reach the bathroom. "I have to get ready. I'm meeting everyone at some retreat tonight. We're planning our tour. You should be thrilled." He took another step but stopped at hearing Morgen's stern voice.

"He would have found you, Night. And if you'd gone there by yourself you would have spent eternity in his basement. Did you know you had a basement?" Congestion hampered his speech like never before. "He's been trying to get to you since you left. Therefore, I saved your ass, and who knows how many other asses by knocking Gramps off."

"I'm not happy about it, Morgen...but you only killed him because of what he did to me, right, so thanks."

Morgen barely nodded. "Don't mention it."

****

At the bathroom sink, Night pushed a clean blade into the handle of his razor. He opened the faucet, glanced into the mirror, and did a double take. The razor hit the mirror as he spun and ran back into the guestroom where Morgen stood coughing into his arms.

"Morgen, look at this...!"

But Morgen bolted past him, smashing doors aside as he tore through the suite. Night chased after him, but only to have the bedroom door thrown in his face while Morgen, on the other side of it, burst into an even greater coughing frenzy. Night charged in, causing Morgen to cringe the other way while blood from his mouth leached from between his fingers and trickled to his elbow.

Night's whole demeanor sank as his brother swiped copious amounts of tissues from a nearby table to clean himself up.

"You're getting worse really fast."

"Excellent report, brain surgeon. What do you want?"

Night felt awkward announcing his lucky break, but he couldn't contain it. "I think my hair is turning white! Look at my face. Look at my scalp." He flipped his head down and parted his mop. "Do I have any roots—because I should have some by now?"

Morgen stepped closer and peeked indifferently. "No."

"Well, how could this happen?"

"How the hell should I know? Mother Nature just finally realized you should have been a blond all along, so just be grateful. Now, for Christ's sake, leave me alone!"

****

At one o'clock in the morning, Sandy approached his surveillance station and rewound the tape in his VCR. The live action monitor revealed nothing but a still form on Morgen's bed, made visible only by the moonlight through the window. When Sandy pressed play, the black and white scene on his television flickered into a picture of an empty room. He advanced the tape, stopping where he caught the image of one of the twins entering.

Sandy could only see the subject from behind, bending over to rifle through the nightstand drawer. He decided this had to be Morgen, when the subject exposed a syringe and vial in his hands, after turning on the lights.

Plopped on the edge of his bed, and turned halfway toward the camera, the weary-looking Morgen pushed the needle into his arm, before tossing everything back into the drawer and leaving the room.

Sandy gripped both sides of the television with his eyes wide and his lips halfway to forming a smile. As a bonus to his mercenary achievements, he could probably get the prick charged for possession. He stepped away from the screen and had to advance the tape another two times before he glimpsed some further action.

For about a minute, Sandy watched Morgen cringing and hacking at the edge of his bed, but the event that followed had Sandy throwing up his arms in celebration. Night burst into the room to share his astounding hair phenomenon. Every word was clear, along with the details of their physical likenesses. Even if he never had a chance to record anything else, this alone would be enough. It was only the ensuing footage that almost blew down his mighty sails.

He watched Morgen turn the white tissues black as he wiped the blood from his hands and arms. After Morgen's phantom brother vanished from the room, Sandy raised his finger to the screen. "I don't give a damn in what shape I have to sell you, you mangy fuck. I finally got you where I want you, and soon both of you will know exactly where that is."

****

Night dropped Morgen off at the park to meet Steve before making his way to the exclusive conference resort that Gin had booked for the band and its entourage.

After hours in a boardroom, the whole troop headed outside for the cushioned, wrought iron chairs at one round extension of the massive, illuminated pool. Gin wrapped up one final debate, now under twilight, amongst palms, ferns, and chirping crickets.

"If nobody has any more suggestions, then maybe we can just enjoy the rest of the night." He turned to the occupied loveseat beside him. "Morgen and Doris...maybe the two of you can hold off on enjoying each other for the evening. My hopes are that each of you will bond intimately with one another while we're here."

Doris bit down on her lip and smiled at the imposter Morgen. "So, what are we going to do?" she asked behind the straw of her margarita, her voice sultry like the air of a true jungle. "Are we going to play Truth or Dare or something like that? ...In any case, I don't think Morgen will be bonding too intimately with anyone else but me tonight."

Sean, who'd long pushed himself back from everyone else, set down his beer bottle. "Get a life, Doris. We're about to go on tour. Do you really think such devotion is going to last once the first curtain falls? Me thinks your time is finally up." He cackled. "We got what we wanted, but there's always a price, darling."

Doris glanced around for support while Night tried not to grin at the deluge of toasts to their drummer.

"Look at him..." Sean persisted, shifting his crosshairs on Night. "What was *your* price, Morgen? What did you trade to the devil to get here...your personality? What the hell's the matter with you?"

Aden's tranquility finally broke. "Like you said, Sean, we got what we wanted. I don't really care what's up with Morgen, as long as he can work the stage. And that's all you should care about."

"No, I want to find out what the hell's up with that guy. I know Morgen, and that stiff sitting there ain't him!"

Night narrowed his eyes at the drummer, unable to see how playing it cool, in Morgen's true form, could have given him away already. "I don't know what you mean."

Sean began laughing. "'*I don't know what you mean?*' Is this what you're like when you're more high or less high, Morgen? Or are you really Morgen's twin? You do look a little different lately."

"Of course he looks different," Brandt piped up as he reached for his drink. "He spends hours in my studio, week after week, being reinvented. I mean, of course it shows." He winked at Night and then scanned the group smugly.

Brandt rarely left him alone in any capacity, and Night didn't mind. This style guru had even taken over Morgen's coaching role, now that he had to venture out from under Morgen's wing more and more.

The sky switched from indigo to black, and a cool breeze passed over the urban oasis, but some of the guests couldn't be dissuaded from using the pool. Night admired both the sinuous and the muscular forms cutting through what looked like liquid glass.

"Shall we join them?" Doris enticed, dropping her wrap and tugging at Night's open flannel shirt that he wore over a tee.

Once again, Brandt came to the rescue. "He can't, Doris. He's...allergic to...the pool chemicals."

Doris chortled. "Really? But you have a pool..."

"Beth uses it more than anyone. I can't really—"

"Yeah, it's incredible. I even had to change the makeup I use on him. We'll have to treat this one special."

"I'll do my best," Doris surrendered with a shrug.

As Doris sat down, their manager, Gin, stood up with an eye on the bar. He took one step, then leaned over Night's shoulder. "You really are awfully quiet. If this isn't you, should we expect your return anytime soon?"

Night replied with an emphatic shudder. Nothing from his past would ever be coming back if he had any say about it.

"Well, I've seen you the other way. Whatever it is you're on, stay on it," Gin said, only half in jest. "But whatever our drummer's on, he can't handle it. Talk to him." He slapped Night's shoulder before heading off to the bar.

Night hadn't counted on ever having to acquaint himself with Morgen's medication. He never would have guessed that the bonding experience with his new career family would involve passing around a straw with several rails of cocaine.

It was pleasurable to sit amongst the people whose job it was to judge him and, for once, just laugh with them—even roll against the shoulder of one of them as the substance gripped him most intensely. Then again, that moment might have been during the second round when he began to fear everything around him—as though the world had fractured into a kaleidoscope of Andrews. Sean's jeering in the background only heightened the effect.

Night stood up—he didn't know why—and stumbled forward. Gin reached out for him, full of concern, but this made him spring backward like a crayfish, and he ended up treading water after all.

"I told you!" Sean cried, half delirious. "Morgen's not green to this stuff. Who the hell is that guy? Identify yourself!"

Brandt slammed down his drink and rushed to the edge of the pool while Night responded, only with semi-compliance, to the many arms all coaxing him to grab on. He still averted everyone's hands when he found his footing on the tiled ground, but Brandt boldly clutched the hotel key dangling from a cord around Night's neck and read the room number. Hauling him past the others, he muttered, "This is just terrific. Maybe it's funny to you guys, but I'll be the one who has to deal with the rash before the photo-shoot."

The next morning, Night remembered Doris touching his face and prattling into it, and he remembered being helped to his hotel room, not by Doris, but by someone who was able to manage most of his weight. His friends recounted the events to him, in lavish detail, over breakfast.

"Morgen Dahlsi...not so notorious after all," Brandt professed in closing.

Night sat back from the table, annoyed at being picked on, but also in an effort to avert Sean's eyes. He sensed the time had come to start worrying.

# Chapter Twenty

"Get a new drummer," Morgen suggested, or it might have been an order. "Sean's worn out his usefulness as a dealer. He's become a bloody liability, and if he's really onto us, you have to take him out of the picture."

"How?"

Morgen explained between labored breaths. "Let him know that it's not working out and that it's his own fault. Tell him he's bringing everyone down and risking your success. And if he argues, tell him you'll expose his already lucrative business, along with all of his contacts. Ask him if he prefers jail."

Night's eyes grew large. He should say this...he who narrowly escaped this fate himself? "But Sean's your friend..."

"Do you want him to ruin everything? Do you really want to argue about this? Do you want the police to add impersonation to your list of crimes—not to mention what happened to your daddy? You're the one with all the motives for revenge."

"You wouldn't do that to me. Not anymore...?"

"You have one purpose, and if you're going to allow him to fuck everything up, you bet. Just do it, Night."

The distinct sound of Brigitte's heeled footsteps reached them from the far end of the hallway and Morgen ran for his bedroom, but his coughing could not be locked behind the door. Night made his mind up in a hurry and slipped into the hallway before Brigitte could enter the suite.

"Well hello, superstar. I just came to check on you. Weren't you going to tell me how everything went?"

"I was just coming down to get something to eat."

"I thought they would have fed you guys through the entire thing," she remarked, trying to keep up with him until he slowed down on the staircase. "Well, if you're hungry, you can tell me all about it in the kitchen."

He told Brigitte about Gin's plans for the tour and answered her questions while she waited for her tea water to boil.

Sandy strolled into the kitchen, grinning. He didn't head for the fridge; he just stood against the wall and fixed his gaze on Night, who eyed him uncomfortably over his toast. The water in the kettle started to roll, and the housekeeper just crossed his arms as Night's words awkwardly faded to nothing. Brigitte excused herself, smiled at Sandy, and headed for the counter to prepare her tea. Only then did Sandy approach Night. He leaned over his shoulder to slip a Polaroid photograph in front of him.

At one look, Night felt his blood freeze. He read the date and time that had been written on the white portion at the bottom—today's date, and a time of only a few minutes ago. The picture, taken from an awkward angle, revealed Morgen curled up on his bed. He looked up at Sandy, lost for words.

"Don't run to him about this," Sandy whispered. "We'll talk later." As Brigitte made her way back to the table, Sandy tucked the picture away and let out a dramatic sigh. "Sometimes I wish there were two of me. Then I could always be in two places at once and get so much more done." He snapped his fingers in mock regret and walked out before Brigitte could question him about his apparent troubles.

****

Car horns, engines, and faulty mufflers polluted the air outside a lively bar where Morgen arranged for Night to meet Sean. The inside had its own share of noise with cue balls slamming into one another and people shouting over the loud music.

Sean sat down in front of Night. "What's so important?"

"I want you to leave the band."

"Now, you're definitely high..."

"I mean it." Morgen's words ran through his head...

*"Don't ramble. Be firm. Less is best."*

"So, now that we've made it, you want to cut me out? ...Fuck you."

"Everyone is tired of you, Sean, especially me. You're a wreck, and sooner or later you're going to bring us down. I just can't let that happen."

"It's not your choice anymore. I've got a contract, just like you."

"I know, and I want you to break it."

Sean wiggled his head as he stood up. "See you in the studio."

Beneath the table, Night's knuckles were turning white. "Sit down! You have a choice. You either get out like it was your idea, or the cops are going to find out about your other business." He took a deep breath and tried to keep his lines straight. "I'll have half your customers as witnesses against you after I report them too...and I'm sure they'll do anything for a deal."

"You never had a problem with my business. What is this really about, Dahlsi?"

Again, Night followed Morgen's advice to remain cool. He said nothing.

Sean swooped forward and spat on him before he reeled from the table. "*Whatever.* I'm done with you—all of you—but I want compensation or I'm going to make your life hell! And that is not negotiable!"

He watched Sean barge into the daylight while he felt for the gift Sean had left in his hair. He'd predicted Sean's wrath, but not his payoff demand. How was he going to tell Morgen that Sean wasn't going down that easy...and that Sandy may have just become his biggest threat yet?

****

Night emerged from the darkness of Morgen's private stairwell only to be ushered back into it by the housekeeper. Sandy shushed Night as he closed the door to the hallway.

On the narrow landing, Night ripped into Sandy, first. "Tell me how you got that picture!"

"Now, now," said the housekeeper. "Before I get to the important stuff, just let me assure you that I know what's going on."

Night flexed one forearm between their chests. "Going on with what?"

Sandy ignored him. He'd obviously written his script and wouldn't deviate from it. "I'm assuming Morgen is the sick one... Have a look."

Night shuffled through a series of shots that Sandy had snapped off the television, many revealing proof of there being twins in the house. "How'd you get these?"

"That's my secret. As for your secret, let me share my thoughts on how you can keep it safe. Tip number one... I hate your brother, and I don't plan on liking you, so if you think I'll be forgiving if you screw up, you're dead wrong. Two... If you tell your brother about any of this, you guys won't have a secret anymore. Three... Don't bother looking for the evidence in my possession because you won't find it. Where are we? Number four... If something mysterious happens to me, like I disappear, or I get fired, then Plan B will take over and, guess... You won't have a secret anymore. And last tip, there will be an end to this, so don't lose too much sleep over it. You have to look good for the public."

Night stood in the murky light, paralyzed. He hadn't worked this hard with Morgen to have everything ruined by the family housekeeper. He also wanted to throttle him for the tabloid incident, but that would undoubtedly backfire.

"But you can protect yourself," Sandy announced. "What I want is money. Big shocker, huh? Weekly payments will be fine. Let's say a thousand bucks a week, every Saturday?"

230

Night scrunched his face. "What if I can't...?"

"Don't kid me...Night," said Sandy with dissolving whim. "I'm sure that Morgen shoots more than a thousand dollars into his veins every week."

Night surrendered a peeved sigh. "What are you doing? You're our housekeeper..."

"I'm looking to change careers."

"I don't think you know what's going on. Morgen's really sick, and neither of us are doing this for fun."

Sandy twisted around and opened the door. "I don't care. Just do what you're told and don't be late with your payments." Then he closed the door in Night's face.

****

The telephone began ringing the moment Night entered the suite and he ran to answer it.

Sean's voice immediately belched into his ear. "Just listening to my radio, here, rubbing our success into my face!"

Night swallowed the lump in his throat that still hadn't dissipated since his exchange with Sandy.

"So, let's talk about cash," Sean continued. "You realize, by fucking me over this way, I won't even get my rightful dues as a leaving member—and you owe me at least that?"

"What exactly do you want?" Night asked, afraid that he might not understand the answer.

"This isn't going to be a one-time transaction, asshole. You may want me out of the band—and you got it—but you will never have me out of your life! From now on, I'll be expecting a steady stream of royalty money. So, once you have a new drummer, consider me the fifth member of the band! Do your math, asshole, and then be in touch—or I will."

Night set the dead receiver down against the cradle, with two hands, and then pressed them both against his head. He couldn't talk to Morgen just yet, so he trudged down to the kitchen and returned with a bowl of soup that he garnished with a parsley sprig. Once in a while, he liked to remember his restaurant days.

"I thought you might be able to have soup," he said to Morgen, who didn't even look alive in his bed.

Morgen blinked and then answered him with dry sarcasm. "That's great, Night. Soup always makes everything better."

"You better have some, Morgen." Night's voice was shaking as he scanned the room for any sign of how Sandy might have obtained the pictures. "I'm trying to take care of everything, and I was thinking...you really should've been nicer to Sandy. I also think—"

"I should have found a way to have him fired. And thinking really isn't your strength."

"Morgen, I'm in charge now, and if you want things to work out, then you better start to listen to everything I say."

Morgen balked and then struggled to sit up at the edge of the bed. "Where'd Corbin take you guys? Dictator Boot Camp? I suppose I get how you got this way, but stick it somewhere, and get it through your head...there doesn't always have to be somebody in charge."

"I don't understand that. There always is, everywhere. Even in the studio. Even in your family. And between us, it used to be you, but it isn't now."

"Well, suck me if you think it's you." Morgen's legs collapsed when he tried to stand up. He simply gave into his pain and doubled over his knees. He couldn't move as he tried to recover the air his lungs ejected on the way down.

Night placed the soup on Morgen's nightstand. "See? You need me, very much." He squatted and reached out to offer his assistance, but Morgen pushed his hands away. After watching another pathetic attempt to rise, Night lifted him up by the armpits and dropped him back on the bed. "Just eat what I brought you and maybe you'll be able to stand again."

Morgen inched up onto his pillow and closed himself to any further discussion.

"I know you don't believe me," Night persisted, "but I know what I'm doing, and I think you need to stay in the guestroom, from now on. We'll switch. There's no reason for anyone to go in there, so there'll be a lesser chance of someone finding you like this."

"Like what?" Morgen asked malignantly, but he gave in when Night answered him with a deadpan stare. "Whatever you think, Night. ...You're the one in charge."

****

The first day of video-production arrived big and fast. Between the sets, the costumes, and the energy, the experience turned out to be as surreal as the final product that included a great deal of superimposition of shadow images and animation. The group's first concert, under their big-time management, also left Night dazed, but here he also received his first real criticism. Apparently, he didn't know how to move on a stage, so just after graduating from voice lessons, he had to start with a new coach.

Night could feel Morgen's heart swell with all the glory that was truly his, but the rush couldn't last. It got to the point where Morgen struggled just to talk, and unless he prepared himself by clearing his lungs first, he didn't even bother to try.

Therefore, it surprised Night when he came home, on one occasion, to find his brother in the common room, sitting up, and staring at a piece of mail. Slouching over his knees in obvious discomfort, he greeted Night with relative pleasantness. Night walked over to take in Morgen's view of the black and white portrait-postcard that he held in one hand.

Morgen flipped the card over and his eyes narrowed, but he didn't comment.

Night thought he'd recognized the image. "Who is that?"

"I told you about him," Morgen replied in a raspy whisper. "One of the greatest people in music history."

Night plucked the card out of Morgen's tense grip and read the tiny print on the back. "John Lennon..." Night's stare shifted to the handwritten message in the open area. "'May you follow in his footsteps.' Oh, that's so nice."

Morgen glanced up at Night. "Yeah," he choked out. "Nice."

Night studied the card again. "Look at this. Why is that, there?" he asked, showing Morgen the clock face sketched in one corner. The hands indicated a few minutes past eleven.

"How should I know?" Morgen stood up and swayed, which made him sit down again. "Do you remember what you have to do when the time comes?"

Morgen sounded more like ninety than nineteen. Night nodded shortly as the sum of their efforts poured from the radio in the corner of the room.

Morgen continued. "You've done it...and from here...you can go anywhere—do anything. Don't let your past, anybody—not even Sean—stand in your way."

Night tried not to look at Morgen. Seeing him like this was worse than in any nightmare in which he'd appeared. He couldn't burden his brother with his updates about Sandy and Sean, but Morgen already knew something or Sean's name wouldn't have popped out of his brother's mouth, in such a random way, a few seconds ago. What really surprised Night was how Morgen wanted to protect him in precisely the same way.

***

"You're looking good out there," Brandt commented from the doorway when Night finished his lesson with the choreographer. "You're really hopping along." He laughed infectiously, then stopped when Night started to grin. "So, what's changed you, Morgen? Sean made me believe that you would be incredibly difficult to work with, and Aden didn't exactly come to your defense, but so far it's been a pleasure. Sure, you threw this at me," he broached, slapping Night on the back as they left the foyer of the dance studio. "But other than that..."

234

"Well, what did Sean tell you?" Night questioned, equally curious about his brother's notorious reputation.

"He said you're bitchy, self-serving, stubborn, impulsive... He said you've shown up for rehearsals stoned, and I even heard that, not so long ago, you lost an opportunity for a big break because you just didn't show up. You know, you're lucky to be here today."

"That wasn't me."

"I'm glad to hear that," Brandt replied, obliviously. "You were quite sick for a while too, I heard. Are you still sick?"

"No," Night churned out, as though he'd just been kicked in the stomach.

"Good. I guess you're one of the luckiest people around. You're going to need your health in the next few months. Touring can be rough, so don't put any unnecessary strikes against yourself, if you can help it."

Over coffee, Night tapped Brandt for his knowledge about the music industry, instead of bringing his questions to Morgen as he would have in the past. Reading didn't pose much of a problem anymore, except when it came to deciphering his contract.

"So, what do these letters mean?" He began reading them off the page. "A-S-C..."

"It's one of the performing rights societies. Didn't Chandler go over this with you?"

"I can't remember."

With one hand Brandt seized the papers, and with the other he pressed Night's hands to the table.

"Will you just relax? You've got a great lawyer and a great manager, and it's their job to worry about this. Anyway, at this rate, you're going to trick me into revealing the secret of life, and you know what the penalty for that is?"

Night shook his head.

Brandt flung his clenched fists against his chest to represent the plunge of a dagger. "And then who is going to take care of you?"

"I don't need you to take care of me," Night retorted, but it relieved him to know that Brandt thought he did.

****

Between work at the studio and their small-venue performances that their booking agent called rehearsal, Night found himself removed from his secret responsibilities more than he wanted to be. Morgen needed his help constantly, even for the simplest tasks.

"Just stop...I don't care anymore," Morgen declared one day after Night spent almost a half hour pounding on his back. "I can't breathe...and I'm tired of trying."

As Night irritably brushed Morgen's shabby dye-stripped hair, he started to notice how much of it remained in the bristles. He couldn't imagine that, in a short time, this life, this body, this replica of his own that had once housed so much ambition, would just cease to exist. He felt himself missing him in the past, and missing him in the future, and missing the soul that had always supplemented his own. But he didn't say a word as he continued to work dutifully in both areas of his new life.

The music scene became Night's welcome escape from the morbidity of his private life. It baffled him how he could be earning so much money for doing something he gladly would have paid to do. But he rarely had a chance to spend these staggering gratuities, and many of his smaller royalty checks went directly into the Sandy extortion fund.

****

Sandy had caught on to the fact that Morgen now resided in the guestroom. He realized this after sifting through his latest volume of recorded video, so he finally snuck back into Morgen's suite to retrieve his camera unit. It all didn't matter anymore since he'd already acquired enough evidence to cram every single page of every tabloid in the state for a year. He would hold out for a bit longer, probably until the tour, for the big splash.

236

****

One evening, Night arrived home from the studio to find a tacky, gold, chocolate-filled Valentine heart in front of Morgen's garage door. He assumed Doris had left it there since it only made sense from what he'd learned about the occasion. Morgen would only throw up at the sight of them, so he tucked the gift under his arm and carried it up to his suite where he planned to dig into it as soon as he set down his keys.

As he wriggled off the heart-shaped lid, he considered that the gesture could even have come from Beth—until he saw the contents that caused him to flinch and hurl the whole thing straight off the end of the coffee table. The dead scorpion tumbled across the carpet and came to rest against a baseboard. Night stared at it for a while, not really trusting it to stay inert.

He found Sandy in the third place he checked—the kitchen— leaning over a pot on the stove. He turned around to receive the back of Night's hand across his face, right before Night seized his hair and drove him facedown onto the kitchen floor.

"What do you want from me?" Night roared. "I'm giving you what you want!"

Sandy flipped himself over. "What the hell is your problem, you little faggot?"

"What's yours?" Night tackled him on the stone-tile floor, dropping his forearm against his throat. "What did you mean by giving me the big ugly bug?"

"What the hell are you talking about?"

"As if you don't know! Come and take it back!" After lifting his arm, Night rocked back on his heels and stood up. "Come on, and get it out of my room!"

Sandy scrambled onto his feet and straightened his shirt before reasoning out loud. "As much as I'd like to know what you're talking about, I can't really go into your room—I mean, with your brother crashed out in there an' all."

Night ran from the kitchen and returned to the suite by himself. He used the empty heart-shaped box and strewn lid to scoop the creature inside, and then he marched it back to the kitchen where Sandy had resumed his work. This time, he had Sandy's attention right away. Night ripped off the lid and shoved the box in Sandy's face, sending the housekeeper recoiling against the boiling pot on the stove.

Springing forward, Sandy snatched the box and lid from Night and, at arm's length, attempted to put the two back together. "Well..." he remarked, "I see I'm not the only one who Morgen has pissed off. Big surprise. Believe me...I did not send him this."

Sandy's frankness made Night believe him, but it brought on a new conclusion. As Sandy implied, the heart, and likely the postcard, had come from somebody else who hated Morgen...someone like Sean.

Night collided with Beth, in the south hallway, at the top of the stairs. They hadn't been alone together since before the tabloid scandal, and with that still weighing oppressively over the household, they backed away from one another.

"Now, do you understand why we can't...you know...?"

He nodded, but it wasn't the scandal that strained his features.

"What's going on, Night?"

Beth was more than helpful when he asked her what he couldn't, as Morgen, ask anyone else.

She looked at him with surprise. "'What happened to John Lennon'? Well, he was shot a few years back, if that's what you're asking?"

Night nodded and walked away, having reaped all he needed from this consultation with Beth. If Sean thought he was going to pull a trigger on him, literally, or figuratively, then he was dead wrong. Sean didn't realize he was matched against a new opponent—one that with all of his feral inadequacies considered few restrictions when it came to his own survival.

238

# Chapter Twenty-One

In the twilight hours, Sandy looked out of his window and watched a figure drawing closer, scuttling through the bushes along the south driveway of the Dahlsi mansion. He couldn't make out a lot of detail from his midpoint window, at the front of the house, but he could tell by the figure's massive size that it wasn't either of the twins.

Sandy activated his video equipment and aimed the camera out the window, just in time to record the intruder literally leaving his mark on the garage door like a tomcat. Tonight, he would allow the offender to complete his task, which included scrawling something on Morgen's garage door, but next time, he would confront the intruder with the means to extort a few bucks from him. Then, taking into account the weekly payments from Night, he'd be raking in money, hand over fist.

**\*\*\*\***

Night didn't say anything about the ugly bug gesture when he saw Morgen at the end of the day. That morning, he'd already erased the familiar clock-face that had been sketched, in chalk, on the garage door. Night figured out that the hands on Sean's signature clock held the greatest significance, moving through the hour of eleven, toward a moment of certain doom at the top of the hour.

He also answered a few telephone calls that complemented the offerings from Sean, but Night always hung up before any threat could be spoken. Another clock-face arrived in the mail, and again, the minute hand had moved inexorably onward.

Morgen didn't witness these things or much of anything anymore, except with Night's help. Morgen's unmistakable nervousness also made Night feel uneasy. Perhaps Morgen saw the worry in his face, but he couldn't be sure if Morgen knew about Sean or Sandy's threats with neither of them willing to bring up the subject.

"Everything is going well," Night reported as he injected morphine into his brother's vein.

Morgen glanced down at the needle in his arm. "Isn't that a little much...or are you trying to hurry things along?"

"You need it. I thought you said you're in a lot of pain."

"I'm almost out, aren't I?"

Night nodded. His brother could no longer venture out of the house to take care of his own business, so Night anticipated his request.

"If I tell you where to go and who to see, do you think you can do it?"

****

After the evening routine was completed, Night made a telephone call and then left the house to find Morgen's illicit contact. He parked his brother's white convertible under the sapphire sky, not far from the unfamiliar nightclub on the outskirts of town. A strong electronic beat pounded through the glass doors and exploded on him as he entered. He found it difficult to navigate the room between the crowds and strobe-lights.

Morgen had assured him that he wouldn't be dealing with any of Sean's pals tonight—that Sean had only been useful for cocaine. But all Morgen really needed anymore was morphine.

As the blue and yellow lights flashed in time with the music, he stood face-to-face with Edward, the morphine guy, who Morgen had described meticulously. Night offered him a quick signal and then a handshake with a palm loaded with a tight roll of green bills. Edward placed his hand inside his own jacket and drew out what appeared to be a candy bar, then another. After that, the man turned and danced back to the bar as though nothing had happened.

In the car, Night ripped open one of the candy bar wrappers and a series of small glass vials, filled with clear liquid, spilled out of a roll of cardboard, and onto his lap. Headlights from another vehicle flashed into his eyes, sparking an entire scheme.

Through all the big hair and black leather, he sought out the morphine guy for a second time tonight, This time, Night asserted himself, demanding that Edward follow him.

"Is there a problem?" Edward assumed, stuffing his hands into his purple sport coat that hung loosely over his beige slacks.

"I want to buy something else," Night stated. "I want to know if you can help me."

After hearing Night out, the man nodded and offered him some instructions. They parted ways, with Night returning to his car and the morphine-guy heading for a telephone booth. If all went as planned, the morphine guy would come out of the booth with his arms crossed, indicating that arrangements had been made for the imposter-Morgen to meet with a second contact tonight.

****

Twenty minutes later, at a roadside lookout, Night waited for a man on a motorcycle to show up. When a bike finally pulled in, he admired how easily this slight person managed to climb off and settle such a large bike. But the final surprise came when the rider in the tight jeans and the black leather jacket took her helmet off.

"Hey Doll," she started in a syrupy drawl. "It's late. Did yer car break down or are you maybe lookin' for somethin' here?"

He nodded and stepped away from his car.

"I hoped so." She flicked back her layers of two-tone hair before she sauntered over to the railing and pulled a small pistol out of her jacket. Night took it into his hands as though it were literally burning hot.

She peered at him, up and down. "D'ya know how to use it?"

He looked from the revolver to her face, still mute.

Grinning, she took back the weapon and aimed it into the blackness over the railing. He flinched and she laughed. "Here," she said, releasing the thumb catch and flipping out the cylinder. "See? It's already loaded. Should do ya unless yer a real bad shot, or yer plannin' some kinda killin' spree." She pointed out the main parts and showed him how to cock the gun and release the hammer, before placing it back into his hand. "No harder than firing a toy gun. But it ain't a present, Doll."

The scent of leather and cigarettes swelled between them as he leaned toward her and began placing one bill after another into her gloved hand. She closed her fingers abruptly at the correct sum and slid the money into her jacket.

"That was fun...and you're cute," she purred near his ear. "Might ya be lookin' for somethin' else tonight...somethin' for free?"

He barely heard a word she said. "No, that's it. Thank you."

"Got nothin' but killin' on yer mind tonight, huh?" She spun the other way and shrugged. "You take care, y'hear."

****

Andrew decided it was time to exchange the broom he'd been using as a crutch for something he could use in public, like a real cane. The bullet that had ripped through his leg might have only been half so damaging if it hadn't shattered his fibula. But walking had become bearable again, and he could now pull off a steady gait, at least for short distances. He cloaked his other wounds beneath fine attire and masked his emotional insult behind a proud face and eloquent words...at least around others.

He managed to get from his car, into the drugstore, without the help of his broom. A saleswoman approached him, eager to assist the distinguished gentleman with his purchase of a walking stick.

As he passed the rack of magazines near the front checkout, he stopped and leaned heavily on the brown stick to peer at one particular cover. The title of *Morning's Desire* drew his attention to the glossy teen magazine. He scanned all four faces that made up this rock group, but his eyes returned to only one.

He leaned his cane against the rack and picked up the magazine. Below the group's name, right beside the tagline: "Their Upcoming Tour," was a page number. He stared at the familiar image, but it frustrated him that he couldn't quite determine if it was Night or Morgen. From what he knew, it had to be Morgen, but his expression revealed a softness, or rather a stunnedness, that clearly screamed Night.

For just a moment, Andrew considered stashing the magazine inside his overcoat, but he laid it on the checkout counter, instead, and muttered, "My niece likes these...these..."

The woman smiled, dispelling his rare feeling of awkwardness. "I have teenagers myself—and they are both *mad* for this guy," she added, tapping the image of his bastard grandchild.

In the car, he didn't start the engine until he'd fully inspected this "special edition". He turned to page forty-two and read the lengthy article about *Morning's Desire's* upcoming tour, including the interview with the band's lead singer-guitarist.

Q: Did you expect such amazing success so soon after you were signed?

A: I didn't even know what success meant and then suddenly I was in the middle of it. I'm just so thankful...and I'm not the only one.

\*\*\*\*

Q: What is the best part of this whirlwind success you've achieved?

A: Everyone is finally happy and I feel like I've accomplished what I was always meant to do. The concerts are great, and the people I get to work with are great. I still can't believe it's real.

\*\*\*\*

Q: Your lyrics hold a lot of mystery. Everybody speculates about the meaning of your songs.

Can you explain, for instance, what *"My Other Side"* is really about? Are you referring to yourself, a friend, or perhaps a girlfriend?

A: I don't think I should tell everybody that. (laughing) When something is truly your other side, there's hardly a difference. It's all those things. You can't hide from it, or ignore it. It finds you, even if it has to visit you when you're asleep.

****

Q: What advice do you have for bands out there that dream of making it, like *Morning's Desire*?

A: No matter who you are, or what your situation is, it can happen. I mean, if it could happen to me... (Pause) You have no idea.

****

Andrew put the folded magazine on the seat next to him. Night just told him what was real—right off the page! It made him steam. After all the effort he'd expended to keep Night out of the relative handful of hearts around town, he'd somehow succeeded in making himself central in an orgy with the entire continent! Night was probably laughing at the reality of this every day as he flaunted his breath in every cardinal point on the compass. The speedometer shot up with Andrew's blood pressure, but he had to keep it together. By the end of this tedious scavenger hunt, that he vowed would lead him to Night, neither of them would be laughing.

****

While the world grew fevered at the mention of Morgen Dahlsi, Doris cooled toward "him" more with each passing day.

In the studio, she brushed past him when he tried to say hello. He regretted having to distance himself from a beautiful girl who had no qualms about showing him affection, but he didn't have a choice if he didn't want to jeopardize his own future and his brother's legacy. Morgen had, once again, supplied him with an excuse, albeit a lame one.

"We're in a group, and we're all supposed to be equal. I think that's what Aden wanted us to see since the beginning."

"That's just great, Morgen. What was I thinking?" Doris muttered while checking over the connections on her keyboard. "Who ever heard of a rock star being involved with another band member? Just say it, if you want to play the field."

244

Whatever she was suggesting sounded all right, but he did wish he could make her a part of it.

****

Their new drummer, Colby Field, had taken the band by storm and today's dinner meeting had everything to do with honoring him. Gin called on the band members, and most of their extended team, to hear out a list of Colby's ace recommendations, and to officially assign him with the task of standing next to their lead in all the formal interviews. Aden pointed out that Colby would also have to handle all the usual questions about fitting into the shadowy tracks of a leaving member.

Colby did fit in. He consistently played cleaner and harder than their former drummer, but he also dared to bring his own backup and supporting vocals into songs that Morgen had already perceived as perfect. His considerable experience might have funneled him into his lofty standing, but as Morgen called it, from afar, Colby was another musical prodigy.

A final item hit the agenda with Brandt's suggestion to throw a real white tiger into part of their show. The white tiger, the band's emblem, would be led onto the stage by their platinum-haired lead singer in select performances. Despite the extra work and red-tape, their publicist, manager, and even their lawyer, quickly got on board to make it happen.

Brandt elaborated. "This could put the band over the top, if we make this stunt into a cause, like saving endangered species, and we donate a percentage of the ticket sales to some wildlife foundation. *Morning's Desire* will be more than a rock group...these guys will be heroes."

Their publicist nodded explicitly. "It's perfect. Brilliant. We can call this their *Roaring Desire* Tour." He looked at the group's manager. "What do you think?"

Gin shrugged. "Yeah... We'd have to limit it to one, maybe two, shows—team up with a local handler in those states, make sure the animal doesn't get exposed to too much noise or travel. We don't want the animal welfare groups to end up turning this against us, right? Beyond that, it's perfect. Brilliant...like you said."

Night glanced at his watch, wondering how Morgen had managed today. He wasn't quite sure how to deal with this recent problem of Morgen expecting, and truly needing, him to be in two places all the time. He shuffled in his seat, no longer able to ignore the clamoring at his consciousness that sounded a lot like Morgen ordering him to get his ass home.

****

Tonight, the nameless intruder appeared to make it his mission to leave a more persuasive and permanent message on Morgen's garage. He whirled around at hearing Sandy's voice through the darkness.

"Hey..." barked Sandy. "Was this work contracted by the owner of the house? I'm guessing not, but I can make sure you get recognized for your work." He ignored the man's serpent-like glare as he held up some snapshots, all fanned out, in front of the trespasser.

"Can you see that...?" He pointed to a window, on the second floor, where a small square box peeped over the ledge. "It's too bad that I'm down here because I'd rather be watching this on my monitor, upstairs."

The man's jaw finally gave like a seized-up metal hinge. "I can make it worth it to you not to talk."

"I thought you could. It won't cost you much. A couple hundred dollars, every Friday, behind that gatepost over there... Mister Dahlsi won't ever have to see your image. By the way, I like what you've done here. Kind of reminds me of Morgen."

The intruder backed away, nodding, his eyes still piercing Sandy's face before he turned and ran across the property, and through the open gates.

****

Night's anxiety level climbed as he approached what he now called home. After any long day, he feared what he might find inside

246

his brother's guestroom. He sped down Morgen's driveway, but then he slammed on the brakes so everything loose inside the car showered against the dash. He left the engine running as he stumbled toward the strange, grotesque-looking object suspended on the garage door. It turned out to be the poorly de-boned rib cage of an animal—presumably just some grocery store poultry—but it was unsettling nonetheless, and it made Sean's intentions unmistakable.

The minute hand was now only a hair away from twelve o'clock—not on his wristwatch, but on the notorious clock that the messenger had boldly drawn on his garage door in red spray paint. Night pitched the corpse into the trashcan in Morgen's garage and bounded up the steps, two at a time.

He dashed to Morgen's bedside to find him, as feared, battling for air, and convulsing uncontrollably. Night leapt onto the bed, without a thought, and hoisted him upright.

"Stop it," he yelled, clutching Morgen's wet face to search for signs of awareness. Like other times, but more desperately now, he reached for some towels that he kept near the bed, pushed Morgen forward and thumped on his back until he lurched up all the fluid that tried to solidify his lungs.

"You're going to break my fucking back," Morgen managed through his violent tremors and gasps. "Where'd you put the morphine? I need it. You got it, didn't you?"

Night ignored him and drew up a syringe, using one of the many vials he'd placed in the usual drawer. Morgen had entered delirium, and with both of them now shaking, it amazed Night that the needle still found his brother's vein on the first try.

The infusion had a quick effect, allowing Morgen to relax enough to start pacing his tortured breaths. Night sat on the edge of the bed and waited for the morphine to deliver his brother into unconsciousness before he wiped his brow, paused, and then kissed his mouth.

The telephone rang and Night grabbed it in the common room before it could ring again.

"Yeah?" he said softly.

"The one and only Morgen Dahlsi, I assume?"

"Uh..." Night glanced at his watch. "Yes, it's Morgen."

"I hope you're not working yourself too hard, Morgen," said the voice...a man's voice.

"Who's—?"

"That would leave very little time for you to reflect on who you once were."

"Sean?"

"Just make sure it's not too difficult to come home when it's all over."

He was having a waking nightmare while every aspect of his being fought to deny the source.

"I'm your biggest fan," the man continued, "and I'll be watching you... 'Every move you make. Every step you take'..."

These words ended with a click. Night looked behind him as though he expected to see eyes already there. He didn't see any, but he could feel them. He shuddered before he began his mission to find Morgen's address book, which he now did with extra determination.

Sean's messily-written name jumped off the page and Night tore the whole page out. Morgen had credited him with having a photographic memory, and this might have been true, but he didn't want to take any chances when it came to shooting the right person.

Night's last chore of the day involved visiting Morgen's car, one more time. He opened the glove compartment and placed the address book entry, completed with driving directions, on top of his gun. Now, he simply had to take action, before Sean's sinister cartoon clock could strike midnight.

# Chapter Twenty-Two

Nothing induced more panic in Night than the threat of someone invading his suite. He'd just completed the new, more involved, morning routine with Morgen when he heard Frederick's assertive footsteps slowing down in the hallway. Night tore through the bathroom to meet him.

"Hi son," Frederick greeted as Night burst into the common room. "I want you to know that someone will be coming by the house, today, to refinish your garage door... I assume you've seen it."

Night nodded.

Frederick glanced at his watch as though every minute mattered, yet he took the time to perform a cursory inspection of the bar. He gave Night a distrustful smirk when he found nothing.

"Maybe you should keep your gates locked from now on," he continued. "I don't understand. Such a curious gesture, to paint a clock face on the door. It almost seems personal."

"Yes, maybe someone made a mistake." Night aimed his gaze at the south-facing window, the direction of Sean's address. "It won't happen again."

"Just lock your gates from now on."

\*\*\*\*

After Night pulled out of the driveway to meet with his latest coach, the animal trainer, Sandy looked for his first deposit of two hundred dollars around the gatepost. When he didn't find it, he figured it would show up after dark, and he headed for the beach. There, he sprawled himself on a park bench with a beer in one hand, savoring his mercenary achievements—even daring to imagine what it would feel like to take over the world.

The sun touched the horizon before Sandy put the newspaper down and abandoned his bench. The comics had blurred in front of him, all afternoon, as he kept envisioning various scandalous headlines at the top of the page.

In waning light, he strolled back to the parking lot that stretched for a mile along the beachside road and brilliant sunset. He took little notice of the silver Challenger that had parked next to him, on the driver's side—at least not until its passenger door flew open, right beside him, and knocked him onto his hands. In a flash, he was reliving the grocery store incident as the knee of a hefty assailant crashed down on his back; only, this time, no knife touched his rear to silence him, just a hand over his mouth. He heard a set of heavy heels on the concrete behind him, which signaled that a second perpetrator had just joined the party.

"So you like to play with cameras?" a male voice with a slight drawl initiated, after squatting beside his left shoulder. "You're some cocky son-of-a-bitch. But you gotta learn when it ain't so smart to show it. I can certainly get why Morgen paid to have your ass whooped. Anyway, about the camera... I guess we all have a secret. Morgen's obviously got a secret, I got a secret, and if you don't keep your secret," the man spat at his ear, "then nobody'll have a goddamn secret!"

Sean sprang up and left Sandy with the human boulder on his back. A few seconds later, Sean's Challenger started up and reversed, in a wide arc, out of its parking spot. Sean's cohort picked up his struggling victim, ripped down his jacket to trap his arms, and hauled him into Sean's trajectory.

Sandy both felt and saw lightning when the thug heaved him to the ground. The second bolt came as the car's right wheels thumped over his legs, rolling him over twice as it sped away.

If timing hadn't been on Sean's side, someone might have noticed his burly associate sprinting away from the crime scene, before catching up with the Challenger on the southbound lane. But any potential witnesses were absent at this time, still leisurely roaming the beaches.

\*\*\*\*

With Morgen's old directions on the seat beside him, Night found his way to the deserted country road where Sean lived. He slowed down to scan the property before speeding around the bend to park where the car couldn't be seen from the house.

The wildflowers dotting the landscape struck him as eerie. Tumbleweed rolled across the barren front yard of Sean's ranch-style house. It looked neglected, which whispered to Night that Sean didn't care about his home and perhaps not even about his life...an asset for both of them if it were true.

He crouched behind a crest of rock and spied on the house. His hands clenched the grip of the pistol that he rested on the surface of the ridge, and he stayed this way until the last shred of daylight faded on the horizon. It became clear that Sean wasn't home when no lights came on in the house.

As he rolled back on his heels, prepared to accept failure, headlights beamed into his face.

The Challenger pulled into the driveway—after having passed Morgen's glaring white car around the bend—so as Night saw it, he now had very little choice. He couldn't steady his aim before Sean walked into the house, but then the lights came on outside, the door creaked open, and his target stepped out again.

Night lifted the muzzle and aligned the front ramp sight with his target. Fear overflowed his crystal eyes and sweat formed on the bridge of his nose. He released the safety—quickly this time—but he recoiled as though he'd just fired the gun when a large dog charged from the house. It bounded past his owner and galloped in circles in the front yard. The pistol skipped from Night's hands and bounced off the rocky ledge, to his knees. The animal looked his way and growled, but became distracted when Sean tossed a stick.

Night swept the gun up with one hand and took aim. He adjusted his pressure on the trigger, a few times, always sure the next second would be the right one.

Sean grabbed the dog's collar and guided it toward the open doorway. Panicked, Night tensed his finger and the result shocked him like a wallop from thunder itself. Numbness swept his entire body. His hands quivered, his heart felt like the lead slug he'd just released, and it hurt to breathe, as though his lungs had petrified. Then, every one of these sensations slammed him a second time as he realized Sean had made it through the front door.

Night stood up and shot across the landscape like a bullet himself, to reach his car. He drove for some time without turning on the headlights and as the city lights emerged in the distance, he once again dreaded his homecoming...but much more than usual.

Deferring his responsibilities, he sat in the foyer and sifted through today's pile of mail—mostly from girl fans who'd managed to circumvent the fan club. He took a bit longer examining the postcards that showed him glimpses of different parts of the country, but one picture, a shot of some rugged coastline, caused a new lump to form in his throat, especially when he flipped the card over and confirmed that it had come from Oregon.

"I would do anything to meet you," the sender had written in the message space. "I bet I have more of your stuff than any other fan in the whole world! Maybe soon. Love YF"

He shuffled this postcard to the bottom of the bundle, which he carried upstairs and tossed on a chair in Morgen's common room. He had to control his paranoia. Naturally, he would also have countless fans in Oregon...

He approached Morgen cautiously and placed the thirty-eight revolver on the bed. "I went to kill Sean," he said, "...before he could do it to one of us who you know would be me. But I didn't get him, and now I made things worse. I know he saw the car."

Morgen clenched his fists over his eyes. "Fuck, Night..." he intoned above a whisper, which Night recognized took a great deal of effort. "You can't...go around *killing* people."

"Well, Sean wanted to kill you, and you killed Andrew, and he killed at least—"

"No..." Morgen groaned, which made him choke. If he had been capable, he surely would have been yelling. "You can't just kill a person—no matter what I did or anybody else did."

"I can do anything I want now."

"Oh, God...you don't even know what you've done." Morgen's hands melted flat over his face. "You shot at him... Do you think he's going to forget about that? Sean knows people—like the people who messed up Sandy's face—the kind of people that will do the same thing to you, but twenty times over. Even if you elude them until the tour, they'll still be here when you come back..."

Night felt his body numbing more with every word that managed to escape from Morgen's lips.

"This is just great, Night. How am I going to fix this?"

Night shook his head. He doubted Morgen could fix anything as he watched the skeleton hacking away in his bed.

"Maybe...maybe if I confess what's been going on," Morgen sputtered between gasps. "I'll explain that you don't understand things. Hurry... Bring the phone closer to me."

Night had abandoned the bedside. He stood at the dresser, a few feet away, and drew some morphine into a syringe with which he returned.

"Don't bother with that, right now. I told you, I have to do something and I can't be falling asleep..."

"It's a stupid idea." Night clamped his brother's closest arm against the bed and plunged the needle straight through an old puncture mark. "There's no way for you to fix it...but I can."

****

The lights were all on when Night returned to Sean's isolated house and pulled into his driveway. He slammed the car door, with all his strength, stomped up the path, and hammered on the front door when he tried the handle and found it locked.

"Open it, Sean! We need to talk!"

Sean thrust the door wide open, barreled into him, and shoved him against a post on his veranda. "I was expecting one of my guys—who I called right after you shot at my head, asshole!" Sean's dog could only bark through the mesh on the door. "Why on earth would you come back here?"

"Sean, I want you to know something. You were right every time you said 'that guy ain't Morgen.' I found out this year that I have a brother, and you should know it was my brother who tried to kill you—because you were threatening his life and everything we've worked for."

Sean looked uncertain, even a bit frantic.

"It's true. Only thing is..." Night pulled the gun from his back pocket, "*I'm* the brother."

Sean scrambled backward, but the piece fired. Night felt confused in the proximate aftermath. Sean continued to stand. His gaze aimed vacantly into Night's face...

Then, blood leached through the stonewashed denim of Sean's jacket's breast pocket. A short cough sent more blood to trickle from his mouth, and finally, he collapsed onto the wooden planks of his shallow deck.

****

He didn't expect Morgen to be conscious when he got back to the house, but through deep, precise breaths, Morgen peered upward and waited for Night to speak.

"Sean's not going to ruin anything now."

Morgen's eyes squeezed shut and his head rolled to one side.

"You said it yourself, Morgen. Sean wouldn't just forget what I did. He only came to the door because he thought I was the guy who he already called to deal with you."

"You shot him?"

"Yes, and I already got rid of the gun...like on TV."

Morgen's chin lifted and fell as his lungs jerked and a tear ran from each eye.

"Why aren't you happy?"

Morgen's whole body shuddered. "Oh, my God...!" His voice came out full-bodied, a sound he hadn't produced in over a month. "Sean used to be my friend—and yet we got to this point where he wanted to kill me. And you...you just killed a man and seem fine with it. And what can I do about any of it? Even if I could change what you just did, I can't think of anything else that would've guaranteed you'd stay safe...you, the psychopath." His voice wasted steadily back to a whisper. "And I'm not forgetting what you keep doing to me with the morphine. You just do whatever you want, with no regard for decency, you freak...psychopath."

"Stop it." Night sat down and grasped Morgen's head between his palms. "I didn't want to kill Sean, but I didn't want him to kill me either, because I still have to be here for you. And what would have happened to me if I had let you call Sean?"

Wheezing, Morgen started to nod in the way that he did when his lungs got too full to speak.

Night reached for a fresh towel, pushed Morgen forward and walloped his back in the precise way that instantly saved him from drowning. "Good thing you have this freak to keep you breathing long enough for you to see him complete all your unreasonable requests...every one of *Morning's* greedy desires."

# Chapter Twenty-Three

"Dahlsi Family Housekeeper: Victim of Hit and Run."

The article contained little substance with respect to the assault on Sandy since he refused to share anything. Consequently, it had to be inflated with Frederick's campaign statistics and facts about the band's tour. Reporters clamored for more information, both at the house and in the hospital, hoping the family might elaborate on the story.

Night tagged along with Frederick and Brigitte when the hospital informed them that Sandy was alert enough to receive visitors. The doctor informed them that Sandy's concussion had diminished already, but his broken femurs would not be better anytime soon. His legs would stay in traction for weeks and his humor, according to the doctor, had probably taken the hardest hit.

"Why don't you help them write their article?" Frederick quipped. "God only knows what they'll print if left to their own devices...and I'll take the sympathy votes." He pressed his hand on Sandy's shoulder as though acknowledging he'd made a joke in bad taste, but then he grew serious. "How could this happen to you a second time? Are you sure there isn't something you want to tell *us*, at least?"

Sandy's eyelids closed as though he'd heard nothing except for the call of his sedatives.

Brigitte gave his hand a sympathetic squeeze before she followed Frederick out of the room. Only Night lingered behind.

"You have to tell me where you put the pictures."

"Go to hell," Sandy muttered, barely opening his eyes. "And don't forget to make your payments to me while I'm in here."

"Morgen's going to die, and I never did anything to you, so why do you have to be so mean? Maybe if you were nicer these things would stop happening to you."

"Yeah...okay," Sandy grunted, rolling his head the other way.

Night's fists tightened. "I'm going to find them. And you'd better be scared if I don't!" He thumped Sandy's shoulder and then elbowed the traction pole as he ran for the hallway, slamming the door on Sandy's cries.

****

Night tried not to panic when he got the call from Gin Corbin, the following day, about another major headline: *"Morning's Desire's Ex Drummer Shot Dead"*. Gin had been tasked with getting all the band members together for a police interview, that afternoon.

Everyone sat in the room, wide-eyed, even before the investigators arrived. Doris was the first to offer more than a burst of expletives.

"I wasn't completely on board, Morgen, when you insisted we had to lose Sean. I'm sorry. I had no idea he was in that deep."

When the interview began, one officer pulled out a list of phone records that exposed all the recent calls from Sean to Morgen Dahlsi's personal number, but Night managed to stay collected. "He did call a few times, but he didn't care about the band. He just wanted to make a deal with me, to sell his stuff to the band." Morgen had supplied him with that one. "Of course, I didn't agree."

A policeman explained they would be remiss if they didn't check out every lead, especially in light of Sean's recent dismissal from a thriving band. Luckily, their investigation had already uncovered a more compelling lead and the air did not feel suspicious.

Along with Night, Gin exhaled as the interview wrapped up with the consensus that Sean's murder had everything to do with his extensive drug affiliations and his shooter would likely never be identified.

****

With Sean now crossed off from their list of worries, the key point—that Morgen was actually going to die—stabbed through every level of Night's awareness. Decisions had to be made about his brother's care before the tour whisked his sole caregiver away. Morgen insisted that a hefty dose of morphine would fix the problem, but Night refused to hear it or even grant Morgen access to his own vials, so nothing came close to being resolved.

"Beth wants to come in to see you," Night informed, one day, as he administered his brother's drug. Morgen had snubbed her ever since the tabloid incident, but now he barely had the cognizance to argue.

"Don't let her in," Morgen pleaded. "Don't do this to me or I'll haunt you for the rest of your life."

He would too, Night imagined, but he couldn't imagine life any other way. "She wants to see you. She loves you, Morgen."

A surprisingly healthy grunt escaped from Morgen's lungs and he turned his face to the wall.

"Well, don't expect me to stop her." Night started to walk out, but he suddenly remembered what he'd initially come in to do. He returned to Morgen with a handful of photographs that Brandt had taken during the making of their last video and he dropped them all on the bed. While Morgen struggled to focus on them, Night crept toward the door, turning around a couple of times along the way.

Morgen rarely got to behold his dream through some tangible means. He studied each picture until they tumbled from his unwilling fingers, and just for once, he looked blissful as he lost consciousness.

****

"You're getting a reputation," Brandt reported on a Monday afternoon, after watching Night guide a giant white tiger around a ring in a specific format. "People think you're a ghost. You appear for work, but nobody knows where you go after that."

Night replied, "I go home."

"Don't worry. Your mystery is part of your image. People create fantasies about icons like you...and when you appear, it's like they're seeing a god." Brandt started to laugh. "Imagine that...going home instead of partying with the celebrities is making you irresistible. Did it also work for you in high-school?"

It relieved him when Brandt didn't wait for an answer. Brandt's focus switched as he witnessed the trainer walk up to Night and hand him the object of his next lesson: a short range projector pistol.

The trainer's shoulders dropped. "It isn't loaded, but didn't I tell you last time never to hold it like that—no matter what?"

Night straightened his elbow and let the muzzle hang down.

"I'll tell you again. Always assume that you've got a lethal dose of Hellabrun sitting in there. The rest of us aren't tigers and I assure you if there was an accident, any one of us would end up dead from respiratory shut down before you could even utter the word antidote."

Brandt smiled and waved Night off. "Go learn your stuff, tiger."

Night glanced back and shrugged before he followed the trainer to the building's side exit, ready to assimilate yet one more arbitrary talent.

****

Beth twisted a bobby-pin around in the door handle of Morgen's common room. She didn't go straight for the guestroom, afraid that her struggling effort might provide her brother with a potentially never-ending warning to her intrusion. It did take several minutes and a few beads of sweat to gain entry into Morgen's suite, and she called his name softly as she entered from the conjoining bathroom.

Night's account of Morgen's condition had not prepared her for the remnants of skin and bone that now replaced her brother. She crept alongside the bed until she reached his shoulders.

"Morgen...open your eyes. Look at me." She waited but he didn't respond. "Night told me you still talk to him, so talk to me!"

The mangled sheet that covered most of his body continued to rise and fall and she sensed his frustration at not being able to keep all signs of life from her.

"I miss you. I didn't want to believe this—I didn't want to find out it was true. Morgen, why won't you talk to me—even now? She crashed down on the edge of the bed and leaned over his chest until it dawned on her that he could suffocate under the slightest weight.

"I love you, Morgen. I love you like a sister—only like a sister— and I'll always be exactly that to Night from now on. I'm sorry, I'm so sorry." She sniffed as she endured another silence, but she noticed his hand looked unnaturally tense. She also noticed how the bed sheets were clean, except for the damage from Morgen's constant perspiring, which boosted her respect for Night even more. "Oh, come on, Morgen. I don't know how you can be so stubborn, right to your last breath."

When he still didn't react, she touched his arm and ran from the room, wishing she had just barged into the suite, a long time ago, when he could not have gotten away with this act.

****

Beneath the afternoon sun, the front garden looked electric when Night pulled into the driveway. The breeze ruffled the glistening foliage surrounding the lawn statue that, with its blind eyes and trace grin, appeared to be concealing something today. A second glance revealed the sculpture's secret, a human companion cowering behind leaves and alabaster.

With thoughts of Sean's cronies, Night killed the engine and charged from the car, but the intruder didn't make a break for it.

Steve's dark eyes quickly scanned his face, after Night aborted his attack.

"I wanna see Morgen," Steve blurted. "He don' let me see him no more, but maybe I know why now."

Night had no defense and Steve also impressed him so much that it left him speechless. It only took this fellow an instant to see what none of Morgen's friends or family had the time, imagination, or guts to perceive in over half a year.

Steve's head tilted beseechingly. "Come on. You're not my friend, man. You're not Morgen and I know he's sick. I try to help him before but he don' listen. Look...I can still help him, but you will have to let me see him."

Night scowled. "Why were you hiding if—?"

"I was not hiding—I was jus' waiting and I jus' got scared when you come out of the car so angry. Believe me, if Morgen is sick, I can help him," Steve persisted, slightly bouncing from the knees. "I can take him to someone who can make him better."

"Nothing can make him better!"

"Look man, after I done this big favor for you guys in Oregon, you should believe I jus' wanna help. Whatever's your secret, I will keep it."

Night eyed the familiar fellow. What would he be risking if he allowed Steve to confirm what he already knew?

"I swear..." Steve hammered. "I swear, I mean it." He looked around himself before dropping to his knees. His fingers fumbled inside the collar of his top until he pulled out a gold cross on a chain that hung around his neck. Without looking up, he squeezed the cross in his fist. "I swear...I swear to God and to Jesus, to Santa Maria, and to all the saints, I mean it. I can help him...or at least, I know someone who can try."

Night gazed down at Steve, amazed by the display of devotion for his thankless brother.

"Please. I mean it. I swear."

"All right. Fine. Whatever!" It frustrated him to think how he might still be gullible, but he didn't say another word. He simply beckoned Steve to follow him through the entrance beside the recently refinished garage door.

Morgen's eyes flew open when two sets of footsteps approached his bed, and the shock catastrophically derailed his carefully paced breaths, just as Night had anticipated.

"Jesus..." Steve slurred.

Night managed to get his brother's lungs back on track with a recent trick that involved close eye-contact and a breath-mirroring technique.

Steve obviously couldn't wait to speak. "It's okay, man. I needed to talk to you before I went. I knew there was something more wrong." He glanced at his guard uneasily, but the words continued to flow. "I try to tell you before about my aunt—who I'm going to stay with for a while. I think it will help me...after what happened, you know, in Oregon. She lives in Chihuahua Mexico and she learned from the different yerberos and curanderos their art. She's a healer."

"A healer? Morgen sounded delirious. "She'd have to be God."

"No, my friend, but she can help you."

Morgen turned his face into his pillow as though it helped him to reflect on the offer. "Mexico...?"

"I can take you to her," Steve continued like he'd never missed a beat. "She lives in the mountains...and nobody will know you are there," he added intuitively. "Maybe she will make you better because I seen her do it for others."

Morgen's harsh air of rejection started to dissipate.

Still seated at the edge of the bed, Night nodded at both of them. This would solve his colossal problem of what to do with Morgen when the tour took him away. He didn't have any confidence in Steve's aunt as a healer, but at least nobody would be the wiser if his brother died in the remote mountains of Mexico.

Morgen cleared his throat to speak and Steve had to lean in to decipher his pause-riddled speech that only came out in whispers.

"It's all...shit, Steve...but...I'll go."

"What about your brother?"

"It's...all good. Just don't...tell anyone...anything...when you come back."

Steve shook his head. "Why didn' you trus' me with your secret, even when I tol' you a hundred times that I knew?" But he let it rest when Night's glare reinforced how little energy Morgen had to argue. "Can he walk? I left my car—"

"Go get your car," Night snapped. "I left the gate open."

Steve nodded and fled the suite and Night turned to Morgen. "Maybe he means it. You never know."

"Just help me...get ready."

Night helped Morgen clear his lungs, for the very last time, and this offered his speech a limited reprieve. "Pack me some clothes, and some money, and a few checks... Make them out to Steve...a couple thousand each, and put today's date. And pack all that shit you've hidden from me," he said, referring to his morphine.

Changing Morgen's position, drastically, always threatened to be fatal. Even Night held his breath when he transferred him twice, first into the bathroom, and then to the common room couch.

Morgen looked like a wet kitten as they waited in the room that had witnessed every change in both himself and his brother since the day he'd arrived. They barely resembled one another now. Morgen's stringy, poorly bleached hair fell into his gaunt face as he curled against the backrest. His eyes were glazed, likely from both the inside and outside perspective, and he wheezed incessantly as Night cozied in beside him.

"What am I going to do without you, Morgen...alone?"

"You've already been alone for months," Morgen answered in his certain whisper that sent chills through Night's body.

He sensed Morgen's desire to impart strength to him that he really couldn't spare in any capacity. "I need you here, Morgen. I wish there was no tour."

"Stop it. The tour is everything...and the last thing you need, anymore, is *me*."

"You're my other side, Morgen..." Night struggled not to say it, but then it all just poured out. "I'm never going to see you again, and I don't want it to be like before...just nightmares."

Morgen laid his head back and closed his eyes. "So much for your faith in Steve's aunt."

Night became frantic as the Steve's footsteps returned in the hallway. Morgen was leaving him, ready or not.

Steve burst through the door. His black ponytail jumped on his back as he spun around to close it. "Let's go, my friend?" he said as though they were leaving on a joyous adventure.

Ignoring the whimpers, Night scooped his longtime patient up with both arms—Morgen now weighing little more than a child. As he carried him into the hallway, he ordered Steve to follow with the luggage. He couldn't help but resent Morgen's friend, at the moment, for taking away what belonged to him.

Night unloaded Morgen into the passenger seat of Steve's Datsun and Morgen's hands peeled off his shoulders, steadily, as he faded in and out of consciousness. Night stepped back and squinted in the sunlight. This moment nearly destroyed him, but he maintained a well-trained stoicism. He didn't expect Morgen to revive when he leaned in to place sunglasses beneath his loose fingers.

"Come here..." Morgen requested as he fought to place the designer shades on his nose with one trembling hand. At last, he fixed his concealed gaze on Night. "You were handed a raw deal, no doubt, and I know it haunts you. But I've seen your two sides, and you have a choice. Don't go the wrong way. Don't even try to be just like me, but whatever you do, Night, don't become like Andrew Shannien...whatever the impulse."

Night's jaw loosened as he withdrew from the window. The car rolled out of the driveway, and though it didn't seem real, unlike his parting words, Morgen was gone.

# Chapter Twenty-Four

Sandy's stash of evidence weighed heavy on Night's mind, especially without Morgen around to focus on. He'd already found the suspicious drill hole in the wall, along with the camera system on the bookshelf in Sandy's suite, but the pictures remained hidden, as Sandy swore they would. Night never gave up, though, and as he entered Sandy's suite, for the third time in one day, an unfamiliar face startled him.

"Hello," greeted a middle-aged woman from the middle of the room. "I'm Helen, the replacement...until your regular housekeeper is able to come back. Poor thing." She seemed undaunted by Night's horrified expression. Her next line didn't help. "Your parents didn't mention you had a twin. I assume he doesn't live here?"

His mind raced. *What did she know?* Housekeepers seemed to be a lot of trouble, and now he understood why Andrew had never employed a consistent one. "Twin?"

"Well, yes. I went to sit down on the sofa," she said, pointing to the one behind her, "when I heard something crack underneath me and I soon realized the cushion was loaded with cassettes and pictures, all stuffed inside the foam."

Night exhaled with relief. "There is no twin," he professed. "He's just a friend. We were trying to see if we could make it look that way on camera for some project of his. So...you think we look the same?"

"Except that the other fellow seemed awfully thin. You will have to tell him to start eating more if you guys really want to pull it off."

"Can I get those from you?" His voice quivered. "I've been using this room since Sandy's accident, and nobody said you were coming."

Helen led him directly to the loaded sofa cushion and even got ahead of him in pulling all the evidence out through the pocket Sandy had sliced into the foam. "They're awfully dismal images. I hope your friend is just making a horror film—but who am I to offer you advice?

You're a superstar. I heard all about you before I even came here, from my sister's girls, and I'm sure they'll just worship me if I bring them a signed poster of you."

Night would have given her anything she wanted. He thanked her profusely as he beckoned her to follow him to his suite. On the way, he asked about the girls' names. From a folder beneath the bar, he dug out one of the group's new photos, one with a white tiger, and signed it with a flourish: "*Thanks, really truly, Carrie-Anne & Jenny – Morgen*".

****

Night burst into Sandy's private hospital room and flung the loaded drawstring bag at his throat. "Look inside, asshole!"

Sandy had been asleep. The sedatives in his blood delayed his reaction, so Night grabbed the bag himself and dumped the contents all over the bedcover.

Even Sandy's enfeebled voice wielded an edge. "Do you think I didn't make copies of those?"

"If there's more, you better tell me." Night caressed one of the pulleys that he knew did something to service Sandy's broken bones, but it was Night who jumped when Sandy pulled a cord and set off an alarm.

"That's right. Get out of here quick, you stupid fuck, or I'll tell them I think it was a white convertible that ran me over!"

Through sheer panic, Night scraped all the strewn evidence into the bag with no regard for Sandy's legs beneath them. He cinched the bag and still afforded himself an extra second to thump Sandy's closest leg with his fist, before colliding with a nurse on his way out.

"What's going on here?"

"Give him something for his pain," Night directed, firmly.

"Nurse..." Sandy choked. "Make it something strong."

The ache in Sandy's voice hinted at more than physical pain and Night closed the door confident he didn't have to worry about copies.

That same afternoon, Beth came home from school, prepared to break into Morgen's guestroom again, only to find the door ajar. She ran to both ends of the suite, finally bursting into tears in the middle of the empty bedroom. Night came in, moments later, and held her tightly.

"He's not dead, I promise. He's with Steve, who's going to get him some help in Mexico. He's going to be just fine."

Since Morgen could never be convinced to admit himself into a hospital, Beth accepted this move as the next best thing. Even after hearing the details, she held to the fantasy that a miracle could still happen.

"But I can't believe he wouldn't talk to me. He didn't even want to say bye."

"There wasn't time," Night explained, sounding a bit patronizing. "But he wanted to. He told me to tell you he was sorry about the other day. Yeah..." he mused while she chose to believe, "he really wanted to see you."

****

Morgen woke up as Steve began to ease his pressure on the gas pedal. Things had become tense during his last conscious spell when he witnessed Steve dumping all his medication out onto the side of the road.

*"I don' think you should have this when we cross the border, and you won' need it when we get there,"* he'd stated, nervously.

*"You're right...only because I'll probably be dead!"*

Now, as Steve veered onto a narrower mountain road, it felt like they'd broken away from earth's stratosphere and the car was drifting into outer space. The frequency of the stillness increased as they rose in altitude. The Sierra Madré Occidental screamed against civilization and had staved it off, rather successfully, to this day. For a long time, they were surrounded by nothing but dramatic crests, gorges, and greenery; unimaginable north of the border.

A village appeared, freckling a valley still far ahead of them. Only now did Morgen's eyelids stay open. The scene came into vivid focus, gradually, like a developing Polaroid image. Around them, the sharp rocky peaks were covered by a brilliant haze of green made up of thornscrub, outside the pockets of pine and Chihuahua oak. The clouds dipped in and out between these giant mossy-looking peaks and blue sky appeared to be falling like water into the ravines.

"Am I dead?" Morgen uttered, barely producing sound.

"I thought maybe, but no... We made it, my friend." Steve's voice fell on Morgen's ears warmly like the sun's rays that filtered through their rolled-up windows.

The temperature climbed as the car descended into the valley. There were tiny stone cottages and shacks strewn all over the land, and one was their destination. Morgen felt too weak to smile...but it was the perfect place to die.

The road, more of a cow path, was narrow and unpaved. Broken stone fragments bumped beneath the wheels of Steve's car and long grass grew up the middle. He brought his vehicle to rest beside his aunt's cottage, in the shadow of the mountain's backdrop. A tanned face appeared in a window that had no glass or screen, only wide-open shutters.

"*Esteban!*"

"*Hola,*" Steve answered before he reached Morgen's side and tried to drag him out.

The woman from the window rushed outside to assist her nephew.

"My friend...this is my aunt, Nita."

"*Quién es?*"

"*Es mi amigo, se llama Morgen. Está muy enfermo.*"

"*Es muy flaco!*"

"What's she saying?" Morgen peeped, feeling himself losing consciousness again.

"She says you're skinny."

Nita was not, however. Over her stout figure, she wore a bright blue skirt, with a berry pattern, and a red blouse that matched the berries. Hoop earrings dangled below her short black hair. In addition to the string of pearls around her neck, Nita had many beaded strings hanging around her home. There were countless herbs and powders suspended from hooks or in canisters she kept on open wooden shelves. Nita's dried garden, inside the house, filled the room with scents that sweetened the earthy smell from outside.

Nita helped her nephew guide Morgen into a small room at the rear of the house. The bed consisted of a narrow mattress, on a shallow wooden frame, covered with vividly dyed covers. Morgen's head came down on a small pillow that Nita quickly pulled under him. Congestion set in immediately and he could only wheeze as Steve and his aunt debated his fate.

"Can you help him?" Steve asked his aunt, in English.

"You used to bring me chinchillas," Nita remarked, "now you bring me people. ...I don't know, *Esteban*."

She pulled a crucifix from one wall and carried it back to Morgen's bedside. She hung it by its cloth hook onto a nail in the clay wall above the bed. Next, she picked up a string of beads that encircled a sprig of dry herbs and she began moving it, up and down, over Morgen's body.

Morgen could no longer keep his eyes open, but he could still hear.

"I have to find out what ails him and then I will try, but I don' know, *Esteban*. Your friend is almost dead."

****

The days before the tour saw Night floundering in a new world where he had no one to take care of and no one to answer to. He often sifted through the photographs he'd confiscated from Sandy, not sure if he would ever be able to dispose of them like he knew he should.

272

For now, he stashed them in the ceiling of Morgen's bedroom closet where he discovered a loose panel.

Eventually, the tour stepped in and saved him from having to contemplate anything further. Gin Corbin had arranged for their pickup and delivery to the airport. The entire household gathered in the foyer to see him off and Beth put herself first in line to say farewell.

"When you come back, do you think you can sneak me into your week somewhere?"

"I don't think it'll be like that, Beth," Night stated calmly, maturely. He embraced her and she gave him a quick kiss on the cheek.

Brigitte coaxed him into her arms and prefaced her short valedictory with a kiss. "Oh, Morgen, you've made it all the way to the top, even with so much thrown against you. We're so proud."

Her gaze lingered on his face, verging on a double-take.

Frederick also embraced him genuinely and then looked into his face with soft eyes. "We can get so caught up in what we want very badly... You understand?"

Night nodded. He knew this was Frederick's conditional apology, implying that they could both do a bit better in certain respects.

The aggressive honk of a stretch limousine hurried their parting and Night climbed inside. His friends had already set some iced glasses, filled with tequila and margarita mix, out on a table, ready for him to lift the first glass and inaugurate the tour.

****

By the time the pilot announced their descent into Atlanta, Night's eyelids nearly met in the middle—a combination of the long flight and Brandt's endless lecturing about his conduct on the tour. In return, Night accepted everything that was offered to him during their flight: every drink, every refill, every treat, and of course, every first-class meal.

Deliverance came in the peace of his hotel suite, except for the self-inflicted nausea. He had to overcome it by the evening, for their first performance at a small venue that their agents referred to as warm-up, as opposed to a publicity stunt. The size of the nightclub crowd impressed Night, so when he walked into the Omni Coliseum, the next evening, the reality of his new status finally set in. Sixteen thousand seemed like a big enough number in words, but he hadn't quite imagined what it would look like in seats, or sound like in the form of human voices.

The opening band, that Night privately envied for having more of a metal sound, met him backstage, and each member shook his hand briskly.

"Hey, Morgen," Gin called out abruptly, "we've got a couple of backstage passes coming up here in a minute. Don't take too long with them. You guys got less than ten minutes." He took off, probably to find Doris, who had a habit of meeting her fans off stage.

The three girls and one guy immediately flocked around Aden and Colby, but when Night stepped out from the sidelines, the same girls nearly barreled him over. One girl, who could easily have passed as Daphne, latched her arms around his neck, crying, but she was ousted by another who came at him with a permanent marker, begging him to sign his name above her left breast as she exposed most of it. He did this while the other band members signed various paraphernalia and body parts as well.

Security soon hustled the backstage visitors to the stairs and someone yelled: "Five minutes!" Night felt perspiration break across his face and, for a moment, he feared for Brandt's make-up job: liquid and powder foundation, black eyeliner—with the smoky effect—frosty-white eye shadow and mascara—all of it in jeopardy! Brandt fussed over him for a minute with tinted lip gloss and, at last, he was "Good to go."

When he walked into the spotlight and seized the microphone, the cheering made his eyes well up with Morgen's tears. Every muscle in his arm showed as he fingered the frets of his guitar beneath the lights that obliterated his view of the audience. The small chains and

274

buttons on his tattered costume caught the light so, each time he adjusted his hold on the guitar, the cheering surged like he was, in fact, doing something spectacular. He couldn't wait to bring the tiger out in the second half of the show, with himself dressed in black vinyl that reflected electric tiger stripes in the intermittent black stage lighting.

As Night popped backstage for some water, his manager cut in front of him and yelled in his face: "You're everybody's fantasy! And most importantly, you're the record company's fantasy! When you scream like that, out there, you bring out the devil in those girls! They want to ravage the tiger, save the tiger, tame the tiger! Each and every one of them just wants to fuck you! And those guys out there are all dreaming they can have that kind of power—not to mention there's a whole crew of them out there who just want to fuck you too!"

Through his smile, he lit up from top to bottom. It tickled him to hear that everyone thought he possessed all this power. All he wanted to do, suddenly, was rush to the front of the stage and bathe in a vainglorious shower of it.

One of his little trademarks, at any venue, was to play a classical excerpt between songs. Doris came to expect the intrusion on her keyboard, as much as his fans anticipated it, and every time he did it, the crowd went berserk. It amused him to be overtly stealing from the meager bag of tricks that Andrew had granted him, and now to flaunt these tricks in front of a global audience.

****

Andrew tried again to cross his living room without the aid of his cane. He growled when, as usual, a snap of pain caused him to collapse before he even reached the corridor. His plans would have to wait a bit longer.

From the armchair, he snatched up his cane before hobbling over to his den where he'd posted a calendar. In March, he'd crossed off the days that would not see his fulfillment. Atlanta, Jacksonville, Seattle... He had the whole tour schedule, including inane trivia, and rare behind-the-scenes photos. It paid to be a member of the fan club.

275

Night could pour his lungs out for now, but he was quickly running out of those blissful hours. So nobody could ever link him to the call, Andrew drove to a payphone, in town, and had an operator connect him to the hotel currently hosting *Morning's Desire,* in Atlanta. He held the magazine in front of him to read off their manager's name, unwilling to honor the idiot by remembering it.

"Yeah, I have a message for Gin Corbin, if you can put me through... I'm calling from," he cleared his throat, "...*Detonic Records.*"

****

When all their PR duties were completed, after the concert, Doris squeezed Night's arm. "We did our first stadium tonight, Morgen. You must feel different...actualized. I've been listening to you talk about this day for years. Don't you think we should celebrate, together, even if you still think it's wrong?"

He saw her point and considered the offer as they stepped into the hotel lobby.

"Your place or mine," Doris said with a triumphant grin, but she stopped and let go of Night when Gin pushed through the security to reach him.

"Before you go off to get wasted, Morgen, I just picked up a strange message from the front desk. Someone claiming to be from the record company said it was imperative for Morgen Dahlsi to know there might be consequences for assuming 'your other side.' Any idea what that would be about? Have you had any threats from a nut-job before?"

Night gawked at him and backed right into Doris. "No..."

"You didn't rip off someone's song or anything, did you?"

"*My Other Side*...? No, that's all mine." Regardless, the caller's message would replay in his head for the rest of the night. "I'll see you tomorrow," he said to Doris before picking up his pace. He barely noticed his private security staff clearing his path to the elevator.

Between the Daphne lookalike he saw today and a message that struck him as one from beyond the grave, he had little consideration left for what should have mattered to him tonight: the world that was finally his...the world of a living, breathing star.

# Chapter Twenty-Five

Their short time in Jacksonville passed without incident, in the way of creepy messages from mysterious callers. No matter how Night tried to rationalize every freakish call to date, he couldn't dismiss his instinct. Did Morgen truly know the outcome of his visit to Oregon? Would it matter if Andrew wasn't dead? Night had already determined that he would gladly bleed for the opportunity to throw his success in Andrew's living face, but not knowing if he had survived gave Andrew the upper hand, once again...even perhaps in death.

Night sat pensively in his chair while Brandt retraced the charcoal liner around his eyes with a smudge brush, but then a thought escaped.

"Why would someone try to stop another person from being happy?"

Brandt flinched. "Maybe if someone is acting on justifiable revenge... Why, what's going on, Morgen?"

"No. Not revenge. What if the person really didn't deserve what someone did?"

"Then, I would say it's this certain someone you're talking about who's probably a bit messed up."

"Right...so why would a person still care about someone like that?"

Brandt grinned. "This someone must be pretty significant, and can't be all bad, or this person wouldn't care so much, would he?"

"I'm not sure," Night debated, still remarkably on track. "If someone thinks they're giving a person everything, but lies and hurts people to make sure they get what they want...is that all right?"

"What exactly are we talking about here? It's not all right—"

"But if someone actually believes they did everything to help the other person and made sure that nothing ever took that person away...it must mean that they really loved the person?"

"I don't know. Maybe in some twisted way." Brandt scowled. "But it sounds like someone has some serious—"

"So why do people hurt other people if they love them?" Night stared straight up into a handful of brushes.

"Well, not all people *do*. I guess some people just have a lot of issues and by the time their love filters through, it just comes out all warped. They become incapable of real love. Why are you asking me these things, Morgen?"

Inside his own head, Night fiercely confronted the scenes of his past. "Why would a person be so stupid as to go through so many years without realizing what you just said about someone's love?"

Brandt shrugged in exhaustion. "I suppose that after such a long time, the person would no longer know what love is."

"So you think that's it...that the person doesn't really know what love is?"

"Sounds like it, Morgen."

"Well, how can a person know if it's real?"

"It's not hard to know love when it's real." Brandt leaned over and lightly placed a kiss on Night's temple, and then he walked away.

****

On a cool, drizzly Sunday in April, Beth paid Sandy a personal visit in the hospital.

Sandy rolled his head toward her, barely taking his eyes off the small television monitor on the window side of his bed.

"My mom told me your legs are healing pretty good."

"Yeah," he grunted.

"Morgen called me from his hotel this weekend and we were talking about you."

Sandy refused to turn his eyes away from the TV. "Don't you mean Night?"

"No, he called this morning," she replied, tossing her head back in a mock laugh, but he seemed oblivious.

"What I'm saying is, don't you mean Night called this morning?" He rattled his head. "Is the other little fuck finally dead so Night can be Morgen permanently now?"

Beth's eyes narrowed at Sandy. "What are they giving you in here? I don't know what you're talking about. I just came to find out if you're planning to work for us again because me and my brother don't think it would be such a good idea after what you did, spying on him to make some money, like a big creep."

The features of Sandy's face screwed together. He appeared to be pondering the proportion of her naivety to her intelligence.

"Well, anyway," Beth continued, "don't think of coming back, or next time *you'll* end up the front page scandal of the day—not my brother. We have all the proof we need, which includes the hole you drilled into Morgen's room. Don't forget, my whole family is very popular right now." Heading for the door, she added, "So call and let me know what you decide...you little fuck."

****

Aden peered through the clouds from the airplane window when he nudged Night. "We still got something to aim for, and I'd like to know why we haven't heard it from you."

"What do you mean?"

"Next time," he declared, "I want Madison Square Garden. Do you see that name on our itinerary?"

"I don't understand. Didn't we make it?"

"Dahlsi, whatever happened to your crazy-psycho ambition? What happened to our leader since we got our record deal?"

Night searched his intuitive mind for any faint signal from their leader, but unlike the old days, Morgen chose to remain aloof. Night tried to draw a clue from his last dream that left him with the sense that Morgen had undergone some kind of change and was somehow at peace. Logically, this implied that Morgen had passed on, but something kept him from grieving just yet.

****

Halfway through their week in New York State, following another public interview, a nightclub near their hotel became the scene of yet another memorable bash. They would be admitting only the first two-hundred and fifty fans who showed their *Morning's Desire* concert ticket stubs, as well as a few privileged guests who uttered passwords given to them by the band members themselves. Night had given these special keys to five girls whose friends would not be denied entry.

"Hey..." Gin called when Night walked into the private back lounge with Colby. "If it isn't the man who spurns parties and covets the medal for the world's most mysterious rock star."

*Not on this occasion*, Night thought, accepting a drink from a server with one hand and a spliff *en route* from Aden with the other. He tried to mimic his friend but didn't inhale properly, therefore wasting his turn.

A man came into the room, delivered a message to Gin, and walked out again.

"Hey, Morgen...your password-babes are being checked in at the front."

Night abandoned his razzing companions in the private party room to submerge himself in the chaotic atmosphere of the main hall. His vision clouded amidst the various forms of smoke and dry ice oozing from somewhere. Fans decked out in new-wave style danced past him and, in light of his choreography lessons, he was able to show up every move as he crossed the room on his way to the front.

He typically felt the alcohol in his blood more than anyone else and, already, the world seemed ten times friendlier, and another ten times freer. He kissed the dark girl, and then the fair one who he'd met behind the stage—the one who reminded him of Daphne. She

282

began combing her hands up his chest while her friend grazed his neck from behind. He didn't even care that his T-shirt was rising precariously high over his back... after all, it was dark, and the tireless flashing of colored lights made it challenging to see any details.

Doris walked over, at the edge of her own group, and paused beside him. She flung her hair and walked past him and his followers. He noticed Doris and Brandt exchanging a concurring sneer before continuing on their separate ways.

Night could tell that almost everybody in the place was deeply intoxicated by something or other. Having consumed hardly anything himself, he wondered about his excuse as his inhibitions drifted off like the puffs of mist around the room.

"Do you like it?" asked a redheaded girl when she noticed him staring at the trim on her corset-bra.

He was held speechless by the memory of Daphne's pink ensemble from that night on the bridge. His lips went straight for her cleavage, then traveled up to her mouth, and back down again, deep inside the boned cups of her bra.

"What's your fantasy?" asked the young woman. "Whatever you want..." All of her bracelets tumbled to her wrists as she guided his hands from her chest to her hips and then behind them where she pressed his palms to the bare skin beneath her miniskirt.

His left hand circled to find the slightest strip of lace along her hipline and running through her fold. He pictured his fantasy, Daphne, as he closed his eyes and clutched her to himself, but he allowed somebody else to oust her.

This new girl brought a fancy drink to his lips before replacing the glass with her mouth. This continued until she wore out every trace of her lipstick and they could taste nothing but each other's chemistry. He felt the envy of others through their greedy hands on his back, arms—and someone even dared to sweep his groin.

But in the end, all this fervor gave way to a surprising truce. They all moved to the back room and, for a full hour, he just chatted with his intimate audience and answered their many questions as he

283

upped the ratio of alcohol to blood in his system. It stunned him when he reflected on his own learning curve and remembered the inane questions he used to ask Morgen about the industry. Someone in the group wanted to know if he would play a song, just for them, and Night had to do little more than look up and point to get started. A crewmember closed the door to the back room and another brought him a guitar.

Slurring somewhat as he added the words, he played acoustically, creating whole new renditions of Morgen's mellower songs. His solos generated a resurgence of lust making it difficult to play with arms groping him from all sides, mouths nuzzling his studded earlobes, and faces with pleading eyes appearing around his knees.

Akin to Daphne's shoe falling off the bridge, an alarm suddenly blasted through the building. Most of his followers sprang up and looked to him before an explanation came from the far side of the door.

*"Fire!"*

A crewmember hustled people out through the back entrance while the scene in the main hall turned into pandemonium. The music stopped and, through the backroom door, Night could hear guests screaming and personnel shouting, trying to establish order.

"Who set it?" Night demanded when Colby came alongside him and pushed him toward the back exit.

"Nobody *set it*, dummy. Something just went wrong with the light show."

The main street looked like a concert ground. Night sprinted toward the throng, out of range of some scolding shouts warning him to stay put. Two fire trucks soared past him and stopped close to the main doors that now spewed boundless amounts of black smoke, along with the venue's guests. He scanned the crowd before getting mobbed by fans, but adrenaline made it possible to escape, to tear away from everyone, and slip back into the private lounge at the back of the failing building.

Images from the last minutes of the *Emerald Shore* raced through his mind and merged with his present perception that at least half the band and crew had not made it out. He couldn't imagine why more people hadn't come through the back room to flee the building—until he opened the inner door and got bowled over by smoke, heat, and fire.

Meanwhile, people still pushed through the front doors. With the fire now infesting the backroom, he stumbled into the main hall, already nauseous and virtually blind. Someone grabbed him from behind—someone in full fire-protective gear who pulled him into the back room before resealing the inner door and the back exit.

Fire and EMT personnel escorted him into an ambulance where he instantly received oxygen, interspersed with puffs of medication from inhalers while his manager insisted they do everything in their power to allow the show to go on at their next venue. Gin calmed down when one of the EMTs deemed his smoke inhalation to be "mild to moderate" and only recommended some blood work and a thorough follow-up assessment.

Night still threatened to bolt as Gin and a flock of security transferred him to the limousine. "But what about the others...?"

"They're fine," Gin barked, scrambling in beside Night, after shoving him into a vehicle that already seated the other band members.

****

Andrew stoked the flames in his fireplace, then sat down to read the entertainment section of the newspaper—the column about the *Morning's Desire* tour. The interview clips at the end of these stories were always the best.

****

*Q: Morgen, is there a particular kind of girl that really draws your eye?*

*A: Well...I'm not sure. But if they're especially nice and really fun...long hair...blond—but red's good too—and freckles...I like that. That's really special."*

****

Andrew reflected on Night's reply. There was little mistaking the childish descriptiveness of his answer. It begged for a simpler truth: One that looks like Daphne: a homely, cheap, shameless slut.

The column also confirmed that Boston came next on the band's itinerary. "Night...how did you ever manage this?" Andrew muttered at the flames.

He absently closed the newspaper, then glanced down doing a double-take. The headline took another second to digest. A massive nightclub fire involving *Morning's Desire*...? He grimaced as he grinned. "Don't tell me... Did you burn down another building?" he asked as though Night was right there.

But the article disclosed the truth about the club's overzealous pyrotechnics. He lowered the paper as his mind went on a tangent. He'd had a few radical ideas, but he'd never thought of "smoking the band out" of a venue. The wasted opportunity pained him.

In another week, he would be ready to throw away his cane and make the shorter trip to Chicago. He still had to commit to one believable disguise before pursuing the great imposter...this magician he'd somehow cultivated.

Studying Night's magazine photo again, he allowed himself one more shot of cognac over which to reflect. At one time, it had sufficed to stifle Night's voice behind a lie, but now it would have to be choked out and buried, or else every *Morning's Desire* song would be an ode to his failure.

# Chapter Twenty-Six

With fingers pressed against his aching throat, Night squinted against the fluorescent lights that surrounded his hotel bathroom mirror. His residual eye makeup and crunchy hair confirmed what he so often needed to verify: that his new life was real, and he had some extra proof this morning. He felt queasy from the anti-cyanide-poisoning medication he'd received at the clinic, and somewhere between last night's energetic concert and the smoke inhalation, he'd blown out his voice.

A knock on the door pulled him away from the mirror to confront another familiar face.

"How's your voice this morning?"

"Fine," Night rasped, dressed in a hotel bathrobe.

"Glad to *almost* hear that." Brandt lifted the steaming cup in his hand a little higher. "Here. I brought you some herbal tea. Believe it or not, this really helps."

Night took it to a table and sat down. He anticipated a comment, from Brandt, on last night's disaster.

"Hey, the fire actually gave our tour another boost. They're calling you a hero for going back in to check on your band mates and fans. I don't know what you were thinking, but we're lucky nothing happened to you, or anybody else. Now, go get ready. You're a bloody mess. We have plans for today, and I want to get out of here before anyone tries to change them. Pack what you need for a sleepover."

Night took another sip and tested his voice. "I need a break, so it better not involve a gig."

"Hell, no, I have friends near Boston. Tonight we're guests at a home that will impress even you, Morgen Dahlsi."

Brandt left a message with the front desk before he escorted Night to a rental car. Heading toward Plymouth, Brandt drove from ramp to ramp, switching Massachusetts' highways as though he'd come back to his hometown.

"These are all nature reserves," he pointed out. "When was the last time you saw so much green?"

Night had already noticed the green, the pines—the cool, briny morning air that made him expect to see his old driveway at any moment. "I don't remember."

"Then take it all in. It can't all be stadiums and bright lights. Today, you get to ground yourself."

Brandt stopped the car near a dilapidated boardwalk. "Follow me... There is one thing that should be part of any cross-country tour." He slammed the car door, then hurdled over some rocks to reach the ocean. He squatted at the water's edge and peered over his shoulder. "Come here, Morgen, and shake hands with the Atlantic Ocean."

Night mimicked him, watching his hand beneath the surface as sheets of cloudy water swilled forward and ebbed. With the tide also came a thought—how so many people had died in the past year as he evolved. Had he unwittingly bargained for knowledge in exchange for the lives of everyone he knew, and did it matter if he didn't regret any of it?

"Who are you?" Brandt demanded, shattering Night's reverie. "I would do anything to find out. Sometimes you're like a child, still learning about the world. Yet you're a genius in your own right, and also private and mature...when you're not obligated to put on a show." He rose and climbed onto the boardwalk, only a few feet away.

Night joined him at the railing and leaned on one hand in the identical fashion. Several moments passed before he responded. "There are things that nobody in the world can know," he stated, still guarding his voice, "...but I would tell you."

"Oh?"

Night continued evenly. "You've taught me so much. You care about what I do, but not like some people—in a good way, like you really care."

Brandt's face brightened with amusement as he watched Night chase after every elusive word. "I do, Morgen. So, what's this secret you keep alluding to?"

"It's just that...I want to tell you something...that I'm...I'm really..." He scratched his head.

Brandt's simper broke into a laugh. "Please, Morgen. You're putting me through a slow death, here."

Night recognized the pain that ripped through his hip for what it probably was: a warning from Morgen. Dead or alive, he was telling him to stop right there.

"I'm really just glad I met you."

Brandt's posture collapsed. "Pretty loaded intro if that's all you meant to say, you liar. But I'll get it out of you yet. Let's go."

After a day of tourist attractions, Brandt's travel route had boomeranged from Boston to Plymouth, then along the Blue Hills to Milton. Brandt found his friend's sprawling residence effortlessly, and the pale stone house, with its impressive gardens, did not betray his earlier account of its grandeur.

They sat down for a late dinner with Brandt's friend Keith and his new wife, Jacqueline. They were served like patrons in a restaurant. Night also noticed the enormous house had several staff to support it—undoubtedly all better qualified than Sandy.

"So how's the Boston theater industry?" Brandt asked, changing the subject from their past association through the Hollywood scene.

"Not as good as the New York modeling game," Keith replied, winking at Jacqueline.

"I'll bet," Brandt mused, his words leaving behind a hint of frost that Night could easily detect, sitting right beside him. "I'm sure your wife could raise the standards in both."

Jacqueline grinned his way, but her eyes bounced back to the rock star. "I just bought your record. It's really good. Amazing. And your lyrics are very clever."

"I had a lot of help," Night confessed.

"You're too modest."

There was little mistaking anymore when a person really wanted him, but these opportunities had become strangely meaningless, somewhere down the line. The people that wanted him included almost everybody—a conquest he decided he would have exchanged in an instant for an encounter with just one person who he actually wanted in return.

Shortly after dinner, Jacqueline slid back her chair. "Please, excuse me, but I have to get ready for this evening."

Brandt nodded as Keith explained.

"It could be another big contract for Jacqueline. You understand. We both regret that the tour couldn't part with you a day earlier, or later, but that's how it goes. So, make yourselves at home...Brandt, my friend. You know the place. And when you're ready, just ask one of the staff to prepare your rooms or room, or whatever."

"Yeah, great. Thanks."

****

Brandt watched Night walk away as one of the servants led him to the nearest washroom.

"He's intriguing," Keith remarked. "Maybe after the tour is finished he would be interested in trying some local alternative theater for a change. Or maybe both of you can come back here for a visit and the four of us can just entertain each other."

Brandt hesitated. "I don't think so and no."

Keith shook his head. "That's always been your problem, Brandt...everything belongs to you."

Brandt's manner grew testy. "I prefer it to your philosophy that everything belongs to everybody."

290

"Well, that's a shame." Keith grinned lightly and stood up. "Enjoy your evening, Brandt."

****

The evening was one to enjoy. The outside temperature had dropped, but the ground surrendered the heat it had absorbed during the day. This created a sub-tropical evening in the grand garden of dark foliage and flowering hibiscus trees.

On the banks of a manmade stream, both of them paused to admire one of the many imported sculptures. A number of birdbaths and fountains also asked to be spotted, between the shrubs and lanterns, but Brandt didn't notice them in the presence of the human sculpture right next to him.

From the textured iridescence that bordered Night's youthful face to the faultless lines of his body, Brandt could no longer resist satisfying his fantasy inside this Garden of Eden. He turned and placed his hand on the open collar of Night's shirt and caressed the seam.

"I'd like to actually see what I see in my head... May I?" Brandt asked, releasing the next button over Night's chest. "Can I undress you?"

"You don't usually ask."

"We're not working."

Night straightened his shoulders and gazed into the distance, like a mannequin ready to be made over. The cotton shirt landed around Night's hikers, along with Brandt, who dropped to one knee to loosen the laces. Brandt sensed no resistance from his human artwork that waited, with soles bare against the tepid flagstones, for the rest of his clothing to be peeled away in ritualistic measure.

The moonlight reflected off every waxy leaf around them, the celestial glow painting Night's skin a homogeneous stony gray and his loose hair a complimentary mineral white.

"You look like you were stolen from Versailles," Brandt offered gently, "...a monument that has come to life. Let me see. Step back a little. Tilt your hip into those vines a bit more... Even more. Now, look over this way. Put that arm slightly behind you. Perfect."

A mild snicker shook Night's silhouette, and Brandt felt a hunger pang surge through his gut as he feasted on the sculpture he'd created.

"Ah..." Brandt sighed, feigning a stumble. "He stands before me with the radiance of Apollo, the dilemma of Narcissus and the burden of Atlas. Tell me," Brandt implored, "what is it exactly that weighs upon your shoulders? ...You still haven't told me."

Night released his pose and flashed a coy grin. "You wouldn't believe me."

"I'd believe anything from you. What wouldn't I believe?"

"That I'm not who everyone thinks."

"Yeah, now tell me something I don't know."

****

Night had eluded temptation, for the second time in one day, through Brandt's misunderstanding, but he so wanted to pour his story out to him. He bowed his head in shame to Morgen, although it was Brandt in front of him, picking up his chin.

"You live in your own secret world." Brandt felt his face with one hand. "Where is it?" The blaze of scarlet hair over Brandt's head gave the illusion of being connected to the explosiveness behind his pupils. "I want to go there, Morgen. Tell me about that place."

Brandt deserved to know the truth...his best friend who had welcomed him into the real world more genuinely than anyone from his old life, new life, or even his dream world. Night allowed their lips to join and he started to kiss Brandt in just the way he was first taught by Daphne, but he stopped, abruptly.

"Do you mind?" Night asked on the fuel of that thought. "Can we go up there?" He gestured at a low bridge that arched over a manmade stream.

"After you..."

292

****

On the summit of the stone bridge, Brandt's exquisite, unreal monument raised its arms, in slow motion, then locked them behind the shoulders of the mortal caught in its sight.

But Night's mortality was revealed through the pulsing Brandt felt as his mouth traveled up his neck. He nuzzled the diamond-studded ear before he bit into the silvery-white wisps behind it and ran them through his lips.

Brandt ripped open the first few buttons on his own shirt, then waited for Night to completely remove it before he resumed his exploration of almost superhuman perfection. He clutched Night's platinum head against himself and peeked over his shoulder. He found the marks on the star's back were nearly washed away by the grace of the moon.

"What kind of idiot... You actually wanted this?"

"*No,*" Night snapped.

"Then how could you let somebody do that to you?"

"I didn't. I was kind of asleep."

"Oh, that's right, because you were drugged out of your skull in bad company?" Brandt's chin swayed against his hair. "What you did was plain stupid. I could just spank you—for real!" Brandt brought back his hand, only to have his friend turn his chest into a springboard.

"Relax, Morgen. Help me out a little. You like this sort of thing?" he asserted a little more than questioned. He pressed down on Night's arms until the body attached to them sank to its knees. "Would you like me to take control?"

Night's face tilted up. "Yes."

Brandt kneeled as well and leaned forward, wordlessly persuading his submissive to lay back. He guided Night's wrists between two sets of teardrop-shaped bridge rails while he searched out Night's tongue with his own. Yet, the moment he found it he withdrew to say something else.

"Don't move?" Night guessed.

Brandt didn't realize how often he must have said this in the dressing room. "Well..." he returned in a mock huff, "not until I say it's okay." Straddling Night's hips, he sat up to slip the thin leather belt from his own waist.

Through anticipation, his subject gripped the backs of the rails with the intensity of his stare as Brandt leaned down and threaded the end of his belt through the buckle and pulled it tight around one of Night's wrists. Two rails over, he trapped the other one in a simple overhand knot and fastened the remaining length to the rail. "How's that?"

Night chortled. "How should it be? Why am I letting you do this?"

Brandt, briefly, placed one finger over Night's lips. "I'm serving you, aren't I? I'm pleasing you, am I not? You already know you like it."

"Then I don't understand myself."

"I understand you, Morgen." Brandt picked up his strewn plaid shirt and ripped a strip off along the base. "You hold many burdens inside you, and every so often you want to surrender them, even if just for a short time." He snapped the material taut to tease him again.

"What are you going to do with that?"

"That depends. I suggest you shut up now and just respond where appropriate." Then he leaned in to wrap the cloth around Night's eyes.

"Right now you can forget everything. You don't have to concentrate on anything except for what you want to see in your own mind. You don't have to think about the things you haven't done, or should be doing, not even how you could be pleasing me...not when you simply...can't. Sometimes we need a little help to achieve this for

294

ourselves." He brushed his hands up Night's forearms and clasped both of his hands inside of his own.

"You get to shut out all your responsibilities, without any guilt, without any choice." He opened his fingers against one of Night's palms and silently admired the smaller hand span of his young superstar lover. He sent his other hand to the back of Night's thigh. "In these moments, the whole world can turn without you because you've left it. Nobody expects anything from you at all, and that is a rare ecstasy...isn't it?"

"Yes. It's like being back..."

"In time?" Brandt supplied. He skimmed Night's throat with his lower lip, until he reached his mouth, and then he sat up. "There doesn't have to be any pain, except for the wonderful agony of feeling yourself stripped of all responsibility."

Night's face revealed acquiescence, despite his words. "And control?"

"Semantics, Morgen. You're simply allowing someone else to drive, to choose for you, think for you, work for you—do your bidding without you even having to ask."

****

His head weighed heavily in Brandt's hand, but he still nodded. It was the past. It was a taste of his old life in the *emerald shore*line, but without any of the misery.

Every second brought with it another surprise and fresh expectations. Brandt's massaging expertise turned every journey, over any part of his body, into erotic bliss. Brandt used several elements to create pleasure. His fingers plied the muscles in his thighs and rear while his lips, tongue, and even his teased hair played a part in arousing what nobody was ever supposed to see...according to someone he didn't care to remember right now. But as Brandt kept pointing out, he had no choice. It would not only be seen; it would be grasped, caressed, and tasted.

His heartbeat became amplified all around him, pounding almost in stereo with Brandt's. His whole body coursed with electricity when his friend's tongue delivered a barrage of tormenting little sweeps to his fully alert private part. His own hands longed to jump down there too. The fact that they couldn't, snatched the air from his lungs and intensified the pleasurable prickling that traveled from his scalp to all the way down his legs.

He felt some aversion when Brandt's finger went into his mouth, but he soon realized that the more he hated it, the more he liked it. The finger left his mouth anyway as the hand attached to it dove between his legs and made him jolt.

Night pressed against the weathered marble as Brandt made him sweat, his fingertip casting a numbing effect on its mark. Night stirred his hips to either displace it or invite it in deeper inside. His chest began blazing at the sensation of hot breath, and a rough chin between his pelvis, and the anticipation of action on both top and bottom. He bucked again as Brandt's finger finally attempted to go deeper, raising him from the inside.

"Morgen, you're either extremely resilient or you have uncharted territory here."

"I don't know what you're saying, Brandt. Just show me everything."

Brandt chuckled. "I'm not one to show you *everything*, but it's nice that you're signing up for a few more nights."

That was all he said, and then his mouth touched down to mercifully complete the hardening that had threatened to reverse itself. Night gasped and then cried out as Brandt drew against him and entered him, both at the same time. Brandt started to grant deeper access to his throat, which overrode any pain he felt as Brandt curled his finger inside him. Then, all at once, Brandt withdrew. He unfastened one wrist and then directed him to turn over, but Night stopped halfway and pulled his other wrist free before tearing off his blindfold.

"I want to try without," Night declared, flushed and dizzy. He reached out for an embrace, but Brandt lowered Night's arms and, with a melancholy stare, pressed him down to where he wanted him right now.

"You're exactly what I contemplated..."

****

Brandt didn't finish his thought out loud, but the fact was he knew the divines of legend and they were selfish and fickle in their ways. And likely by daytime tomorrow, this particular one would return to being a stone sculpture in his presence, only to thaw into flesh for some new gods or goddesses.

# Chapter Twenty-Seven

Night's identity went on trial within an hour of his return to the hotel.

"Something's happened to you. You're not my Morgen," Doris charged and convicted. "I used to know you. I used to know exactly what you wanted, and now...that's anybody's guess."

"What do you mean? I thought I was doing a great job."

"A great job? *That's* what I mean! That barely even makes sense. So, what is it exactly, huh? Head injury? Lobotomy? Body snatchers? Or are you really Morgen's twin? At least, that would make some sense!"

Night turned his face away. Everybody suspected it. They just didn't dare believe it.

Doris sighed; her whole body sighed. "And what happened this weekend? You split from the group to sneak away with Brandt—who we both know didn't take you out for a good time with the women of Boston."

"So, what? I can do whatever I want."

"Morgen, when did what we want and what you want become two different things? Just help me understand what's happened. You used to want *me*."

Night did regret having to insult his brother's uncanny loyalty to Doris, but it came down to one point: Andrew had largely achieved his goal by marking him. One intimate encounter with Doris could end the performance of his lifetime. He'd thought about telling her the truth, but he felt he owed it to Morgen to wait, at least until after the tour. "I guess I've changed."

Night could see the lava churning behind Doris's glare and he knew they were heading toward an inevitable blast.

"How, Morgen? What the hell could have changed in a matter of months—pardon me—other than you becoming a switch-hitter?"

"A what?"

"Oh, come on! You fuck around with Brandt for two days and a night, yet you have no problem offering yourself to every scavenging slut—"

There was a bump and a crash as Doris's head hit the wall, causing a framed picture to fracture on the baseboard. Night glanced down at his hand that now stung as much as Doris's words. For several racing heartbeats, they just stared at one another.

When Doris finally recovered, both her balance and her breath, she made a decree. "Sean was right. You're not Morgen Dahlsi...not in heart, not in soul... And as much as I wanted to change him at times..." her eyes and voice welled up so she could barely finish, "now, all I want is to have him back."

****

The atmosphere was similar in the dressing room, before the band's second Chicago performance.

Aden leaned forward in his chair, to see around Brandt, and he pointed at Night. "What happened at the hotel was shit! We're in a fucking band, not a goddamn soap opera, so can the drama before we lose everything we've worked for."

Night pushed Brandt's arm out of his face. "You don't really know what happened."

"Whatever, Dahlsi, but this is why I didn't want a chick in the band. She's good, so I got over it, but since she was *your* choice, you better figure out how to fix everything—and fast!"

Aden appeared to be finished, so Brandt decided to offer his two cents. "What I don't understand is, where's the anger coming from? You really behaved like an asshole and I never took you for a guy who had such a lack of respect for females."

"Why would you say that?"

Aden piped up again. "Because you slugged Doris into a wall—for saying the same thing that Sean and I have been saying for months."

"No..." Night rattled his head. "You guys never said it like she did—that all the girls I like are sluts."

Aden looked over and Brandt stifled a laugh. "You're a conundrum, Morgen. Now, it almost sounds like you were sticking up for women. Commendable...but you might have given Doris the wrong impression when you smacked her. Don't you think?"

"I wasn't even thinking, just reacting."

"Like Aden said, just 'fix it,' rock star, and fix it fast.

**** 

Andrew tried to recall the circumstances surrounding his last trip by air as he boarded the plane. It had been well over thirty years ago when Brigitte insisted they fly to one of the sunny destinations she so preferred over Oregon—the dismal place she'd committed herself to by marrying him.

Her excuses for leaving were plenty, he recalled: the weather, the miles from her family, his devotion to his dead wife, and finally, the strain caused by Reade's suicide. He leaned back in his soft leather seat and tried to imagine the excuses she'd invent when she realized that, for almost a year, she'd been unable to distinguish Night from the poisonous snake she'd originally imported from *that dismal place.*

**** 

Behind the massive backdrop, Night gripped the rungs of the ladder attached to the scaffolding that would facilitate his grand aerial arrival onto the stage. Doris glanced his way in the same moment that he peeked over at her.

"What I did was an accident!" he yelled to her, and still his voice dissolved in the ocean of voices on the other side of the screen. "For a moment I thought you were somebody else...someone who used to say things like that to me!"

She also had to shout. "That's an interesting story, Morgen, but I'm half tempted to go with it." She came closer. "I was a bit out of my mind myself. I think we both need some sleep. I mean, if I'm out of my mind and you're hallucinating..." She offered him a strained smile. "Let's do our song tonight, Morgen. Let's sing it like we mean it, like we used to."

He nodded at her and quickly continued up the ladder. Aden and Colby had already started the intro and all hands would be required on deck in less than thirty seconds. At the top, Night reached for his support tackle that was doubled over the lighting grid. His fingerless gloves allowed him to comfortably grip and slide down the ragged length of hemp that delivered him, in a spiral descent, onto the stage. The instrumental bass enveloped him as he clutched the microphone.

With his free hand, he pulled the net over the grid and let it pool all over the stage. A technician handed him his guitar from the sidelines as he jogged around the net's perimeter. He felt a rush greater than his audience—a runner's high from outrunning his past. Everything and everyone he'd known there had been eradicated and the future looked infinitely better.

"This is for you!" he yelled into the microphone and his fans collectively detonated. They didn't have a clue that his call was really to someone else. "Do you hear me? This is for you...my other side!"

The stage had a renewed energy tonight. It was as though every band member saw this performance as their new start. With the stadiums and arenas filled to capacity, everywhere they went, it looked as though Aden would also have his desire, soon enough. Their second tour would see them perform in the largest stadiums in the country and, according to Gin, in other countries as well.

****

Andrew nodded at the doorman who cleared his way into the lobby of the luxury hotel. Under the reception sign, he reached over the marble countertop and showed the desk clerk a fancy business card through the window inside his wallet.

"I'm Andrew Thompson from the AHA..."

"Oh..." The young woman sounded both enthusiastic and nervous.

Andrew's gold and silver tiepin, in the vicinity of a matching pen, flashed beneath the tempered lights of the front desk. "I understand you're hosting some important guests at this time. I'm here to conduct a survey for the department of consumer relations to find out how your administration handles such affairs."

"I should get the manager."

"That won't be necessary...quite yet. I always prefer to carry out this work from a relaxed standpoint, through the frontline staff, and that's difficult to accomplish when the manager is delivering a running sales pitch on a guided tour." It was probably the right time to drop the name he'd been given over the phone, a few days ago. "Mister Couthier shouldn't have any objections to my plan to add this hotel to the list of top celebrity picks of America. I'll look forward to speaking with him later. Actually, if you have no objection, I'd prefer to make a formal announcement to Mister Couthier, about my decision, once everything has been approved by the association."

Sufficiently baffled, the young woman nodded. "I'll have a concierge escort you to wherever you want to go."

"I'll tell you this...'Nancy,'" he read from her nameplate, "so far I'm giving the reception here top marks."

****

Andrew never heard the commotion as *Morning's Desire*, and a flock of their crew entered the hotel lobby. Security had the throngs of fans thinned out by the time they reached the elevator. Doris clutched Night's arm with an air of concern.

"Are you feeling any better?"

Night shook his head. He'd behaved like a storm, all evening— having gained momentum from every increment of glory and power he'd assimilated since his soles hit the stage—but now came the upshot.

"I think my voice is going again." He paced his words, speaking as though he didn't want anyone to overhear him.

"I can't believe you're going to pass up this big house party. Don't you want to have fun?"

"I just want to sit down and drink some tea." He grinned at his private memory of Brandt at his door with this remedy.

The band members all had a key that allowed the elevator to open on the tenth floor. Doris followed him to his room and kissed him before sauntering off to prepare for her next showing.

"You rest up then," she called over her shoulder, "and I'll go order you up a big, strong, sinful pot of tea, okay?"

****

"Don't announce me," Andrew requested, in front of the kitchen doors. He strode in, visualizing his own anger boiling from his ears as he witnessed the steam rising from a pot on the massive stove. He had to remind himself to smile so he could pull off the second phase of his mission.

He grinned genuinely, for a second. If he had in fact been an inspector, he would have been impressed by this kitchen. He noted the cleaning products in easy reach of the three deep sinks meant for manual disinfecting, and the staff all presented as institutionally clean and organized. He announced his phony name and duty to the room, then walked over to one of the cooks.

"Do you check the temperatures of the frozen meats you receive before you store them?"

The man glanced over his shoulder. "I don't. But somebody does." Then he turned around. "Are you from the Health Board? I don't think you'll find any problems here. Not while I'm in charge."

Andrew's jaw tensed. This one was going to be harder to foil. "Not exactly. AHA&LA."

"Rhonda, could you please help this gentleman complete his assessment and answer any questions he may have?"

A woman in a black and white uniform approached him from across the room. His first plan was to make her feel so inept, she would tell him anything, or take him anywhere, if it proved to him she had some knowledge or influence in her position. He had a list of questions prepared, based on regulations he knew well from having managed the ill-fated *Emerald Shore*. It sped things up, considerably, when someone interrupted.

"Hey, Rhonda..." another male kitchen attendant called out playfully. "Do you want to take some tea up to the tenth floor?"

She gaped at him and proceeded to fan herself. "Really...? Which one?"

"Which one do you think needs the herbal tea for his voice?"

Andrew's chest tightened. He almost choked as he inhaled. "That will be fine. We're really quite through here and perhaps I can wrap up my report once I've accompanied you on this delivery—I assume, to one of your special guests? I'm required to meet with only one of them before my job here is completed."

The woman didn't hide her displeasure, but she stopped short of telling 'Mister Thompson of the AHA' that he wasn't allowed to do his job.

"Like I told them in the last department, I have a feeling this hotel will be highly recommended in my next publication. You..." Andrew called to the back of the room, "make sure that water comes to a full boil before you pour it."

****

To find the lead singer, after chatting with the drummer, Brandt simply had walked through a door in Colby's adjoining suite. He found Night in his bedroom, wearing an old T-shirt and sweatpants, in complete contrast to his flashy costumes of earlier. From his king-size bed, he just continued to lifelessly flick through the channels on his large television.

"Hey, Morgen... I didn't feel much like partying either. Mind if I join you?"

Night shrugged.

"Great, thanks." Brandt helped himself to the bathrobe in the bedroom closet and put it on after stripping down to his underpants. "I'm beat," he said, eyeing the area for a friendly place to sit.

"I am too. You can't sleep here, Brandt."

Brandt tilted his head. "So it looks like you and Doris are getting along much better already."

"Yes."

"That's good, that's really good. I'm just curious..." Brandt persisted, plunking himself down in an armchair. "What exactly does Doris have to say about your mysterious tiger stripes?"

Night didn't turn his head, although the question seemed to rattle him. "Nothing. She's never seen them."

Brandt flinched. "That's impossible. Weren't you two..."

"No."

"No?"

"Don't ask, Brandt."

"Of course. Why would I ask...you with all your little secrets and riddles and double-meanings? Does anybody really hold a backstage pass to your show, Morgen?"

The knock on the door stopped the exchange from escalating.

"I asked for some tea," Night informed. "My voice is going again."

Brandt's wounded countenance broke with laughter as he swept into the main room to answer the door. "I'm glad you listen to me about some things."

His stare dropped to the cart that supported a teapot, under the tea cozy, while Andrew's focus barreled up and down Brandt, twice over.

The woman's face also revealed uncertainty over who she was actually face-to-face with. "Room service for Morgen Dahlsi..."

"Yeah. Great," Brandt replied, grabbing the cart so he could pull it into the room.

Andrew held it back and glanced at the employee at his side. "It seems we have the right room. Thank you for escorting me up, Rhonda. I'll just stay here and complete my business—and you can go back to your own. Goodnight."

The woman glanced at both stubborn faces and then walked away, but nobody missed her glare.

Andrew's petulance now spilled into his eyes as he locked them on Brandt. "Excuse me?" he reopened. "Who might you be?"

"My name is Brandt. Can I ask you the same question?"

"I'm here to speak with Morgen." He dug into his suit jacket and dropped open his wallet. "I'm conducting a survey for the American Hotel and Lodging Association."

"Hm," Brandt responded, unimpressed. "You know, I don't think this is a very good time. Maybe you can talk to our manager—or even Colby in 1006. He's just as important."

"I'm sure, but I prefer to speak with Morgen. We've spoken before, and this will save me an introduction. Who are you again...in relation to Morgen?"

Brandt began to adopt Andrew's snooty tone. "I'm his friend, and I'm the one who makes him look hot for the stage. I do his makeup, his hair, I dress him, and I undress him—"

"Fine!" Andrew snapped while Brandt smirked. "Now, if you'll excuse me." He pushed the cart over the threshold, but Brandt blocked Andrew from entering. "Look, I have a job as well and you...you're interfering with it."

Brandt extended his neck to peer in the direction of the bedroom. "Hey, babe... Do you want to talk to this guy from the American Hotel Association who says you're expecting him?"

"I'm not expecting any...body..."

The star's strained holler crumbled into a cough and Brandt scowled at Andrew. "I don't think Morgen's really up to using his voice right now. He just gave it up completely at his last performance."

"That's a shame. I wish I'd learned sign language."

Brandt winced. "What was your name again?"

"...Thompson."

"I'm sorry, Thompson. I can't help you." Brandt almost shut the door but Andrew's hand cut in.

"I don't think I've made myself clear. I know Morgen, personally, and I don't think you want to deprive him of my visit."

"Then you better think again. Look, I doubt very much that you're from any hotel association, but congratulations on making it this far if you're press. Now, are you going to leave or do I have to call security?" Brandt's hand settled on the wall phone beside the door.

"There's no need. I still have other departments to visit, but as for security, I'll be happy to report that I've observed absolutely no lack of security in this hotel—only an abundance of disrespect for one of its associations."

"Go fuck the hell off! Now, your report will be accurate."

Brandt kept the cart but slammed the door. When he looked in on Night, he found him clutching the phone to his ear. In his heated final moments with "Thompson", the incoming call had barely registered.

****

"I said it's Morgen. Who's this?" Night cringed at the static on the line.

"Can you hear? I tol' you, it's Steve...calling from Mexico?"

Night's lungs started to heave. "*Steve?*"

"Yeah, I'm sorry to bother you on your tour, but I should tell you about your brother... Your brother is..."

"What? ...*Hey!*" Night pulled the dead receiver from his ear and throttled it with both hands.

"Another nut-job call? Brandt pried.

Night shook his head, his answer breaking-thin. "No."

"Well, *I* just finished dealing with a nut-job."

Brandt recapped most of the conversation he'd had with the so-called AHA rep. His skepticism about the man's motives compounded all the freakish high points for Night—like the strange and pointless reference to sign-language. But that alone didn't compare to Night's excruciating dilemma of which horrendous possibility to focus on: his brother's passing or Andrew's resurrection.

Colby suddenly appeared in the doorway. "Uh, hey Brandt. Sure you guys don't want to come with us? You look a little stressed, Morgen. Maybe what you need, instead of laying low tonight, is to get yourself utterly and intolerably stoned."

Night nodded feverishly. He had to get out of his own head, and for once, not settle for anything short of the drummer's suggestion. "Help me get there, Colby, because, right now...I really need to know what that feels like."

# Chapter Twenty-Eight

Two days later, the tour landed in Wisconsin, and Brandt plunged into the sunshine through the lobby doors of his Milwaukee hotel. He inhaled the fresh air, enjoying the freedom of not being a core member of *Morning's Desire*. The band would be stuck in interviews all morning and, beyond that, would never really shake security. He, on the other hand, could mosey down to any local coffee shop without being recognized.

He veered off the main road to cut through an alley between two high buildings when something bashed him over the head. He wanted to blame a piece of concrete for falling off one of the old buildings, but he already sensed the human culprit.

Someone ripped a dark cover over his head and kicked him in his stomach. Before he could stand up by himself, arms doubled across his neck and yanked him into an even narrower side-alley, on his right. He realized there were two attackers when a second perpetrator kneed him in the stomach while the first still held him up from behind. Except for his own cough, he didn't hear another man's voice until he rammed his elbow into the rack of lower ribs behind him.

The injured party shoved him forward, tripping him into the trajectory of the second assailant who could be heard scraping a metal object off the pavement. The anticipated blow fell across his shoulders and made him crumble, while a steel-toed boot kicked him in the groin, paralyzing him throughout a spectacular show of colors.

Brandt clawed the bag off his head to the thumping of two sets of fleeing footsteps. His eyes uncrossed, but his assailants had already vanished onto the main street. Against all instincts, he took his time in standing up, but he realized it would be a few minutes before he could walk, let alone run.

The attack was unexpected enough, but the biggest surprise came when he felt his back pockets and confirmed that they hadn't even bothered to steal his wallet.

****

Andrew glanced at his watch. His plane was scheduled to land at Portland International in less than ten minutes. He could have waited for the tour to bring Night back to Oregon, before making any kind of move, but by venturing to Illinois, he'd managed to identify another major foe in the ever-expanding chronicles of Night.

Before this trip, he'd never given the band's entourage much thought, but after having met Brandt, and verifying he was the group's key image consultant, and Night's personal stylist, he was glad for the wake-up call. At least he'd delivered one strike against this queer prick who had so pompously, with his housecoat gaping at the chest, guarded Night from the man who had raised and owned him first.

Andrew tried not to think about how many others deserved to have thugs-for-hire stuck on their trail. He cringed at his surreal nightmare of the multitudes of Aileens, Daphnes—and now Brandts—in Night's daily experience, and tried to see the additional trip to Milwaukee, and the shady business he'd conducted there on a downtown strip, as time and money well spent.

****

When Night decided to visit Brandt, in the afternoon, he walked in on a scene disconcertingly reminiscent of Sandy's homecoming, after his grocery store incident. Brandt didn't have the colors of violence all over his face, but his limp and his reaction to the incident made it comparable.

"Morgen...don't worry about it. I don't need to go to the hospital. I'm probably going to live," he added, sounding more than a little bit like Sandy. "Don't you think it would be pretty cheap of me to take attention away from the tour's success when I'm going to be just dandy in a few days. Look...I'm fine right now...perhaps a little sore in places, but I'll live!"

"Who would do this to you?"

Brandt waved him off and hobbled toward the washroom. "I could think of a couple people, but not any in Wisconsin. I'll see you before the show tonight. Don't even think about this. I'll be fine."

****

"You're definitely different, Morgen, but I think I'm beginning to like the changes," Doris broadcasted backstage as she skipped toward Night.

"Since when?"

"Since I heard about what you said in the dressing room. I didn't know you were so sensitive about certain things. But maybe you're right about what you suggested to me—that we should both go with other people for a while. I think that when we're both all screwed up and screwed out, we'll come looking for one another. You think I haven't noticed that your groupies are starting to bore you. You're not lost out there. You're still right here, attached to me, and the rest of the home crowd."

He felt she was right, in a way. He could hear his fans in the arena and he couldn't deny they excited him—on the whole—but individually, not so much. The few exceptions consisted of people who he could never see again or who refused to have him. This thought led him straight to Morgen.

His brother's life mission had been to get to this moment—either himself or through the only other person who could. Often, Night hoped he'd get a message in his sleep that would assure him that his brother was satisfied. Tears threatened Brandt's make-up job again. Life without Morgen wouldn't have been his choice, but without that choice, it was time to fully accept all he'd earned.

"Are you okay, Morgen?"

He clutched Doris to his ragged costume and kissed her—until he'd surpassed his efforts with anyone so far. Doris looked puzzled when he backed away.

"Wow. I really didn't expect you back so soon."

Night's hand slipped from her arm as he heard his cue. "I've decided...you should be mine."

She laughed, despite his seriousness. "I always have been, you asshole."

Night turned his head and saw Brandt in the sidelines staring back at him. For once, the make-up artist didn't bother to do a single last-minute touch-up, leaving Night to freely ascend to the platform.

In this non-tiger performance, the star alone wore the black and white stripes. They stood out plainly on the tatters Brandt called a top, but on his loose-legged black pants, the stripes had to catch the light to be visible. For the first time since the start of the tour, his earlobes showed plainly beneath freshly cut and teased layers of platinum hair, revealing all three earrings on either side: one hoop and five studs, in total. He had to agree with Brandt. The times, as well as his profession, did allow for a lot of fun...a whole lot of "whatever."

Gripping the rope and crouching at the top of the removable staircase, he left the scaffold and spiraled onto the forestage where a microphone waited for him. He poured his best roar into it and then waited for his fan's screams to dwindle, but after pacing back and forth, several times, he realized this would take a while. It took Aden and Colby's explosive intro to conquer the crowd.

Night waited out the beats before he had to fire his own voice into the mix. He grabbed his guitar from a crewmember in the sidelines and positioned it while he absorbed the sights from the stage. He stared into the thousands of open-mouthed faces and beheld the scene completely without sound as he tried to imagine it being his very last show. It was a heart-wrenching thought—that Morgen's survival would have condemned him to a kind of death—and it hit him. He wasn't doing any of it for his brother anymore. In essence, it was Morgen who had done this for him.

"I love you!" he called out as the sound returned to ears. "If my other side can hear me now...thank you!"

What he could hear, loud and clear, was many of his fans answering that they loved him too, just before he drowned them all out with the cry that opened his song.

After the concert, it seemed everyone in the audience had a backstage pass, and the rest of the band didn't appear to be in any great hurry to leave. This set the tone for the next couple of days, especially in light of one prestigious party invitation.

****

Night realized he hadn't made much of an effort to speak to any member of Morgen's household since he'd started the tour. He still faltered when it came to remembering his responsibilities to Morgen's family, which were quite different from the ones he'd always had to Morgen.

His call to the house was received by the temporary housekeeper, Helen, who gushed for over a minute about how much her nieces loved the poster she'd begged him to sign for them. He planned to talk to Morgen's parents if they were home, but he asked for Beth first.

After the initial thrill of his phone call subsided, Beth approached a topic that neither of them wanted to touch. "Have you heard from...you know...?"

He understood that she didn't want to say Morgen's name on the chance that some unscrupulous source could be listening or recording the call. His heart plunged at the thought of telling her about Steve's call...and he also didn't want to make it real. "It would be very hard to reach me," he half lied.

"Yeah, maybe he did try. Well, guess what..." Beth perked up on the wave of denial he sent her way. "It looks like Dad's going to win the election. For a while, it was close against that Malcarek guy, but people are talking like it's already a done deal that Dad's going to win...even after the tabloid scandal...imagine that," she remarked. "Well, Dad's not here, but let me go get Mum. She's been dying for a phone call from you. Hang on..."

Two minutes later, Brigitte's voice came through the line. "Morgen, we miss you around here. Beth makes sure we see all the coverage from your tour and I think your father can only dream of that kind of popularity. And let me tell you, your success hasn't hurt Beth's popularity either. I don't know how you even managed to call home with so many people fighting for your attention. I hope we'll still get to see the old Morgen when you come back."

Now that he'd opened up to integrating the old Morgen, he thought it might be a possibility.

****

"Brandt!" Night shouted over the chatter on the TV, after bursting into his friend's suite. "I want you to do my makeup, right now."

Lying on the couch, Brandt pivoted slightly toward him. "Why? You starting to feel naked without it, even offstage?"

"I mean the makeup on my body."

"Oh? Is that foreplay to getting naughty with me, like the last time, because I have to say, my balls and their friend are still killing me since the Milwaukie incident—?"

"Brandt, I want to do it with somebody else. I'm going to that party, and first, I would like you to do my makeup."

Brandt glared at the television, but then he stood up and wobbled over to the bar. "No," he replied, without turning his head.

Night stomped further into the room. "No? What do you mean 'no'?"

"It's not my job to do your pre-sex makeup, Morgen. At least, I didn't see it in the contract."

Night's face flushed and his whole body tensed. "That's not fair. I can't do it myself, and you're the only one who can."

"Aw, that's right."

"Brandt! You always help me. Why won't you help me now?"

"Oh, for Pete's sake, Morgen, you're not an idiot. Figure it out yourself and then go screw whoever you want—and best of luck to you—but I'm not your goddamn servant."

"Brandt? ...Brandt!"

But Brandt wouldn't look at him as he poured himself a drink.

"It's your job to look after my image, but if you don't care, why should I?" Night waited for a response that didn't appear forthcoming. "Okay, fine! Well, fuck you, Brandt...fuck you!" He ran into the hallway and slammed the door behind him, so hard, it sent yet another hotel room picture crashing to the floor.

\*\*\*\*

In spite of everything, Brandt snickered at how Night reminded him of a small child trying to mimic an adult, every so often spewing out an inappropriate phrase that he'd picked up somewhere. But after a few seconds, Brandt's grin fell and he tossed his rye and coke into the sink; then, with his arms folded, he returned to the couch and continued to glare at the television.

\*\*\*\*

The music turned up and the lights dimmed, inside the grand house. Different from the other parties he'd attended, this one catered mainly to personnel of every corner of the music industry, from other bands, to their executives and crew, to bar managers and friends.

Night soon realized he was being tested again, this time by Aden, who kept pushing shots of vodka across the table. His bass player held his stare, threatening to detect the slightest hiccup in his composure.

"You caving already, Morgen?" Aden took another shot himself. "Once again, Sean Durges redeems himself. God rest his soul."

Night shrugged and faced Colby, a bit uncomfortable with the subject of Sean. "I'm glad you're here, Colby. You're a better drummer than he was and he deserved to be killed."

"Shit, Morgen... I hope the rest of us never let you down or get on your bad side."

Aden raised his glass to Colby's words while Night downed another shot.

"I think someone is waiting for you to notice them," Colby announced before Night finished his gulp.

A girl with a crimped ponytail and gold tassel earrings leaned in between them with her eyes on the tiger.

"I wanted to bring you a drink, but it looks like you don't really need one." She stepped back and flicked her head, beckoning him to follow her, which he did.

She led him up an impressive staircase, into a bedroom that turned out to be her own. She turned on the lights, then dimmed them, slightly.

Night adjusted the same dial until the interior of the room resembled his name.

"Not that low," she protested. "I want to see you—"

"No... This is how I want it." It really wasn't, but with Brandt having refused to do his body make-up, he thought he'd exercise his status and show some command.

"Radical, but I'm game." She pushed him backward, onto her black islet bedspread. "Why don't you tell me more about how you want it?"

Her body slinked over him, led by her lips that seemed hungry for his mouth. She tasted the inside of it, stirring the malty remnants of his drink with her tongue, and when she'd had enough, her teeth found his left ear. She plucked one of the tiny silver studs from the back of his earlobes, and with the same efficiency, she drew out the stem with its minuscule diamond.

"May I keep it...as a souvenir?" She obviously sensed his nod against her cheek because she continued, happy. "Now it's your turn to call the sport. What is 'morning's desire' exactly?"

318

"It's this..." Night ran his open mouth, sometimes with teeth, down her neck to her gaping cleavage. His hands explored and eventually tightened over the mounds beneath her gold sequin bodice. This action brought him into a sitting position as he gradually pulled his knees back.

She tugged off his slippery black top and tossed it off the bed. "I'm Sherri," she stated, once they were eye-to-eye. "My dad built the arena that you guys played in yesterday. And I know who *you* are, so I think we're ready to rock." She nipped at his face, all the while fumbling to drag her elasticized top over her head. This left her dressed in only a gold link belt atop a black suede miniskirt.

For a moment, Night secretly implored the ceiling lamp to glow a bit brighter so he could visually inhale the deep pink buds on the girl's small round breasts, but Sherri was clearly jammed on fast-forward because she pressed him back immediately. Her next game involved using only her mouth to open the silver clips on his belt, as well as the button fly beneath it, which put him within an inch of finishing when he wasn't yet willing.

"Here's the best part of my tiger impression," she cooed, clutching his pants and ripping them clear below his knees, and then off with the help of some frenzied kicking from her prey. She mounted him and, to his surprise, she helped him slip right through a slit in the lacy material of her thong.

He'd thought the same thing on other occasions but, once again, this feeling transcended anything he'd experienced so far. It was a sensation he'd often imagined. It had been whispered to him through every similar encounter but had never been fully realized.

He pumped and she stirred and, for a time, he became lost in pseudo-realism—further away than any drug had ever taken him. It had been enjoyable enough, to be taken into somebody's mouth, but it didn't compare to the warmth and tightness of here...

He didn't care or acknowledge when two guests walked in, ended a brief conversation with one another and walked out again. Sherri's counter thrusts consumed him both physically and mentally and he sent a cry into her rhythm of hard breaths, just as somebody walked right up to the bed.

"Oh my God... The queen bee," Sherri blurted, panting and winding down.

Night's tipped his face to the side to see Doris's silhouette beside him.

"Wow. Doris DeCara... I so respect you," Sherri continued, still perched on top of Night and topless except for her jewelry. "I've been trying forever, but I'll never be able to play the keyboard like you."

"Thanks," Doris replied, deadpan.

"Oh, I'm sorry. Here..." Sherri scrambled off him.

Night slowly sat up, rubbing his face as he dropped his legs off the edge of the bed.

While Sherri looked for her sequined top, Doris focused on Night and laughed, frankly. "You know...I could help you out of that state, if you'll let me."

Night looked up as his black top bounced off his face.

"I thought you couldn't wait to get back with me," Doris stated.

He grabbed her extended hand and pulled her close.

"I'm going to join the other party," Sherri peeped, from the far side of the bed, "....unless you want me to stay."

When nobody demurred, she crept back on the bed, beaming with Doris's implied authorization to have sex with the lead singer of *Morning's Desire—and* her female idol.

"This is cozy," Doris drawled before Night kissed her. Mirror images in kneeling, his hands clutched her back as though they were iron on powerfully magnetic skin. The wide-open back of her tight dress tricked his senses into feeling her body naked. His cheek pressed against her thick, strawberry hair as her fingers scrambled up the back of his neck, straight into the turbulent sea of his teased platinum, and then she began kissing him.

320

Sherri positioned herself behind Night, pressing in so her pelvis became his seat. Her body arched backward as she released thrusts against his rear while her fingers on his chest offered different levels of pressure every time they tweaked his nipples.

Doris held both of them between her knees as he entered her. She heightened his sensation through the deliberate muscular contractions she strategically delivered around his member. He leaned forward, to take greater control, and Doris melted all the way onto her back. Sherri climbed off the bed and gently kissed Night's shoulder, and then Doris's forehead, before she slipped into her en suite.

They tumbled around one another, in one complete rotation, and although they'd become disconnected, Night now found himself being pulled inside Doris's eyes. They looked wild, like his, but of a different animal. With his fingers, he touched her eyelids, her lips, her neck. He traced her entire form to reacquaint himself with the softness of a young woman's curves. When his lips took the place of his fingers, he noticed her skin was fragrant with a trace of vanilla body lotion, yet it became seasoned with salt as he descended some more.

His hands slithered and locked behind her legs. With his temple against her thigh, he could feel her hot lifeblood pulsing, and when she placed her fingers around his head, he went in.

Her breathing intensified as his tongue helped him learn about the other sex, but the demands of his own body finally called him back to the surface. She helped him re-enter her, and from there he needed no more assistance. He was fervent, even greedy, as he threw his pelvis, over and over, while she willfully tightened around him again, causing him to arch and almost roar like the tiger he stood in for on stage.

*Fuck*...he thought, as though Morgen had planted the word in his mind. He felt so many good contrasting feelings about this all-physical experience: relaxed and exhilarated, content and ambitious. This was so much better than the pitiful existence he'd known in Oregon...so much better than...than mice.

# Chapter Twenty-Nine

With his doctor insisting on at least one more week of intensive physiotherapy before letting him leave the hospital, Sandy decided to take matters into his own hands. He didn't have much time left to capitalize on the success of the *Morning's Desire* tour. He reached across his nightstand and pulled the telephone onto his hospital bed.

"Give me the number for the tabloid, *Storm*, will you?"

"Oh yeah, I remember you," said his old contact, Oran Twaites, when he got on the line. "Are you finally thinking of talking about what really happened in that hit-and-run? With the Dahlsis constantly in the spotlight, your story is worth a lot right now. Perhaps an interview?"

"An interview would be *great*," he growled through clenched teeth. "But I hope you haven't forgotten about our original agreement?"

"Oh, yeah," the man erupted with a derisive flair. "That's right. I'll be interested in finding out about your celebrity scoop as well."

"I don't talk for free," Sandy stipulated, and when Oran Twaites didn't object to his demand, he continued. "Remember what I said to you last time we talked? I don't want to be a housekeeper anymore—although my days with the Dahlsis are numbered anyway. But you know what I mean."

"Don't get yourself all worked up. You just keep your end of the bargain, and I'll keep mine."

****

Night leaned against his window in the small chartered airplane. "I don't know why we have to go to Oregon."

Beside him, Aden turned his head in the same direction. "Why the hell wouldn't we go to Oregon? And we're breaking our record for ticket sales with these outdoor concerts."

324

"It'll be cold."

Aden became testy. "We'll be under a tent with heaters—and aren't you the one who's always fanning yourself backstage or bugging someone to do it for you? Man...what do you got against Oregon?"

Night shrugged. He glanced around the plane and noticed Doris and Colby comparing drinks and Brandt sitting with their manager, working something out on paper. At that moment, he just wanted Morgen to help him bridge his two lives. Nobody else could.

"I feel like there's something wrong."

Aden glanced at his watch. "Thanks, asshole. I hope you mean something like you forgot your toothbrush, otherwise, keep it to yourself until on the ground."

****

Their two concerts in Portland, at the Memorial Coliseum, were jam-packed with fans from both Portland and Washington State. Gin repeatedly cursed his earlier decision to leave Seattle out of the tour.

While Portland hadn't conjured up any dreaded memories, Night felt the echo of every last one as he looked out at Salem. He requested a map of Oregon, just to confirm he really wasn't in his old backyard, but irrespective of the miles from home, every sight closed the distance a little more.

True to Aden's description, a giant tent had been erected on a vast field of green. Heaters came on, before the show, but just shortly to decrease the humidity and inject some warmth beneath the broad ceiling. The tent masked a permanent structure. An amphitheater had been modified, and partially soundproofed, for the protection and comfort of the white tiger. An air-bridge connected the two structures. Night came to like this setting with its view of the water. In fact, it exhilarated him to pour his voice into the same air that had once held him mute.

It seemed as though the whole of Oregon turned out for the first concert. It amazed Night that there could be another concert of the same magnitude, twenty-four hours later. Unlike the other band members, he didn't feel the need to hit the town after the show. His mind, alone, supplied the entertainment by presenting reruns of his past, only now, he got to watch them through the eyes of a stranger. He spent some time in the amphitheater, playing with the wildcat while the tiger handler stood by and watched.

"He really likes you," the man commented as Night waved a branch across the floor, which the tiger chased like a colossal housecat. "He trusts you. He seems to think you're one of us. He must be a good judge of character—I mean, your band has raised hundreds of thousands of dollars for these beautiful creatures, and other endangered animals, throughout your tour."

"Thank you," Night replied. Half a year ago, he wouldn't have even known about the plight of some wildlife that people referred to as endangered species. Of course, in those days, he also didn't have platinum hair, six earrings, and eye makeup to showcase his uncanny white-tiger eyes. He then grasped the reality: coming back to Oregon was perfect.

****

On that overcast but mild Saturday in May, Brandt coolly carried out his work before the show. "Your marks are really fading. It's hard to see them...without good light."

"Really?"

"Yeah... But you're still too damn pale, and that'll never change."

While Brandt perfected his smoky eye effect, Night fantasized about two things. First, he imagined Andrew standing in the audience, devastated at witnessing his success—and then his deliberate snub from the heights of the stage. Second, he imagined Morgen appearing amongst his fans, alive and well, showing him approval—perhaps through a wink...both fantasies separate, of course.

After his make-up session, Brandt helped him into one of the most maddening costumes he'd ever designed—the scene bordering on vicious when Night repeatedly mistook gaps in the material for

326

armholes. Over a shimmering white tank, a network of black webbing draped over parts of his torso, and spiraled one bicep, in an asymmetrical design. A tarnished silver belt looped twice around his hips. Synthetic black leather pants and boots offset the blatant glamor of the rest of his costume—because real leather remained a no-no on the *Roaring Desire* Tour.

On cue, Night charged onto the stage, in front of the others. He drank in his ocean of fans until their voices reached a zenith, and then he yelled into the microphone: "It's so great to be in Oregon!"

He hated Oregon. Even considering the cathartic potentials of performing here, he still loathed the place.

At the beat, he skipped around the stage before reclaiming the microphone and throwing his voice into the mix. Oregon loved him as it always had when he was only a bartender, but now with a teenage ferocity that didn't compare. It began to feel like any other concert, and by the third song, he finally connected with his Oregon audience. He kneeled at the edge of the stage, made eye contact, smiled openly, and allowed fans to grab his hands.

A few rows from the front, he noticed someone pushing toward him. He was not the typical fan sporting new-wave clothes and teased hair, but someone with silver hair, whose attire struck him as glaringly conservative within the scene.

Night's hands died on his guitar, leaving the re-intro behind.

One by one, his friends on the stage peered in his direction and then followed his gaze into the crowd. As the figure dissolved into the gloom beyond the perimeter of his fans, Night picked up the tune and the music swelled...the synthesizer, the bass, and the snare. Night's voice rushed in as well and the bizarre hiccup in his performance translated into nothing more than a casual interlude at the star's whim.

A smile revitalized his performance, but the catalyst was not so pure. In a reckless way, he hoped Andrew *had* come—his far-fetched but desperate fantasy realized!

He replaced the microphone on its stand, picked up his guitar, and smugly fingered the frets as he sauntered over to Doris's keyboard. She grinned as he handed her the guitar and took command of her synthesizer for a virtuoso rendition of Bach's *"Little" Fugue in G minor*.

The crowd went crazy, his break into a classical number unmistakably the highlight of the evening. He trusted Andrew would appreciate the quality of his performance—the intricacies of the piece, not only learned and mastered, but transcended by his once voiceless slave puppet.

The screaming never wavered as he left Bach and returned to Morgen's masterpiece, improvising a brazen new medley that combined modern and classical. With electric guitar in hand, he danced to the left of the stage and froze solid. He hugged his guitar as if it could shield him from some emerging psychosis. Directly in front of him, his own face—Morgen's face—rendered every other fan faceless. Morgen even winked at him, just like in his alternate fantasy of earlier today.

He could only stare as Morgen pulled a kerchief over his head, pointed to one corner of the stage, and reversed into the mob behind him. That's when Night realized—the worst of all his surreal nightmares—the collision of his two egocentric daydreams!

Night reeled forward imagining Andrew crossing paths with Morgen, who had once left him for dead. He turned around to find his band mates staring at him. Under duress, he hoisted his guitar against his hip and persuaded his numb hands to play. He only had to make it to the end of the song and then he could try to take it all in. In the upcoming intermission, he was expected to collect the white tiger, return to the stage, and recite a few wildlife statistics to the audience, but the plan now stood a good chance of being delayed.

When the song ended, he paused at the steps behind the curtain, expecting Morgen to show himself at any moment. His band members and even some of the crew hounded him for an explanation as to what had happened on stage, but he couldn't come up with a reply before the stage director accosted him.

328

"Morgen, go get the cat! What the hell are you waiting for?"

Nearly out of his mind, Night slapped his sides and ran behind the curtain, through the air-bridge, into the amphitheater. The animal trainer thrust the handle of the tiger's chain into Night's palm and then sprinted ahead of him to join the stage crew already waiting for the star to make his grand entrance.

Night took a few seconds to pet the giant cat before moving to fulfill his duty, but steps from the amphitheater door, he froze as a terrifying variation of hysterical screaming ignited in the distance, somewhere near the foot of the stage.

"Morgen?" he uttered foolishly, right before a searing pain drilled through his abdomen, which dropped him to his knees, beside the tiger.

The garish lights around him faded into an eerie glow and the screeching beyond the amphitheater became muted as though he'd been plucked from the scene and catapulted into cosmic space. With his face hanging only inches above the floor, the tiger began licking his hair, and when he didn't respond, it resorted to using its teeth to gently tug on the back of his neck. His body lay half deserted as his spirit wavered between it and the open air.

"Hey...!" called a man's voice, which made the frantic tiger retreat.

The mystical link that had flash-formed between him and Morgen snapped as his awareness bounced back. Night lifted his head and found the animal handler anxiously staring down at him.

"Are you all right, Morgen? What happened to you? It's utter chaos out front..."

Night scrambled to his feet and leapt at the door to the air-bridge. He peered through the small, mesh-enforced window when the face of his living nightmare jammed his view.

Andrew shoved his way in while the handler elbowed past Night.

"Sir, I'm sure you're not supposed to be back here..."

"Hi, I'm from Animal Control…" Andrew quipped, seizing the confused tiger man by the face and slamming his head against the concrete wall.

Night snatched the tiger's chain and shuffled backward.

"Don't worry, he'll live." Andrew shrugged as he turned around. "I'm very disappointed, Night. Aren't you happy to see your biggest fan in the whole world, Y.F. —*Your Father!*"

Night looked away with glacial indifference. "I knew it was you all this time."

"Of course you did, Night." Andrew's forward amble caused the tiger to arch and growl as its cerulean eyes locked on the potential threat. "Do you see it now? I'm still in control—just as I have been by weighing on your thoughts, every day and hour since you left."

Night flicked his gaze up. "Do I look like I've been thinking about you?"

"Undeniably. Look at you…you're wearing your pitiful mutiny all over your body."

Glancing around, Night tried to figure out how everyone could have left him alone. He let the tiger's chain slip through his hand to its full length. "How did you get back here? Everyone's going to start looking for me, any second. Where *is* security…?"

Andrew chuckled. "I think they're kind of busy."

"What do you mean?"

"I mean, they can't even hold back your crew—let alone the fans—all trying to see the *Morning's Desire* lead singer lookalike lying on the grass with a tent stake through his gut."

This confirmation pierced Night in the gut for a second time. Nothing in his arsenal of contempt could outshine Andrew's victory— not if Morgen had been miraculously cured in Mexico, only to meet his demise through the freakish coincidence of both him and Andrew showing up at the same concert.

"Face it, Night, it's over! It's time for you to leave this circus, so say a little goodbye..." Andrew signed three letters in the way of Night's historic rendition from the day he walked out of the *Emerald Shore*.

The atomic blast behind Night's gaze gave way to a physical eruption as he struck Andrew full in the jaw, knocking him against the door. Night dropped the chain and tackled him against the steel surface, but Andrew latched onto a multi-studded earlobe and extracted a shriek out of Night as two earrings ripped through his flesh. The pain made him double over as he tried to staunch the blood streaming down his neck.

Andrew hustled to thread the tiger's chain through a bracket on the wall and when the animal lunged at him before he was finished, the chain links jammed tight. Andrew smiled as he calmly advanced, repelling Night into a stumble.

"Why don't you just admit it..." Night screamed as the blood in his hand splattered on the ground, "you did it all for nothing! *You're* the one who's pathetic and a freak!"

"Are you sure about that...?"

Night spat in Andrew's face. "You saw me out there! Why don't you just admit that I won?"

"Won what, you stupid brat?" The back of Andrew's leaden hand landed across Night's other ear. "Are we anywhere near finished?"

They lunged at one another and the tiger burst into a frenzy, held back only by the seized link. Andrew reveled in mocking both the beast and its master as he swayed forward and tore the thick silver choker from Night's throat.

Night struck back crosswise. His knuckles, inside a fingerless glove, ripped across Andrew's eyeball, forcing him to strike back blindly. Through pinched eyelids and Night's combative hands, Andrew managed to latch onto a fistful of platinum hair as the stalemate between two chain links suddenly gave way.

Night's scalp began to tear, but his brittle yelp was obliterated by Andrew's multi-octave cry as the tiger plunged both sets of front claws into his shoulders and raked them down the entire length of his back. With Andrew writhing on the floor, Night had clear passage to run, but he didn't.

"Yeah, I know... Hurts," Night taunted, giving the giant cat an affectionate stroke with his trembling hand. "'But that will go away.'" He spun toward the exit, but Andrew caught one of his ankles and dragged him back, now growling like an animal himself.

Several grunts escaped Night as he flipped himself over and kicked at Andrew, while the animal handler started to wake up, near the exit.

The agitated tiger did a careful inspection of the semi-conscious man, then returned to the conflict, just as Andrew's hands closed on Night's throat. The animal pawed and butted Andrew's head in an attempt to expose the back of his neck, but Andrew stayed dead set on placing his own death grip on Night.

Under his rival's full weight—and some of the tiger's—Night's words still grated through Andrew's calculated chokehold. "You can't handle that I won."

"Tell me a little more about your victory..." Andrew's hands tightened, but his fingers began sliding in the blood of his victim's mangled earlobe.

The tiger also botched its death move when Andrew viciously elbowed the creature, but then it sank its teeth in, beside his neck, and began thrashing him around. The tiger's ferocious flailing lifted Andrew enough for Night to wedge his knee between them and free his emergency tranquilizer pistol. Through all the bumping, the muzzle lodged itself below Andrew's ribs.

"I want to hear you say it..." Night exacted in a shot up whisper as he pulled the cocking mechanism back to maximum range. "Say that I won."

Andrew's strangling grip loosened and his eyes glazed. "Yes, you won, Night...but do you have any idea what you cost those you loved?"

"*You* set the price." Night flicked the safety off and fired the dart. A few seconds later, Andrew collapsed next to him, beneath the nose of the wary tiger.

Shivering and disoriented, Night crawled through the bloody paw prints, stroked the tiger, and gave it a kiss on the head, before he remembered Morgen.

He stumbled through the doors to the back of the stage. Emergency vehicles had arrived on the field and he staggered toward their lights. An officer was speaking over his radio as Night approached.

"I have a young male stabbed and the EMTs are in attendance. Hold on... A second male victim, possibly another 217, just surfaced. Stand by." He turned to Night. "Morgen Dahlsi?"

Night stared into the distance where an ambulance, with lights flashing, began to drive away as he shot forward. Someone who turned out to be Aden caught him and they both nearly toppled.

"Where're you going—and what the hell happened to you?"

He pushed Aden's hands off, suddenly realizing he was surrounded by his band, and the rest of the world, all leaning in to hear him say anything.

Several members of the press pushed microphones into his face.

"Mister Dahlsi, what happened here?"

"Do you know the stabbing victim?"

"Do you have a statement for your public?"

With charcoal smudges in his eye sockets and bloodstains, highlighted by the camera's flash, all over his face, he painfully enunciated each word of his reply.

"Tell them...I fucking won."

# Chapter Thirty

Gin struggled to get Night out of the concert grounds and into the limousine. "Not now. Not right now. Move out of the way!"

The noise from the crowd became muted as the limousine door slammed shut. Gin's manner bounced between his frustration and his genuine concern. "Some kid got stabbed, you got strangled... Your voice better recover because somebody needs to explain to me what the hell just happened at our concert!"

Doris leaned into Night and placed her cool hands on his face, but in a peculiar way, like she was looking for something; then she sat back in silence.

On Night's opposite side, the borrowed paramedic sifted through his medical kit. "Our dispatcher arranged for you to arrive at a clinic so you won't be subjected to any public hospital, but first, let's get you fixed up, okay?"

Night acknowledged with a scant nod as he held a compress against the side of his head. Now that the bleeding had stopped, from what was left of his earlobe, the paramedic began taping it up.

After a silence, Gin noted, "I guess the tour's over. Let's just thank God we're near the end of it. As soon as we're in the clear, health-wise, we'll try to reschedule the canceled shows." Night thought Gin had finished, but then he started up again. "What the hell happened? You shot a man with the tranquilizer pistol. Did you know who he was?"

The only safe answer was a lie. "No," he stated thinly.

The paramedic gave the singing star some advice before moving to a less prominent seat within the limousine. "Don't speak until you've had your pipes checked out, or you might cause more damage."

****

Into the early morning, Colby and Aden waited at the hotel for everyone to return from the clinic. They followed Gin, Doris, and Night into the hotel's finest suite.

Gin gripped Night's arm. "I'm out of here, Morgen, but before I send you home tomorrow, I'm going to arrange for you to see a voice specialist. You just take it easy because you won't get that chance again for a while."

Night groped for the armchair as though he couldn't quite see beyond the turmoil in his mind. His face sank into his palms. Doris and the others gathered around him.

"Who are you?" she pleaded. When he didn't answer her, she didn't stop. "I saw him on the grass, and I knew, right away, that it was Morgen."

"What are you talking about?" Colby sneered.

Night refused to look at any of their faces and Aden stood transfixed.

"Just stop it...*please!*" She squatted before him and tugged at his wrists. "You can stop pretending. I've wondered about the changes ever since we played at the New Year's party, but I couldn't *seriously* accuse you of being Morgen's twin...not until tonight. I saw him—I saw my Morgen, and you are not him."

As Doris pulled her hands away and stood up, Night pressed his palms into his lap and looked up. "Morgen wanted this."

"Holy shit!" Aden reeled back and paced in a complete circle while Colby interjected.

"Look, obviously there's a reason for this, but you have to tell us who you are."

Night stood up and shoved past everyone. He ended up in the kitchenette where he slumped over the countertop.

Doris followed him, halfway. "I want to say something to you before we go on. I want to thank you for fending me off for as long as you did. I mean, you could have just jumped right into bed with me, but you didn't. And as for the other night...I think that was real."

"Oh, that's so sweet, Doris," Aden groaned. "But I think we should be getting a nice fat explanation for everything that went down, right here, right now! Who the hell are you, man, and why would you guys pull a stunt like this?"

"Leave him alone. He shouldn't be trying to talk right now—and he may have just lost his brother..."

"Oh, come on! We just want a name!"

Night looked up. "Morgen..." he pronounced in an icy whisper. "That's the only name you'll ever get." Then he marched into his bedroom and locked the door.

****

At the Dahlsi mansion, the following afternoon, Night was sure he wouldn't get away with his silent treatment, once Morgen's parents entered the forum.

Brigitte clamped her arms around him, in the foyer. Her whole body shook with dry sobs that Night imagined were fueled by turmoil, rather than relief at his homecoming in light of his close call with death. His belief was confirmed when Brigitte led him into the living room and Frederick came at him as though he wanted to blast him clear through the wall.

But Frederick broke one step short of Night and threw a newspaper headline in front of his face.

Night scowled at how Frederick could think he needed a reminder about yesterday's mayhem, but when he finally focused on the words, his expression melted.

"'*Morning's Desire Stabbing Victim Dies,*'" Frederick broadcasted, dropping his arm with the paper.

Brigitte, who'd been pacing near the back of the room, began to cry again, and Frederick grew more agitated with him for managing to keep a straight face.

"It says here the victim looked a lot like Morgen Dahlsi...but I think these pictures say it all!" He flashed the lower half of the page in front of Night, indicating the portrait shot of him, next to a grainy shot of Morgen on the stretcher. "Everything makes sense now! Come on! How about you show us your chipped tooth?"

Night's chest began to heave. Each breath brought him closer to seething. "Of course I'm not Morgen! And I know you saw it...but did you really not believe it until now?"

"Don't turn this on us!" Frederick warned. After a long silence, his manner softened. "Just tell me how it came to pass that Andrew Shannien targeted my son when he could only have been connected to *you*?"

Confusion washed out Night's heated countenance as he reflected on the latest word from police. His attacker had carried no ID, and no abandoned car had been found on site. "How'd you know it was Andrew?"

Brigitte stopped pacing and answered him boldly. "Because I was warned!"

"*What?*" For a moment, Frederick looked as disgusted as Night.

"A woman called here, about a year ago. She said we were connected through Andrew Shannien. Then, said she was trying to assist someone who was with her and she mentioned Morgen's birth mother... I hung up...because I thought she was speaking for her, but she wasn't. She was calling about *you*."

Night could have nodded, but he just let her continue.

"That's why we haven't been able to recognize our own son in months... Everything came together when I saw the newspaper, this morning." Brigitte's voice dropped two octaves. "Just tell me Andrew didn't raise you."

Even while it consoled him to know, at long last, that Brigitte hadn't meant to leave him behind, Night answered her with a scathing blink.

338

Frederick's unstable expression exposed both his sympathy and rage, but he was saved from having to comment from either standpoint when the doorbell rang. "It's Charles... He said he'd be over as soon as possible."

****

The lawyer invited everyone to sit down as though they were *his* guests. He nodded at Night, coldly, before turning to Frederick.

"Tell me, how's your housekeeper doing?"

Frederick balked. "Sandy? He's recovering. He should be back with us very soon..."

"Well, I'm quite sure he won't be. It's about an article—"

"What article?"

"Another tabloid thing, Fred. It hit the stands in the latter half of the *Morning's Desire* tour."

Night felt the urge to run.

"Your housekeeper claimed to have been tracking two Morgens inside this house...until he got hit. He mentioned having pictures—and other evidence that never surfaced—so like everybody else, I didn't think anything of it until all this shit hit the fan, last evening."

Night knew he looked distraught, but he quietly waited for the lawyer to finish piling all the damage onto the table.

"Your children are adopted, and that's not a crime," Lehman continued. "But you made a statement to the public, after that sex scandal you called a hoax, to say your children are both Dahlsis. Now, can you imagine the impact on your political career if pictures were to surface that proved Morgen had a twin after you continually denied the possibility? I'm looking out for you, Fred. I'm doing everything I can to deal with this—but you have to deal with your housekeeper, and find those pictures, if they exist."

While Brigitte held onto her throat, Fred struggled to cough up the right words, sighing several times over. "Charles...the best thing you could do for us, right now, is find out for sure if...Morgen's twin is really dead. What if he's not, because I may just want to come clean about my family's history and welcome him into—"

"Relax, Fred. That's what I've been doing all morning, and I can guarantee he won't be back. I'm the one who informed the media of his status, early this morning. I'm sorry you had to see it in the paper before I could get here, but this twin rumor is being shut down.

"I can always get an official death certificate in case the Oregon police get tempted to probe this—no matter what links they make later on. Now...my advice to everyone in this house is to get your stories straight. I don't need to know what really happened here, but I need to know that we are all moving forward from the same page." He threw another derisive glance at Night. "As for your housekeeper, as long as no pictures show up, he'll be remembered as nothing more than another celebrity chaser."

****

"Okay, now talk!" Frederick bellowed in Night's face, the moment Lehman walked out the door. "I still need to know how Morgen became involved in a man's vendetta against *you*."

"It wasn't just me," Night retorted, his damaged voice still breaking in and out of a whisper. "Morgen drove to Oregon, one time, and he said he got back at Andrew for all the things he did to me."

Brigitte winced. "All the things...?"

Night ignored her. "I never wanted to take Morgen's place. He begged me to do that. I can show you."

Night led Frederick and Brigitte to Morgen's suite where he showed them Sandy's confiscated videos and photographs. On Morgen's TV, he showed them video clips that detailed Morgen's late stage illness.

At the same time, Frederick shuffled through the photographs and his complexion ran pink. A tear exploded on one of the photos Sandy had snapped off his television screen. "God...! Why didn't he just tell us he was sick? I suspected it—more than a few times—and he always denied it. That visit to the doctor...of course it was you."

340

Night nodded and glanced down.

Frederick shook his head, clearly embarrassed, and frustrated. "Lehman's right. We have to destroy these. I'll do whatever it takes to preserve this family, and that means you will remain Morgen Dahlsi, but after today, there will be no way to go back on that decision. Do you understand? Does everybody understand?"

Brigitte placed a reassuring hand on her husband's arm, then the other on Night's, although she looked as though she might lose it again at any second.

"This discussion isn't finished, but it'll have to continue later. I don't even know who I'm talking to when I look at you." Frederick set his glare on Night. "You don't talk like my son, or act like my son— and even though I haven't really seen Morgen in months, I still convinced myself it was his image I was seeing almost daily on the TV—and I still see him in front of me right now... I still see him. I still see Morgen!"

This was the first time Night had seen a grown man cry, but Frederick pulled himself together quickly.

"How am I supposed to feel? You deceived us for almost a year— and all the while you were making us feel closer to our son than ever. What should I think of you? I don't even know what to call you!" Frederick threw down the photographs.

"Right now...I think it's time I pay another visit to our housekeeper in the hospital. I swear, if I had learned about what he was hiding from me, earlier, I would have taken my car and run over his goddamn fucking legs myself!"

****

Beth had been on a school trip when she received the news. She arrived at the house to discover that Brigitte had taken Night onto the lanai to get acquainted with the child Aileen Coleman had failed to tell anyone about. She'd overheard much, by the time she reached them at the patio table and, instantly, her mission became to not lose her substitute brother as well.

Her mother leapt up and embraced her before offering her a seat and a summary of events, which included everything Lehman had divulged about Sandy.

It didn't really surprise her. Morgen had always disliked the guy, whether this transpired through experience or intuition, and now she knew he'd always been a step ahead of everyone else. When her mother asked how long she'd known about the twins, she didn't lie.

"For a long time. It was stupid and I didn't want to keep it a secret, but if you saw how much Morgen wanted this..." Through her tears, she pleaded for understanding. "And Night actually did it... He did it for Morgen."

Not feeling much like talking, Beth excused herself and started for her room, but someone grunting in Morgen's hallway froze Beth on the staircase. For a few seconds, she dared to hope she would see Morgen, but a peek through the rail posts quickly ended that fantasy.

If her father had been volatile when he left the house, he was really going to combust when he reached the hospital and found out that the vermin he'd come to exterminate had just slinked back to their home. She watched Sandy propelling himself down the hallway with his new titanium forearm crutches and she strategized for a minute.

She rummaged through her bedroom to find her camera and then raced down the south hallway, halting abruptly at the threshold of Morgen's breached doorway.

"Hello, Sandy. Say 'cheese'."

Sandy spun around with his hands between two sofa cushions, only to have his eyes kissed by her camera's flash.

"Gee, Sandy, think of the headline: *Dahlsi's Housekeeper Caught Stealing from Private Rooms.*" With that, Sandy picked up his crutches and tried to follow her.

"Fuck, Beth...it's not like you guys didn't steal anything from me!" But Sandy couldn't keep up. "Fuck your stupid picture. It doesn't prove anything anyway!"

342

Beth tossed the camera on her bed then retraced her steps as she decided she wasn't finished with Sandy. Not finding him back in Morgen's common room, she dashed straight into Sandy's old suite. He'd left his bathroom door open and she could hear him urinating.

He didn't have a chance to react to the intrusion before Beth kicked him in the back. He crashed forward, over the toilet bowl, and corkscrewed into a wet landing between the bowl and the wall.

"Crazy bitch!"

"Asshole!"

She grabbed one of his crutches while he scrambled to get up. "They say Morgen's dead! Can't you just leave us alone? And *this* is for last Christmas!" She jabbed at him heedlessly as he retreated into a protective ball.

"Chill out, bitch. I was just packing!" he yelled as he literally packed himself inside his pants and did up the zipper.

Night charged in behind her, shouldered past Beth, and dragged Sandy into the main room where he chucked him onto the window ledge.

Sandy only became vocal again as he lost touch with the floor. "Let go of me, you psychotic little faggot! You're the last one around here to be calling the shots!"

"I can do anything I want," Night stated, pressing on Sandy's shoulders until his legs tipped up.

"Night, stop!" Beth shrieked as Sandy's desperate hold on Night's shirt became the only thing keeping him in one piece. "I want to kill him too—but you'll go to jail!"

Night yanked him forward and Sandy dropped inside the room.

Beth offered him his crutches, which he ripped out of her hands.

"Where are your car keys?" Night demanded.

"On my bed. Just leave me alone. I'm going!"

Night grabbed the keys and hurled them out the window. He then pushed Beth aside and prodded Sandy through two hallways and down the garage access staircase.

"What about my stuff!"

"Use your blood money and buy yourself some new goddamn stuff," Beth muttered as she got ahead of Night to hold open the door to the driveway.

"You're the ones who should be thrown out of this house, not me!" Sandy persisted as he crossed the threshold. "I just showed this family how you were fucking them all—some literally!"

Without warning, Night clutched Beth against his chest and kissed her full on the mouth, before he gave Sandy a syrupy blink and slammed the door.

In the dim light, Beth looked up at Night, but neither of them smiled. She needed this day to confirm that Night was not a substitute for Morgen, and she now wanted her real brother back, more than ever before.

****

As predicted, the world demanded to hear from Morgen Dahlsi about recent events. A little over a week after the tragedy—after littering their home state of California with canceled shows—Gin was eager to hold a press conference as a surrogate form of entertainment. To reflect the sober theme of this particular conference, Brandt had to tone down his creativity before sending the star to the podium.

"They wouldn't let me near you since that night. Is that what you wanted?"

Night recoiled from the comb that came precariously close to his stitched earlobe. He already had to suffer it tugging on his torn scalp, countless times.

"Do you really think I got anything I wanted in the last few days?"

"You've been through a hell of a lot," Brandt conceded. "I heard some stuff on shortwave, this morning, from Oregon...about that guy who attacked you. They think he might have been a former restaurant owner named Andrew Shannien. Apparently, they found a car on his property that belonged to a missing girl."

Night glanced up but said nothing.

"The girl was dating the man's son who's also missing, and who the police briefly thought might be the stabbing victim. See, the police knew the man's son had some distinguishing marks on his body..."

Peeking at the mirror, Night confirmed he actually looked bored.

"But their lead went cold when they followed up at the hospital and were told that the stabbing guy had no unusual marks. It's interesting, isn't it?"

"Brandt, use a bandana—do something to hide my ear. I hate how it looks."

"I should call you Raggedy Andy," Brandt digressed with a grin, even as his brow furrowed. "So, the police are assuming the missing parties have been dead all along. I heard they're even questioning whether this nurse, who the man dated, really died in an accident like they first thought. All I can say is, whoever his son was, I hope he experienced *some* light since the day he burned down his father's restaurant and fled...because it sounds like he came from a pretty dark place if he lived with that psychopath."

Gazing straight ahead, Night reached up to guide Brandt's hand down to his shoulder and then kissed the top of it. "Psychopaths, freaks... Maybe they all have a reason."

****

Night resisted the snippets of advice that Gin Corbin on his right and Charles Lehman on his left whispered in his ears, just about every time a journalist asked him a question.

"Morgen, what was your impression of the man who attacked you at the concert? Did you sense what he was capable of?"

"A bit too late, but I finally did."

"What did he say to you?"

"He said something about being in control...but he got that wrong, didn't he?"

An uneasy silence swept the room while, beyond the range of the microphones, the lawyer cautioned the superstar about his attitude.

"Did you mean to kill him?"

"I did the only thing I could." He caught Lehman nodding at finally hearing the words come out of his mouth exactly as prescribed. "I had to use the tranquilizer pistol or I would have been the one killed."

The barrage of questions and comments that followed left him speechless.

"Do you believe your lookalike fan was an unsuspecting victim? ...There are rumors you seriously acknowledged him from the stage that night. ...Morgen, could he have been your brother—I mean, are you in fact a Dahlsi or—?"

Lehman lurched forward in his chair. "His family has already provided a statement in that regard. Of course he is a Dahlsi. The victim was nothing more than an obsessed fan."

"Mister Dahlsi, can you verify for all of us that you did not know the victim?"

Gin whispered through clenched teeth. "You don't have to keep answering that."

Night barely heard his manager over the eerie silence of the lawyer saying nothing. He followed Lehman's wild stare to a male figure, with platinum-blond hair and tinted glasses, weaving along the back of the room. Night pushed himself from his chair and bolted for the door, behind the podium, that led to an antechamber.

Gin was left trapped at the microphone when Lehman abandoned his seat as well.

A side door opened into the hotel corridor and Night ran the length of the conference hall to the rear entrance. He could hear Gin appeasing the crowd and Lehman closing in on his heels. "Morgen, we have to deal with this!"

Night spun around and shoved Lehman in the chest. "Deal with what? Just go do your job!"

"I've been doing my job—cleaning up after every fucking mess you've thrown at your family! Now, let me handle this."

They both peered into the room to scan the back rows, but there was no sign of the mysterious Morgen-figure. Night turned away from Lehman and found himself face-to-face with a security guard.

"Mister Dahlsi, I can escort you wherever you need to go."

Night pointed at Lehman. "Just keep *him* here so I can have some privacy...maybe I just need to have a piss!" He narrowly escaped being followed by another guard, but it took both of them to hold Lehman back and, Night guessed, that wouldn't be for very long.

"Do you know what you're doing, Morgen? For God's sake, you better deal with it! Morgen...!"

Night reached the elevators and slammed the up-button with his fist. In an attempt to keep everyone, especially the lawyer, off his trail, he got off on a high floor and then took the stairs down to P3 where he'd parked Morgen's car.

Perched on the driver's seat, Night tried to catch his breath. Lehman's reaction, not his own eyes, had just verified that the mysterious figure they'd both seen in the back of the conference room was Morgen. Now, he hoped Morgen would think to look for him here. For either of them to squirrel away to some random spot in the hotel would make no sense, and Morgen would know they'd both be mobbed if they were spotted in the open. Despite this reasoning, he still jumped when somebody tapped on the windshield.

"You just ruined everything! Why'd you run?" Morgen, very stiffly, pried the passenger door open, got inside, then scowled at the concrete wall in front of them. "I practically killed myself to get here and you make me chase you through the building like you want to finish me off!"

Night ignored every word. "How could you be here?"

"It wasn't easy," Morgen confessed. He lifted his shirt to reveal, or perhaps check on, his abdominal wound. Blood soaked the white bandages that seemed clumsily wrapped around his waist. "Try scaling a wall with this..."

The glaring red blood barely stood out for Night. What did register loudly was everything else about Morgen. He'd gained weight and a bit of color—and he could walk and talk. Night couldn't understand the rush of mixed feelings that swept through him, but he surrendered to the happy ones by throwing his arms around his brother's neck.

"Not this again..." Morgen pushed him back. "Listen...Steve was right about his aunt. She really is some kind of a miracle worker. I couldn't believe it when I got there. She has herbs and beads hanging all over her house, and she uses crystals, and candles, and peyote... I'll tell you, the stuff she gave me was way better than anything Sean ever came up with. But she says that's not what worked. She used something like hypnosis. She called it a spiritual journey—I don't know—but I started getting better after the first weird trip. I don't think Steve even expected the outcome."

Night spoke without turning his head. "Steve called me on the tour and I thought—"

"Steve almost blew my cover. It wasn't time for you to know, and I'm sorry... I had to disconnect that call."

"*You* did that?" Night's emotions flipped. "Why wouldn't you want to tell me if you were getting better? Don't even answer—you're just going to say something stupid. So, what happened to you after the Oregon concert?"

"Yeah...don't remember much about that night, but I found out, later, that Daddy's campaign manager—or rather, Lehman's operative—was all over the situation before I even got to the hospital.

Lehman flew to Oregon and did his slimy lawyer thing to have me transferred to a private clinic down here—that same night."

"He told the press you were dead. It was in the newspapers the very next morning."

Morgen rattled his head. "If the trip didn't kill me, he was going to. Lehman's been onto us for weeks—ever since Sandy released some article about us. Did you know about that?"

Night shuddered. "I took away his proof...all his pictures of us. But I didn't know he told anyone what he knew until I got back."

"Well, I know that Lehman talked to Sandy, and he obviously didn't want an adoption scandal to burn down the Dahlsi family tree—not to mention your criminal past if it became known that my dad—his meal ticket—was connected to Night Shannien. So, yeah...he needed one of us to be dead."

Morgen clutched his midriff and aborted a chuckle. "Lehman picked a shady enough clinic to deal with, then he pinned me with serious drug and psych issues and told them he was representing some big-shot who wanted to keep my identity private—at all costs. And I never said a word, even in Oregon, which only helped his case."

"Why?"

"Night, I didn't know what you admitted to after the concert, so I couldn't risk blowing our cover."

"I didn't admit to anything."

"Then it was all worth it. We beat all the odds. I just can't get over Lehman being one of them. The creep dropped by, early in the week, walked right up to my bed, and told me he wished my quiet act was enough. I don't want to sound paranoid, but I think he was going to end it right there, but a nurse came in."

"I'm going to kill him," Night declared. "I *will*," he added when Morgen sighed.

"Luckily, we shouldn't have a problem, after today, but I had a few reasons to worry when I was still in that place. I knew there was going to be a next time, and if he couldn't make it look natural, I'm sure it would only have been a matter of time before he staged my suicide.

"Even if I chose to talk, with the whole place already convinced I was crazy, I couldn't chance it that anyone would listen to me. So, I thought I'd better just make a break for it. I figured out where I was by reading a worker's ID badge. Then I called Steve, and he came and got me—literally from the bushes at the side of the road since I didn't even have real clothes. Good old Steve..."

Night's anger coursed beneath his exterior like lava gunning for the surface. He glanced around fretfully, then focused and slapped Morgen as hard as he could.

Behind his own hand, Morgen looked more confused than angry.

"We thought you were dead! You should have called me from the clinic—*not Steve!* You have no idea what you've done! You should have seen what you did to Beth, and to Brigitte, and Doris—and even Frederick was crying!"

"You're kidding."

"I'm not!"

Morgen's whole head circled as he rolled his eyes. "Look...My original plan would have been good for all of us, but I didn't expect Gramps to show up at a concert in Oregon and almost kill me. I tried to join you on the stage where I would have introduced myself as Luis Prieto, which is Steve's middle name and his aunt's last name. Steve thought it would be hard to disprove if I said I grew up with his aunt, south of the border. Not true, though, since my Spanish is shit... And not that this matters, but *'Prieto'* is actually a nickname for a guy with dark skin and hair..."

Morgen's flagrant amusement stirred Night's anger.

"So, here I am. I came to see my plan through today...get on a stage and tell the world I recently found out I was your brother—and promise that I'm every bit as rock star as you. After that, the whole country would *demand* to see us perform together. Why did you have to leave the podium? You fucked it all up, the same way Andrew fucked it up in Oregon."

The numbness in Night's body tried to stifle his speech. "You don't understand what you've done."

"My plan helps you the most, Night. Did you want to go back to being Night Shannien when I came back? Instead, I found a way to launch you as someone who isn't on a nationwide wanted list...and I found a way to launch *Us*."

As Night's senses returned, he could hardly stop shaking his head. "You don't get it? Nobody is ever going to forgive you now. Don't you get how we were all forced to make a choice...your family, and even the band? Your parents swore to the world, twice now, that Morgen Dahlsi is their real and only son. And the lie was worth it—when we thought you were dead! Now, everyone's going to know that we all lied!"

"You're as bad as Lehman..."

"At least, he just wanted to fix this—but *you* didn't think any of it through!"

"Night, it can all work out."

"*Really?* All of Sandy's stories are going to be confirmed now! It's going to kill your family—and *Morning's Desire* is finished! They will hate us...do you hear me? They will *hate* us—and we are not walking out there together so everybody can think that I had some part in your stupid plan!"

"Come on, Night. We'll help them understand you just freaked out when you saw me—that you weren't part of any scheme—but you made it more complicated by running off like you did. Now, as anticlimactic as it may be, we have to go up there and face them. We can't sit here forever...and don't you want to walk onto that platform and watch Lehman's face?"

"I don't know how you can joke about this, Morgen. You weren't there this week. There's no way to undo this, and I finally like who I am and what I've got."

351

"Everything you've got is *mine*, so sorry for living. Look...you'll be fine once the dust settles. Maybe I'll even let you join the band."

Night felt his face flush hot. "The deal was that I would make Morgen Dahlsi a star, and in return, you would give me everything...your name, your life, everything! That's what you told me. That's what you said!"

"Yes, Night," Morgen replied, a bit too sweetly. "And you accomplished the impossible. I mean, really...I can't even believe it. But that was the arrangement when I wasn't coming back. Come on, Night. They're all up there waiting for a show, so let's give it to them."

Night felt frantic now—cornered. Worse than Sean, Morgen threatened to rip out his core, everything he'd earned in the past year, and leave him to linger as only the shell of his vulturine twin. He squirmed, sickened by the impulse overtaking him. His hands tensed and his vision became a narrow tunnel with Morgen at the end of it.

"Night, I'm starting to think you really wish I was dead, and it's a little disconcerting. Do you remember the last thing I told you before I left for Mexico, because I don't think you listened? Please don't go that way. I know you have every reason to be fucked up, but Steve's aunt can help you like she helped me. I could take you to her. Either way, Night, you have to get over it. There can only be one Morgen Dahlsi, and I didn't die..."

****

As he ran through the garage, he had flashbacks of their only visit to the empty grave in the mountains. He never expected to see this plan to the end: to place his brother's body in the trunk of a car and illicitly offer another soul to the Angeles National Forest...not that it would ever stay there.

In the stairwell, on his way back to the press conference, he crashed to his knees and threw up on the landing. With eyes closed, he glimpsed a series of memories, from their many nightmare *rendezvous*, to their first physical meeting, to the months of caregiving they both endured. These flashes ended abruptly with a stab of understanding of how Andrew could have claimed to love the same person whom he would later attempt to choke the life out of. He knew this with resounding certainty because he'd just done exactly that to someone he truly loved.

A security man opened the exit door. "Is that you, Mister Dahlsi? I'll call for help. I will also inform Mister Corbin that you won't be able to proceed with the press conference?"

"No...don't. I'll finish the conference." He got to his feet and wiped his mouth with his wrist. "...But first, I need to speak with Charles Lehman."

****

The so-called lawyer swaggered around the backstage door with his usual arrogant flair. "If this is going to be a preamble to you and your shadow sticking it to me out there, keep in mind that your stunt will have a devastating effect on—"

"I killed him."

Lehman's expression brightened. "Where, may I ask?"

"In the parking garage."

"What are you saying—in front of the security cameras?"

"It all happened inside my car, in dim light, behind tinted windows. And to alleviate your next concern, I can pull the back seats down and push things into the trunk from the inside. ...Look, it wasn't exactly my choice that this happened."

"No, no, of course not. I've already been in your shoes, but failed, so you spared me a very difficult task. It's unfortunate, but there cannot be two of you. I don't know how he left that clinic, but at least, now, they'll be more than willing to produce any document I desire, after I threaten to sue their asses for allowing my prominent client's wayward son to slip out of their custody."

They nodded at one another.

"I guess this explains your partial wardrobe change. Got blood on your clothes, did you? We'll just tell them you were unexpectedly sick."

"I know what you did, Lehman...and my father is going to murder you when he finds out."

"Not likely, kiddo. I don't think he shares that homicidal gene with you...Shanniens. And I know what *you* did. So, unless you want to traumatize your family, all over again, by forcing me to divulge that you killed your own twin, just let them go on believing your brother sadly died from his stab wound.

"As for the public, they can now receive the same confirmation about their delusional *Morning's Desire* fan. End of story. They're all waiting for us out there, and we can take care of the whatever mess you made, after the conference. Come now..."

The lawyer opened the door to the stage and dared to drape his arm around the star.

Once seated, Morgen tugged on his stolen head-wrap that held his hair in place, over his unscathed ear, and he watched as a melancholy hush worked its way through the room.

He wanted to tell the world he'd always felt a connection to someone unseen, somebody he'd never met. He also wanted to confess how his chart-topping song, *My Other Side*, had been inspired by this overwhelming force, and that he hoped to find the real person someday.

But Morgen could already sense him—even more profoundly than the pain from his mending stab wound. In front of everyone, the nightmare he'd spawned had found a way to invade the material realm of the conference hall. He could feel Night's shallow breath moving in from behind him, and in spite of what he'd done, he could feel the arms of his inexorable other half cinching around him in a parasitic embrace...just hanging on.

END

# About the Author

Tina Amiri is originally from Sudbury, Ontario, but now lives in Barrie, just north of Toronto. She began writing stories before she could spell and never lost interest, so launched into the medical field. She continues to work as a low vision specialist while pursuing her interest in fiction—most recently, providing intensive book-doctoring and editing services, mostly over e-mail, to people in several countries. Other passions include supporting animal and environmental causes. To balance all the computer time, she tried her hand—and other limbs—at martial arts, but finally found her comfort zone in fair-weather distance running.

Blog:
whatevertheimpulse/Facebook

Book Email:
whatevertheimpulse@bell.net

Facebook:
www.Facebook.com/whatevertheimpulse

Twitter:
@WTIbook

Book's Website:
www.whatevertheimpulse.com

Instagram:
whatevertheimpulse

CPSIA information can be obtained at www.ICGtesting.com
Printed in the USA
LVOW10s0540010316

477268LV00005B/14/P